# MIAMI MARRIAGE PACT

## NADINE GONZALEZ

# OVERNIGHT INHERITANCE

## RACHEL BAILEY

MILLS & BOON

First Published in Great Britain 2023
by Mills & Boon, an imprint of HarperCollins*Publishers* Ltd
1 London Bridge Street, London, SE1 9GF

www.harpercollins.co.uk

HarperCollins*Publishers*
Macken House, 39/40 Mayor Street Upper,
Dublin 1, D01 C9W8, Ireland

*Miami Marriage Pact* © 2023 Nadine Seide
*Overnight Inheritance* © 2023 Rachel Robinson

ISBN: 978-0-263-31773-2

1223

This book is produced from independently certified FSC™ paper
to ensure responsible forest management.

For more information visit: www.harpercollins.co.uk/green

Printed and Bound in the UK using 100% Renewable Electricity at
CPI Group (UK) Ltd, Croydon, CR0 4YY

**Nadine Gonzalez** writes joyous multicultural contemporary romance. Until Hollywood comes calling, Nadine will keep her day job as a lawyer while crafting modern love stories featuring diverse casts of characters. When not working or writing, she's cataloguing her life through photography, so be sure to follow along on Instagram and TikTok @_nadine_novelist

**Rachel Bailey** lives on the Sunshine Coast, Australia, with her partner and dogs, each of whom are essential to her books: the dogs supervise the writing process (by napping on or under the desk) and her partner supplies the chocolate. She loves to hear from readers, and you can visit her at rachelbailey.com or on Facebook.

# MIAMI
# MARRIAGE PACT

## NADINE GONZALEZ

For Ariel and Nathaniel, always and forever.

## ACT I, SCENE I

*Scene: Interior. Night.*

"Are you proposing marriage, Ms. Garcia?"

"I am."

"We just met. I hardly know you."

"You know what I have to offer."

"And what's that?"

"Your wildest dreams on a silver platter."

"I don't have wild dreams, only attainable ones."

"I can change that."

"I'd say yes, just to see you try."

"Say yes, anyway."

"My answer is no."

"Why? Give me one reason."

"We'd be using each other. That's not my style."

"Correction: we'd be *useful* to each other. And really, is that so bad? Marriages have thrived on less."

"When you put it like that, it all sounds so simple."

"It is that simple. So, you'll marry me?"

"No."

# One

When had her life turned into a Hollywood production? Conditions imposed on inheritance? A marriage of convenience to sort it out? Those were tropes best left to romantic comedy scripts, and yet, here Gigi was, shopping around for a husband, her best friend acting as her middleman. The drama had started with a familiar scene: The Reading of the Will.

They'd gathered in the lawyer's office. Not in a wood-paneled suite, like moviegoers have grown accustomed to. The law firm occupied the top floors of a downtown Miami high-rise with water views that made a mockery of her misery.

Seated beside her on the white leather couch was her mother, Elizabeth Brooks-Garcia, better known as "the former top model from Texas, Beth Brooks." She wore black from head to toe, in case anyone should question her grief. Gigi's half brother, Gabriel Garcia, sat facing them in a wingback armchair. He stared at her with his own mother's mossy brown eyes. Behind a sleek desk sat attorney Andrew Row. All three seemed to be holding their breaths, waiting for her tantrum to pass.

Not one of them was in her corner.

"What do you mean I have to wait five years before I can touch my inheritance?" Gigi exploded. A five-year wait for fifty million dollars? Even a saint wouldn't agree to that, and she was no saint.

"Or marry," Row specified. "Wait five years or marry. Those are the terms."

"How long does my mother have to wait?" Gigi asked.

"She doesn't."

Gigi pointed to Gabriel. "What about him?"

"He doesn't have to wait, either."

"So, it's just me?"

"Just you."

"Georgina!" Beth wailed. "Your father had his reasons."

Her mother wailed far too often now. Gigi struggled to keep her voice calm. "Did he? I'd like to hear them."

"He was looking out for you."

"He was trying to control me, even from the grave!"

"Don't be so dramatic!" Beth scolded.

"Two things can be right at the same time," Gabe explained. "He was looking out for you...*and* he was trying to control you. That's what you get for being the favorite."

"Thanks for that insightful analysis, Gabe." You'd think at a time like this, they could set their sibling rivalry aside for like a fraction of a second. They never got along, and likely never would. In fairness, their dad had left his mom for hers, so...there was that.

Gabe grinned. "Anytime."

Row intervened. "We've been at this for a while now. Would anyone like a refreshment? Coffee? Tea?"

Beth opted for coffee. "Black. No sugar, please."

"Water," Gabe said.

Gigi sighed, deflated. "A margarita on the rocks with salt on the rim."

"Georgina!" Beth wailed once more.

Okay, she'd asked for that one. Something about this whole situation and being powerless reduced her to a rebellious teen, and her instinct was to lash out. The person responsible for this mess, the only one with the power to *do* something about it, was long gone, singing hymns with the angels or reincarnated into a butterfly. Either way, her father was enjoying his afterlife while his family hashed out his last will and testament. Apparently, his last will, his parting wish, was to screw his only daughter out of tens of millions of dollars. And all anyone could offer her now was refreshments and pity.

"Sorry, Mom," Gigi said sweetly. "It's not every day I'm forced into marriage."

"No one is forcing you into anything," Beth retorted. "Your father wanted what's best for you."

"I'm pretty sure that's the official motto of the patriarchy," Gigi muttered.

Beth pinched the bridge of her nose. "Heaven help me."

Gigi turned to the lawyer. "What are my options?"

"Florida laws are strict," Row said. "There is ample evidence Mr. Garcia was of sound mind until the end. His cognitive abilities are documented in the extensive medical record."

Her dad's mind had remained sharp even as his body was crippled with disease. He'd kept managing his affairs from his hospice bed. The former Major League All-Star remained a champion to his dying day.

"And I'll testify, if it comes to that," Beth said. "Your father was an extraordinary man. I won't have his legacy watered down just so you can collect early."

Before she could lash out at her mother for practically calling her a gold digger, Gabe jumped in, adding insult to injury.

"That profile in *Vanities* did you no favors. I'm sure that's why Dad did it."

Gigi's heart tanked just at the mention of the article. "Layoffs and Pay Cuts at GG Cinema." The trade magazine had pronounced her career dead after a string of box office flops, all critically acclaimed, but flops nonetheless.

"Since when do you read *Vanities*?" she asked.

"A copy was lying around my dentist's office," Gabe replied.

"Oh, sure."

"It's not like you'll go hungry," Beth said. "You're a savvy businesswoman. Plus, your monthly income is more than enough to tide you over. Your father didn't touch that. Isn't that right, Mr. Row?"

"Yes, that's correct."

Income wasn't the problem. Gigi didn't need an allowance; she needed *capital*, enough funds to cut ties with her main investors and chart her own course.

Gabe had a suggestion. "Maybe auction off your collection of Oscars."

Her brother reclined in his wingback chair with the nonchalance of a man who stood to inherit millions without having to jump through a single hoop. Gigi did not take the bait.

"I guess I have no choice but to get married," she muttered to herself.

"How will you swing that?" Gabe asked. "You've been single for a while."

That was a bold assumption! What did he know? "I'm seeing someone."

"You are?" Beth asked. "Where was he on your birthday? All your friends were at your dinner."

"We're discreet. I don't parade around my secret lovers."

Gabe laughed. "Nobody says 'secret lover.' You've been in Hollywood too long."

"Call him what you like," Beth said stonily. "But for the love of God, don't marry him. Marrying for money is tasteless."

Gabe made no effort to stifle his laugh. Truth be told, Beth's lack of self-awareness was hilarious. Eighteen years younger than her late husband, she was instantly branded a trophy wife. Only Gigi knew the truth: her parents adored each other.

Row cleared his throat to remind them all of his presence. Gigi had a question for him. "Does the will say I have to marry for love?"

"No," he replied. "It doesn't."

"That's enough now," Beth snapped. "I won't stand for this."

"Is my mother's approval necessary?" Gigi asked the attorney.

He appeared amused. "No, it's not."

"It settled! I'll be married by the end of the month."

Her declaration was met with dry, brittle laughter all around.

"You think this is funny?" Gigi asked.

"We think it's tragic," Beth retorted. "The one time you don't get your way, you resort to pulling stunts. When will you grow up?"

NADINE GONZALEZ                    13

"Careful you don't end up having to pay some guy spousal support," Gabe added. "It sort of defeats the purpose. Make sure to get an airtight prenup."

"An airtight prenup…" Gigi mimed taking notes. "Got it! Good looking out, big bro."

Gabriel was her half brother, but she couldn't afford to splice and dice the only sibling she had. Growing up, she'd admired him. Gabe was athletic and handsome, and all her girlfriends had crushes on him. Too bad he considered Gigi the enemy. She didn't take it personally. She'd understood, even at a young age, that her brother's resentment rested squarely on Beth for allegedly wrecking his home.

Juan Pedro Garcia was still married to Gabe's mother when he'd met Beth, yet he swore up and down that he hadn't "declared his love" until after he was legally separated. "I respect the sanctity of marriage," he'd say to anyone who'd listen. Decades later, when he was terminally ill, he became obsessed with finding his only daughter a husband. "I won't get to see you married," he'd say. Gigi had always tried to make light of it. "You got to see me win an Oscar. How many dads can say that?"

It wouldn't have mattered if she'd won a Nobel Peace Prize. Her father wished only to see her "settled."

Beth reached over and touched her arm. "Gabe is right. Your life is not a romantic comedy. Getting married for the wrong reasons is a terrible mistake."

Seriously, what was her family's obsession with the film industry? They tossed her career in her face at every opportunity. Everything—every setback, every bout of bad luck, no matter how trivial, the flu or whatever—came down to her so-called Hollywood lifestyle. If they were taking bets on when her career would collapse, she would not give them the satisfaction.

"As long as you're entertained, Mom. Don't forget the popcorn."

"I prefer Raisinets," Beth said smoothly.

"To each her own." Gigi stood and smoothed down her skirt. "I'll leave you two to discuss your affairs. Keep an eye out for the wedding invite."

With those words, she strode out of the lawyer's office and made a beeline toward the elevator bank. Gabe chased after her. "Hold on, Georgina!"

Increasingly, he favored their dad. With his hair cropped short, he looked like a young Pedro Garcia, the cocky shortstop newly recruited by Houston.

She pressed the elevator button. "Go away!"

"Just give me a second, will you?" he said. "It's no wonder he treated you like a child. You act like one!"

Gigi whirled around, primed for a fight. "What are you going to do with your money, huh? Buy a boat? Another condo on the beach? Invest in crypto?"

The elevator came and went as she waited for an answer. Gabe's face reddened. "It's none of your business what I do with it."

"That's my point," she said through clenched teeth. "It's *your* prerogative. What a privilege that is!"

"Believe it or not, I'm on your side," he said. "You have every right to be upset, but please, don't do anything you'll regret."

No one was on her side; they'd made that plain. She was alone in this. "I'll do what I have to."

Gigi turned her back on her brother and caught the next elevator. She was met by her reflection in the mirrored walls and her mask of self-confidence nearly fell away. Tall, slim, she had her father's golden brown complexion and her mother's chiseled cheekbones. More importantly, she had her father's head for business and her mother's cunning. She would figure a way out of this. No one, not her mother, brother, or ghost of her father, would stop her.

Outside, she waited patiently for the valet to bring around the powder blue Bentley that had once belonged to Beth. She slid behind the wheel and veered onto Biscayne Boulevard only to pull over to the side of the road when her vision suddenly blurred with tears.

She gripped the steering wheel. *Shit! What am I going to do now?*

Fate threw Gigi a lifeline. Just as panic threatened to choke her, her phone rang. The name on the dashboard display sent a jolt of relief down her spine. A second later, the warm voice of one of her dearest friends filled the car. "I've been trying to reach you. What's going on? How's your day?"

Her heart rate steadied. "Miserable. You won't believe what I've been through."

"What happened? What's wrong?"

Most people were lucky if they had one person in their lives who would rush into a burning building to save them. Gigi had a handful. One of them was Oscar-winning actor Alessandro Cardenas, "Sandro" for short. He'd flown in to attend her father's funeral and checked in on her daily.

Although she and the actor had Miami roots, their paths had crossed in LA. Sandro had auditioned for a small role in one of the first films she'd produced. His portrayal of a queer Cuban activist had made him a star. The film was nominated for an Oscar, and Sandro went on to win many prestigious awards. They'd been in each other's lives ever since. What a shame he was engaged to a talented artist with whom he was very much in love. If not, Gigi would have proposed to him on the spot.

"Don't worry," she sighed. "I'm fine."

"You don't sound fine," he said. "Let's have lunch. I'll pick you up. Just tell me where you are."

Where was she, even? Somewhere near a strip mall. A group of school kids eyed her car as they crossed the street, backpacks slung over their shoulders. The Bentley attracted way too much attention. She fired up the engine. "Never mind that. I'll come to you."

"All right," he said. "I'm headed to Diablo. Meet me there."

After the morning she'd had, a noisy, happening restaurant was the last place she wanted to be. "I don't want to be around people right now. Can't we meet somewhere private?"

"Diablo is my second home," he assured her. "We'll hang out in the kitchen, sample the food and talk. I promise they'll leave us alone."

That sounded wonderful, actually. She was starving. A good meal and chance to vent would get her back on track. "What's the address?"

Sandro went quiet for a bit. "Are you joking?"

"Fine!" she cried. "I'll look up the directions! No need to be rude."

"I can't believe this," Sandro said. "You've never been to Diablo?"

"Sorry, no."

Gigi wasn't sorry at all. She didn't have time to make the rounds of every trendy bar and restaurant that popped up in Miami. Unlike his other freewheeling friends, she had a company to run to the ground.

"Hold on," he said, more forcefully than the circumstances required. "You've never met Myles?"

"Maybe… I don't know."

She met so many people; how could she know for sure? However, she now understood why Sandro was upset. Myles was his childhood friend. He talked about the guy nonstop. Ah, yes! He was a chef, of some sort. He must cook at Diablo, or maybe he owned the place.

"Never mind," he said. "Head over to NE 40th Street. It's on the corner—you can't miss it. Ask for the chef's table, and they'll take you back."

"See you soon."

She made it there in no time. Removed from the busy street and surrounded by palm trees, Diablo was not what she'd expected. The architecture was reminiscent of old-style Florida with its white facade, jalousie windows and angled roof. Just before darting inside, she stole a moment to type "Chef Myles Diablo" into her phone's search engine. Maybe Sandro would forgive her if she showed some interest in his friend's career.

The search results were slim. The restaurant's official website came up, but she was hunting for links to his personal Instagram or TikTok. The chef was apparently social media averse. However, she stumbled across an interesting profile in *Let's Spoon,* a culinary magazine.

> *Myles V. Paris, the so-called "MVP" of fusion cuisine, is named the Hottest Chef in the Kitchen. The Miami native of Haitian decent heats up the culinary scene, but remains focused on his career. "I'm single, and okay with it." Update: We at* Let's Spoon *are not okay.*

Gigi tapped on the accompanying thumbnail photo to enlarge it. Dark skin, light eyes, wearing chef whites, a butcher knife clutched in one hand, Chef Myles was strikingly handsome. She took in his even features, the set of his jaw, the cocky half tilt of his smile. And those eyes! They drilled straight into her.

One of her many gifts was her uncanny ability to read people. Granted, she hadn't yet met the man, but this one photo told her everything she needed to know: smart, stubborn, sexy, steadfast… She dropped her phone into her bag and reached for a tube of lipstick. She had her work cut out for her.

# Two

"Chef's table, party of one!"

The hostess had to hop out of the way of waiters swirling in and out of the kitchen twice in the time it took her to finish her announcement. From his stool at the bar-height table by the lone window, Sandro called out, "She's with me! Let her through!"

Myles looked up from the menu he was revising. There was no chef's table at Diablo. It was code for close family and friends, usually on off-hours. At the moment, it was the height of lunch hour. His patrons tended to linger, order coffee, flirt or catch up. The main dining room was lively, brimming with chatter, which meant the kitchen was chaotic. Why would Sandro bring anyone into this hellscape?

"Are you taking meetings here now?" Myles asked.

"Don't put ideas in my head," Sandro replied. "This would be the best spot to talk numbers with my manager."

Myles doubted it. They'd barely be able to hear each other over the clamor. "Now isn't exactly the best time to entertain."

"Sorry, man." Sandro offered a sheepish grin. "She's going through some things and we need to talk privately."

"Who's she?" Myles asked. It wasn't Sandro's fiancée, that much was sure. The entire staff knew Angel by name and she had access to the kitchen, no code word required.

"Georgina Garcia," Sandro answered. "My friend, the producer."

Myles assessed the consistency of a line cook's béchamel. "Don't think I've met her before."

"I'm actually upset about that," Sandro said.

Myles frowned. The béchamel was too thin, and his best friend wasn't making sense. "Why have you been hiding her?"

"I'm curious, too."

The answer did not come from Sandro, who was chewing on a chunk of artisanal bread, but from the woman who'd made a smooth entrance, ducking out of the way of two waiters, in a body-hugging dress and high heels. Red pepper lips, cinnamon skin, and chocolate hair to her waist, she assaulted his senses.

"Myles, this is Gigi," Sandro said finally.

The famous Gigi, Myles mused. Visionary maverick, shatterer of glass ceilings. The local press had adored her dad. The baseball legend turned real estate mogul had left his imprint on South Florida. There were libraries, museum pavilions and hospital wings named after him—no doubt after sizable donations. Gigi had her father's height, his smile and his presence minus the brash showmanship that had turned some people off. Her gaze was fluid, honey in an airtight jar. Emotion made them hazy. It looked to him like desperation, or was he imagining it?

"It's good to meet you," she said. "Sandro says you're like a brother to him. I'm like his big, bossy sister."

"Does that mean you and I are related?"

"No," she said firmly. "It doesn't."

Good, Myles thought. He already had a big sister.

"It's nice to meet you, too, Georgina," he said.

"Please, just call me Gigi," she replied. "Everyone does."

"Is this your first time eating with us?" he asked.

"It is," she said. "Let's blame that on Sandro."

"No doubt I blame him," Myles said. "I've met all his other friends."

Gigi frowned. "Sounds like gatekeeping to me."

"You two are ganging up on me?" Sandro said. "You've only known each other five minutes!"

"That's more than enough time to catch a vibe," she said. "I already know that I like your friend, this restaurant is great, and I'm going to love it here."

Even as Georgina "Call me Gigi" Garcia teased their friend, she kept her gaze on Myles, eyes sparkling with interest. Nervous, he shifted the conversation to more neutral territory.

"Are you hungry?" he asked.

She laid a hand on the flat of her stomach. "Starving."

"What are you in the mood for?"

"Anything," she said. "Last night I had a bag of popcorn for dinner."

"Jesus… Don't say that."

"It's true."

"Any food restrictions?"

"None."

"Adventurous?"

"Absolutely."

"All right." Myles nodded. "I'll take care of you."

Sandro tore another piece of bread. "Is it me, or is it getting hot in here?"

"It's you," Myles replied. "Show your guest to the chef's table."

"Send over more bread, and we'll be out of your hair," Sandro promised. "You won't even know we're here."

Myles doubted that very much. Gigi was magnetic. In a short time, she'd changed the chemistry of the room.

He had a waiter set their table with fresh linens and sent over a bottle of red wine and a bowl of Sandro's favorite olives. Then he went to work, putting together a tasting menu. He would start them off with his snapper ceviche. For the main dish, he liked the braised rib, but would give them the option of the house favorite, seared scallops on jasmine rice. He'd finish with the coconut flan, which was Sandro's absolute favorite. That ought to do it. The last time he'd put this much care into anything, he was a finalist in a cooking competition, which he'd won. From time to time, he stole a glance their way. Huddled together, voices deliberately low, they looked more like coconspirators than friends or old colleagues. It made him feel out of place in his own kitchen.

He saw Gigi nodding and listening to Sandro, even as her gaze skimmed the kitchen. Myles had no doubt she was searching for him. When their eyes met, a new conversation began just between the two of them, overriding everything else.

Why was she here, and what did she want from him?

# Three

Sandro reached over table and squeezed her hand. "I'll be honest," he said. "You look a little unhinged. What do you need? Water? Wine? Something stronger? There's an open bottle of whiskey somewhere."

"What I need is a husband."

Sandro let a moment pass. "I'm engaged. You know that, right?"

"Not *you*!" she said.

"Why not?" Sandro asked, suddenly offended. "I'd make a great husband."

She didn't need a great husband, only a discreet one. His one marital duty would be to keep his mouth shut. For that, she was ready to pay him handsomely.

"I know, sweetheart," she said reassuringly. Men were fragile and constantly needed coddling, even those with a fan base. "Your fiancée is one lucky woman. It doesn't change the fact that I need a fiancé of my own."

"Since when are you interested in marriage?" he asked.

It was a fair question. She'd never expressed any desire in getting hitched, even when her friends shoved sparkling engagement rings under her nose. In the olden days, women had to marry to solidify their positions in society and secure fortunes. Seemed like everything old was new again, because here she was, out in these streets, seeking a "good match" to secure her future.

"Since the great Pedro Garcia added a marriage stipulation to his will."

Sandro furrowed his brows in confusion. "Break this down for me. I don't get it."

Gigi gave him a quick and dirty summary.

"Why would he do that?" Sandro asked. "You needed that money to invest in GG Cinema, right?"

"I still need it."

"Did he know? Or did he think you were going to spend it on Birkin bags?"

"Oh, he knew."

That was the worst part. She'd visited him in the hospital shortly after the *Vanities* article was published, and they'd had a private chat. Gigi didn't bullshit him. She owned up to her mistakes and shared her plans to restructure her company. She'd even asked for his advice. But he had no wisdom to impart. He only listened, nodded and patted her hand. He told her that he loved her and believed she'd do great things with her life. He was dying, so she didn't press him for more. She'd walked away feeling empowered, only to learn, today, that he'd called his lawyer as soon as she'd left him. Could anyone blame her for feeling betrayed? Her father had deliberately sabotaged her. The five-year "cooling period," as Andrew Row had put it, was a fatal blow to GG Cinema.

"Gigi, please don't tell me you're willing to marry some random person to get the money."

"What choice do I have?"

"The choice to say 'fuck it' and let it go."

"I can't do that."

Myles approached the table and set a dish of butter between them.

She perked up. "What's this?"

"Truffle butter for the bread."

"Delicious," she said.

"Unless you prefer olive oil."

She smiled, wanting to say, *I prefer you.*

"Butter is good," Sandro replied.

Myles left them. He was good-looking in the photo but heart-stopping in person, with soulful eyes in stark contrast with his strong brows, nose and jaw. His thick black hair curled softly away from his angular face. He moved with grace. Where Sandro was lively, always down to party, Myles was calm and spoke with quiet confidence. She better understood the role he played in Sandro's hectic life: Myles was his safe space.

"Wait five years," Sandro said, once Myles was out of earshot. "That's the choice you have. Something else will come up."

"I can't afford to wait."

"Call me crazy, but I'm pretty sure you can."

"No one can afford to waste time, Sandro. Not even me."

"Come on, Gigi. I didn't mean it like that."

"Yes, you did."

"All right, yes," he conceded. "I don't want to be a prick about this, but it's not a question of life or death. You can afford to wait."

"The company—"

"G, I know all about the company. Still, I say it's not worth it," Sandro said. "A bad marriage can wreck your life."

Gigi slathered a bit of bread with truffle butter. "It doesn't have to be complicated. We won't have to stay together 'til death or whatever else fuckery marriage involves."

Sandro cocked a brow. "Oh yeah? What about good, old-fashioned fuckery? Will you be doing any of that?"

"Shh!" She looked about to make sure no one had overheard them. Her eyes scanned the crowded kitchen, resting finally on Myles. She mentally revised the answer to his question from a "Hell no," to a "Maybe."

Sandro dropped his butter knife. "Hold on," he said. "If you think that guy, the one you're making eyes at, is the solution to your problem, you're dead wrong."

That was exactly what she was thinking. Myles was vetted, so to speak. And with Sandro hovering over them like a satellite orbiting Earth, what could go wrong?

"What's the issue?" she asked. "I read he was single."

"Where did you read that?" Sandro asked.

"Online! Where do you think? God, you're protective of him."

"Get used to it," Sandro retorted.

"Is he single or not?"

"He is."

"No one on the side?"

"None that I know of." He paused. "Well, not since Natalie."

*Natalie? Hmm...*

"But he's stubborn, G. No way he'll agree to any kind of scheme."

"Out of principle?" Gigi asked.

"Yes."

"Oh, God..." Was there anything worse than a principled man?

Sandro shrugged as though to say he didn't understand it, either.

Gigi was close to giving up when Myles looked up from his task and glanced her way. Briefly, they locked eyes. She plucked an olive from the bowl and popped it in her mouth. The tangy blue cheese stuffing felt velvety on the tongue. No way she was giving up.

"I'll make it worth his while," Gigi said to Sandro. "Any man who marries me will likely get a lot of attention in the press. It'll be good for business. I'll bring half of young Hollywood to this restaurant."

"So could I," Sandro said. "He doesn't want that."

"What does he want?"

"To be left alone."

Gigi refused to believe it. "That's not how the world works. Everybody wants something."

"Everyone except Myles," Sandro said flatly. "I know you're in a bind, Gigi. I'm not trying to block you or anything, I swear. What could be better than my two favorite people getting together? I bet you'd throw the best parties. But Myles is not that guy. He's serious and focused and doesn't put up with nonsense. He barely puts up with me."

Gigi chewed on that for a while, but soon let it go as small plates of dishes started to arrive at their table, everything from cauliflower to couscous plus an amazing ceviche. Gigi nearly forgot her father, the will, her failing company, all of it, until Sandro brought it up again.

"Your dad screwed you over," he said. "I don't blame you for wanting to get the last word."

"That's not what this is about."

"Sure."

"Fine!" she conceded. "That's not what it's *only* about. I was counting on that money to hold on to my staff, to fund my next project."

"I'll fund your next film," Sandro said, as if it were as easy as that.

"I'm not taking your money."

"It's a loan."

Loans were what had gotten her into this mess. Her last two movies did not perform as well as she'd hoped. Meanwhile, her financiers were waiting for returns on their investment. She had to balance her books before taking on any new projects. Once those debts were settled, she would self-finance any future projects. That was the plan.

"I don't want a loan," she said. "I'm sitting on a pot of gold. I need to access it."

"You'd marry a total stranger?"

"Myles isn't a stranger, is he?"

"To you, he is."

Gigi took a gulp of the cabernet Myles had selected for them. He might be a stranger, but he knew her taste in wine. Sadly, it did nothing to soothe her. She was nervous. She'd expected pushback from her family, but not Sandro, her wingman, her partner in crime. They couldn't all be wrong. Was she deluding herself? A bad business merger could destroy a company. How much more damage could a bad marriage do?

Myles checked on them during dessert, a tasty fruit tart with a side of mango sorbet. Gigi was licking pomegranate sauce off the back of a spoon.

"Could we have whatever this is at our wedding?" Sandro asked, as if the wedding weren't one year away.

"Can't promise that," Myles said. "Depends what's in season, what we find."

"Are you catering?" Gigi asked.

"Among other things," he replied.

"Oh? What other things?"

"He's also my best man," Sandro said.

"I'll gladly give that up that role to be in the kitchen," Myles said. "You know I have your back. You don't need me standing there."

"I need you at that altar," Sandro said. "You better be there."

"I should be officiating this thing," Gigi said. "I was *instrumental* in getting you and Angel together."

She'd practically had to point the poor girl in Sandro's direction. The prospect of dating a world-famous movie star would daunt anyone, but Angel was terrified.

Sandro gave Gigi a look, to which she responded, "What? You know I'm right!"

"And that's why you're the maid of honor."

Gigi flushed. "Really?"

"Yes, really," Sandro affirmed. "Angel will ask you sooner or later, so act surprised when she does."

"Count on it. You're not the only one with acting skills."

Jokes aside, Gigi was moved. Every time a friend married, there was the risk of losing them to the coupledom. It was reassuring to be included in this way.

Myles grinned. "Guess I'll meet you at the altar, Gigi."

*Yes,* she thought. *Yes, you will.*

# Four

"Hey, Eddy, get out of here!" Myles ordered the young dishwasher later that night. "Don't you have school in the morning?"

The high school senior had dreams of attending culinary school, but first he had to graduate.

"Nah," Eddy replied. "Teacher planning day. You know how it goes."

He continued to stack clean plates on shelves, at 11 p.m., as if he had nowhere better to be. Myles wasn't fooled. Even though no formal announcement had been made, the staff was aware of the restaurant's imminent closure. They were coasting on borrowed time. One cook had quit. The others, strangely enough, had leaned in. They'd started showing up early, staying late, even volunteering for double shifts. For most of them, Myles included, this kitchen was a home away from home. It was going to rip him in half to lose this team, but nothing could be done to stop it. Diablo didn't belong to him, and never would. Once, he'd been fool enough to hope. He wasn't a fool anymore.

"Go home anyway," Myles told Eddy. He grabbed a to-go bag with some leftovers off the baker's rack and handed it to him. "Go catch up on homework if you're bored."

"Good one, Chef," he said, chuckling. "See you Friday."

Eddy shuffled out of the kitchen, and nearly ran into Sandro on his way in.

"What are you doing back here?" Myles asked.

Sandro's visits were never spontaneous. They required planning and forethought. His fame was limiting. He lived on a tiny, private island off the coast of Miami, accessible only by air or sea. Wherever he went, so went his driver/bodyguard, Gus.

"Wanted to check in before flying out tomorrow."

Sandro dragged a stool up to the counter and got settled, which meant he was going to stay a while. Something must be weighing on his mind. They made small talk until the kitchen cleared out. Myles trusted his people; they wouldn't repeat anything they'd overheard. Sandro, though, needed the extra privacy that his fame and celebrity had robbed him of.

"Where are you off to this time?" Myles asked.

"Toronto," Sandro replied. "I'll be gone six weeks."

He was due on set for his next film. This new role was a challenge. He'd had to work with a dialogue coach as his character, a CIA agent, was fluent in several languages. Genuinely interested, Myles asked questions even though he was stalling for time. Finally, the last of the crew straightened up their stations and, one by one, filed out. Myles locked the door. "We're good," he said. "Why are you back here? Is something wrong?"

"Nothing's wrong. We didn't get to talk earlier."

"You were here to meet with Gigi," Myles said.

"Not true," Sandro said. "That was a last-minute decision, but I'm glad you got to meet her. She's a good person."

"Good-looking, too," Myles said under his breath.

"You noticed?"

"Hard not to."

"Does that mean you're ready to break your vow of celibacy?"

"What are you talking about? I'm no monk!"

"You could've fooled me," Sandro said. "Here's some good news—she's not seeing anyone, either, and hasn't been for a while. You've got that in common."

That was possibly all they had in common. "Is this what you came here to talk about?"

"Maybe."

"In that case, I won't waste your time. It's a hard pass."

Sandro folded his arms. "Why?"

"No time." With all the shit he had going on, dating was the last thing on his mind. "Don't get me wrong. I appreciate you trying to fix me up with your rich, gorgeous friends."

"The more I think about it, the more I like the idea," Sandro said. "You'd be great together."

"Stop thinking," Myles suggested. "What would she need with a guy like me?"

"You'd be surprised what she needs."

In all honesty, Myles would rather not think about Gigi's needs for fear of where his thoughts would go. "Why not tell me why you're really here?" Myles asked.

"First, I need a snack," Sandro replied. "Feed me."

"Goddamn it," Myles mumbled, even though he secretly loved feeding his friends.

A moment later they were munching on the last of the *churros*. It was like old times. Myles and Sandro had grown up together like brothers, biking to and from school, playing soccer in the street, hanging out in their secret clubhouse in Sandro's backyard, dreaming of a future that would take them beyond their little neighborhood. After high school, they each had gone their separate ways. Sandro had taken off to study acting in New York and LA, while Myles gained admission to culinary school in France. After years apart, they'd reconnected in this kitchen. Whenever Sandro was in Miami, he'd stop by to eat, talk, complain about a part he'd lost, or cry about some girl— most recently his fiancée, Angel. Myles had convinced himself that nights like these, hanging out with people he loved, in a space he loved, was tied to this restaurant. That was why he'd fought so hard to keep it.

"Actually, I'm here for an update," Sandro said. "It's been a while since you put an offer on this place. What happened? Didn't you hear back?"

Myles turned away from him and busied himself with the day's receipts. "Yeah, I heard back."

"And?"

"They turned it down."

"That's not how it works," Sandro said. "They should counter your offer."

"Is that how it works?" Myles asked. "Shit. I didn't know."

He didn't mean to come off as bitter, but in truth he was more bitter than gas station coffee. He'd put forward a solid offer on the restaurant, only for it to be laughed off the table.

"You'd be pretty much where you are now," Sandro said. "Stuck."

Myles pulled a jar of Nutella from the pantry and set it before Sandro as a sort of peace offering. Sandro accepted it gladly. "Don't forget I'm on your side."

"I know," Myles said quietly.

Sandro slathered the hazelnut spread on his pastry. "They turned down your offer. What happened then?"

"I returned with a higher number."

"Yeah? How much higher?"

"Five hundred thousand."

Sandro nodded approvingly. "That would put you somewhere in the two million range. Solid. What happened next?"

"It was turned down flat, and before you ask, there was no counter."

Sandro lost it. "What the fuck, man?"

"It's a seller's market," Myles replied, with a cool detachment he was far from feeling. The way he was dismissed had felt personal.

"This is bullshit," Sandro said. "Cut out the middlemen and talk to the guy. You've worked for him for, like, what? Eight years?"

The guy Sandro was referring to was Lou Palmer. He'd inherited the family-owned restaurant and kept it running despite little to no interest in the food industry. He'd hired Myles straight out of culinary school. Lou's general lack of interest and his hands-off management style worked well for Myles, who had the liberty to do whatever with Diablo. He could change the menu on a whim, experiment with flavors, adjust prices. The freedom had allowed him to perfect his signature style and, soon enough, his reputation had grown. Now, sadly, he couldn't imagine working anywhere else.

"Ask him what his bottom line is and we'll meet it."

"*We* won't be doing anything," Myles said. "This is my problem."

Sandro had made this offer many times before. Myles had considered it from every angle, always coming to one conclusion: he could not take his friend's money. Their friendship worked because it was disinterested. The world demanded so much from the actor—time, money, endorsements, details of his personal life. He would not be one of those people.

"You don't have to do this alone," Sandro said. "I don't want to lose this place, either. It's our spot."

"We don't need a spot," Myles said. "And we don't need a secret clubhouse. We're adults."

Sandro tossed him a quizzical look. "Speak for yourself."

"We're gonna be fine," Myles assured him.

"So, what's the plan?"

It was time to come clean. "I've got a couple offers lined up in Vegas."

"Vegas? Are you joking?"

"You're out there all the time."

"To party or promote stuff, rarely for very long."

Myles felt a tightening in his chest. "It's a temporary thing. Three to four years, max. Then I'll return and open my own place."

"Why go at all?" Sandro asked. "There are more restaurants than we know what to do with in Miami."

"For the money. The goal is to open my own place in five years."

"What about your family?" Sandro asked. "You're just going to leave Michelle?"

"Michelle is grown, engaged and doing great," Myles said. "She'll understand."

"Yes, but it's just the two of you now."

"I'll visit often."

That was a load of crap. Once he stepped into the role of executive chef at any restaurant chasing Michelin glory, they'd be no time to breathe.

Sandro looked crushed. "Are you sure about this?"

"I don't have a lot of good choices right now."

"That's not true," Sandro scoffed. "Screw Vegas! Your family is here, your new house…your life!"

Myles shoved the stack of receipts in a drawer and locked it. He was desperate to change the subject. "How early is your flight?"

"Stupid early." Sandro made no move to leave. "Listen, I'm in no position to talk. I get that. I'm hardly ever around. But hear me out. Angel and I can't wait to start a family. Now that I don't have to troll around Hollywood for auditions anymore, we're free to move back after the wedding."

"That isn't until next year."

"I'm just saying, we want you in the kid's life."

Coming from anyone else, this would be classic emotional blackmail. However, Myles knew where this was coming from. Sandro had a deep-rooted need for family and community. His parents had not wanted him. To his father, he'd been a burden, and to his mother, a mistake. For most of his life, it was just him and his grandfather—and a dick of a half brother from whom he was now estranged.

"Don't worry so much," Myles said. "I'm not headed to Mars. And I promise to take my role of honorary uncle seriously."

"It's not a fake title," Sandro said. "You're the uncle, plain and simple. The only one the kid will have."

"I love the kid already, and I promise to spoil him rotten."

Sandro cooled down, but Myles couldn't. His chest felt as hollow as his promises.

Sandro stood and stretched. "Hey, will you do me a favor?"

"Anything," Myles answered, eager to get off the topic of Vegas. "What do you need?"

"It's not for me," he said. "It's Gigi. She's going through a lot, and I'm leaving her just when she could use a friend."

Myles nodded. "She's grieving the loss of her dad."

"It's more complicated than that. He left her in a…difficult position."

Dads dying and leaving their kids in sticky situations was a thing both he and Sandro knew too well. Sandro's dad had abandoned him long before he'd died, but his financial support was sorely missed. Myles's own father had passed away the day after he turned thirteen. Overnight, he was expected to be the "man of the house" even though his sister, Michelle, was older by two years.

"Could you maybe give her a call and check in on her?" Sandro asked.

Here it was, at last, what Sandro had come to ask of him. The guy was an excellent actor, but a lousy liar. He was still trying to fix them up.

Myles was too tired to argue. "Sure. Why not?"

Sandro grinned, triumphant. "Cool. I'll send you her number."

# Five

A text message quietly lit up her phone screen. It was past midnight and, had Gigi been asleep, like well-adjusted people, she would've missed it. However, she was wide-awake, curled up in bed with a bowl of ice cream, watching *I Love Lucy* reruns with the sound muted. Even laughter from a studio audience was unwelcome in a house in mourning. The house howled with sadness, just the way Beth liked it. Gigi was suddenly aware of how unnecessarily large their home was, and how vacant the rooms felt. She wondered if her mother would keep it. It was too much house for one person.

She set the bowl of ice cream on the nightstand and reached for her phone. The message better not be a last-minute invitation to anywhere fun. She'd promised her mother to stay out of the limelight, out of respect for her father. The social media captions would be ruthless. *Party Girl Seen Out Partying after Famous Papa Passes Away.*

The message was from Sandro. It was as short as it was vague. You're right

No punctuation. No context. She took a moment to puzzle out the message's meaning, and drew a blank. She texted back: I usually am. What exactly am I right about this time?

Sandro: Everybody wants something

Her father had drilled that in her head. She could hear his voice: "Everybody wants something in this life. Don't trust anyone who pretends they don't." Slowly, realization dawned on her.

Gigi: Are you talking about Myles?

Sandro: Yes

Excitement and curiosity rushed straight to her head. What could the hot chef possibly want? She was aching to know.

Gigi: Want to clue me in?

His response came in fits.

Sandro: Sorry

Sandro: Can't

Sandro: It's confidential

"Come on!" she balked. "What's the point of this?"

Gigi: Bro! You've got to give me something to work with!

Sandro: You're smart. You figure it out.

Gigi: How???

This was beyond outrageous. Sandro was leaving for Canada in…a few hours. When would she have a chance to meet with Myles again? Honestly, what reason was there to dangle this carrot before her nose? She'd already given up hope, hence the comfort food and comfort television.

Sandro: Wait for his call.

She gasped. Sandro had come through! Why had she ever doubted him? But wait… With trembling fingers, she resumed typing.

Gigi: What did you tell him?

Sandro: That you could use a friend. He doesn't know you want to trap him into marriage.

Relieved, Gigi took a breath and collected herself. It would be good to meet with Myles one-on-one, get to know the man better and figure out what, if anything, he might want from her, before moving forward with her plan. After all, marriage was not to be entered into lightly.

Gigi: THANK YOU

Sandro: Good luck

Gigi clutched the phone to her chest. She needed all the luck she could get.

Too excited to sleep, she kicked back the sheets and took the empty bowl of ice cream to the kitchen. She found a half bottle of chardonnay in her mother's wine fridge and a sleeve of gourmet crackers in the pantry. She smuggled the loot back to her room. There, in the light of the muted TV, she munched on crackers and took swigs from the bottle, mapping out a strategy in her mind. She had to be ready for her meeting with Myles. At the end of the day, there was no trap without bait. She had to lure him with the promise of money; that was a given. Cash was king. Last year she'd sold some stocks, which meant she had a little money to play with, enough to get the ball rolling, anyway. It depended on what Myles had in mind. Did he want to expand the restaurant? Open a new location? Or simply take a year off to write a cookbook? What did chefs dream of, anyway? Whatever it was, one million, flat, should take care of it. Half up-front and the balance when they divorced in a year's time or earlier, should she suddenly crave her freedom. Divorcing too soon would draw suspicion. A yearlong marriage was just about average in her industry. They'd blame their hectic schedules for their breakup, and no one would bat an eye.

*Oh, wow. This just might work.*

Hysterical laughter bubbled up to her throat. She clamped a hand on her mouth to keep it from spilling out. Her mother's bedroom was at the opposite end of the hall. She'd likely taken a pill to help her sleep, yet she couldn't risk it. Lately, her mood swings were legendary.

Gigi wondered what her mother would do with the rest of her life. She was still young. Would she start a charity? Join a reality TV franchise? It was never too late to start over, to reinvent oneself. However, she doubted Beth would put in the effort. Her identity was grafted onto her famous husband's. She took pride in his accomplishments, as if they were her own. His legacy was hers to uphold. Her mother could have been one of the great models, yet she'd willingly given up her career for marriage. Gigi would only consider marriage to save her career. Their differences didn't end there. She and her mother didn't think the same, dream the same, vote the same or hustle the same. There was never a time when they weren't at the opposite ends of any given spectrum, and now was no exception. Her mother had lost a husband. Gigi—fingers crossed—had found one.

The very next day, around noon, Gigi received a text from an unknown number.

This is Myles. May I call you today?

Myles asking to call felt like a privilege only a few people enjoyed. Although Sandro had likely twisted his arm, she felt special anyway. She replied: I'd love that. Whenever you like.

How about now? Are you free?

I am.

She was not. With many apologies, she ended a virtual meeting with her assistant who was basically holding down the fort of GG Cinema while she was away. She deserved a raise and would get one if Gigi didn't have to lay her off at the end of the quarter. "Sorry, Zerlina! Got to go! We'll circle back, touch base, all those things. Bye! Thanks for everything! Bye!"

Her phone buzzed in her hand and sent an electric current straight to her heart. For whatever reason, she smoothed back her hair before answering the call.

"This is an unexpected pleasure, Chef. What's on the menu today?"

She heard him laugh softly and felt sure that, too, was a privilege few enjoyed. "Sandro gave me your number. I hope that's okay."

"More than okay. He said you'd call."

"What else did he say?"

"That you'd take me out for dinner."

"He said that?" he asked.

"Oh, yes," Gigi replied. "He said you'd take me somewhere quiet where we can get to know each other."

"Funny. He didn't mention that to me."

"That's odd."

He laughed again. Her cheeks were warm with pleasure.

"Obviously, you don't have to take me out," she said. "Just know I'd be crushed."

"I couldn't live with myself."

"Well, there you go."

"Someplace quiet?" he said. "Are you sure about that? Because a new hotel bar is opening on South Beach tonight."

Her party girl reputation must have preceded her. Myles likely thought she needed a red-carpet situation to enjoy herself. "No grand openings, I beg you."

"Christ, I'm sorry," he said. "I didn't think that through. You're going through a tough time. That's the last thing you need. Where are you staying? If you like, I could come over and cook for you."

As delicious as that sounded, she would have to pass. She couldn't have him over at the House of Sorrows. Besides, she'd been cooped up in her room all day, reading scripts, taking meetings and calls. "I'm staying with my mother, and I desperately need to get out of this house. I need fresh air, fresh food and a cocktail."

"Ten Eighty Riverside Drive," he said simply.

She was familiar with the little neighborhood that skirted the Miami River. There were some good places to eat there. "Say when. I'll meet you there."

"If we get there by five, we'll beat the crowd and get the best table."

Gigi could have screamed with joy. "Meet you at five, and thanks! I appreciate this."

"Don't thank me now," he said. "Wait until you see where I'm taking you."

Sandro called minutes later. "I got a text from Myles. He's taking you to dinner. Like what?"

Gigi didn't think that warranted a five-star alarm call. "It's just dinner."

"You don't get it," Sandro said. "Last I talked to him, he was too busy, focused on his future, and all that bullshit."

She let him in on a secret. "I lied through my teeth."

"Makes sense."

This got her thinking: if he agreed to this one "date," out of politeness or duty to Sandro, she might not get another chance.

"Will you pop the question tonight?" Sandro asked.

"I might have to."

"Hate to pressure you, but you might," Sandro agreed.

She'd get a sense of him by the appetizers and propose during dessert. That should make for a hot first date. "Should I slip a ring in his champagne flute, like in the movies?"

"No, but some champagne would be nice," Sandro said. "You're going to have to sweet-talk the guy."

"Why don't you just tell me what it is he wants?" Gigi implored. "It would make life so much easier."

"What kind of friend do you think I am?" Sandro asked, indignant. "You two could marry and have ten kids, and I still wouldn't tell you what Myles tells me in confidence. He and I go way back. Bro code and all that."

"Fuck bro code," she mumbled.

Sandro laughed. He was enjoying this way too much. "Let me know how it goes down," he said.

"Sure thing," she said with a sigh. "I'll call you tomorrow."

"Tomorrow? Hell no!" he balked. "Call me tonight. I don't care how late. I'm invested in this. I won't sleep until I know."

By four in the afternoon, Gigi was out of her loose pajamas and in a clingy black T-shirt dress with long sleeves and a micro-miniskirt that struck the right balance between sexy and casual, particularly when paired with a pair of limited-edition embroidered designer flats she'd picked up in Tokyo. She'd looked up the address and as far as she could tell, it was a family-owned seafood restaurant best known for its fried calamari, which made things tricky. She had to seduce Myles without scandalizing the regulars. Seduction was the wrong word. That wasn't her objective. Yet, when she recalled Myles's laugh swirling in her ear, the way it made her shiver, she wondered how she could possibly resist.

Gigi grabbed the purse that matched the shoes and headed out. From down the hall, her mother's voice scratched through the silence. "This is the powder room," she was saying. "The marble is exceptionally rare and imported from Italy."

Gigi sincerely hoped whoever was on the receiving end of that flow of information was actually interested, and her mother wasn't rambling on at some unsuspecting person's request to use the bathroom.

Before she knew it, her mother and her guest, a young man in a suit, were upon her.

"Georgina!" Beth exclaimed. "You're home!"

"I've been home all day."

Her mother eyed her outfit. "Are you going somewhere?"

"I am." Gigi eyed the man in the suit. No strangers had been in the house since her father had taken ill. "Who's this?"

"This is my Realtor, Arturo Ortiz."

"Hello, Ms. Garcia," Arturo the Realtor said. "I was a big fan of your father's."

"Yeah, thanks," Gigi said. "Excuse me. I'm confused. Mom, are you selling the house?"

"You don't expect me to live here alone, do you?" Beth asked. "The expense alone! Besides, I may not stay in Miami. Your father liked it here. I don't. I prefer Palm Beach. Or maybe I'll move back to Texas. Anyway, once I sell the house, I'll have a better idea of what to do next."

"Now is the perfect time to sell," Arturo said. "It's a seller's market. Besides, with the golf course, the church, the schools, this neighborhood is very much in demand."

Lovely! This very private family conversation was being moderated by the friendly local real estate agent.

"If it's no trouble, Georgina, may I show Arturo your room?" Beth asked.

"Will you be taking photos for the listing?" Gigi asked.

"We're not listing yet," Beth said, in a tone that Gigi was growing weary of.

"Just a quick glance," Arturo added hastily. "I want an idea of the layout of the bedrooms, that's all. Your mother hasn't hired me. There is no listing yet."

"Go ahead," Gigi said. "Close the door when you're done. I have to go."

She hurried down the hall and out the front door, giving in to a sudden urge to run and leave this house and everyone in it behind.

# Six

The billionaire heiress pulled into the restaurant's parking lot in a powder blue Porsche. Myles had arrived ahead of time. Through a window, he watched her climb out of the sports car, one shapely, tawny brown, outstretched leg at a time. She wore a simple, black mini and the most extravagant shoes. When she slipped off her sunglasses and took in the worn-down building with its chipped paint and pothole-ridden parking lot, he wondered if inviting her to The Heron had been a mistake.

He loved the place. The dishes were simple and the seafood beyond fresh. He often dined with family or friends, but never a date. With its kitschy, aquatic-themed decor and its main entrance accessible only through a fish market, it wasn't in the running for one of Miami's hot spots. He reminded himself that she'd requested someplace quiet to talk. This fit the bill. Then he reminded himself that this wasn't a date. He was doing a friend a favor. That was it.

If the bell above the door hadn't chimed, he would have missed the split second when she peeked inside the market and turned to leave.

He moved away from the window display and chased after her. "Hey, wait!"

She tossed a look over her shoulder and skidded to a stop. "Oh, thank God!" she exclaimed. "I thought I was at the wrong place."

Gigi could not hide her emotions, he found. A moment ago, her face had betrayed her confusion and now her brown eyes shone with relief.

"Do you know there's no sign out front?"

"There used to be," he said. "It got knocked off during the last hurricane."

"Should we donate a new one?" she asked.

"Nah," he said. "I think they like it better this way."

"Where do we eat?" she asked, some of that earlier doubt flooding back.

He pointed to a closed door. "Through there."

"Wait," she said. "Is this a private club? Do we need a special password or key?"

"If the fish market doesn't scare you away, you're in."

"I don't scare easily."

He should have known that about her. "Are you hungry?"

"Starving," she replied. "All I had for lunch was a bag of chips. And before you ask, I have no allergies. I love all types of seafood."

"You're in luck," he said. "The oysters are fantastic, and worth the trouble of finding this place."

"I heard good things about the fried calamari."

Myles let out a groan. "Not the fried calamari, Gigi."

"What exactly do you have against calamari?"

If Florida could ban the popular appetizer, he wouldn't object. It took him back to the good old days, working as a cook, frying batches of the stuff for the happy hour crowd.

"At seventeen, I worked at a sports bar that served cheap beer and fried calamari every evening from four to six. Forgive me, I just can't enjoy them."

Laughing, she reached for his arm. "We'll have the oysters!"

Their table bumped against a chipped wooden rail and overlooked the river, ablaze from the glow of the setting sun. Between them, resting on ice, was a sample of oysters from various regions. He pointed out his favorites from the East Coast and the West.

"You're the expert and a culinary professional," she said. "Anything to the theory that oysters are an aphrodisiac?"

"Science backs the claim."

Mischief lit up her face. "Are you up for a science experiment?"

They should've gone with the calamari. That was his mistake.

The waiter arrived with their drinks. A margarita for her, and a beer for him. She tasted the salted rim with a flick of her pink tongue. Myles admitted to himself that he'd misjudged her. She was easygoing, with none of the pretentiousness he'd expected from a sports legend's only daughter. Myles set aside his apprehensions. He could relax and be himself now. The only way he knew to do that was to be as direct and forthright as possible.

"I told Sandro I was meeting you tonight," he said. "To be honest, he has certain expectations on how this evening will go."

She stirred the ice in her glass. "So do I."

"This is a conspiracy, then?"

She denied nothing. "We may have been plotting something that involves you. Would that be so wrong?"

"Not wrong," he said. "Just a waste of your time. Nothing personal. I've got a lot going on, and Sandro knows it."

"I get that." With long, delicate, gold-ring-clad fingers, she picked up an oyster, drizzled it with lemon, knocked it back, and dropped the shell with a clatter into an empty bowl. "All I ask is that you keep an open mind."

He tore his gaze away. A slender heron, perched on a neighboring dock, locked eyes with him. The bird was known for its wisdom, and likely questioned why Myles, a clueless male human, was on the fence when a stunning female of the species was making such aggressive moves. He questioned it himself.

Myles wasn't a dreamer, like Sandro or Gigi. They could plot all they wanted, but nothing would come of it. He and Gigi were far too different. If you took Sandro out of the equation, what did they have in common? Gigi was a celebrity in her own right, her life documented in the press and social media. She was always front row at some fashion show or walking a red carpet in Venice or Cannes—not that he kept up with those things. She made all the lists: whether it be 30 under 30 or Hollywood's Nepo Babies, she was on it. Besides, she lived clear across the country and moved in circles that he avoided.

He paused, exhausted from the mental gymnastics. He'd never had to work so hard to talk himself out of anything.

Right then, Sandro sent him a text message. It read simply: So?

Reminded of his true mission, Myles said, "I never got to tell you how sorry I am for your loss."

"Thanks," she said quietly. "It was a long time coming. I was prepared. His health was failing, and he hated being stuck in bed."

Myles knew something about loss and grief. No matter how prepared you were, the blow could knock you off-balance. "It still hurts."

"Oh, it does," she admitted, her gaze skimming the river. "Some days if feels like I'm losing everything."

"You're not," he said. "It only feels that way."

"Trust me," she said. "I'm not being dramatic. In a matter of months, I've lost my dad, my home and…"

"Your home?"

"My mother is selling the house," she explained. "Thought I was prepared for that, too. Sometimes it's hard to let go."

It seemed like in a short time, her life had shattered. If he could go on a scavenger hunt and collect the pieces, he would. "What else did you lose?"

A flash of panic, and then a smile. "Never mind! I'm really killing the vibe. We're supposed to be getting to know each other."

"We are." If the vibe was made of fake smiles and small talk, he'd gladly kill it himself. "Pedro Garcia was so famous, so liked… Having to mourn him alongside his fans has to be draining."

She picked up the plain butter knife and gripped the handle.

"He's an icon and a legend, and to say anything negative about him is blasphemous."

"Were you close?" he asked.

She weighed his question. "I thought so, but…" A fishing boat motored past and drowned her words. When silence returned, she said. "Closeness requires mutual respect and admiration. It can't go one way."

Myles tried to make sense of that. "Are you saying he wasn't proud of you?"

She leaned forward, brows drawn. "Are you sure this is what you want to talk about? It's such a nice day and—"

"I'm sure."

"Okay." She took in a sharp breath and let it out. "It's my fault. I didn't come into my own until I moved to California. Before that I was an international It Girl, like the Hiltons and the Hadids. Every relationship I had, every fun night out, every friend I made and lost, it was all documented in the tabloids. To my parents, I'm still that wild little girl, that rebellious teen who grew up to be a reckless young woman. I never grew up in their eyes, and they treat me accordingly."

"It's not your fault."

Everything that she was—smart, confident, successful—was obvious to anyone. If her parents didn't see it, they chose not to.

"How about you?" she asked, tentatively. "Are you close to your father?"

"He passed away before I could figure that out," he replied frankly.

She went still. "I'm sorry."

"It was a long time ago."

Myles had the opposite problem to hers. His parents had put an end to his childhood as soon as he turned ten. From then on, he was "a little man." When his father died, some three years later, he was named the "man of the house." He'd never had a rebellious teen phase; there was no time. He had responsibilities no kid should bear. It was only at Sandro's house that he could kick back.

"When we lost him, my mother, in a way, sort of lost it," he said. "She didn't trust that she could carry on alone, without some protective male figure. One day, she took me to see a pastor for a talk. He told me to set aside childish things."

Gigi stared at him, her vivid eyes questioning. "That's a lot of pressure. How did you cope?"

"Hanging out with Sandro after school," he said. "That's where I learned how to cook, making nachos and burgers. At home, my mother forced my sister to cook, yet kicked me out of the kitchen. Sandro's grandfather didn't care what we did. He was the best. This is not to say I didn't love my mother. I did."

"I understand," she said. "I loved my dad."

Myles felt as though the river rushed through him. He hadn't opened up like this with anyone for years.

Gigi raised a toast. "To our dads… May they rest in peace."

It was morbid for a toast, but fitting. He could do better, though. "To killing the vibe, and getting to know each other."

"Fair warning," she said teasingly. "To know me is to love me."

He had no doubt this was true. "I believe it."

He raised his glass. *"Santé!"*

Her smile widened. *"¡Salud!"*

They went to work on the oysters.

"I have a question," she said. "What's your favorite movie?"

"I don't have one," he replied.

"That's insane! Everybody has at least one favorite movie."

"I like anything Sandro is in." He never had a chance to attend the premieres, but he made a point to watch at home. *"Downward Spiral* was the best. He made that one with you, right?"

"Good answer," she said. "Now tell me the truth."

*"The Godfather… I* and *II."*

"Aha!" She winked. "There you go!"

"Your turn," he said.

"You won't judge?"

"I absolutely will," he assured her. "Count on it."

"I didn't judge you for your classic dude movie choices!" she protested. "The first two *Godfathers*. Really? What a surprise!"

"Sounds like judgment to me."

"No judgment. Now, if you had said *Scarface*, well…"

He smiled and handed her a perfectly balanced dressed oyster. "For you."

She accepted the offering. He watched her throat constrict and relax as she swallowed. She dropped the shell in the bowl with a flourish.

"I'm waiting," he said.

"I like any movie where the big city girl falls for the small-town boy."

He groaned. "God help me."

"I like slasher movies, spy thrillers and family sagas."

"Okay…"

"I like pretentious, art house films with tortured dialogue and confusing endings."

"Anything else?"

"Foreign films with subtitles."

"Just say you like movies, Gigi."

"It's true," she said. "I love them all. It's an escape to another world."

"You're in the right line of work."

"I think so," she said. "Okay. Let's see… What's your favorite food? No, wait! You're a chef. What's your favorite meal to cook?"

"I cook to make people happy," he said. "To please and surprise them. Whatever you like to eat is what I like to cook."

Her face was rosy with pleasure. "It's your love language!"

"Maybe," he said with a laugh.

"Is that why Diablo is so successful?" she asked.

"No, when it comes to the restaurant, I can't lose sight of the business end of things. The more…innovative a dish is, the more attention it gets. The buzzword is 'fusion.' So, I push the envelope, but it's work."

"And when you're not working?" she asked.

"I'm always working," he said. "But I like to have my good friends over and make simple food."

"Would you have me over?" she asked.

It was almost a plea. The yearning in her voice stopped his heart. "Anytime you like," he said. "You're a friend."

The pinkish color spread down her neck, exactly where he wanted to kiss her.

"What's yours?" he asked.

She blinked at him. "My what?"

"Love language."

"Telling people what to do," she said. "Some call it pestering. I call it nurturing."

"Yeah. I totally get that."

Gigi methodically squeezed lemon juice on the very last oyster, then followed with a dollop of horseradish. Myles was getting a sense of her palate. Nothing subtle or sweet. Citrus factored first, from the tart margarita to the choice of dressing. Next came the heat of the horseradish. She was bold, frank, and not at all shy, so this mix of flavors made sense.

Myles took a sip of beer. He did not want her to catch him staring.

"Next topic?" she proposed.

"Go ahead."

"What are your goals?"

"Professional goals?" he asked, confused.

"Yes."

"I don't get it," he said. "Is this a job interview or a date?"

"I don't date."

"Uh… That can't be true."

"It's true," she affirmed. "Dating sucks. When was the last time you were on a hot date?"

"What makes for a hot date, in your opinion?"

Her answer was oddly specific. "When you're out with someone clever, who listens, and has insightful things to say, yet while they're talking, in the back of your mind, all you can think about is kissing them."

By that definition, he likely never had been on a hot date—if he ruled out this non-date. "You set the bar high."

"I'd settle for less, trust me," she said. "But every date I've been on in the last few years has felt transactional. So I gave up."

"Transactional in what sense?" Myles asked.

For some reason, she hesitated before saying, "Everybody wants something."

He grabbed a napkin, reached over and dabbed a bit of horseradish off the tip of her nose. "Why is that so bad?" he asked. "It's human nature."

His phone buzzed with another text message from Sandro. Well???

Myles lost his patience and pocketed the phone.

"Is that important?" she asked. "I don't mind if you take the call."

"Trust me, it can wait."

The busboy cleared the table and filled their water glasses. Myles thought they could try the grilled snapper for dinner. All the while he was thinking of kissing her. And then it clicked. "If this isn't a date, it's a job interview."

She bit her lower lip to control a smile. "I wouldn't put it that way. Let's call it an audition."

He was on to something. Interesting. "What role do you want me to fill?"

"Hold on," she said. "You may not be the right man for the job."

The right man? Suddenly, he was focused on proving her wrong. "I don't think you could do better than me. I'm a quick study. I think on my feet. I work well with others. I'm an excellent leader."

"Myles! I didn't mean to rattle your ego!"

She had a point. Ego had him fighting for something he was almost certain he didn't want. But there was nothing he could do to stop it.

"Test me," he said. "You wanted to know my goals, right?"

"Yes, that's important," she said. "Where do you see your-self in a year?"

"You mean five years," he corrected. "Isn't that the standard interview question?"

"This isn't a standard interview," she replied. "You're auditioning for a limited run. One year is all I need."

Their waiter approached, presumably to take their order. Only, he arrived with a magnum of champagne and two glasses. "Compliments of Mr. Cardenas."

Myles couldn't believe it. "You've got to be kidding."

"Not at all, sir," the waiter said cheerfully. "Congratulations on your engagement!"

"What the—"

*POP!*

# Seven

With the uncorking of a fine bottle of champagne, a lovely dinner plunged into chaos. Panicked, Gigi started babbling to the waiter. "Oh, wow! Just leave it. We'll take care of it."

"Not a chance, miss!" He dutifully filled two flutes and nestled the bottle into a standing silver bucket. Before retreating, he said, "Your father was one of the greats. We're so honored to have you. Congratulations!"

Gigi, who prided herself in never losing her composure, lost it completely. "Oh, God," she whispered. "Oh, God… Oh, God…"

"Gigi, it's okay!" Myles said. "Don't look so terrified. I'm not going to propose."

*No, but she might.*

"This is classic Sandro," he said. "The guy is on a movie set somewhere, laughing at us."

She flashed her red-carpet smile. "A joke! I get it!"

He did not look convinced. "You don't look well. Let's go."

"No! Wait!"

He leaned forward and studied her with concern. Gigi had to admit, he was stunning when he was serious. This wasn't a date and for once she hadn't put on a fun, flirty persona. Miraculously they'd clicked. Often, Gigi was either too much or not enough. Most people approached her with preconceived notions. Spin the wheel! She was either a nepo baby, a brat, a bad bitch, a boss babe or a bimbo. But with Myles, she felt like a normal person, a regular girl getting to know a guy. Sadly, she was going to put on her boss babe hat and ruin it all.

It was now or never.

Gigi took a sip of champagne—she might as well—and,

summoning the audaciousness of bad bitches everywhere, she said, "Myles, will you marry me?"

Myles looked at her expectantly. He was waiting for a punch line, she realized.

"This isn't a joke," she said.

"Are you sure?" he asked, affording her the benefit of doubt.

"I'm sure," she said.

"Well, I'm lost," he admitted. "What's going on?"

She managed a wobbly smile. "Everybody's looking for something, right?"

"I didn't think you were one of them," he replied.

Every ounce of badassery drained from her soul right then and there. She saw herself through his big soulful eyes, a greedy opportunist. To think she could arrange a marriage of convenience over a meal! Was Gabe right about her? Had she been in Hollywood too long?

"Just hear me out," she said. "I can explain."

"Don't," he said gently. "Whatever you and Sandro are up to, I'd rather not get involved."

Put in her place, Gigi sat with her hands on her lap as Myles tried settling a tab, which, as it turned out, Sandro had already settled. The most he could do was add a generous tip. Once that was sorted, he stood. "We should go."

"Please, let's not end it this way. We were having such a good time."

"That was before I knew you had an agenda."

He shouldn't underestimate her. She had more than one agenda, but she kept that to herself. "Could I at least share it with you?"

Who knew what he'd think of her if she didn't have a chance to explain?

He searched her face a while. Gigi held her breath, but she did not hide. Her secrets, her schemes, he might as well see it all. There was no point in hiding.

Finally, he caved. "We can't talk here. Would you like to go to my place?"

She sprung to her feet. "I'd like that. Where is it?"

"Not far." He pointed across the river to a low-slung house with a yard that backed onto the riverbank, complete with a dock. "I'll take you. Let's leave your car here."

By that, he meant, he'd take her via Jet Ski. Without question, she took his outstretched hand and let him guide her down a flight of rickety wooden stairs to the dock, under the watchful eye of a slim heron bird. He guided her onto the tethered watercraft with care, a hand on her waist. A sweet but unnecessary gesture. Some girls grew up riding ponies, but she'd grown up on the water. They took off, her chest to his back, her hair in the wind. This felt like the start of an adventure, not an end to their story.

The short ride from dock to dock took all of five minutes. Gigi reluctantly let Myles go. He slipped out of her arms and smoothly leaped onto the seawall. No way she was going to leap in limited edition Dior slingbacks. That much was settled in her mind. So, when Myles reached for her, she handed over her purse and shoes instead. "Here! Take these!"

That split decision set in motion a series of unfortunate events. Only her purse made it safely to Myles. The limited edition slingbacks slipped from her hands and plunged soundlessly into the water. Gigi was galvanized into action. She sprang off the Jet Ski and ended up waist-deep in the cold, murky river. It was worth it when she excavated a soggy shoe from the muddy riverbed.

"I got it!" she cried, and held it up to show Myles, but he was no longer on the dock. He was wading in the water, coming to her rescue—or to the rescue of the other shoe, which he found.

Gigi was speechless. *This is the man I want to marry.*

A hot shower later, wearing an oversize sweatshirt and the shame of her latest stunt, Gigi joined Myles in the kitchen. It was dark out. Recessed lighting cast a soft glow over the butcher-block countertop where he was busy chopping something into bits. It was all so very cozy.

"Should I toss your dress in the dryer?" he asked without looking up.

The idea of the vintage silk jersey dress shrinking to a doll's size made her shudder. How could she survive it after the near destruction of her shoes? "Not unless you want to break me."

"Glad I asked."

He presented her with an honest-to-goodness charcuterie board with sausage, cheese, olives, tomatoes, various crudités and crackers. While she gawked at it, he opened a nice bottle of red. "What are you and Sandro up to?" he asked.

She spread brie on a cracker. "Please don't blame Sandro. I dragged him into this. He would do anything to help a friend."

"All right." He set a glass of wine before her. "What are *you* up to?"

Gigi held his gaze. She'd misjudged this man and mistaken his calm, quiet demeanor for softness. At his core, he was granite. There was nothing soft about him.

"Earlier, you said you liked the film I made with Sandro. Did you mean it?"

"I meant it," he said. "He says it was his best work, and I agree."

"It was my best work, too," she admitted. "I poured everything I had into that production and bawled like a baby when I watched the final cut. It was a commercial *and* critical success. Nothing I've done so far has matched it, but I'm not ready to give up trying."

"Why should you give up?" he asked. "You're obviously very talented."

"Talent isn't enough."

"What's stopping you, then?"

"What stops anyone from doing anything they want?" she asked. "A critical lack of funds."

"You have funding issues?" he said incredulously. "Come on."

"I do."

She sipped her wine and let him come to terms with reality.

Yes, she had access to resources and, it had to be said, immeasurable privilege, but everything had its limits.

"Go on," he said.

"I've been running in the red. My only option is to settle my debts, cut ties with my financiers and restructure my business. Going forward, I plan on self-financing. That'll give me more control over the projects I choose."

"Aren't you worth millions?" he asked.

"Yes and no."

He stuck a cocktail pick into a stuffed olive and offered it to her. Their fingers brushed, and for a moment she forgot what they were talking about. It was just the two of them, standing in his kitchen, eating premium cheese, on a summer night.

"I'm having a tough time figuring out where I fit in," he said.

"My father left me enough money to fund my business, but there's a catch."

"There usually is."

"Wait five years or get married."

"What?"

She popped the olive in her mouth. There was no need to repeat herself.

"Are you serious?" he asked, still grappling with her revelation.

"I am."

Myles scratched at the fresh stubble at his jawline. "So… you want to marry me?"

"I do."

"Gigi, that's crazy."

"Think about it. I can deliver your wildest dreams."

He tempered the bitterness of her tone with a sweet smile. "Good thing I don't have wild dreams."

She found that hard to believe. He had the eyes of a dreamer. "Liar."

"I don't lie," he said simply. "For one thing, I've never had to. You'll always know where you stand with me."

If that wasn't husband material, Gigi thought, what was?

"Hmm… How can I rephrase this?" she wondered aloud, fingers curled around the wineglass's long stem. "Is there nothing you want? Nothing you yearn for?"

"Anything I yearn for," he said, "any dream I cook up, I make it happen on my own. I don't owe anything to anyone— ever."

Gigi respected that. "Good answer. You and I aren't so different."

"We couldn't be more different, Gigi."

She resumed spreading brie on a cracker and changed tactics. "Forget dreams. Let's talk next steps. What's in the cards for you? The restaurant is extremely popular. Are you looking to expand your business, open a second location, maybe?"

A shadow passed through those eyes. "I can't expand on what's not mine."

Gigi froze, the loaded cracker halfway to her parted lips. Without realizing, Myles had revealed his hand. The thing he yearned for, his wildest dream, was the very restaurant to which he'd already given his all. God help her, she intended to serve it to him, with a flourish, on a silver platter.

# Eight

When Gigi had stepped out of his bedroom, barefoot, wearing nothing but his sweatshirt—as far as he could tell—hair dripping wet, long, brown legs still glistening from the shower, Myles couldn't look at her and he couldn't look away. Standing now on the knife's edge of desire, he was this close to saying yes to any half-baked plan she and Sandro whipped up.

"I'd marry you for this charcuterie board alone," she said. "But I need a husband to access my inheritance."

Myles tried to make sense of her words. "Have you talked to your money manager? I'm pretty sure that's not how it works."

Her pretty, pouty mouth tightened to a thin line. "My father's attorney would disagree."

"Did you lawyer up?"

"I don't have time," she replied. "I'm getting married—that's the plan."

He wasn't sold. "I get that you'd like to invest in your business, but—"

She laughed bitterly. "I need the money to *save* my business."

"From what?"

"Bankruptcy."

This was inconceivable to Myles. "You won an Oscar or two. Isn't that the equivalent of a Michelin star in your industry?"

She laughed darkly and ran her fingertips through her wet hair. "Not really. I know a sound editor who slept in his car cradling his Oscar."

"That's horrible."

"That's the industry."

He took away the charcuterie platter. "I'm hungry for real

food," he said. "All we've had are appetizers and I'm still upset we didn't get to try the snapper. Dinner?"

She offered to order in food. "I've put you through enough."

"No," he said grimly. "I need to cook." He reached for a copper pot from the hanging rack. "Everyone gets their hands dirty in my kitchen. Come grate cheese."

"Yes, Chef!"

He set up a station with a bowl, a grater and a wedge of Parmigiano-Reggiano. "At the restaurant, I experiment with pasta dishes. At home, I keep it simple with cheese, good butter, salt, pepper and fresh pasta."

"I like simple," she said.

He filled a pot with water. "I keep my life simple, too. I'd love to help you, but I can't. A fake marriage is not my style."

"It's not a designer bag!" she said. "Who's to say what's real or fake? I'd make a great partner."

She was grating his beautiful wedge of cheese with such savagery he could not stand by and let it happen. He reached for her wrist and begged her to stop. "Show mercy. You're killing it."

"I watched every episode of *Martha Stewart Living*," she proclaimed. "I know how to grate cheese."

"Watching and doing are two different things." He demonstrated, showing her the right pressure and pace. "Look what you get—fluffy, stress-free, grated cheese."

She folded her arms. "Okay. Fine!"

Myles grabbed a pinch and held it up to her mouth. She very readily parted her lips. Every nerve ending in his body snapped and cracked.

"Delicious," she said.

Myles felt a tightening in his chest. He wouldn't marry her, but what he wouldn't do to her if given the chance.

"Marrying for money is one of life's oldest hacks," she said.

She'd resumed grating, but her technique had not improved. Myles took the bowl away. "I think we have enough cheese."

"You can never have enough," she said. "In the DR, we fry

chunks of white cheese. My grandmother would make it whenever I visited."

"I can make it better than your grandmother."

"Oh, I forgot!" she exclaimed. "You're the MVP of world cuisine!"

"That's *fusion* cuisine." He would never live down that stupid title. That didn't mean he couldn't have fun with it. "So…" He checked on the pasta water, adjusted the flame. "You went to Sandro with this idea, and he offered to set us up? I thought he knew me better than that."

"That's not what happened," she said. "The moment I met you, I knew you were the one."

He glanced at her. "That's romantic, in a perverted way."

She blushed and turned away.

The pasta water came to a boil, and Myles focused on preparing the meal. For some reason, he wanted to impress her, to make her the best damn pasta dish she'd ever had. Years from now, he wanted her to remember this night, the simple meal they'd prepared together in his kitchen, and how it had made her feel.

When he was done, he loaded two bowls with creamy pasta topped with caviar.

"Now you're just showing off," she said.

"You had a long day," he said. "You fell into a river. I want you to eat well."

"You're wrong about one thing," she said. "I very deliberately jumped into that river."

"I hope those shoes were worth it."

"I just pray they're not ruined!" she exclaimed. "Thanks for helping me, by the way."

He topped her wineglass. "You're welcome."

She took her first taste of pasta and moaned. "You're a genius."

"Yeah, well…maybe…"

"So modest!"

They remained at the counter, side by side, eating, sipping, laughing. Finally, she said, "Don't you want to hear the offer before you turn it down?"

"You're persistent." How many ways would he have to say no?

"And you're just as stubborn as Sandro said."

He was having too much of a good time to put up a fight. "Go on. Make me an offer."

"About twelve months of marriage in exchange for a fixed amount."

"Oh yeah? What's the going rate?"

"It's negotiable. How much do you need?"

He didn't need any money—if you excluded the funding for a new restaurant. And he did exclude it. It was an enviable position to be in, and he'd worked his ass off for it. That aside, he hated that she was in the crappy position of having to entertain this idea.

"Gigi, it won't work," he said. "Do you know how risky your plan is?"

"Not with you," she replied. "I can trust you. That's the beauty of it. The only person I trust more is Sandro."

"I'm not your first choice, then?"

"You may be my only choice," she said. "Wouldn't you like to set up a restaurant or buy out the owner of your current one? Marry me, and we'll make it happen. You'll never work for anyone ever again."

"I'd be working for you."

"Don't think of it that way."

"How should I think of it?"

"Like a short-term loan," she said with a shrug. "I promise you. We'll both win in the end."

"You can't promise that."

"I just did." She reached for his hand and squeezed. "Marry me, and I'll deliver your dreams on a silver platter."

"I'd say yes, just to see you try."

"Say yes, anyway."

"No." He took their empty bowls to a sink.

"Why? Give me one reason."

"We'd be using each other."

"We'd be *useful* to each other," she said. "And really, is that so bad? Marriages have thrived on less."

Myles laughed. "You make it sound so simple."

"It is simple. Will you think about it?"

"No, gorgeous," he said. "I won't marry you. Not under any circumstances, and certainly not under these."

Myles brought her hand to his lips and sealed this dark promise with a light kiss.

# Nine

"What the fuck, man?"

That was all Myles could say when he finally confronted Sandro. The showdown happened via FaceTime. The actor was on set and had barricaded himself in his trailer between takes to make the call. Myles was at Diablo. It was past midnight, and he had the kitchen to himself. Finally, he could unleash his frustrations. How could his best, and some may say his only, friend set him up like that?

Sandro attempted to explain. "Honestly, I think you two would be good together."

"You think marrying an heiress so she can get a hold of her dad's money is a good idea?"

"That's not what I meant," Sandro said. "Anyway, I told her you wouldn't go for it, but then I got to thinking—"

"That was your first mistake!" Myles cried. "Don't over-think it. Your first instinct was spot-on."

"Bro...chill..."

Sandro was far too chill, in Myles's opinion. Or maybe the actor was in character. He was playing the lead in a 1950s period piece set in New York City but filmed in Toronto. He wore a smartly tilted fedora hat, which Myles wished he could stuff down his throat. He had to remind Sandro of the gravity of the situation.

"Bro, you pimped me out!"

"And for that I deserve a thank-you. Gigi is one of the best people I know. She's smart, loyal, caring. She needs a little help right now. If you weren't so thickheaded, you'd admit to need-ing a little help yourself. You two could work something out."

A little help? It's not like the woman was asking for a ride to the airport or help moving apartments. She wanted a temporary sham of a marriage. He'd have to lie to everyone he knew, family included, to keep up the ruse, and then he'd have to take her money, something he would never do. For the rest of his life, he'd be known as Gigi Garcia's ex-husband.

Sandro laid out the plan. "Marry her. Play house for a year and walk away the proud owner of a restaurant. It's that simple."

It was not simple! "And lie to my family, and everyone I know?"

"You don't have to lie," Sandro said. "You don't owe anyone an explanation. If anyone asks, tell them it's none of their business."

Myles shook his head. "That'll go over well with Michelle."

His older sister was his only close relative. They trusted each other. He would not jeopardize that.

"Gigi is tons of fun," Sandro said. "Who knows? It could be just the thing to knock Natalie out of your head."

Myles ignored that last part. Natalie was his ex, and had long been knocked from his heart and mind. Instead, he focused on the fun part: he and Gigi eating pasta on their feet, laughing until well in the night. Even though he'd turned her down, she hadn't turned on him. She'd taken her defeat with grace, then forced him to watch a movie. He couldn't remember the last time he'd brought a woman back to his place, not after Natalie, and usually it was strictly for sex. They didn't hang out in his kitchen, discussing their dreams, their fears, and least of all marriage. What he'd experienced with Gigi was far more intimate than it had any right to be considering they'd only just met and would likely never meet again.

She'd spent the night in his guest room to sleep off the wine, but he'd slept hardly at all. In the morning, she'd stuffed her damp dress and soggy shoes in a shopping bag. She'd kept his sweatshirt, which fit her like a dress, a very short one. Then he'd driven her to her car and paid the premium for the overnight stay.

"You'll be all right?" he asked once she was settled behind the wheel.

"I'll be fine."

Although she smiled sunnily, something ripped inside of him. He wanted more for her than "fine." Where would she go from here? Would she get Sandro to recruit another potential husband? The questions burned with urgency, yet he'd forfeited the right to ask.

"Come here," she'd said.

He'd leaned low, stealing a moment to take in that face, those clear brown eyes, the natural wave of her hair that returned as soon as she hit the water. She smelled of his soap.

That was his very last thought before she cupped his face and brushed a kiss against his lips. "Thank you," she whispered.

"For what?" he asked.

"Last night."

She took off in that ridiculous car, and he'd stood on the sidewalk a long while wrestling with the feeling that he might be making a mistake.

"I didn't like Natalie," Sandro said. "Did I ever tell you that?"

Sandro's question pulled Myles back. "It was mutual."

"Fair enough."

"Hold on a second."

Myles thought he heard footsteps in the main dining room even though he was alone. The last of the cooks had locked up before leaving. A quick inspection showed nothing out of order. It was quiet. The tables were set with fresh linens for the next day. The bar was polished. As always, whenever he had the space to himself, he was seduced by its magic. Then he remembered Sandro waiting on the video call and rushed back.

"Sorry about that. Thought I heard something."

"No problem," Sandro said. "Anyway, I gotta go. They need me on set."

Her first Zoom call of the day was with Emily, her lead project developer. She encouraged Gigi to explore the book-club-to-big-screen pipeline that had proven lucrative for two major competitors. "It's a no brainer, and frankly I'm upset we didn't think of this earlier. We grab a book with the right buzz, shop it around to a streaming service and give it the GG Cinema treatment!"

That treatment consisted of casting little-known actors in key roles. Their cohort of stylists and publicists turned them into stars.

"If we do it right, the book fans alone will give us the ratings."

Emily's idea was a good one. They could pick a popular novel and produce a gorgeous film. When Emily suggested scouting picturesque European locations, Gigi snapped out of it. She did not want a no-brainer project. "I don't think so, Em."

"Trust me on this," Emily said. "Everyone I know is dreaming of Italy and Stanley Tucci."

"Oh, God, me, too," Gigi blurted. "It's just…our next project has to be something original to help us stand out."

"All right," Emily said. "Forget Italy."

"Yes, please," she said. "We probably couldn't afford it anyway."

"Oh…right." Emily tucked a stray lock of red hair behind her ear, a nervous tic Gigi knew well.

"Listen," Gigi said. "I can't keep pretending like this. I owe you the truth."

In her last staff meeting, before leaving for her father's funeral, she'd assured her team that she had a plan to get the company back on track. It was high time she admitted the plan had failed.

"Don't," Emily said, blue eyes wide in panic. "I can't handle the truth."

"Yes, you can," Gigi replied. "There may not be a next project at all."

Emily shook her head. "I don't accept that."

"You have to. This may be the end of GG Cinema."

"This is the best job I've ever had," Emily said. "I won't accept that it's over. You can turn it around. I believe in you."

This was what you got when you hired a former professional

cheerleader. This never-say-die attitude was great, but it could only take you so far.

Gigi's phone rang. The caller ID flashed Sandro's name. He was in Canada filming yet another remake of a Hitchcock classic, but that was no excuse for making her wait a whole day before returning her call. She was in a crisis, for heaven's sake!

"Em, I've got to take this call."

"I'll send you a few books with promise," Emily said. "Don't freak out if a few are set in Italy. It can't be avoided. Which format do you prefer, print, digital, or audio?"

"All of the above!" Gigi answered. "Talk soon!"

She slammed the laptop shut and answered Sandro's call. *"Finally!"*

"Settle down," he said. "I meant to call sooner, but it's been busy. No French hours on this set."

And yet he'd found time to track her and Myles down at the riverfront restaurant and drop a champagne bomb. "What were you thinking, sending over that bottle?"

"I got a little excited, I won't lie," he said. "Dumb of me to count on the waiter's discretion, though."

"You think? Now Myles is convinced we're plotting against him."

"Oh, I know."

"You spoke with him?"

"I listened as he ranted, but yeah, we spoke."

"Is he mad?"

"Not at you. He thinks I pimped him out, which is the truth."

"Oh, God…" She buried her face in her hands and mumbled, "I'm so sorry for dragging you into this mess."

"Don't be," Sandro said. "I'm having a blast. I am curious, though. How was it before the champagne arrived? Were you clicking?"

"Definitely!" Gigi cried. "Even after he turned me down, we managed to have a good time."

"Is that right?" Sandro said dryly. "What did he say when you revealed your plan?"

Gigi made a face. "Reveal my plan? Like a scheming villain?"

"Yeah."

She sighed. "He said he wouldn't marry me under *any* circumstances!"

"Whoa! That's harsh."

"But then he kissed me."

"Kissed you?"

"He kissed my hand."

Without thinking, Gigi touched the exact spot on the back of her hand where his lips had brushed her skin. She had to give it to the man: she'd never been rejected with such finesse.

"He kissed you," Sandro repeated in disbelief.

"The thing is, I know he's the one."

"The…one?"

"Myles would be the perfect husband," she explained. "He's kind and caring. Do you know how rare that is?"

"I do. Why do you think he's my best friend?"

"He jumped in the river to save my shoes."

"The…river?"

"You know, the one behind his house."

"Yeah… I'm familiar with the river."

"Could you talk to him?" she asked.

"He kissed you, and you think he's the one. What do I have to add to this conversation?"

"Please let him know that I have no hard feelings," she said. "I'm grateful he listened to me at all. I'd hate for him to think I was only interested in using him."

"Since when do you care what people think about you?"

"I only care about what *he* thinks."

"All right," Sandro said. "I'll tell him."

Gigi blew him a kiss. "Thanks! Love you!"

"Yeah, right," he said. "Listen, I gotta run. They need me on set."

Long after the call ended, Gigi turned Sandro's words in her mind. Was it odd that she wanted Myles to like her even if nothing would come of it? Sandro certainly made it seem so. She pondered this on her way to the kitchen for a second cup of coffee.

Her mother was at the table with her usual cup of tea, aggressively flipping through a copy of *Architectural Digest*. She greeted Gigi with a scowl.

Gigi went to the coffee station and pushed a pod in the espresso machine. She could feel her mother's eyes on her. "Why are you looking at me like that?" she asked.

"Because there's security camera footage of you sneaking in at dawn wearing only an oversize sweatshirt," Beth replied.

"Ah, yes..." Gigi laughed softly as the memory flooded back. She'd never return that sweatshirt. "I wasn't sneaking, by the way."

"You think it's funny?"

"It *was* fun. I'll say that."

"We just buried your father, Georgina. Couldn't you take a break?"

Her father would have wanted her to enjoy her life. He'd always cheered her on and bragged about her exploits. Yet, if the last few days had taught her anything, it was that she hadn't known the man quite as well as she'd thought. On the other hand, her mother remained the same judgmental person she'd always been. Gigi caught her disapproving stare. It might be time for her to head back to LA. With so many aspiring actors wandering about, she might have a better chance roping in a husband.

As if she'd read Gigi's mind, her mother said, "Your father wanted you to come home and take over the charity arm of his organization. He wanted you to build on his legacy, not squander it chasing dreams in Hollywood."

Gigi's reaction was violent. This was the first she was hearing of this. Take over what? Did such a thing even exist? "I might be wrong, but the business doesn't have a charity arm. Anyway, it sounds like a job for you. Fundraisers and luncheons are more your thing."

"It could be your thing, too," her mother said. "We discussed it, and we think it's a good fit for you and your particular skill set."

Signing checks made out to children's hospitals didn't require any particular skill, only the will and an open heart. "Sorry to crush your dream, but I'll be heading back to California soon. I stayed for you, but I think we could use some time apart."

"Fine." Beth stood and tucked the magazine under her arm. "Honestly, I don't care what you do with your free time. But while you're here, please keep your clothes on."

"I'll try," Gigi quipped.

"Oh, one more thing," Beth said.

"What's that?"

"We have a buyer for the house."

"Already? Did Arturo even get a chance to list it?"

"Arturo was my plan B."

"What was plan A?"

"Selling directly to a developer."

Gigi held on to the granite countertops as if for the last time. "But they'll tear down the place."

"It's for the best," Beth said. "Too many memories live here."

Built in the eighties, the McMansion was as ostentatious as it was outdated. Its only appeal for Gigi was the memories: lazy Sunday afternoons by the pool, birthday dinners, Christmas mornings, creeping out at midnight and, yes, sneaking in at dawn. Her roots were buried in the backyard beneath the mini golf course.

Jesus, she was going to miss it. She was going to miss the home her father had loved and the family unit he'd kept together. Without his embrace, Gigi and her mother were destined to drift apart. She saw that clearly now.

# Ten

*What now?*

That was the first question that popped in Myles's head when his boss, Lou Palmer, strode into the kitchen early on a Monday morning. The next question was: *How much more of this bullshit can I take?*

Diablo was closed for the day. Yet, anyone who knew Myles, Lou included, knew where to find him. The kitchen was his sanctuary. Some people woke up at dawn to run a mile or two before work or cleared their minds with yoga. Myles preferred the quiet of his kitchen. On Mondays, he planned his week, tested new recipes and refreshed the menu. It was his private time and he guarded it jealously, but he couldn't toss out his boss without risking his job, even if the job was soon coming to an end.

"There you are!" Lou said, striking a jovial note. "Glad I caught you, at last."

Myles wasn't fooled by the cheery tone. In his late sixties, short, balding, always in a tight-fitted suit, Lou appeared harmless, almost comical. But he was, in fact, cynical, distrusting and a touch paranoid. He was also a pathological liar.

"Have you been trying to reach me?" Myles asked.

"I came around last night, but you were long gone," he said.

That couldn't be true. He'd stayed late. After his talk with Sandro, he was too worked up to drive home. He'd spent an hour rearranging the pantry, which was pretty sad when you thought about it.

"Well, we lost the buyer," Lou announced.

"Did we?" Myles wasn't aware they were in this together. "What happened? I thought you closed last week."

Lou spat out his one-word response. "No."

Myles sat at the corner of his desk. "What went wrong?"

"Ah...you know how it goes."

"Well, my offer is still solid."

Lou squinted, as if it pained him to disappoint Myles. "I'm hunting for big game," he said. "No offense."

"None taken."

They knew where they stood with each other. The disdain was palpable: Myles could cut it with a knife.

Lou had the carelessness of a man who hadn't truly worked for anything. The property he was so desperate to offload had belonged in his family for a generation. An uncle had started the restaurant, run it for a decade, lost interest and passed it on to Lou. Hiring Myles straight out of culinary school was a stroke of luck, rather than genius. Myles had been the first scheduled interview. Unwilling to waste a day sifting through candidates, Lou had offered him the job on the spot. In addition, he'd offered Myles the freedom to do as he pleased with the failing restaurant, and for that Myles would always be grateful. It had allowed him to stand out in the crowded Miami culinary scene. Yet, his success seemed to have only earned him Lou's resentment. The magazine profiles, the endorsements, the proximity to fame through Sandro only made Lou jealous, even though it made him money.

"Nothing's changed," Lou added. "We're shutting down at the end of summer. We'll likely find a buyer by then. Maybe it's time to tell the staff."

"They already know," Myles said. "Most of the staff have jobs lined up."

No formal announcement had been made; however, rumors of the restaurant's imminent closure had been swirling for months. It kept everyone, including Myles, on edge. When finally, the headwaiter had asked, Myles did not withhold the truth. Lou was looking to sell, and the future was uncertain for them all.

"I'll need a formal date," Myles said.

"August 31st."

That gave them six short weeks. "Noted."

Lou made a big show of checking his vintage Rolex. "Okay. That's all I got."

Myles nodded curtly. "Good talk."

For such a busy man, Lou did not seem eager to leave. He was waiting for something more.

"Anything else?" Myles prodded.

"No, that's all. I…uh…promise to keep you posted."

Lou exited the kitchen through the main dining room. Myles grabbed a knife and viciously started chopping celery, carrots, onion. It worked better than meditation to calm him down. The way his thoughts had run to her, to her kiss, to her light-filled eyes.

*Your wildest dreams on a silver platter.*

Late that night, Gigi sat up in bed eating corn puffs from a bag and listening to the patter of rain. Every drop mocked her. Why was she still in Miami, cut off from her work and her life? After the funeral, her mother had implored her to stay on a few weeks. She'd readily accepted, no questions asked. Of course, she would stay! Their little family had suffered a blow, and she, too, needed the emotional support. It was becoming painfully obvious that her mother had only intended to use this time to implement her father's plan: force her to give up her business and get busy upholding his legacy. Brilliant.

Suddenly, her childhood room felt like a prison from which she had to escape. Where could she go at this time? It was raining and past ten. If Sandro were in town, there would be no question where she could go. But now?

Of course, her thoughts ran straight to the cozy spare bedroom she'd had to herself at Myles's home. She thought of the meal they'd cooked and shared, to the bottle of wine they'd emptied, to the conversation that had spilled late into the night. Like her, he was not an early-to-bed, early-to-rise type of person. He'd told her that he barely slept at all. He said his mind was always working, racing on three tracks all at once. She understood.

She sent him a text.

GIGI: I can't sleep. Want company?

MVP: Depends. Will I have to marry you?

GIGI: No, you won't even have to cook. I've had a crappy day, and I just want to talk.

MVP: Come over. I'll take care of you.

GIGI: Thanks!

MVP: It's raining. Should I come get you instead?

GIGI: Myles, I'm a Miami girl. I can drive through a tropical storm.

An hour later, when she pulled through his gate, it was still raining, but her cloudy disposition had cleared. Myles was waiting under a large black umbrella. He directed her to the open garage. She parked and climbed out of her car, her pulse erratic, and popped open the trunk. "I brought a change of clothes, just in case."

"Safe bet." He set aside the umbrella and pulled her overnight bag out of the trunk. "I didn't think I'd see you again."

"You fed me cheese after midnight. That was your first mistake."

"Gremlins, a classic! You little movie geek!" he teased. "Didn't think I got the reference?"

"Wow! I'm impressed."

"Come inside."

He led her into the house, switched on lights and tossed her bag onto the couch. Then he filled a kettle with water. On this rainy night, she'd take tea and warm bread over wine and caviar. The man just knew how to do things right.

Even so, when he retrieved a jar of loose leaves from the pantry, she couldn't help but tease him. "You know, Lipton sells convenient little tea bags."

"Don't push my buttons, Gigi. It's late."

"Hey, I had a thought," she said. "Let's start over, wipe the slate clean. There's no reason we can't be friends."

She meant it. She wanted his friendship. The way he made her feel warm and welcomed was priceless. She could not buy this feeling and couldn't hire anyone to recreate it.

He ignored her suggestion and pointed to the couch. "Get settled."

She moved her travel bag to the floor and got comfortable. A while later, when he brought over a fragrant cup of mint and lavender tea and motioned for her to set her feet on his lap, she could not hold back. "This could be our life, you know. A year's worth of cozy nights like this."

"Sounds ideal," he said.

"Our fake marriage would put real marriages to shame!" she declared.

"People would come to us for advice."

"Exactly!"

"What about the messy divorce down the line?" he asked.

"There'd be no mess," she assured him. "That's the beauty of an ironclad prenup."

He nodded. "You think of everything."

"I do," Gigi said. "Before I forget, I meant to congratulate you. I read about your deal with a leading Japanese knife company. That's wonderful. Even I've heard of them, and I don't even cook."

"That deal has been pushed back a year and a half due to production delays," he admitted.

"And patent issues," she added. Her research was thorough. "A delayed deal is still a deal. You can use it to negotiate others.

Think of TV appearances and book deals. Who's your agent, by the way? Should we get you a new one?"

This was a narrow space where their worlds overlapped. If he wanted, she could make him a star.

"Now you sound like our best friend Sandro," he said.

"Maybe it's time you started listening to your friends. We know something about striking the iron when it's hot. And you, my friend, are very hot."

"Wait. Is this how fucking good it feels to have a supportive spouse?"

Gigi burst out laughing, coming close to spilling tea down her shirt. "How do you like it?"

"More than I thought," he said. "Now tell me what kept you up tonight. Why couldn't you sleep?"

"My mother."

"Is she giving you a hard time?" he asked.

She shared her mother's plans for her future. "She wants me to take over the so-called charity arm of my father's organization. You know what truly annoys me? I could run that entire organization as well as or better than the man my father appointed."

"I don't doubt it," Myles said.

"Also, she found a buyer for the house," Gigi said. "I didn't expect it to happen so soon."

"You can stay here," he offered. "For as long as you like."

"I couldn't."

"Really, it's okay. I like having you around."

"That's sweet," she said. "But I'm heading back to LA next week. It's time to face the music." Gigi hadn't made up her mind until right then. There was no point dragging her feet. "My team is still trying to bring projects into development. They're so hopeful. I owe them the truth—we're likely closing shop."

Myles wrapped a hand around her ankle and rubbed a thumb along the inner curve, coaxing her to relax. "What's next for you?"

"I don't know," she admitted. "I'll try to get a development deal with a streaming service, but if there is one thing Hollywood hates, it's failure. Oscars or no Oscars. It kills me because I know I could turn things around. With a smaller team, less overhead, less useless expenses and the right projects, I would drag us out of the red. I can't tell you how frustrating it is when you have a vision, you see it clearly, yet no one believes in you, not even your own father." She glanced nervously at Myles. He was listening intently, his long, black brows knitted like when he was focused on a task—a look that she now knew well. "I'm sorry. I'll shut up now."

"Don't apologize," he said. "I want to hear it all."

"That's all there is." She finished her tea in silence, enjoying the taste of lavender and mint, and set the cup on a side table. "I'm exhausted just thinking about it."

"Sandro and I grew up together," he said. "We were neighbors, and we kicked a soccer ball around after school, but it wasn't until we shared our plans for the future—and didn't laugh or poke fun at each other—that we truly became friends. Back then, Sandro wanted to sing, and I wanted to be a celebrity chef with a catchphrase and everything."

"You?" Gigi cried. "I don't believe it. You're so publicity adverse! What happened to change your mind?"

He kept on stroking her ankle, drawing loose circles with his thumb. His thoughts were elsewhere. "My dad died, and catchphrases became meaningless."

"I know how that feels," she said quietly.

"How did it all start for you?" he asked. "How does the daughter of a baseball legend choose the film industry over… I don't know…sportscasting?"

"My father had a cameo in a movie, a shitty movie, but still," she said. "We went to the premiere and walked the red carpet. My parents were giddy. My mother wore a gown, and she never looked more glamorous. I was only twelve, and it was all so exciting. I truly believed they'd approve my career choice. I thought they'd be proud."

"They never are," Myles said.

"Did your mother encourage you?" she asked.

"To leave the family, move to Paris and study cooking at some fancy school? Of course not," he said. "She wanted me to get a job at a bank. She had her reasons."

Gigi yawned despite herself, fatigue sinking in. "I'm sure she did."

Myles whispered her name and she perked right up. "Yes?"

"I think we're friends now."

She eased back into the cushions, smiling, content. "You know what? I think so, too."

# Eleven

8:30 a.m. Angel to Gigi:

Dinner at Diablo? I have big news AND a big ask. Tonight at 7 okay?

Gigi was lapping up the last of her poached egg when Angel's text came through. For one thing, she hadn't known Sandro's fiancée was in Miami. For another, dinner at Diablo? Just the two of them? They'd never hung out without a group or Sandro to buffer any awkward silences. She liked Angel, very much, but they weren't "let's meet for dinner" sort of friends. She took a sip of the coffee Myles had brewed for her and finally woke up. The big ask! Oh, yes! Angel was going to ask her to be her maid of honor. How could she have forgotten?

*I'll meet you at the altar,* Myles had said. Well, at least there was that to look forward to.

The house was still when she'd ventured out of her room this morning. Myles had left for work. On the kitchen island, she found a basket with fresh bread, a poached egg and a bowl of berries. There was even a note saying he didn't know how she liked her eggs, but he took a chance with a classic recipe. "Raid the kitchen. Take what you want. Everything I have is yours."

Gigi stared at the note a long while. What the hell kind of unicorn was Myles? All the time she'd wasted dating moody film industry types when she should have ducked out of the banquets and checked out the chefs. Was this the standard, or was he the exception?

Munching on blueberries, Gigi explored the house. His home was an updated 1920s' Spanish-style villa with arched windows that overlooked a vegetable garden. Naturally, he grew his own vegetables. There were three bedrooms, one converted into an office—the tidy state suggested it did not get much use. The guest bedroom was neutral and calm and, down the hall from it, the door ajar, inviting, was the main bedroom.

She hesitated before going in, but only for a second. Heart pounding, she eased open the door and stepped inside. Her first observation was that the bed was unmade. What a relief! Myles wasn't perfect. God knew she wasn't. This could be the bed where she ate cheese puffs late at night. She considered the soft linen sheets and stretched her imagination, cooked up other possibilities. Cheeks burning, she looked away.

Next to grab her attention was the cluster of framed paintings on the opposite wall. She recognized the style straight away. Angel no longer used oil paint as a medium and her focus had shifted from the Caribbean landscapes of Haiti, where her parents were from, to the streets of Miami where she'd come into her own. Here, though, was either a collection of her earlier work or a series created just for Myles. The paintings focused on food, from a ripe mango to a simple Caribbean-style tablescape. So, they had that in common: Myles and Angel were from the same island, which was also her island—the Dominican Republic was just next door. Did they all dream of that uncompromising heat? The beaches and the mountains in the distance? Maybe Myles could prepare *queso frito* better than her grandmother. Maybe he had an instinctual understanding of the island's food. Maybe he, she, Angel, were all connected.

Angel… She hadn't responded to her text. She returned to the kitchen, found her phone and typed a response. Meet you there!

She followed with a message to Myles. Thanks for breakfast. Looks like you'll be making me dinner as well. Meeting Angel at Diablo tonight.

For a casual dinner, Gigi had overdone it, showing up at Diablo in a fire-red dress and lipstick to match. Blending in with the crowd wasn't an option. She wanted Myles to spot her right away.

Angel was at a table, looking smart in a loose blouse and jeans, and only the faintest makeup to accentuate her copper complexion. She was really very lovely, with a heart-shaped face and dreamy brown eyes fringed with long lashes. For Sandro it had been love at first sight, but the gallery girl turned artist had needed more time and encouragement to fall in love.

"Am I late?" Gigi asked. "Have you been waiting long?"

In her furious determination to show up looking stunning, she'd lost track of time.

"Not at all." Angel stood to welcome her with a hug. "I came early to check in on Myles. He's having a rough time."

"Is he?" Gigi asked.

"Oh, yes." Angel pulled Gigi into the booth. In a hushed tone, she said. "He lost the restaurant."

"Lost it? How?"

"It sold."

"But he said Diablo wasn't for sale."

"Because they sold it right from under him!"

"Did he get a chance to put in an offer?"

"Uh-huh, and they rejected him twice!" Angel paused to catch her breath, clearly outraged. "Anyway, that's why I wanted to meet here tonight. Myles says they're closing at the end of summer. Sandro and I have so many good memories at this restaurant. It breaks my heart."

Gigi was crumbling inside. Why hadn't her new *friend* told her any of this?

She picked up the menu; the leather cover was just as red as her nails and the word *Diablo* was written in cursive gold letters. She now had a better understanding of the situation. This battle over the restaurant was personal. Myles wanted it, and yet his offer was rejected. Why hadn't the owner worked with him? Diablo would have stayed open, and his legacy preserved. Or was not everyone as obsessed with legacy as her family?

"Now I hear he's branching out to Vegas," Angel added.

"If the owner thinks he can crack the Vegas market, he's in for a rude awakening," Gigi said. "The restaurant scene is oversaturated. Celebrity chefs are a dime a dozen."

"Not the owner," Angel said. "Myles! He's going to join all those celebrity chefs."

Gigi slammed the menu onto the table. "You're kidding."

"I wish." Angel shook her head slowly. "A shame, too. He just finished renovating the house on the river. I wonder if he'll sell it."

"He'd sell the house?" Gigi blurted.

"Who knows!" Angel exclaimed. "It's a great house, isn't it? Myles throws the best dinner parties. Sometimes, he'll make a paella and we'll sit outside and have a little wine. The paella is always so flavorful. Chef's kiss!"

The paella was beside the point. Myles was leaving Miami for Vegas, giving up his darling house on the river with a vegetable garden for a desert landscape? What the hell was going on?

The waiter approached with a tray of drinks. "I ordered us spicy margaritas," Angel said. "I know you love a classic, but trust me, these are awesome."

"Thanks." Gigi took a sip from the glass rimmed with Tajin. All she could think of was Vegas.

"So, on to my big news," Angel said. "Is that okay?"

Gigi forced a smile. "Oh, yes!"

"I have a solo show in Paris next summer," Angel said. "Yay me!"

"Congrats to you!" Gigi cried. "That's excellent news! When next summer? I'll add it to my calendar."

"In June," Angel replied. "You'd come?"

*"¡Claro!"*

"It's a midsized gallery on the Left Bank, nothing extravagant."

"I don't care if it's under a bridge," Gigi said. "I'm coming."

"Thanks," she said with a wobbly smile. "The more fabulous people show up, the more buzz for the show. I need the exposure."

"If that's all you need, leave it to me," Gigi said. "I'll make sure everyone who's anyone makes it to the gallery. We'll sell out the show."

"You don't have to do that," Angel said.

Here, again, was the shy Angel she'd met two years back. "Yes, I do," Gigi said. "If we don't support each other, particularly in the arts, we'll never be seen. Trust me. I've been doing this a long time."

"Thank you!" Angel raised her glass. "To Paris!"

They toasted to Paris and to Angel's success. "That was the big news," Gigi said. "What's the big ask?"

Angel laughed. "You don't waste time, do you?"

"I try not to."

"Okay." Angel joined her hands on the table and sat up straighter. "So, as you know, Sandro and I are getting married next year."

"I'm aware," Gigi said, mimicking her tone.

"We've settled on a Christmas wedding. We met in December, so it feels right."

"Perfect."

"We love you and want so much for you to be a part of the ceremony," Angel said. "Gigi Garcia, will you be my maid of honor?"

Although Gigi had been expecting this, she was unexpectedly moved. Tears sprang to her eyes. To be loved, to be wanted, it shocked her how desperately she wanted that.

"Don't cry!" Angel said, laughing. "You still haven't said yes."

"Yes," she said. "I'd be honored."

Without her friends, Gigi would be completely lost.

"The wedding is in Lake Como."

"Italy? Really?"

"We're taking over a lakeside hotel," Angel said.

"I guess everyone really is dreaming of Italy."

"Wait until I show you the photos. It's dreamy."

Before Gigi had a chance to pivot back to Myles and his potential move to Las Vegas, there he was, coming out of the kitchen carrying a tray. She couldn't tear her gaze away from him. Lean and tall in his chef's whites, he was so incredibly elegant. He moved with confidence through the dining room, stopping to greet the patrons along the way, graciously accepting compliments, even posing for photos when asked. Gigi was completely taken. Her cheeks were as red as her dress—she was sure of it. Another thing she was sure of: she wanted Myles. If she couldn't marry him, she could sleep with him, no contract necessary—just good old-fashioned out-of-wedlock-sex.

"What do you have for us?" Angel asked, when Myles approached their table.

"A special appetizer for our special guest, Ms. Garcia," he replied. "My take on a traditional Dominican recipe."

The fire within Gigi consumed her completely. She brought a hand to her throat. "I don't know what to say."

"She's an emotional wreck this evening," Angel explained.

"What's wrong?" Myles asked.

"Nothing's wrong. I'm fine," she assured him. "What do you have for me?"

Myles set a platter of *queso frito* on the table. The cheese was fried, cubed and served with a mango sauce. Abuela Silvia served it the traditional way, with eggs for breakfast. She would have likely gagged at this presentation, but Gigi was not her grandmother. She loved it.

"For you, Angel, I have one of your favorites."

He set down a second platter of fried goodness.

"This is *Accras*, a Haitian classic," Angel explained. "It's made from a root vegetable. My mother would always fry a batch for parties. Saulty and spicy! So good!"

"Can't wait to try all this," Gigi said. "Thank you, Chef Myles."

"You're welcome," Myles said.

So much passed between them with that exchange. Their little budding friendship was theirs to nurture.

"Are you okay with drinks?" Myles asked.

"I'm okay with this," Angel replied. "I've got to get up early in the morning."

"I'm good for now," Gigi said.

"All right. Enjoy this, and I'll send out your main dishes."

Her gaze trailed after him until he disappeared into the kitchen. Then she tasted a piece of fried cheese and melted. When she met Angel's eyes, she realized that the future Mrs. Cardenas hadn't missed a thing.

"Is it true you've never had dinner here?" Angel asked.

Chewing, Gigi nodded yes.

"Like I said, I've been coming here fairly regularly, and Myles has never made anything off the menu," she said. "Then again, I don't look at him the way you do."

Gigi nearly choked. How devilish of Angel to use her own words against her. Two years back, at a hotel rooftop party in Miami Beach, Gigi had said something similar to Angel regarding Sandro. That night, Gigi admitted that her short-lived crush on Sandro had never amounted to anything. *"I never looked at him the way you do, so maybe that was my mistake."*

"I'll never forget that night," Angel said, lips curled in a mischievous smile. "It changed my life. You made me acknowledge my feelings for Sandro."

"What are friends for?" Gigi said. "Anyway, you would've figured it out, eventually."

"I'm not so sure!" Angel said. "Everyone fantasizes about falling in love with a famous movie star. It's daunting when it actually happens. There's so much to deal with—the press, the paparazzi, the fandom calling you out as basic."

"Basic? Who would dare?"

"Anyone with an Instagram account."

"Who cares about the haters," Gigi said. "Look at you now, planning your Lake Como wedding. Nothing basic about that."

"You know... I'm starting to think Sandro is on to something."

"On to what, exactly?"

"He senses there's something between you and Myles."

"He senses this all the way from Toronto?"

Angel shrugged in a show of false modesty. "What can I say? He's extremely intuitive."

"Has he considered starting a psychic hotline?" Gigi asked.

"Joke all you want," Angel said. "There's enough electricity between you and Myles to wean us off fossil fuels."

"Well," Gigi said with a nervous laugh. "I am a big fan of renewable energy."

"I'm just saying," Angel said sweetly.

"It doesn't matter," Gigi said. "We probably wouldn't work out, not in the long term. He's so calm and steady, and I'm a hot mess right now."

"Stop! You're the coolest girl I know!"

Gigi rolled the footage of the last few days in her mind and, sadly, could not find a shred of evidence to support that. "Yes, but he's exceptional. I may not be the right fit for him."

She could sleep with Myles, she could marry him for the sake of money, but under no circumstances could she fall in love with him. For his sake, as well as hers, she had to draw a line somewhere.

"Anyway," Angel said. "Think about it."

Gigi thought of little else all through dinner, dessert and later, while she and Angel waited at the valet station for their cars. Angel's sports car arrived first. She left Gigi with a kiss on both cheeks and a promise to catch up. The attendant assured Gigi that her vehicle was on the way, but she had another idea. She reached into her purse for a fifty-dollar bill. "Do me a favor, will you? Park it somewhere. I'll be right back."

"Will do, ma'am!"

Gigi turned on her heels and rushed back inside the restaurant. The hostess accosted her in the lobby. "Miss Garcia!

You're back. Is everything all right? Did you leave something behind at your table? Would you like a seat at the bar?"

Gigi did not have time for twenty questions. "Take me to the chef's table, please."

"Ah," the woman said, nodding with understanding. "Come this way."

# Twelve

"Chef's table, party of one!" Tatiana announced from the door.

With those words, Gigi stormed his kitchen, heels clicking on the concrete floor. Myles nearly doubled over with relief. The crushing dinner rush had made it impossible for him to return to her table. She and Angel had left by the time he could check on them. His disappointment had soured his mood. Would he see her again? If so, when? He had made up his mind to call her when the swinging door blew open and she made her grand entrance. Gigi Garcia was so wickedly beautiful the last embers of his self-restraint flickered and died.

Myles wiped his hands on a towel and led her to a quiet corner away from the curious eyes of the sous-chef, line cooks, dishwashers—just about everyone.

"Thought you left without saying good-night," he said.

"I wouldn't do that," she said hotly. "I'm a lot of things, but flighty isn't one of them."

"What's the matter? Are you angry?"

"Yes, I'm angry."

If the blaze in her eyes was an indication, she was furious. "What did I do? Fry cheese better than your grandmother?"

"Leave Abuela Silvia out of this," she hissed. "You're leaving for Vegas."

Myles stepped back. "Ah… Angel told you."

"Obviously, you're under no obligation to tell me anything," she continued hotly. "I'm only the best fiancée you never had, but still, you could have said something. I opened up to you."

"It's not definite," Myles admitted. He couldn't bring himself to commit to the plan. He liked his life and did not want to give it up.

"It's a terrible idea if you ask me, which you didn't."

"Thanks for sharing, anyway."

"You know, between me and Sandro, we can find you another job, a better one, right here in Miami. No Vegas residency required. You wouldn't have to sell your house."

That was news to Myles. "Who said anything about selling the house?"

"What option would you have?" she asked. "If you rented it out, who would tend to your garden?"

"Gigi… I didn't know you cared so much about heirloom tomatoes."

"I don't," she said. "I care about you."

As soon as she said the words, she looked panic-stricken. Myles, though, gloried in this revelation. Gigi wanted him for something other than what he could procure her. That was worth something.

"Where are you spending the night?" he asked.

"My cold and lonely teenage bedroom," she replied.

"Can't we do better than that?"

She raised her chin. "You tell me."

Myles looked at her upturned face, delicate and determined. "Come home with me. We'll talk. I'll tell you everything."

"Everything?" she asked, skeptical.

"It's a whole lot of nothing, Gigi," he said while freeing a key from a ring. "I've no definite plans, but I won't do anything without first running it by the closest thing I have to a wife." He handed over the key. "Keep this."

She closed her hand around it, clutching the bit of metal tightly as if it were solid gold. It broke his heart.

He lowered his head to kiss her, caught himself, murmured, "Fuck," pulled back, and did not get far. She threw her arms around his neck and yanked him close. "Don't do that," she whispered. "Don't second-guess yourself."

"Who jumps off a cliff without taking a second to think it over?"

She reached up and traced his jaw with the tip of her finger. "I do."

The kitchen noises dimmed. All Myles heard was the blood rushing through his veins.

He drew her close. Their first kiss was deep and frenzied. They explored each other with reckless abandon. A moment later, he had her back to a wall. Who knew what they would have done if a loud sound didn't jolt them apart. A mixing bowl clattered to the floor. That, coupled with the uproar of his staff, raucous laughter, pots beating on pans, cries of "Get a room, Chef!" pushed them part. Myles didn't let her go, though. He clutched the hand that clutched the key.

"Get back to work, clowns!"

Their sommelier, Juan, stuck his head through the pass-through window. "Guys! We got the mayor out here. Tone it down!"

Gigi hid her face with her one free hand. "Not the mayor! I donated to her campaign!"

Myles slipped off his white coat and called out to his sous-chef. "Rudy, you got this?"

"Yeah, I do," Rudy fired back. "Get out of here. You're heating up my kitchen, getting the kids riled up."

Gigi's cheeks were flushed when he turned to her. "Let's go. I'll ride with you."

"Perfect!" she exclaimed. "My car is waiting out front."

On the couch where they'd enjoyed a cozy moment the night before, they tore at each other's clothes now. Myles could not get enough of the feel of her skin. The dress was in the way. He nudged the straps over her rounded shoulders with the tip of his nose and murmured against her skin. "You wore this to kill me."

Gigi laughed and rolled off his lap. Standing before him, she maneuvered the zipper down with expert hands. "I snooped around this morning. I hope you don't mind."

He could not care less. "I doubt you found anything interesting."

"I found your bed very inviting. Bamboo sheets are a nice touch."

"They're soft."

He reached out to touch her, rested a hand on her waist. The bodice of the dress had given way, revealing the softness of her breasts. His fingers dug into her flesh, feverish, as he drew her back to him. Gigi blocked him, her hands on his shoulders. "Some ground rules," she said. "This is important. You can't, under any circumstances, fall in love with me."

Recognizing his own words, he laughed. "I'll give it my all."

"Good," she said. "As for me, I won't ask for anything you can't give."

"You sweet, lying liar." Myles gently moved her hands out of his way and pressed his lips to her navel. "You asked me to marry you before our first kiss."

She straddled him and grabbed a fistful of his hair. "Forget it ever happened," she said. "I'll propose to my personal trainer once I get back to LA."

Myles stiffened. Joke or not, he hated the idea of her out there, still shopping around for a husband. He, stupidly, believed the matter was over. What if it wasn't? She could marry her trainer or just about anyone. Sandro could recommend someone else. Myles wasn't his only friend in the world. The idea bothered him so much that when she moved to kiss him, he moved away. "Hold on," he said. "We came here to talk. Let's talk."

"Oh, no!" she cried. "Let's do this, instead."

He got up and went to the bar cart and filled a shot glass with tequila. When he faced her, she sat with her knees drawn up, looking confused. Confused himself, he said the first thing that came to mind. "Don't go to LA."

"I have to," she said somberly. "I can't fire my employees via Zoom."

He respected that. She took her role seriously. In that way, they were similar.

"What does it matter if you're going to Vegas, anyway?" she asked.

He was never going to Vegas; he knew that now. "Forget Vegas," he said. "I'd miss my garden too much."

"I knew it!" Gigi cried. "There's no shame in admitting that."

He set his glass down with a clink. Then he joined her on the couch. "There's something else you should know."

"What is it?"

"Diablo is still available. The sale fell apart."

"My God, Myles… Does that mean there's still a chance for you?"

He nodded. "A slim one."

She pounced on him. "I want this for you. I don't care what we have to do to make it happen. There are so many options— none involve marrying me."

Myles hadn't expected that. He'd thought, for sure, that she'd take the opportunity to renew her offer and push her agenda, but that wasn't her style.

"What if I wanted to?" he asked.

Her brown eyes widened, eating up her face. "What did you say?"

"I'm asking whether it's too late to accept your proposal?"

"No! Well, yes, but…n-no!" she stammered. "You really want to?"

"I really want to," he assured her.

She grabbed him by his open shirt. "I don't understand. Why this change of heart? You said you wouldn't marry me under *any* circumstances."

A change of heart…that was a good way of putting it.

"I only want to do this with you," he said. "We should both get a chance at our dreams. If it doesn't work out for me, at least you'll be happy."

"Myles…that's the sweetest thing anyone has said to me," she gushed.

"God, I hope not."

"It's true," she said. "You're the most beautiful person I've ever met, and I'd love to be your wife for however long. And you'll see, together we'll make it work."

"I have more hope for you than me. Lou turned me down twice."

"Who's that?" she asked.

"Lou Palmer owns Diablo."

"Hmm… What can we do differently this time around?"

"Make him an offer he can't refuse," he suggested.

She grinned. "I see what you did there, and I like it."

Myles reached for a lock of her glossy brown hair and wrapped it around his finger. "I knew you would. We make quite a pair."

"We do," she said. "That's why I want you to listen to me closely. This Lou Palmer person screwed you over twice. We need a strategy. How much is he asking for?"

"I offered two million, and he turned it down. He's holding out for twice that."

"No fucking way!" she cried. Then caught herself and apologized. "Sorry, bae."

"I'm bae now?"

"You would be by now, if you hadn't insisted on talking."

She had a point. "Fine. Let's wrap this up."

"Four million is a lot. What would that place even be worth without you?"

With that declaration, Myles saw Gigi for the savvy businesswoman she truly was. She would not overpay for anything, except, maybe, shoes.

"I'm flattered," Myles said.

"I'm not trying to flatter you," she said. "I'm being honest."

"Then I'll be honest," Myles said. "The value is in its location, its proximity to the Design District. Whoever buys the property will tear it down, build something else, or even flip it."

Most restaurants operated out of leased venues. This wasn't the case for Diablo. Lou was sitting on a gold mine. Not too long ago, the North Miami neighborhood comprised mostly humble homes and the corner shops that supplied commuters with everything from a quick bite to a lottery card. Now the streets were lined with high-end designer shops and Michelin-starred restaurants. Lou's property value had skyrocketed practically overnight. Even with Myles's pending endorsement deals, it was out of his reach.

"You're up against developers," she said. "My mother is going that route. They'll tear down our old eighties mansion and replace it with an exact same one, except without all the granite."

"I'm sorry, gorgeous."

"I'll get over it," she said. "Do you think that's the only reason he turned you down? He could have easily worked out an agreement with you, a lease-to-own sort of thing."

She was so perceptive, seeing right to the heart of things. "Lou has debts to settle before he can retire. He needs cash and is holding out for a big-time developer."

"Okay, then," she said. "We're big-time developers now. We'll create an LLC, that's a limited liability—"

"I know what an LLC is, Gigi."

She raised a finger, warning him not to interrupt. "If we set it up in Delaware, we can keep our identity secret. We'll call it the Miami Commercial Development Group…or something. Then we'll pool our resources, meet Mr. Palmer's asking price, and buy the restaurant. When you're ready, you'll take full ownership. The lawyers will add a stipulation that I can only sell my stake to you. This way no one—and I do mean no one, not even me—will ever screw you again. What do you think?"

"I think you're sexy when you're scheming."

She grinned. "I can keep it going all night."

Myles whispered in her ear. "Want to take this to my room?"

She made a face. "I want to, so badly…"

He eased her onto her back. "How badly? Show me."

"I can't," she said, even as she wrapped her legs around his. "It'll complicate things. I know this sounds counterintuitive, but if we're going to get married, we should keep things professional."

"Why?" He kissed her throat. "We know what we're doing."

"Myles! How can you say that? We're literally making it up as we go."

She laughed, and before too long, he was laughing, too. This marriage would either ruin him or restore him, maybe a little of both, but he was going to enjoy every minute it lasted.

"Stop laughing," she begged. "I'm trying to be serious. We've picked a lane and can't swerve in and out. We'll end up in a ditch if we do. Going forward, this is a business partnership, a pact to bring us closer to our dreams. We shouldn't walk away heartbroken."

"Like I could break your heart," Myles said. He lowered his head and pressed his forehead to the space just above her beating heart. Her scent enveloped him. Although her body felt soft and inviting under his, he forced himself to pull away. He got up and gave her a hand, helping her onto her feet. "Maybe we'll date after our divorce."

"I'd like that," she said.

He averted his eyes while she smoothed down her dress and adjusted the straps. "What's the next step?" he asked. "Should we go to the courthouse?"

She made a face. Myles was just beginning to read her body language and got the message. "What do you have in mind?"

"Something intimate at a hotel on the beach."

Myles wasn't sure. "There's nothing intimate about a Miami Beach hotel."

"I'm not trying to be a diva," she assured him. "There'll be a press release, and for it to be believable, at least for me, it should say more than they got married at the courthouse. We don't have to go to Lake Como like Sandro and Angel, but maybe something nice by the water."

He didn't think he could say no to her. Still, he had conditions of his own. "I have to tell my family what's going on. I won't lie to them."

"My mother and half brother pretty much know the deal, so that's fair," she said agreeably. "Only they think I'm marrying a secret boyfriend. That would be you. So, you might have to lie about that."

"That's fine," Myles said. He wasn't above a little scheming.

"Do you have a big family?" she asked.

"It's really just my sister," he said. "I don't update my aunts and cousins on my personal life. They don't live in Florida, and it's been a while since I've seen them."

"Beth and Gabe are the only ones we have to worry about," she said. "No one else will question it. An impromptu wedding is very on-brand for me, so long as the aesthetic is right, as terrible as it sounds."

"I get it," he said. "A lot of Sandro's life is for show—viral videos and publicity."

"It won't always be like that," she promised. "Most of the circus is back in LA. I'll head out as soon as I can, take care of work and stuff, and come back to be with you."

Myles took in a breath. "We're engaged. We should celebrate."

"Champagne?" she suggested.

"No," he said. "Gelato."

She joined her hands in glee. "I'm going to love being a chef's wife."

# Thirteen

They broke the news to their inner circle first. Sandro was ecstatic; Angel, too. Her girlfriends Jenny and Rose, a happily married couple, welcomed the news with cautious optimism. They'd met Myles on previous trips to Miami and professed to loving him and his food. However, they warned Gigi to not "F this up." Jenny said, "We don't know what you're up to, and we don't need to know. But if you get us banned from Diablo—"

"I promise that won't happen."

GG Cinema could fail, but Diablo would thrive. She'd make sure of it: Plus, Myles wasn't vindictive or petty—like every guy she'd dated and dumped. He would not turn away her friends because things ended poorly between them. Not that things would end poorly; she was determined to make her fake marriage work.

Not everyone was stoked. Beth was livid and Gabe incensed. Myles's sister remained blissfully in the dark. He was waiting for the right time to tell her. Then she showed up at the house, early on Saturday, unannounced, to find Myles and Gigi, nursing tequila hangovers with coffee, eggs, bacon, and tomatoes from the garden.

The petite woman pushed past Myles and made a beeline to Gigi. "Hi! I'm Michelle," she said brightly. "Myles never said he had a girlfriend. He's so secretive!"

Gigi did not move from behind the kitchen island to better conceal her semi-nakedness. "Nice to meet you. I'm Gigi."

Myles grabbed a T-shirt and pulled it on. "Michelle, this is Georgina Garcia."

"I know who you are," Michelle said. "You're a trailblazer. I read a profile in a magazine. Plus, you're all over Sandro's Instagram."

"That's me!" she said nervously. "Trailblazing on the Instagram. What do you do?"

"She's a nurse practitioner," Myles replied on her behalf. "She saves lives, and I'm very proud of her."

She grinned. "Well, thank you, baby brother!"

At first glance, Michelle looked nothing like Myles. They had the same warm brown complexion, but that was where the similarities ended. Myles's height, stature and dark features gave him a serious air. Whereas Michelle's round eyes and heart-shaped face were expressive and kind. Gigi liked her right away.

"What brings you here?" Myles asked her.

Gigi gathered her showing up like this wasn't a usual occurrence.

Michelle showed off her pink tracksuit. "I joined a 5K run for lung cancer awareness this morning. I was in the neighborhood and thought, maybe, you could make me breakfast. Sorry for interrupting. I would've texted if I'd known you were seeing someone. Should I go?"

"No!" Both Gigi and Myles cried in unison.

"All right, I'll stay! You don't have to twist my arm."

Gigi piled bacon strips on a plate while Myles brewed espresso. She offered the plate to her future sister-in-law. "Here. Munch on this to start."

"Thanks," Michelle said. "I am sorry for barging in like this," Michelle said, although she did not look a bit sorry. "When your brother makes the best breakfast in town, it's hard to settle for drive-through hash browns."

Gigi handed her a set of utensils. "Trust me. I get it."

Michelle chomped on a bit of crunchy bacon, all the while taking Gigi in with eyes sparkling with interest. "How long have you two been seeing each other?"

This was their first real test, and Gigi's stomach tightened with nerves. With the others, they'd conveniently broken the news over the phone. They hadn't had to look anyone in the eye and lie. This was Myles's sister. She would let him take the lead.

"Not long," she answered.

Myles handed her a freshly brewed cup of coffee. "Actually, we're engaged."

Michelle laughed. "That's funny. Have any sugar?"

"It doesn't need sugar," Myles said.

"How do you put up with him? He went to France and came back a purist and a food snob."

"I was living off cheese puffs before I met him," Gigi said. "This is a major upgrade for me. I can't wait until we're married."

"Hold on," Michelle said. "You're actually engaged?"

Myles set a glass of frothed milk before her. "That's right. We're actually engaged."

"When did this happen?" Michelle demanded.

"Tuesday." Gigi turned to Myles. "Or was it Wednesday?"

"Tuesday, definitely."

Michelle checked her pulse. "I'm going to have a heart attack. May I have a glass of water?"

Gigi rushed to fill a glass and brought it to her. "Should I leave you two alone?"

"No," Michelle said. "I'm counting on you to tell me the truth."

"Here's the truth," Myles said. "Gigi makes me happy, and we're getting married. It's really that simple."

Myles's happiness was only one of Michelle's concerns. "Georgina, do you love my brother?"

The answer slipped from her lips. "I do."

Before they knew what hit them, Michelle had darted around the kitchen island and threw her arms around both Myles and Gigi. "Am I dreaming right now? I'm so happy! Myles, you're forgiven. This is the best secret you've ever kept from me!"

For the rest of the visit, Michelle bombarded them with questions. When would the wedding take place? Which venue? What sort of dress would Gigi wear? Who would bake the cake? Thankfully, she couldn't stay too long. She had a nail appointment with a hard-to-book technician.

Myles walked her to the door, shut it behind her and leaned his head against it. "I wasn't prepared for that."

"Not at all," Gigi said in a daze.

"You told her you loved me."

"You told her I made you happy!" she retorted.

"You *do* make me happy," he said. "I wouldn't have agreed to this if you didn't."

"Well, you make me happy, too!"

"That's good," he said. "But you're going to have to pretend to be in love with me whenever she's around."

"If I can fake an orgasm, I can fake being in love."

He narrowed his eyes on her. "You fake orgasms?"

"I've had to, a few times, for the sake of expediency."

"That's sad," he said.

"I'm a busy woman."

"Too busy to—"

Gigi had to put a stop to this. "That's not important. Michelle was the one person you didn't want to lie to. She thinks this is a love marriage."

"After seeing us like this, she wouldn't have believed the truth."

He had a point. The line between the truth and a lie was increasingly blurred. It didn't matter that she slept in the guest bedroom, and they spent their evenings watching classic movies. They looked, suspiciously, like a couple in love.

After breaking the happy news to family and friends, most brides consulted with a pastor or spiritual advisor of some kind, Gigi reached out to her publicist, Stella Horn. "I'm getting married!"

"Gigi, sweetie! Congratulations!" Stella cried. "Who's the lucky man?"

"Myles Paris."

"There's nothing out there linking you to anyone by that name," Stella noted. "Who is he? Have you known him long?"

Gigi could just imagine Stella feverishly taking notes, already twisting the information she fed her into a narrative that would please the public and satisfy the press. "He's a chef and Alessandro's best friend."

"Good…good…"

The din of conversation, laughter and the light clashing of utensils filtered through. Gigi checked the time. It was noon in LA. "Are you at lunch? Am I interrupting?"

"Interrupting? Don't be ridiculous!" Stella shot back. "I'm at a business lunch, but what bigger business than your wedding? If we play our cards right, we can get a feature in *Vogue*."

Stella had missed the point. "I'd rather not talk with loads of people around. I'm counting on your discretion."

"Heading to the restrooms as we speak," Stella said. "Just give me a second to lock the door… Okay. Where were we? Right! Your fabulous wedding."

"Correct."

"Where will this momentous event take place?"

"Miami."

"Oh, good. Florida is a no-fault state. Do you have a date in mind?"

"Not yet."

"A general time frame?" Stella probed.

"Soon."

"How soon is soon?"

"Very soon."

She and Myles had not set a date, but the sooner the better. Her lawyers were working on creating the LLC. They had to act fast before some other bloodthirsty developer moved in on Diablo. Honestly, she wasn't going to let anything, anyone, any dollar amount, stop her from acquiring that restaurant for Myles. It would make the perfect wedding gift.

Stella's response snapped her back to reality. She said only, "Hmm…"

"Hmm…what?"

"Your father hasn't been gone very long. A fabulous wedding featured in *Vogue* might not be the way to go."

It would be in poor taste. "I know. That was never the plan."

Stella, who knew her well, certainly picked up on her disappointment. She would have loved a big celebration, to party until dawn with all her friends. More so, she would've wanted her father to be there, for him to walk her down the aisle, dance with her to the song they'd danced to at her *quinceañera*, and for him to bore the guests with one of his long-winded speeches. As much as she resented him now, she still loved him.

"If you put it off six months or so, you could have the wedding of your dreams," Stella said gently. "The world would celebrate you. Right now, they'll wonder why you're dancing on your father's grave. Not the look we're going for."

"I can't put it off," Gigi said. "It has to be now."

"Why?" Stella asked. "Is there something else I need to know?"

"I'm not pregnant. Don't go there."

"Not even a little pregnant?"

"Not even," she assured her. "Not that that's a thing."

"Something is going on," Stella said. "Whatever it is, please know you can tell me. It's like I always say—"

"You have to know the story to stay ahead of the story," Gigi finished her sentence in a dry monotone.

"As long as you know the score," Stella said. "You don't have to tell me all your business, just give me something to work with."

"Let's just say, it's *convenient* for us to marry now."

"Too cryptic," Stella said. "We need to tell a story."

Gigi floated an idea. "What if I said it was love at first sight?"

It was the one lie that felt closest to the truth. A spark had ignited between her and Myles the day they met. They could fan it and watch it grow or smother it. Either way, it existed and would have to be dealt with.

"No one would believe it," Stella said flatly. "The world is far too jaded. Give me the bare-bones facts."

She offered a watered-down version of the truth. "We met

through Sandro. One day, he invited me to lunch at his restaurant. I met the man, tasted his food and knew right away he was the one."

Stella filled in the blanks. "And you managed to keep your relationship a secret, dating outside of the public eye."

"Yes."

Stella paused a moment to think it over. "Love that you met through a mutual friend. That's the angle we'll go with."

"I like it," Gigi said.

"I'll play with it and send you a draft for approval," Stella said. "I'm really happy for you. Frankly, you're overdue for some good press, after that hit job in *Vanities*."

Gigi wasn't marrying Myles for the good press, but there was nothing she could say to change Stella's mind. As far as the publicist was concerned, life followed a sequence of good and bad news cycles, inevitably ending in oblivion. "Next century, no one will remember who you are," she'd once said over drinks. "Might as well make your mark while you're here."

That wasn't true of everyone. Her father had joined the pantheon of the greats. His legacy would last; her mother would make sure of it. Who would remember the taste of Myles's food or the emotions her art house films had provoked? Likely, no one. Gigi didn't care about legacy. In all honesty, though, some good press wouldn't hurt.

Before Stella ended the call, left the bathroom hideaway, and returned to her usual Cobb salad, she offered Gigi some unsolicited advice. "I won't sleep tonight if I don't get this off my chest."

"Don't be dramatic. What is it?"

"Before you promise to love and obey—"

"Obey?"

"—in sickness and in health, and all of that," Stella motored on, undisturbed. "Get that prenup on lock."

"Of course!" Gigi cried, indignant. "It's not a problem. We've already discussed it."

"Okay. Cool. That leaves one more thing."

"What's that?"

"An NDA."

"Oh, come on!"

This time she was insulted on Myles's behalf. He wasn't the type to sell their story to the tabloids or use it to secure a book deal. Myles wasn't a scammer or a cheater. If anything, she was the corrupting agent in his life.

"I said what I said," Stella insisted. "Just have a clause or two embedded in the prenup. I tell this to all my clients. Trust me. You won't regret it."

Stella might've slept well that night, but Gigi, having spent the night at her mother's house, did not sleep a wink. The next day, she retained the services of attorney Chloe Evens and took the first available appointment. On the drive to the Coral Gables law office, she received a call from her friend Jenny.

"Hey! I need a date for your shotgun wedding!"

"It's not a shotgun wedding!"

"If you say so!" Jenny said. "But I still need a date. Rose and I are booked solid through the month and we want to make sure we can get to Miami in time."

Jenny and Rose were models who'd met in France during fashion week five years prior. Booked in nearly all the same shows, they were a casting director's dream. At the time, Jenny was the All-American Girl, blonde, blue-eyed, tall and curvy, and making her catwalk debut after years of trying to break into high fashion. Rose was the opposite. Tall and slender, the dark Moroccan beauty was a catwalk veteran. She'd been modeling since the age of thirteen.

"I'll get on that," Gigi promised. "Definitely by the end of next week."

She and Myles had not yet taken that final step. Although he seemed committed to their plan, she worried he might back out if she pushed.

"Is it a matter of finding a venue?" Jenny asked.

"It's a matter of finalizing the paperwork. We need a prenup."

"A good lawyer can knock that out. Don't you have one?"

"I'm on my way to meet with her now. But that's not all."

"Pretty sure that's all it takes, even in Florida," Jenny said. "Aside from a marriage license, of course."

Gigi stopped at a red light and out came the truth. "I need an NDA."

Staticky silence filled the car. At last, Jenny cried, "Gigi, girl, what exactly are you plotting?"

"I can't tell you."

Keeping this secret was going to be more difficult than she'd anticipated. If she was going to have Myles sign a document to ensure he kept silent, she couldn't very well confide in her girlfriends. Ultimately, the fewer people who knew the truth, the better off they'd all be.

"Be straight with me—is it legal?"

"It's legal," Gigi assured her. "It's not ethical."

"Will anyone get hurt?"

"No."

The only thing at risk was her mother's pride...and Gigi's reputation, if any of this got out. Myles's reputation, as well. And Sandro's by association. The more accurate answer, then, was yes: a lot of people could get hurt in one way or another.

"But it's a little dicey?"

"Yes."

"In that case, get started on that NDA, girl."

"It's not that easy. The idea alone makes me queasy." Of all things to take with a leap of faith, marriage, fake or not, was one of them. Besides, she wasn't convinced she needed one. "It's the smart thing to do, but..."

"But?" Jenny nudged her.

"I don't think it's necessary. I trust Myles."

Jenny barked out a laugh. "You trust him? When did we start trusting random men?"

"He isn't random!" Gigi said hotly. "Myles is—"

"Myles is what? Different?"

Special. She was going to say he was special. "You've met him. You said you liked him."

"I like him plenty!" Jenny retorted. "I'm not marrying him, though, am I?"

Gigi didn't answer. The light turned green and she hit the gas, realizing too late that she'd passed the address.

"Listen, take my advice for what it's worth," Jenny said. "Men are not my thing. That said, if an NDA is the smart thing to do, then do the smart thing. This plan of yours might not work. Like my grandma used to say, better safe than sorry. Use a condom."

Gigi smoothly executed an illegal U-turn. "Your grandma said that?"

"Grandma Lynn was very progressive."

By the time Gigi pulled into the parking lot, she had to admit the chance of both Stella and Jenny being wrong were slim to none. She rode the elevator to the tenth floor resolved to do what had to be done.

Chloe was a soft-spoken Black woman with keen, sharp eyes. She wasted no time. "Do you and Mr. Paris have any assets in common? Do you own a home? A car? A dog? Anything?"

"Not a single thing."

"A joint account?"

"We haven't been dating long."

Chloe jotted a quick note. "No common property."

"May I invoke attorney-client privilege?" Gigi asked.

"You don't have to invoke it," Chloe replied. "It's a given. This conversation is confidential. Whatever you tell me stays within these walls."

Like Andrew Row's office, Chloe's was in a glittering highrise. Only this one was located in the old money neighborhood of Coral Gables. The new structure mimicked its surroundings with archways, columns and a tiered fountain in the lobby.

Chloe's desk was made of polished reclaimed wood, its edges left raw. On the wall were gold-framed diplomas from UF and Yale. She came highly recommended.

"We haven't been dating that long."

"I see."

Gigi could not bring herself to say the words "marriage of convenience." It sounded crass, even to her own ears. So, she tiptoed around the topic. "We have our reasons for getting married."

"Most people do."

"Even in the event of things going wrong, I want him taken care of."

Chloe ripped off her reading glasses. "Within reason, of course."

"More than that," Gigi said. "He deserves it."

"Spousal support is very common."

Gigi waved a hand, dismissing the suggestion. "He'd never go for that."

"You'd be surprised what people will go for."

For the second—no, fourth—time, counting the heated conversations with Beth and Gabriel, she found herself defending Myles's character. "He's very principled, and he won't accept any money from me."

Myles liked her plenty, but he hated her money. Which was why she'd come up with the LLC for the purchase of the restaurant. It was cleaner this way. Not one single dime would exchange hands. Keeping things aboveboard and professional was the only way to go.

"Most people accept a charitable donation to causes that are dear to them," Chloe suggested. "Scholarships are a good option."

"I like those ideas," Gigi said. "But there's one more thing we need to work on right away."

"What's that?" Chloe asked.

Gigi struggled. It was tough to get the words past her constricted throat. "A nondisclosure agreement. Could we include an addendum to the prenup?"

"Oh, sure," Chloe said, unmoved. "That's one way to go about it. By the look on your face, I thought it was something major. Don't worry. We'll knock that out in no time."

# Fourteen

"People, listen up." Myles punctuated his words with a few knocks on the stainless steel counter. "Gather round."

This was his way of calling a meeting, and he hated meetings. He preferred talking to people one-on-one. Today, though, he had no clear idea what he would say to sweeten the bitter news. His staff had families, bills and other obligations. He wouldn't blame them if they all walked out. At this point, he had no idea what the future held. He and Gigi could buy Diablo from Lou, but that wasn't guaranteed. Another developer could swoop in tomorrow. He refused to peddle false hope.

"Okay," he began. "I got news."

They crowded the back of the kitchen. These were his people, the sous-chef, line cooks, waiters, busboys and hostesses who most days drove him crazy. A lively bunch, they spoke every patois brewing in the Caribbean. Myles had learned to break up fights in three languages. They got along, though, for the most part.

"Looks like we're closing on the last day of August." His announcement was met with stony silence. It wrecked him. He so wanted to do right by them. "This gives you six weeks to get sorted out. If you find something sooner, I understand. It sucks, every way you look at it. I wish I had better news."

Tatiana, ever the cheerleader, cried, "Let's make it a summer to remember!"

Her words were drowned out in moans and groans.

They dispersed and Myles pulled Rudy Green, his most reliable sous-chef, aside. "I promise to find you something. By the end of summer, you'll have a job."

"I'm telling you right now," Rudy said, in his telltale Jamaican accent. "I'm staying until they turn out the lights on this place. You don't have to worry about me."

Myles did worry, though. That was the problem. Rudy had a wife and three small children. He deserved stability. "I appreciate that, but if we find something, you're taking it."

Rudy looked past Myles's shoulder. "We'll talk some other time. You've got a guest."

Myles turned around, and there she was at the door, clutching a binder of some sort to her chest, and looking rather shy. His fiancée. They hadn't seen each other in a couple of days. She'd moved back with her mother under the guise of getting her ducks in order. He suspected she did not want to impose on him any more than she had, which was ridiculous. If they were to be married, even for a short time, they'd have to learn to make space for one another.

He went over and took her by the hand. "Since when are you shy?"

"I'm trying to be respectful. The mood is so solemn," she whispered. "What's going on?"

"I just announced our official closing date."

"Why did you do that? Chances are you won't close at all."

Her voice had spiked dangerously high. Myles looked around to make sure no one had heard her, and then, desperate for privacy, dragged her into the nearest storage room. Anything they said in there would stay within the shelf-lined walls stocked to overflowing with jars of spices, jugs of oil and vinegar, and tins of tomatoes imported from Italy. He had to set things straight with her, but first… Myles crushed her smart-talking mouth with a kiss. He'd missed her. A portfolio slipped from her hands and papers scattered to the floor, but she wrapped her arms around his neck. They kissed until he heard her whimper.

Myles pulled back, out of breath, and said, "They need to know the truth."

"We're going to save the restaurant," she said. "You have to believe that. What else is all this for?"

His hands roamed down her back. "For you to save your company."

"That's not enough." Eyes closed, she brushed the tip of her nose to his. "It has to work for both of us."

"Just so we're clear," Myles said. "This works for me."

She smirked and broke away from him, the crisp documents crunching under her heels. "I'm sure it does."

"What's all this?" he asked.

She glanced down at her feet and up at him, looking uncertain. "The paperwork."

"Ah." Was this why she looked so…official? She wore her hair in a tight low bun. Her clothes were plain, all shades of beige. "We'll get to that," he assured her. "How are you?"

"I've been better," she admitted with a careless shrug. "Honestly, I've been unraveling."

"Is this what happens when I don't see you for a while? You unravel?"

"Maybe?" She laughed. "It was back to cheese puffs for dinner."

He drew her back to him and nuzzled her neck. "Stop it. You're killing me."

"Tonight, it's air popcorn."

He couldn't have that. "No, tonight you'll come to me. I'll cook for you, and you'll walk me through the paperwork."

She sighed. "That sounds nice."

He rocked her slowly. Something was weighing on her mind. They were going to stay in here until he found out. "Talk to me."

"These last few days have been difficult. Turns out it's not so easy deceiving everyone. All this paperwork… I'm scared we're making a mistake. Is it too late to admit that?"

"It's not too late." She could change her mind, right up until the last second. "If you don't want to marry me, just say it."

She rushed to cup his face. To free her hands, she dropped her keys. They joined the mess on the floor with a clatter. "The one good part of this stupid plan is that I get to marry you."

"Because I'll cook for you?" he asked.

"Exactly. Why else?"

"I'm no prize, Gigi," he said, to clip her expectations. "I'm stubborn, bullish, and half the time I smell like garlic and onion."

"Nothing wrong with garlic and onion," she said. "And now you smell fresh, like lemons. What more can a girl want?"

"In that case…" Myles pulled a blue velvet box from his pant pocket and opened it to reveal a ring. "Let's make it official."

The diamond shimmered in the dull overhead light. Gigi gasped. "Myles! What did you do?"

It was a modest ring by heiress standards. Yet, the jeweler Sandro had hooked him up with had assured him that vintage was the way to go. *If she can afford anything off the shelf, your only choice is to pick something unique.*

"Do you like it?"

He heard the uncertainty in his voice and winced.

"I *love* it! But why?"

"Because." Myles removed the ring from the box and presented it to her. "I want you to have something to remind you that we're a team now. This is a messed-up plan, and it may very well blow up in our faces, but why the fuck not?"

"Oh, God! Now you sound like me! I'm a terrible influence."

"What do you say? For better or worse?"

With trembling fingers, she removed a stack of gold rings to make room for his. He slipped it on her finger. The fit was perfect. They stood facing each other, her hand in his, the ring twinkling reassuringly like a candle in the night.

"For richer or poorer is more like it," she replied.

"No." He met her eyes. "We're not doing this for money."

Gigi bit her lower lip. "We're not?"

"We're chasing our dreams," he said. "And I promise you, no one's going to stop us."

She drew a sharp breath. "God, Myles, you're so sexy."

Next thing, the velvet box fell to the floor, joining all the other stuff. Myles backed her up against a baker's rack. It rattled as he claimed her mouth. Somewhere, in the back of his mind, he knew their chemistry was a product of sheer curiosity. They were new to each other and up for new discoveries. It wasn't any more complicated than that. But his curiosity was growing rampant. Kissing her, tasting her, was no longer enough. He wanted to know what she could do with that body. That question dogged him every second they were apart. He wanted her for better or worse and everything in between.

## ACT II, SCENE I


*Scene: Interior. Evening.*


Priest *(speech slurred)*: Should anyone present know of any reason that this couple should not be joined in holy matrimony, speak now or forever hold your peace.

Bride *(whispers)*: We're skipping that part, remember? No audience participation!

*Groom gestures for the priest to keep it moving.*

Brother of the bride *(hand raised)*: I've got something to say!

Bride *(outraged)*: Oh, for fuck's sake!

# Fifteen

Her mother was a no-show. Thank goodness, too, because the priest for hire was a drunk who'd spent all afternoon at the open bar. Sandro had him cut off. With a pat on the back, he said, "Wait until after the ceremony, man!"

Beth had been planning Gigi's wedding for ages. It was all mapped out in one of her journals. The plan was to host a couple hundred guests or so at The Biltmore in Miami or The Breakers in Palm Beach. The ballroom would be anchored by a champagne tower and a chocolate fountain. There would be live entertainment. Gigi's dress would be custom-made in Paris. The wedding would most certainly be featured in *Vogue*. This modest gathering that took all of two weeks to organize would turn Beth's stomach. Gigi could only imagine what she'd say. All of a sudden, she didn't have to imagine. A large bouquet was delivered to the bridal suite. The card read: *I wash my hands of this. Your father would be crushed.*

Gigi fanned her face with the card. "I need champagne!"

The priest had the right idea.

Angel presented her with a flute, filled to the rim with a pink sparkling liquid. "Will rosé do the trick?"

Gigi reached for it. "Anything will do."

"Take a breath," Angel suggested. "You look beautiful, and I've never seen Myles look so happy. Jitters are normal."

Bless her for normalizing this farce. "Angel, you know the deal, right? Nothing about this wedding is normal."

Angel gripped her by the shoulders. "Shut up! I can't testify to what I don't know."

Testify? My Lord… Angel's brush with the FBI over forged art a couple years back must have left her scarred. Or was it stolen art? Gigi was no longer sure. The details were hazy.

Angel wasn't charged with a crime. Plausible deniability had come in handy then. But she and Myles weren't doing anything criminal. Afterward, she'd make this clear with Sandro, lest he and Angel feared they could be charged as coconspirators.

This was a mistake. They should've gone to the courthouse, like Myles had wanted.

They were just a handful gathered at the beachfront villa. Rose and Jenny were on their way from the airport. The rest, Sandro and Angel, Myles's sister Michelle and her fiancé, Carl, and Gabriel who'd showed up without a plus one, were out by the pool. As tradition warranted, Gigi had not seen Myles. They needed all the good luck they could get.

"Could you do me a favor and check on Myles?" Gigi asked Angel. "Make sure he's okay."

"He's with Sandro. He's fine!"

*"Please."*

"If it makes you feel better."

"It does."

"I'll be right back," Angel said, and pointed to the opened bottle of sparkling wine. "Don't drown in that."

"I promise."

Alone, Gigi consulted the grand mirror leaning against a wall. She'd had fun with her look. With no time to go custom, she found a sixties-era minidress online and paired it with the long tulle veil Rose had worn at her wedding last spring. She completed her look with a pair of royal blue pumps. Now she wondered if Myles would have preferred a more traditional bride. She wanted to look beautiful for him.

The way that man kissed her…at least there was that part of the ceremony to look forward to. They'd amended the vows presented by the freelancing priest, booked online, to remove any mention of obeyance and any other superfluous language. Naturally, he was to skip over the part when he asked who, if anyone, was "giving the bride away." The answer was: no one. She was giving herself of her own free will. However, Myles had insisted on the kiss. "Just kiss me that one time," he'd said. "You'll never have to obey me again."

Those words sent a shock wave of desire through her system. Maybe he didn't get it, but she'd do anything he told her to, at this point. She questioned her "hands-off" policy. Was it really necessary? If they were going to forsake all others, did they have to forsake each other, too?

There was a knock on her door. Without waiting for a response, Rose and Jenny flooded in. "We're here!" Jenny cried.

"We ran into Myles," Rose said. "That man is delicious. I'd marry him, too."

"Did he look okay?" Gigi asked, desperate for information.

"He was beaming!" Jenny made this declaration with jazz hands.

"Really?"

Gigi couldn't believe it. She looked down at her engagement ring. He'd been so sweet to get her something she'd cherish when he didn't have to get her anything at all. She could've borrowed a ring from a jeweler or picked up a generic one from Tiffany's, but he was invested in making this special. He'd chosen every item on the menu and had a legendary pastry chef bake their cake. She had no doubt he'd make the most perfect pretend husband. And for however long they remained married, she would never have cheese puffs for dinner again.

God, she was lucky.

"Why do you look so worried?" Rose asked.

"My mother isn't here," she replied. "She doesn't approve, and I'm pretty sure she's putting a curse on me right now."

"Is it because Myles is not part of the one percent?" Rose asked tactfully.

"No," Gigi replied. "Well, yes, obviously, but no. That's not it."

There wasn't much she could add without revealing the whole scheme.

"Your mother will regret missing out on your wedding," Rose said. "You're her only daughter."

Jenny inspected her makeup and fussed with her veil. "I don't think we should dwell on this ten minutes before you walk down the aisle."

"I love you guys," Gigi said. "Thanks for being here. You look amazing."

The couple looked as glamorous as ever. Jenny wore a fitted tuxedo and Rose, a slinky lilac dress that complemented her rich brown skin.

The door swung open again. Angel returned from her errand carrying a small box. "For you."

Gigi eyed the offering with suspicion. From the size of it, she guessed it was jewelry. "What is it?"

"A gift from your future husband."

"Oh no…" she moaned.

All three women started speaking at once. "What do you mean, no?"

"Open it!"

"I think it's Dior!"

Gigi fanned her face again. "Please don't say that."

"The logo pretty much gives it away," Jenny said.

"Since when don't you adore Dior?" Rose asked.

Angel couldn't bear the wait. "Just open it!"

"Don't you see? This *means* something."

Angel rolled her eyes. "Of course, it does!"

"It means he knows your taste," Rose said. "That's a good thing."

It meant much more than that. The night Gigi had first proposed, she'd leaped into the river behind his house to save her favorite shoes from the French design house. This gift was a wink and nod to that night. That was part of their secret history. Her friends knew nothing about it.

Angel placed the box in her open hand. Gigi pulled on the white ribbon. The sides of the box collapsed and inside, a chocolate star with the letters GG in gold leaf where the company's logo might have been.

Her friends gasped. Gigi would have gasped, too, if she had air in her lungs.

"I was wrong," Rose whispered. "This means he loves you."

Jenny agreed. "He's a chef. Food is his love language."

She couldn't say a word. She was stunned by how much she wanted that simple statement to be true. She plucked the pastry out of the box and took a great big bite out of it, much to Angel's horror. "Gigi, no!" she cried. "You'll stain your dress!"

Gigi didn't care. She wanted to feel Myles's love deep inside her. If it tasted like rich milk chocolate, vanilla cream and hazelnut, so much the better.

Ten minutes later, Gigi clutched a bouquet of white roses and purposely walked down the aisle in a stain-free dress. Myles stood waiting under an arch erected by the pool, Sandro at his side. His eyes did not leave her. She was blown away by how handsome he looked in a fresh white suit. Smart, stubborn, sexy, steadfast, and in a matter of minutes, no longer single, Myles Paris was all hers. When she repeated her redacted vows after the priest—*"I, Georgina, take you, Myles, as my lawfully wedded husband"*—she was not acting at all.

# Sixteen

"Should anyone present know of any reason that this couple should not be joined in holy matrimony, speak now or forever hold your peace."

With his fingers intertwined with his bride's, simple gold rings symbolizing a commitment he was only beginning to understand, Myles could not think of a single reason he and Gigi could not be joined in anything. As incongruous as it sounded, he had never felt more at peace with a decision. Chestnut hair swept back, a veil framing her beautiful face, brown eyes swirling with a myriad of emotions, she was soft and vulnerable as he had yet to see her. She was trusting him with her dreams, and he would not let her down. More than that, he vowed to make this short marriage the most wonderful experience of her life. A tall order, but he was up for it.

"We're skipping that part, remember?" Gigi whispered to Father Pete. "No audience participation!"

In all fairness, the man was drunk. He likely did not remember his own last name. Father Pete was not their first or second choice, but he was the only officiant available at such short notice.

Myles made a gesture to say, "Keep it moving."

Father Pete nodded gamely but struggled to find his next words. This gave Gigi's brother, Gabriel, the chance to worm himself into the ceremony. From the second row, he raised his hand. "I've got something to say!"

That, apparently, was his beautiful bride's last straw. "Oh, for fuck's sake!" she cried.

Myles had not met Gabriel before today; he didn't know the man from Adam. He seemed to like attention, though. The timing of this outburst said it all. There had been plenty of time for him to speak up beforehand. He'd arrived an hour early and pretty much kept to himself the whole time, asking only how long Myles and his sister had been involved. Myles kept his answer brief. "A while."

Gabriel now hopped to his feet. "Gigi, this is messed up, and you know it. You're getting married for the wrong reason."

The outcry was instantaneous. Angel buried her face in her hands. Rose and Jenny clung to each other. Gigi gripped his fingers so tightly they could snap. Michelle met Myles's eyes, silently demanding an explanation. Sandro looked as if he were going to punch the man in the face. Myles had to put an end to this.

"Sit down," he ordered.

Gabriel swayed as if hit. "You'll be sorry, Gigi!"

Myles repeated his command, this time through clenched teeth. *"Sit down."*

Sandro took a step toward him, and Gabriel sank back into his seat. Myles gave everyone a chance to collect themselves, checked with Gigi who rewarded him with a wobbly smile, and turned to the flustered priest. "The words you're looking for are 'I pronounce you wife and husband.'"

"By the power vested in me by God and m-man," Father Pete stammered, "I pronounce you wife and husband. What God has joined together, let no man put asunder. You may now kiss the bride."

His new wife, thrilled, tossed her bouquet to Angel and rushed into his arms. Myles pulled her close and kissed her with a deep-rooted devotion he'd never felt for anyone in his life. Thunderous cheers and applause drummed out any last trace of doubt. They were married now for better or worse.

"You taste like chocolate," he murmured against her lips.

Gigi laughed. "Only the best chocolate in the world!"

In a day or two, a photo of their passionate wedding kiss, along with a brief statement, would be released to the press. Right now they were a couple like any other, celebrating the happiest day of their lives.

\* \* \*

Gabriel did not stay for dinner, which was for the best. Myles would've spent the evening wishing the guy would choke on his food. His outburst did force a conversation they'd managed to avoid until now. With no one left but their tight circle of trusted friends, Myles and Gigi decided to come clean.

It made for the oddest wedding toast.

They asked the catering staff for a private moment and Gigi tapped a fork to her champagne flute. "Myles and I would like to say a few words."

Myles rested a hand on the small of her back, a gesture that felt all too natural, and she relaxed against him.

"First, we'd like to thank you for your support these last few weeks. It's meant everything to us."

"Don't mention it, babe!" Jenny said. "We love you!"

Myles loved how devoted her friends were. It said so much about who she was at her core.

"After Gabe's outburst, we owe you the truth," Gigi continued. "We can't keep lying to your faces. Sandro already knows, obviously—"

"Why is that obvious?" Rose demanded. "He knows the whole story, but not us?"

"It just worked out that way."

Michelle joined the swelling protest movement. "You lied to me, Myles? I'm your sister!"

"Ladies!" Sandro intervened in his cajoling way. "We're all friends. Who cares who knew what first?"

"I care!" Rose exclaimed.

"Frankly, so do I," Michelle added.

"Honey, stop," Angel said to Sandro. "You're not helping things."

"Why don't we let them talk?" Jenny suggested. "Go on, Gigi. You were saying?"

Gigi had gone pale. She set down the glass and clasped her hands tightly before her.

Myles couldn't take it. "It was important to Gigi that you be here today," he said. "She loves you, and trusts you, so please don't make this more difficult than it is." He brushed his lips against her temple to encourage her. "Go on."

She beamed up at him. He had to admit, she was killing the role of blushing bride.

"I asked Myles to marry me because otherwise I couldn't touch my inheritance," she said. "That's the truth. It's as basic as it gets. We're marrying for money."

"Don't leave it at that," Sandro said. "Tell them why you need the money."

Gigi swallowed hard. Myles knew it killed her to admit to her failures. "You may have heard my company isn't doing so well. Without an influx of cash, I'll have to close shop."

Her explanation was curiously one-sided. He stood to gain from this arrangement, too. Did she not want her friends to know this? She was making him out to be some kind of saint. "The money will help us both," he said. "If I can't buy Diablo, I'll start a food truck or something."

"There!" Gigi said. "Now you know everything."

Silence spread over the dining room. Gigi stiffened by his side, as if bracing herself before a firing squad. Myles wrapped his arms around her. His instinct now was to keep her safe.

Rose pursed her lips. "If we're being completely honest, I asked Jenny to marry me so I could become a US citizen."

"The work visa thing was getting old," Jenny explained.

Gigi glanced from one to the other. "Not really the same thing, though, is it? You two were a couple for a while."

"I asked Angel to marry me so she could give up her shitty apartment," Sandro said. "But also because I can't live without her."

"Oh, honey," Angel said. "I, too, wanted to give up that shitty apartment."

"Why wouldn't you move in with me?" Sandro asked.

"I did that once and look how that turned out."

"I'm not your ex!" Sandro cried, wounded.

"I know that," Angel said soothingly. "And I love you for it."

"At the end of the day, it all comes down to logistics," Jenny mused.

Michelle touched her fiancé's arm. "I'm marrying Carl to start a family."

"That's actually a lovely reason to get married," Gigi assured her.

"It is, but you know how it is. The biological clock keeps ticking," Michelle said.

"We're trying to tell you that this marriage is a…working arrangement," Myles said as tactfully as he could.

Michelle's fiancé, Carl, a mild-mannered optometrist from Nigeria, spoke up. "I don't see how any of this concerns us. A marriage is what you make of it. As a couple, what you do with your money, inherited or not, is your own affair."

Myles liked that spin on things. If marriage was what they made of it, he'd make theirs beautiful.

Jenny concurred. "It's none of our business."

Sandro tapped his fork to his glass. "You two said your piece, and now I'm reclaiming my time. I'm the best man, remember?"

Gigi grunted in mock disgust and sat down. Myles joined her on the bench for two. "I thought that went well," he whispered.

She rolled her eyes. "They're idiots!"

Sandro cleared his throat. "As an actor, I prefer to stick to the script as much as possible. I had a speech prepared for today. I studied and rehearsed, but nothing in that speech seems relevant now. I'm going to say a few words from the heart."

Angel applauded this initiative. Myles wasn't convinced this was such a good idea. He lowered his head and pinched the bridge of his nose. His wife folded him in her arms. "You're worrying Myles!" she reproached Sandro.

He leaned into her. "That's okay, gorgeous. I can take it."

Sandro tilted his head and appeared to be rethinking his speech, yet again. "You know what?" he said. "I don't have much to say. When you find the right person, everything sorts itself out. I love you guys, and I wish you the best of everything." He raised a glass. "To Myles and Gigi!"

"To Myles and Gigi!" everyone echoed.

Myles squeezed Gigi's hand, then got up and gave his dearest friend, a brother in every way, a warm hug.

# Seventeen

At last, the wedding night.

After dinner, dancing and a midnight snack, a car service returned their guests safely to their homes or hotels. Now it was just the two of them in a big empty villa for the night.

Gigi found Myles alone at the living room bar. The lights were dim and the great windows showcased the beach. Myles had stripped off his suit jacket long ago. In his fitted white shirt and tailored pants, bow tie undone around his neck, he looked at once disheveled and distinguished. He wore the cuff links she'd sent to his room earlier today, a vintage pair that once belonged to her grandfather.

She slid onto the stool next to him. "Thanks for handling Gabe. If it weren't for you, I would've resorted to violence."

"You don't think I was too harsh?" he asked.

"Not at all!" she cried. "Gabe could have made his feelings known with flowers. That's what my mother did."

"That's class," he said. "How do we smooth things over with him? I don't want you two feuding for a whole year."

One year—that was the term limit. They'd agreed on this. Still, him mentioning the end when they'd just begun broke her heart.

"Make him a charcuterie board," she replied. "That's how you won me over."

"That won't work," he said. "You two are nothing alike. You're so easy to care for."

Suddenly, her heart was in good working order again, beating wildly in her chest.

"Look what I have for us," he said.

She hadn't noticed the silver ice bucket fitted with a bottle of champagne, the very same Sandro had sent to their table on their first date.

First the chocolate, now this, Myles's attention to detail was surely what made him stand out among his peers, so good at his craft and so damn irresistible.

He poured her a glass. "After today, do you think you'll ever marry again?"

"I couldn't survive another wedding," she said. "I nearly had a breakdown this morning. How about you?"

"No," he said dryly. "Once is enough."

"You say that now, but…" Her voice trailed. He would find someone, or most likely someone would find him, and he'd give marriage another try. "I'm warning you. I plan on being a difficult ex-wife. I'll show up at your house at all hours demanding tea and comfort."

"It's a little late to tell me this, don't you think?"

"It should've been obvious, Myles."

"Why?" he said. "So far you're the easiest part of my life."

Gigi found that hard to believe, but he'd get no argument out of her tonight.

"My girlfriends sprinkled rose petals on our bed," she said. "Want to see?"

He didn't answer right away. He took a sip of champagne and kept her hanging. "Didn't think we were sharing a bed."

"Well, there's only one."

His brows shot up. "Only one bed in this whole house? There are five bedrooms."

She took away his glass and set it on the bar top. "There's only one with me in it."

"Gigi…"

"Yes?"

"I thought we had an understanding. We set boundaries."

"As I understand it," she said. "This is my wedding night. Possibly, neither you nor I will have another. We're married before God and man—"

"By the power vested in a drunken priest."

"Amen to that," she said. "And to top things off, we have this villa to ourselves. It would be a shame not to take advantage."

"I agree." Myles drew her close and whispered in her ear, "It would be criminal."

"Tomorrow we'll get back to regularly scheduled programming."

"*That* might be difficult."

"Once we get back to real life, it won't be so hard."

In response he let out a low laugh that rolled off the slope of her shoulder.

Shuddering with pleasure, she asked, "What's so funny?"

He lowered his lips to her collar and murmured his words into her skin. "Gigi, you're my quiet obsession. Haven't you figured that out?"

"An obsession?" Her head fell back as he kissed her neck. "Is that good or bad?"

He kissed the corner of her mouth. "It's the worst."

She started to laugh when he kissed her, snuffing it out. Playfulness gave way to passion in an instant. He tugged at her dress. "I want to see you. Last time I didn't get to."

She stepped out of his arms. "This time you do."

"Need help?" he asked.

"No, thanks." The silk dress she'd changed into for the reception had no zippers, hooks or buttons. "It's a slip." She nudged the skinny straps over her shoulders and the fluid fabric dripped and pooled around her waist. "It slips right off."

His eyes glowed as he took her in. "What a lucky bastard I am."

"Don't you dare forget it, Mr. Paris."

He reached out and caught her between his thighs. "I'll never forget."

When he lowered his mouth to her bare nipple, she stopped him. "Hold on!"

Myles jerked his head up. "Something wrong?"

"The bed, the rose petals… Did you forget?"

"Oh…" he said. "I don't need flowers."

"I do!" she cried. "Look, I know it's stupid, but..."

"But what?" he asked, taking her request seriously now.

"It's the sort of thing that happens in movies, but never in real life."

She'd never made love in a bed of rose petals before, and what were the odds she ever would? The men she dated could perfectly cast a romantic comedy but were not romantics themselves.

Myles said nothing for a while, and Gigi felt even more stupid for having made the request. They would've ended up in the bedroom eventually. When he reached for the straps of her dress and slid them up her arms and over her shoulders, she panicked. What was happening? Had she turned him off?

"Do you know what else happens frequently in movies?" he asked.

She shook her head. "No. What?"

In one smooth gesture, Myles swept her off her feet. Gigi cried out in surprise. "What are you doing?"

"The groom carries his bride through the threshold."

Though it thrilled her, she couldn't agree to this. It was taking things too far. "Don't do this! I can walk! Those stairs! Oh my God!"

Her protests fell on deaf ears. Myles effortlessly carried her up the treacherous glass spiral staircase to the second floor. The main bedroom occupied most of it. The wide bed was strewn with red rose petals shaped in a heart. He set her down at its center.

Gigi was ecstatic. For the first time, she acknowledged that her family was right about her. She lived within a Hollywood fantasy. Myles, she discovered, had fantasies of his own.

He kneeled at the foot of the bed and slipped off her satin pumps. "This dress comes off now. Yes?"

"Yes!"

This time he knew how it was done and didn't wait for any further instruction. He glided the silky fabric down the length of her body. When, at last, she lay before him naked, she slipped a jeweled comb out of her hair and tossed it on the side table. "Your turn."

How she managed to sound calm and confident was a mystery. Really, she was craven and nearly delirious with desire.

He ran his hands down the length of her thighs. "Let me taste you first."

Everything came down to taste with this man. "Of course, you'd want that."

"I am who I am."

That half-crooked smile, the one brimming with confidence he'd flashed in that photo for the magazine, there it was! It was magical and it made her whole body tingle. Before she thought better of it, Gigi linked her ankles behind his neck. The smile fell away, and his eyes burned through her.

He gripped her by the hips and drew her to him. With the first flick of his tongue, she cried out in pleasure. With each one that followed, pleasure pulsed through her. She twisted and turned until he reached up and placed the flat of his hand on her navel, coaxing her to lie still. The audacity! The nerve! It was too much; she cried out again, in outrage and in ecstasy. Myles laughed and bit her inner thigh, and then he went on feasting on her.

Gigi raked her fingernails through the thick waves of his hair. She closed her eyes and whispered his name over and over. Her first orgasm was a sudden burst from within, lighting up her inner skies with color. She trembled beneath him and still he did not stop, pinning her to the mattress, sucking on her swollen nub. At some point, the room started to spin. He was on top of her, kissing her deeply. Her legs tightened around his waist, and she returned the kiss with a savagery that came from a deep source she'd never tapped into. She was hungry for him. Her hands gripped his shirt. Frustrated, ineffective, they moved onto the zipper of his pants.

"Wait…" he murmured, easing her hands off him.

"Don't tell me to wait, Myles! I can't any longer!"

There! If he was going to hold her down, naked and shivering, he might as well know the whole truth about her. She was impatient, demanding, and a bit of a brat.

"So bossy," he said with a low laugh.

"Of course, I'm bossy. Don't act so surprised."

He sat up between her knees and undid his shirt buttons, one at a time. "Gorgeous, I'm worth the wait."

"And I'm worth the trouble."

The shirt came off. She pulled herself up and helped him with the undershirt, tugging it over his head. When it fell away, he wrapped an arm around her and kissed her hotly. "You're no trouble."

She had to laugh because…yes, of course, she was. "You have no idea what you've gotten yourself into. If it didn't feel so good, I'd feel bad for you."

He dismissed this. "Half the fun is finding out."

Was there nothing she could throw at this man to faze him? Under his slim, taut body was steel. She could not break Myles. He would not break her. They were, in that way, well matched.

"Myles, please," she relented. "I want you so much."

With a hand to her chest, he eased her onto her back. Their bodies were perfectly aligned. He was hard where she was pulsing and wet. "Don't do that," he said. "Give me my defiant Gigi. Give me your worst. I like it."

She met his eyes, saw the fire there. It mirrored the raging flames inside of her. "I'm hungry," she said simply.

Myles lost any hint of restraint. He buried himself inside of her. She bit into his shoulder as her body took him in. She felt whole. Her fragmented life, the confusion that dogged her, the secret fears that kept her up most nights, all of it, gone. It was just her and Myles in a world they were creating for themselves. The rules changed from moment to moment to suit their needs, desires and wants. She wouldn't have it any other way.

He dug his fingers into the flesh of her hips and dropped his forehead to hers. Then he slowed the pace, taking his time, feeding her bit by bit.

"Anything you need, I'm here for you," he said. "I want you to know that."

It was remarkable that he could talk at all. Her breath was catching and all she could do was whimper as he forged deeper inside her.

"Anything at all," he whispered in her ear.

What if *this* was what she wanted? This chemistry, connection and intimacy she'd never experienced with anyone, and yet always craved. To feel bold and beautiful in his arms, to show her flaws and still be desired. What if she wanted breakfast in the morning and tea at night? He had no idea what he was asking for. She wanted everything.

"And what do you want?" she asked, panting.

He raised himself onto an elbow. She nearly panicked thinking he was going to withdraw, but he only wanted to meet her eyes again. "Come for me. I want to feel it."

That was easy enough to do; she was that close. But she was beginning to understand Myles, and what he wanted was to fight for every good thing he got. "Not a chance," she said through clenched teeth. "Not before you do."

For her daring, she was rewarded. Myles flipped onto his back and positioned her on top of him. Her hair draped over them. He caught her face and brought her close. Their noses touched, their breaths mingled, their hearts pounded as one, and the battle of the wills continued.

"I said come for me."

Myles's voice was quiet, yet it filled the room.

One more thing he'd learn tonight: she loved being told what to do.

## WEDDING ANNOUNCEMENT

After a final farewell to her beloved father, Georgina Garcia turns to a future with chef Myles V. Paris. The two ran in similar circles for years, and yet had never met until a mutual friend, Alessandro Cardenas, made the introductions in Miami. They'd been inseparable ever since. The pair married in an intimate ceremony in Miami Beach surrounded by close family and friends.

# Eighteen

Married or single, absolute silence would always unnerve Gigi.

She stirred awake in the quiet, unfamiliar house, alone in bed, rose petals stuck to her cheeks and thighs. In a panic, she kicked back a hefty duvet and waddled out of the bedroom on shaky legs. "Hello!" she called out from the top of the stairs. "Is anyone here?"

Her answer came in the form of an incredulous laugh. A moment later, Myles was at the foot of the stairs, looking up at her in confused amusement. Meanwhile, she gazed down at him in wonder. He looked handsome and relaxed like she had never seen him.

"*I'm* here," he said. "What kind of question is that?"

Right then, her head cleared. Either it was the sheer relief of seeing him again or the rich aroma of coffee, but the fog of emotions lifted. She pushed out a self-deprecating laugh. "Just kidding, obviously!"

Myles didn't buy into her performance. His face tightened with concern, and he charged up the stairs. Mortified, Gigi held up her hands, ready to fend off his kindness and pity. "Myles, I'm fine! Really! I promise!"

He took her in his arms. "You're trembling."

Was she? And, for God's sake, why? Had she been waited for the morning after her wedding to completely come undone. "I'm sorry! I don't know what's going on with me."

"Don't apologize," he said. "You must be cold."

Actually, she was warm and safe in his arms. It was only when he released her that she felt a chill. Myles slipped off his soft white T-shirt and carefully, affectionately, slipped it on her shivering body. "There you go," he murmured. "Better?"

"Yes," she replied, nodding manically. "And you don't have to worry, I can hold it together. This won't happen again. I don't know what got into me just now."

"*Don't* apologize." He wrapped her in his arms again. "I'm here." He kissed her brow, her temple, the groove just behind her ear. "Your husband is right here."

Those last few words tugged at the string holding her together. She came to pieces in his arms. Every emotion she'd suppressed these past few weeks—sorrow, grief, solitude, fear and desperation—stirred to life. Myles held her and rocked her and whispered to her reassuringly. "You don't have to hold it together," he said. "You can lean on me. No one is here. No one will know."

If this was what it felt like to have a supportive partner, perhaps it wasn't overrated, after all.

Gigi, feeling calmer, and eager to start the day over, stretched up onto the tips of her toes and brushed a kiss on his lips. *"Buenos dias, amor."*

That crooked smile. *"Bonjour, amour."*

"I smell coffee."

"There's breakfast, too."

He took her by the hand and led her down the stairs. Gigi caught her reflection in the floor-to-ceiling windows that opened the first floor to the beach view. She looked a mess. Her hair was frizzy beyond control and her face was puffy. Myles's shirt hung shapelessly off her body. She only wished she didn't look so damn happy.

"What's for breakfast?" she asked.

"Crepes."

"Wow. It's like waking up in the south of France."

In the kitchen, he poured her a cup of coffee. It tasted just as good as the aroma had promised. On the counter was fresh fruit, an open jar of Nutella and a bowl of freshly whipped cream.

"Hold on," Gigi said. "Where did all this food come from?"

The villa did not come fully stocked; she was certain of this. Zerlina, her assistant, had combed through the lease.

"I had groceries delivered this morning," Myles said. "It drives me crazy to see these great big kitchens with all the best appliances standing useless. They're like showrooms."

"In that case, I hope you never come to my LA home."

She must've pushed him too far. He dropped his elbows onto the kitchen island counter and hung his head. She took in his broad shoulders and narrow waist, his taut caramel skin.

"Do you store your shoes in the oven?" he asked.

"My shoes are stored in special acrylic cases," she replied. "My Tupperware is stored in the oven."

"Gigi…my God…"

"I can't cook! Okay?" she cried. "I've tried and everything I touch burns."

"I don't know if this marriage is going to work," he said somberly.

If he had dreams of cooking with his wife, well, frankly, she was going to let him down. But she had other talents. "I'll make up for it," she said. "I love food. I'll eat anything you make or bring home. I'll even wash the dishes!"

He narrowed his eyes at her. "I doubt that."

"Not manually," she said. "I'll load the dishwasher."

"I can live with that."

He went to the stove and placed a large pan on a burner. Gigi recognized a social media–worthy moment when it presented itself. She left the kitchen to find her phone. When she returned, she hopped onto a stool at the island and framed her shot.

"What are you doing?" he asked.

"Soft-launching our happy marriage," she replied. "I hope that's okay?"

"Should I put something on?"

"Oh, no!" Her gaze skimmed over the lines of his torso. "I want people to know I married you for your body and your brains."

He pointed a spatula her way. "As you should."

"And…action!" She hit Record. "Chef Myles, what are you making us for breakfast?"

"I already told you," he replied.

Someone needed media training. "Indulge me."

He faced her, or the camera, and gave her the most soft, indulgent look ever. "I'm making crepes."

"Sounds difficult. Is it?"

"Not at all," he said. "Eggs, milk, flour."

"Only three ingredients. Cool."

"Salt, sugar, vanilla extract."

"Six ingredients, then," she said. "What next?"

"Mix it. Pour it in the pan."

"Go on and show us."

He mixed. He poured. He flipped a golden brown crepe.

"Oh, God! You're showing off!"

"Only for you."

An irrational joy seized her. She no longer felt any desire to share him. "That's a wrap! I'm going to eat crepes now."

While Myles finished a batch of crepes, Gigi edited the video and posted it to her principal social media account along with a cheeky caption. In an instant, reactions, likes and comments flooded her screen—a lot of fire emojis and flaming red hearts. She read through them and laughed. "Take it from an unrepentant wannabe influencer, you'd benefit from having an Instagram account. People love you. You're a thirst trap."

He set a plate before her. "What's that? A hashtag or something?"

"A thirst trap is when a hot person posts a sexy photo or video that draws in all the thirsty people out there."

"I didn't get that," he said distractedly. "What sort of person?"

She glanced up from her phone. "Hot."

"Ah, yes," he said, smiling to himself. "Thanks."

"Myles! You know exactly what a thirst trap is!"

"Why do you think I got off social media?" he asked. "I couldn't keep up with the DMs."

"Sounds like a nightmare," she teased, knowing full well she'd pay hard cash to see those deleted posts.

"I've trolled your socials, you know," he said. "You've set some traps of your own."

The idea that Myles had pored over her photos and videos pleased her to no end. "Is it trolling when you're married?"

"We weren't married then," he admitted. "One thing I noticed—there's never any guy. Plenty of girlfriends, but no boyfriends."

That observation pleased her, too. "I don't post random guys."

The men she dated were never around long enough to warrant any social media attention. Once, she'd made the mistake of documenting a trip to Greece with a charismatic filmmaker who'd won the Jury Prize at Cannes. The relationship ended as soon as they landed stateside. She promptly deleted the posts, which caused a frenzy of speculation and rumors. That was the last time she did anything that stupid.

"You just posted a whole video of me making breakfast," he said.

Gigi set her phone aside. "You're my husband, not some random guy I'll kick out of bed in a week or two."

He came close and spoon-fed her heavenly whipped cream. "You'd do that? Kick some lovesick guy out of bed?"

With a taste of heaven in her mouth, she nearly missed the question. "Mmm… Yes, I absolutely would."

He lowered his head and licked at a bit of cream at the corner of her mouth. "I love how ruthless you are."

Her lips parted. She wanted more.

"Are you hungry?" he asked.

How many times had he asked her this? Each time the question was shaded with new meaning. Gigi knew exactly what he meant.

She met his eyes. "Starving."

"What are you in the mood for?"

"Anything."

He picked up the bowl of cream. "Any food restrictions?"

"None."

"Adventurous?"

"Very."

"I'll take care of you."

"No, it's my turn," she said. "I'll take care of *you*."

She gripped the elastic waistband of his boxers and dragged them low on his narrow hips as she sank onto her knees. Myles took a sharp breath and the muscles of his abdomen tightened. Myles was long, hard and beautiful. She ran her fingertips along the length of him, then followed the path with her tongue. She took him wholly into her mouth, sucked hard until he grunted, then slow until he hissed in agony. When he could no longer take it, he pulled her up to her feet.

"Let's get rid of this." He helped her out of his T-shirt with far less care than when he'd slipped it on. When she was naked and shivering, he pulled back to admire her. "Gorgeous, ruthless Gigi, those guys did not stand a chance."

But he did, and maybe he knew it, judging by the confident way he lifted her onto the countertop, pushed her thighs open, and made her his own. She arched back to take him in. Something fell to the floor with a clamor. Something spilled. Nothing stopped them from riding together, taking their pleasure, unabashedly. Lovers. Husband and wife.

Later, from where they lay on the tile floor, Gigi marveled at how freeing a committed relationship could be. They'd gotten tested the day they applied for their wedding license and Gigi had resumed birth control. All that preparation was paying off big-time.

Myles propped himself up on an elbow. He assessed the mess they'd made even as Gigi clung to him and refused to let him stray. Her body still tingled from the last orgasm, and the one before that. She could not stand on her legs. He held her by the waist and she felt sure that she could only live happily within arm's length of this man.

"I'll clean up," she said. "It's my fault."

"It is your fault for being so beautiful, but this is my kitchen. I'll clean."

"This is *not* your kitchen. You don't make the rules."

"I cooked in it. That makes it mine," he said. "How long do we have it for, anyway? Can we stay for dinner?"

"That's no problem," she said. "I booked the villa for a week."

He dropped a kiss on her shoulder. "I don't understand. Don't we have to leave today?"

"We don't have to do anything," she said. "They only lease this property on a weekly basis. Obviously, we can leave sooner. I thought you might want to get back to work."

"If I walk into that restaurant the day after my wedding, it won't go well," he said. "A cook will throw a knife at me."

"Ah, yes! You're meant to be on your honeymoon."

"So are you, gorgeous."

"It would be odd if we skipped it. People would wonder about us."

There was so much to do. She had to meet with her father's executor, and they had to make a move on Diablo before another buyer swooped in—all very important things. Yet, for whatever reason, honeymooning took top priority.

"Do you know what people do on honeymoons?" Myles asked.

She shrugged. "Take long walks on the beach?"

"They lose their phones. No posting."

She rested a hand on his chest and felt his steady heartbeat. "They lose their phones *and* their inhibitions."

"Is that right?"

"Yes."

If this honeymoon wasn't sweet, she didn't want it.

Myles pulled away from her and went to find the bowl of whipped cream. He returned to kneel between her parted legs. Gigi propped herself up on her elbows and watched, fascinated, as he painted clouds on her body with the sticky, sweet cream. Then, very methodically, working from the bottom up, he licked them all away.

They stayed the week.

# Nineteen

"When do you think you'll be heading back to LA?"

That might've been the wrong question to ask on the last day of their honeymoon. Gigi went pale and murmured, "I'm not sure." Then she shot up from the lounge chair besides his and dove, headfirst, into the lap pool. She could've killed herself; the pool wasn't that deep.

She said nothing or very little after that. It was late in the day, time to pack up and leave the house that had protected their...what, exactly? This honeymoon interlude wasn't part of the original plan. Phase one was to get married. Phase two was to split up. *I won't be in your hair*, she'd said. *I'll head back to LA ASAP, for work. And later, we'll say it was too hard to keep the long-distance thing going.* Only this wasn't a "thing," not to him, anyway. It felt like something precious worth preserving. Something they shouldn't let time or distance erode. But what the hell did he know?

He caught her arm as she brushed past him. For the past quarter hour, she'd been buzzing around in her wet bathing suit, collecting clothes and shoes. "Come on, Gigi," he said. "I only asked what comes next."

"I know."

She eased her arm free and kept right on buzzing. That was when Myles realized that he had an angry wife on his hands.

It was dark when they made it home. The lights switched on automatically and there they were, in the living room with their bags at their feet, facing each other. Because they were home, or at least in his house, he felt more comfortable to speak up. "I can't do the silent treatment thing," he said. "Please, just tell me what you feel."

"I have a headache, that's all. It's been a long week."

Not true. It had been a sweet, sun-drenched week. They talked, he cooked, they swam, they slept in each other's arms. They took all their meals outdoors, uncorked countless bottles, shared stories of their childhoods.

"It's a shame," she'd said one morning. "My mother would've liked you."

Myles found that hard to believe. "What makes you say that?"

"Your character," she replied. "She's very principled, and so are you."

"That's generous of you, gorgeous," he said. "The word you're looking for is pigheaded."

"There's a touch of that, too."

"My mother would've hated you," he said.

"Excuse me, what?" she snapped.

"Nothing personal," he said. "Her default mode was to hate every woman I ever dated. She was the typical Caribbean mother hen."

"Good thing Michelle is on my side," she said.

"Can't say the same for Gabe."

"Family is overrated."

They dropped that subject and discussed their dating lives. He'd even told her about Natalie, who, he'd believed for a while, was the one who'd gotten away. He didn't believe it anymore.

"What went wrong?" she asked.

"I work long hours, had to break too many dates and cancel trips."

He thought of Natalie and her infectious laugh. They'd met at a Super Bowl party. During halftime, they'd made their way to the back porch with a bowl of chips and beer. She was fun-loving and clever, exactly the type of woman he'd wanted to meet for a while. He thought they had a chance, even though that first night the writing was on the wall. "I don't get you," she'd said. "I don't live to work. I work to live." A disillusioned financial advisor, she did not understand his dedication to the restaurant. That fundamental misunderstanding had led to their breakup a year and a half later.

"Are you heartbroken?" Gigi asked.

"Not anymore."

Letting go had been easy. A few sleepless nights, a few restless days, and he'd put it behind him. What other choice did he have?

"Do you want her back?"

"Back where?"

She looked at him pointedly. "In your life."

"I'm a married man, or don't you remember?"

She tucked a damp lock of hair behind her ear. "Yes, but—"

"But nothing, Gigi," he said. "My life is full. There's no room for anything else."

The answer seemed to satisfy her. The honeymoon resumed.

When they weren't eating, swimming, laughing, talking, they were at each other. He could not keep his hands to himself. If she were within arm's length, he was reaching for her. If she stood close, he folded her in his arms. He could not get over the feel of her skin. They'd packed for an overnight stay, which didn't leave them much to wear. Mostly, they spent their days in bathing suits, and nights, naked, in bed.

Who could blame him for not ever wanting it to end? He wasn't an idiot. He knew exactly what this was, understood its limitations. Yet, he did not want to get blindsided. She couldn't resent him for that, but there was no doubt she did.

"I'm going to bed," she declared.

It was only eight o'clock. "Because of your headache."

She raised her pointed chin, defiant. "Yes."

Myles backed away from her, afraid he'd get mauled. "Good night, then."

"Good night."

She grabbed her bag and marched into the guest bedroom. She didn't slam the door. The quiet click shot straight through him.

Myles could not sleep. He worked, answered emails, reviewed

the following week's schedule, approved paid-time-off requests, and combed through the menu. He watched videos of home cooks prepping meals, something that always relaxed him. He believed, firmly, that the best meals were prepared at home, in small kitchens, with fresh ingredients sourced locally. He tried to recreate that simple magic every night at the restaurant. Tonight, he couldn't care less about a young mother's spin on mac and cheese. After a few minutes, he slammed the laptop shut and went to bed. A few minutes later, he switched on the bedside light and grabbed a book. His wife was sleeping in the guest bedroom. He couldn't stand it. Just when he'd had enough, the bedroom door swung open. Gigi filled the doorway. She wore a pair of soft pajamas and clutched a pillow to her chest.

"It's like you want me gone," she said. "Our so-called honeymoon wasn't even over, and you were asking me to leave. Also, that book you're reading is upside down."

Myles glanced at the open novel in his hands. It was, as she'd said, upside down. He tossed it aside. "You're not being fair," he said as calmly as he could. "I thought you'd be eager to get back to your home, your work…your life. A little heads-up is all I'm asking. I've gotten used to having you close."

Her voice cracked when she spoke up. "I don't know what we're doing."

Neither did he. Most people figured this shit out *before* getting married. "Do we have to talk about this now?" he asked.

"No. I'm exhausted," she admitted. "And I really do have a headache."

He lifted the duvet. "Come."

She tossed the pillow at him and crawled onto the bed.

"Did you not think I'd have enough pillows?" he asked.

"I like this one. It's fluffy."

He stroked her hair and kissed her forehead. "Gigi, you're going to drive me crazy."

"I did warn you that could happen."

"Do you want something for your headache?" he asked, concerned. He hated himself for not asking earlier.

"I took an Advil." She snuggled against him. "I'm sorry for giving you the silent treatment. It's a move I picked up from my mother. She never talks about anything."

"Communication is key in marriage," he said. "Open, honest communication."

"Honestly, this is all your fault," she retorted. "You could have expressed yourself clearer."

"What should I have said, according to you?"

"'I want you here with me.'"

"That's it?"

"I'm not an unreasonable person, Myles," she said. "The last day of our honeymoon could have gone a lot better if you'd said the right thing."

"The day isn't over," he said. "There's still time to salvage it."

"Barely!" she scoffed.

He rolled on top of her and scraped her neck with his teeth. "Too bad you have a headache."

"It's gone," she said.

He pinned her hands over her head. "That Advil must have worked."

"Four out of five doctors recommend," she whispered. "Now free my hands."

"Oh, no." Myles tightened his grip on her wrists. "I want you here with me."

Their passionate kiss turned tender. He pulled back to gaze down at her. She was beautiful with her hair spread on the pillow, her eyes bright, and her full lips parted and inviting. Myles came to a quiet realization. Gigi was not a butterfly to pin down. She was a force of nature, freedom itself. He released her wrists. With her free hands, she cupped his face. "Quit daydreaming and make love to me."

"You little—"

"Shut up!"

They came together in a tangle of limbs, laughing, kissing, loving, provoking each other.

The honeymoon resumed.

# Twenty

Family wasn't overrated. Myles had given up on Gigi's brother but was hopeful he could win over her mother.

The idea came to him late in the night, while Gigi slept with her cheek to his chest. The next day, he set out to make it happen. He didn't expect it to be as easy as rolling up to the Garcia estate and politely introducing himself, and yet it was. The gates to the Coral Gables property were wide open to accommodate a massive truck. Movers flowed in and out of the house. Beth Garcia paced the driveway, barefoot and in jeans, hair twisted in a knot. She had Gigi's high cheekbones, long neck and rod-straight posture, plus something else, something unquestionably magnetic. She spotted him right away, narrowed her eyes at him, and did not flinch.

"Mrs. Garcia," he said. "You don't know me, but—"

She cut him off. "I know who you are."

Okay. This was not going to be easy. "That may be true, but you don't know *me*."

Her gaze cut to the movers, three men hauling what looked like a bubble-wrapped baby grand piano. "Be careful with that!" Beth cried. She monitored their movements until the piano was placed without incident in the back of the truck, then she motioned to Myles. "Come with me."

He followed her inside the house, pausing at the entrance to take in Gigi's childhood home, so different from his in every way. He was a tall man and yet the double-height ceiling from which hung a massive crystal chandelier made him feel small. The marble tile underfoot emphasized every step he took. She led him to what used to be a home office or library. The bookshelves were bare. A pair of leather armchairs had not yet been picked up. She eased onto one and signaled that he, too, take a seat.

"I met friends for lunch at your restaurant last year," she said. "They kept gushing over your food. That's how I know you."

"Did you enjoy your meal?" Myles asked.

Beth let out a sharp laugh. "Typical of a man to seek validation."

"It's my life's work," Myles explained. "I take it seriously."

"You sound like Georgina."

"I was wondering when you were going to ask about her. Were you going to give her a chance to clear out her bedroom?"

"I boxed up her things and sent it to her home in LA."

Her home was with him. Myles was convinced of this, but couldn't voice it without coming off as naive.

Beth must have read his thoughts. With a sigh, she said, "You'll soon learn your new wife can take care of herself. She's proven to be more…resourceful than anyone of us thought."

He could not be the only person who saw her vulnerability. "The flowers you sent her on our wedding day were lovely, but she would have appreciated having you there."

"Ha! To support a scam? I don't think so. Her father would be so ashamed."

"He should be, for putting her in that position."

"Don't speak of my husband that way," she fired back. "He was a good man. *I* made him amend the will."

Now, this was a shock. He'd chalked the will nonsense to the desperation of a dying man. This woman was far from desperate. What could be her motivation for screwing her daughter over?

"Why would you do that?" he asked.

"I wasn't born with a silver spoon in my mouth like my daughter," Beth said. "I've been pageanting, modeling, acting, you name it, since I was six. I understand the value of money."

"And Gigi doesn't?"

"Do you know how many cars she's wrecked? Do you know how much money she's wasted on designer bags? Do you know

she leased a yacht off the coast of Majorca for an entire summer to host her friends?"

Beth was describing a very different Gigi. She was not that
girl anymore.

"I'm sorry," he said. "Gigi is an award-winning film producer."

"That's just the latest of her foolish endeavors," Beth cried.
"Those awards have made things worse. They've blinded her
to the fact that her business has failed."

"She hasn't failed."

"Listen, I love my daughter. I really do, but she needs to be
reined in. All she's doing is throwing good money after bad.
With her father gone, how long do you think that money will
last?"

"Your solution was for her to get married?"

"I misjudged her," Beth admitted. "I figured she'd rather
jump out a window than find a husband. She had so much
contempt for people who 'settled down.' Little did I know how
determined she was."

Myles studied Beth awhile. She was very much like his own
mother, reeling after the loss of a husband and provider, unsure
that she could make it on her own.

"You're right," he said. "You misjudged her."

"She has you wrapped around her finger, I see," Beth said.
"I'm not surprised. Georgina has her father's charm. She can
be very persuasive. What's in all this for you?"

Myles steeled himself. He was so far off from his original
goal for this visit.

"Gigi came to me with a business proposition, and I took
it," he answered.

She arched a thin brow. "A business proposition?"

He kept his answer short. "She needed a partner, and so did
I. We worked something out."

It was Beth's turn to study him. Myles did not flinch under
her cool blue gaze. Finally, she asked, "Does my daughter know
you're here?"

"No."

She flashed a grin. "Your wife won't be happy you went behind her back."

Myles understood that nothing positive would come from this meeting. He stood to leave. "Gigi is happy," he said. "That's all I came to tell you."

Gigi was far from happy when he made it home later that night. She was in a panic, screaming, coughing, darting around the kitchen while smoke rose from a pan and quickly spread. The smell of charred meat punched him in the gut. Myles dropped his keys and charged into the kitchen. He caught her just as she was about to douse a small flame with a large pot of water, took her by the waist and pulled her aside. He grabbed the extinguisher from a lower cabinet, safely put out the flame, and switched off the smoke detector that had been chirping like mad. "Gigi, what were you doing?"

She reached for a dish towel and mopped her forehead. Her makeup smeared. Black mascara smudged onto her cheeks. "Making us dinner!"

He removed the pan from the burner. "And what was this, originally?"

"A steak!" she cried, indignant. "A really nice cut of filet."

"Ah… I see."

They both stared at what looked like chunks of charcoal covered in snow, and doubled over, laughing. They held each other, laughing until the lingering smoke filled their lungs and turned their laughter into a heaving, coughing fit. Myles cracked open a window, then then led her by the hand to the garden patio. She took in deep breaths to clear her lungs. He couldn't help but notice the way the damp T-shirt clung to her body and was sheer enough to show the lace of her bra.

"Are you upset?" she asked.

Her question caught him off guard. "No. Why?"

"I trashed your kitchen and destroyed an expensive-looking pan."

He pulled her down onto a chaise and gathered her hair off her neck to help her cool down. The mid-September night was mild, and the sky had the glossy sheen of wet ink. "I think," he said, "we should have roles in this marriage. You leave the cooking to me, and you...file our taxes. I don't know. You decide."

She pouted. "I wanted to do something sweet for you."

"Sweetheart...thought we were clear on our love languages? You just keep bossing me around."

"It isn't getting old yet?" she asked, tentatively. "I sort of bullied you into marrying me."

"You couldn't bully me into anything."

She sat back and stretched her legs onto his lap. "I wanted to cook you a meal to show my gratitude. Honestly, I can't believe how lucky I am."

He glided a hand down her calves. "Luck runs both ways. I needed a business partner, someone other than Sandro, and I found you."

"No, babe, *I* found *you*," she said. "You can't take all the credit."

"I guess you're right," he conceded.

"Why didn't you partner up with Sandro?" she asked. "He'd be wonderful to go into business with."

"Sandro was trying to bail me out."

"Is that so bad?"

"You tell me," he said. "Why didn't you ask him for a loan."

"Because of the risk," she replied sharply. "There's no guarantee GG Films will make it. I have to do this on my own."

"There's your answer," he said. "Restaurants fail at a crazy rate. Even world-famous ones close. I have to do this on my own."

"In that case, I have good news," she said. "I met with the executor today, and the funds will be released to my account by Monday. Plus, our LLC is set up. It's called Miami Realty. We'll be ready to put an aggressive offer on Diablo soon."

"Within reason," he said.

"What's reasonable for the market," she said. "I looked it up. That property will be worth so much more in the coming years with all the surrounding development. Myles, you'll never have to take on a loan again. The equity in the property will keep you afloat for as long as you care to operate Diablo. Should you sell it, years from now, you'll have more than enough to open a new restaurant."

Myles turned away. He could not look at her without an outpouring of love and admiration. More love than admiration, if he were being honest.

"Don't worry," she continued. "We'll consult with a Realtor to put in the right offer, but we are getting you that property."

And she still wondered why he'd picked her. "How do we make sure GG Films stays solvent?"

"Ugh!" She rolled her head back and closed her eyes. "That's the multimillion-dollar question."

"Sorry, I don't know much about the movie business," he said. "I won't be much help."

"Actually...something you said about cooking had me thinking."

"What's that?"

"You're more experimental when you put together a menu for the restaurant, and cook simpler, heartfelt foods for friends and family. I need to do that, not play it so safe. Push the envelope."

"You're remarkable, and you can do it."

"Thank you," she said. "That's why I wanted to cook tonight. To celebrate the good news! We have the money to pursue our dreams, and nothing will get in our way." His expression must have clouded because she rushed to ask, "What's wrong?"

"Unfortunately, I have bad news."

She sat up and stroked his hair. "What is it?"

"I saw your mother today."

"Where?" she asked, confused. "Beth rarely roams the streets of Miami. She's only ever spotted at country clubs."

"I went to see her."

She screeched. "You what?"

"It might've been a dumb idea."

"Myles! What were you thinking?"

Beth had asked him the same thing. "I needed her to know that I wasn't trying to scam you. I'm sorry I went behind your back."

"Oh, Myles," she said. "I could've saved you the trouble. My mother thinks the worst of me. She probably thinks I'm scamming *you*."

"It wasn't a waste," he said. "I got to see the house. I could just picture you running up and down those stairs."

Gigi's expression turned wistful. "Sliding down the rail was more my speed."

"She's moving out, you know."

"So soon? I guess she's finalized the sale."

Myles kissed her shoulder. "There's one more thing."

"Let me guess. She sold my things?"

"No, she shipped them to your LA address."

Gigi rested her palm on his cheek. "Thanks, babe. I'd be in the dark without you."

He couldn't bear to leave her in the dark, so he told her what Beth had said. "We talked a bit, and…"

"And what?"

"She told me that changing the will had been her idea. I thought you might want to know, in case it changes how you remember your father."

Gigi folded her arms tightly across her chest and stared ahead in silence. Myles would not let her struggle on her own. He wrapped her in his arms and rocked her. "It's okay, sweetheart," he murmured. "I'm here."

**BUSINESS NEWS**

Diablo, a popular restaurant in the Design District, has been sold for $4.3 million, according to the *Miami Today Business Journal*. The 7,113-square-foot lot was purchased by Miami Realty LLC. The original owner purchased the site in 1987 for $524,000.

# Twenty-One

Tatiana accosted Gigi the moment she crossed the restaurant's threshold. "Chef says there'll be an announcement before the dinner shift," she said. "My heart can't take another announcement. Do you know anything about it?"

"Maybe," Gigi said coyly.

"Is that all you're going to say?" Tatiana cried.

Barely twenty, sweet and charming, Tatiana had a warm disposition that suited her for the job of lead hostess. Although the staff wore an ocean-blue uniform, Tatiana never missed an opportunity to add personality with bold accessories.

"No, I have something to add." Gigi whipped a scarf out of her bag. "I went home to LA over the weekend and found this in the back of my closet. I thought it would look great on you."

Tatiana held out her open palms to collect the yellow silk square. "Mrs. P," she gasped. "This is Hermes."

"Not your style?" Gigi asked. Legacy design houses could be so boring.

Tatiana clutched the scarf to her chest. "It is now!"

"Great!" Gigi chimed. "Is Myles in the kitchen?"

"Yes, but first, someone at the bar asked to speak with you earlier. She's waiting, I think…"

Tatiana pointed out a statuesque black woman, in jeans and ballet flats, her long hair gathered in a braid down her back. She sipped an espresso martini and munched on Myles's popular oxtail empanada.

"Thanks," Gigi said. "I'll go over and say hello."

Gigi crossed the main dining room to the bar, a flutter of nervousness in her chest. Her time away from the industry had made her a little rusty. She took a breath, smiled and turned on the charm. "Nina Taylor-Knight! What an unexpected pleasure!"

Nina, an acclaimed writer, had married action star turned director Julian Knight. They now lived and worked in a grand mansion on Ocean Drive, a perfect setting for their collection of awards.

"I'm so glad I caught you," Nina said. "We have a friend in common. Angel Louis mentioned I could find you here. So, I took a chance and stopped by. Do you have a minute? I'll be quick. I'm expected somewhere at five."

"Of course!"

Gigi slipped onto the vacant stool next to hers and ordered a ginger soda. It was just her luck: marry a chef and immediately develop digestive problems. She used to brag about eating just about anything, and now she could stomach nothing.

"I'm working on a script and would love to pitch it to you."

"Yes, please!"

"It's set right here in Miami and features a woman who inherits a family business only to find out that it has deep ties with the mob," Nina said.

Gigi sipped on ginger soda, nodding her approval.

"At first, she's outraged and tries to get out of it," Nina continued. "Then she finds a way to get the upper hand. She becomes one of the biggest players in the game."

"Go on."

"There's a love story, there's action, and it's based on a true story."

"Love it."

"Do you?" Nina asked, skeptically. "It's dark and I'm having trouble getting anyone to take it seriously."

Gigi found the darkness refreshing. She was halfway through the novel set in Italy Stella had sent her and weeping with boredom. No one could argue against the restorative properties of fresh pasta, mozzarella, olive oil and San Marzano tomatoes, but Gigi doubted she had anything to add to the discourse.

"I love that it's dark."

A female antihero was the sort of bold character she wanted to put out in the world.

"I would be directing," Nina said cautiously. "It would be my debut."

To launch the career of a female director would be a dream. "I love it even more!"

"Don't get too excited. There's one last thing," Nina blurted. "Julian plays the morally gray love interest. I wrote the role for him."

Gigi tried to picture it. There was no role too complex for the black British actor. It was a shame that he'd wasted so many years on films better known for epic action sequences than good acting. "A sort of charming con artist?"

"Exactly."

"Love that for him. Show me the material, please!"

Nina squealed with delight. "I was so worried about approaching you like this."

This made no sense to Gigi. "You're an award-winning screenwriter."

"I know, but in my head I'm still a struggling short story writer," Nina replied. "It's called imposter syndrome. Look into it."

"Never."

If there was one thing she had in spades, it was a stupid amount of self-confidence. Even her high-profile failures couldn't rattle her. However, since Nina was being honest, she might as well, too. "I'm in the process of restructuring and it'll be a while before I can start work on any projects. Plus, my budget might not be what you're looking for. If I were you, I'd keep my options open and shop around."

While in LA over the weekend, she'd learned that breaking ties with her financiers was more complicated than cutting a check. Her lawyers had recommended that she pause all transactions until contracts were reviewed and revoked.

Nina took a last sip of her martini and grabbed her keys off the wood bar top. "That's not how we do things, Julian and I," she said. "We work with people, and *work around* budgets."

"Wow," Gigi said. "Sounds like a winning strategy."

"It hasn't failed us yet."

Nina transformed from a nervous creative to confident businesswoman right before Gigi's eyes. They exchanged numbers and Gigi left her at the door with a promise to meet for lunch soon. When she joined Myles in the kitchen, her head was spinning. Everything was coming together in the most unexpected ways.

"Gather around, everyone! My wife has an announcement to make. I could tell you myself, but she could do it better."

Gigi climbed onto the stepladder that Myles held steady. She was taller than most people, but not taller than the gargantuan cooks or even the gawky waiters who played hoops in the back alley on their breaks. She needed their full attention. A month had passed since she and Sandro first shared a meal at the "chef's table." By now, she knew everyone by name and they insisted on calling her Mrs. P. She hoped this announcement would be received with the joy it was communicated.

"This won't take long," she promised. They were all so busy. The doors would be opening soon, and they were booked solid for dinner. "I have good news, and even better news!"

"Are you pregnant?"

Someone shouted the question from the back of the room. They were immediately shot down by a resounding uproar.

"If she were pregnant, would she be standing on a ladder in heels?" a waiter quipped.

"She's not pregnant," Myles snapped. "Quit asking."

"Wait." Gigi dropped a hand on Myles's shoulder. "They've been asking?"

When she was joyfully single, people couldn't wait for her to get married. Now that she was married, they were eager for her to start having babies, and cautioned her not to wait too long.

Myles draped an arm around her waist. "Never mind that, gorgeous. Just get down from that ladder."

She took a step down just to appease her solicitous husband, not that she was feeling light-headed or anything. "As I was saying, we have big news! For months, you've heard the rumors. Mr. Lou Palmer was actively looking to sell the restaurant. Well, it's finally happened. The restaurant is sold. As of today, Diablo is under new ownership."

A moan of apprehension rumbled through the kitchen. Myles squeezed her hand. "Gigi, honey, just tell them."

"Don't worry! It's Myles! Your beloved chef is now the owner of Diablo."

"We own it jointly," Myles said seconds before thunderous applause rocked the room.

One of the busboys cried: "Change the name! Diablo is dumb."

Myles's sous-chef, a sweetheart named Rudy, cut through the noise. "Does that mean we're not closing at the end of summer? I sort of made plans."

Everyone quieted down and turned to Gigi and Myles, their faces strained, which made the news she had yet to share even sweeter. "We're closing at the end of the month, as previously announced, but only for a couple of weeks to paint and refresh the main dining room. You'll be compensated! Consider it a paid vacation. Relax and come back ready for the grand re-opening!"

The announcement was met with cries, cheers, whistles, "Hallelujahs!" Myles lifted Gigi and spun her around, which made her feel a little nauseous, but once he set her down, pulled her close, kissed her hair and whispered "thank you" into her skin, Gigi glowed from the inside out. If he wanted a restaurant, if he wanted chain of them, whatever he wanted, in that moment, she was ready to go to the ends of the earth to deliver. It was becoming painfully clear that her life's purpose was to pamper this man. He deserved the world.

"A grand opening is great for the VIPs, but *we* need a grand closing!" Eddy cried. "Party on the deck next Friday night?"

While party planning spun out of control, Gigi met Myles's eyes. Their hands still linked, he led her to the storage room, the one with the dim light and the walls lined with tins of imported oils and tomatoes, the one in which he'd offered her a ring and proposed. Without a word, he locked the door, pressed her against it. His hands slipped under her frilly blouse and equally frilly bra. Gigi found his zipper. The key to a successful marriage was creativity. She could make the storage room work.

"I love how much they love you," he said.

"Me? No!" She raised her hands, as if accused of a crime. "It's *you*. They love you."

"No, baby," he whispered. "It's you."

Sometimes he spoke to her so lovingly it made her quiver, inside and out. So much so, she ignored the light knock on the door, mistaking it for the beat of her heart.

"Hey! We're out of olive oil!" Rudy called out from the other side of the locked door. "I'm coming in. It's nothing I haven't seen before."

Myles swore and stepped away from her, leaving her body aching for attention. "I gotta get back to work," he said, smoothing down her blouse. "Don't go. I'll make us dinner."

Where would she go? There was no place else she wanted to be.

Gigi slipped out to make a phone call. The Porsche was parked in a reserved spot. She locked herself in and got Sandro on the phone.

"We did it!" she cried. "We officially own Diablo!"

Sandro appropriately responded with a famous line from a film. "Always be closing!"

"We're going to give it a minor face-lift, make it fabulous and reopen a month later. Can we count on you to be there?"

"For the grand opening?" Sandro said. "For sure."

"Good."

"You sound funny. What's the matter?"

"Nothing," she said breezily. "Just, you know, relief. What if we couldn't close?"

"But you did, and fast, too."

"But if we'd lost the restaurant?"

"Why are we playing what-if games?" Sandro asked. "Lou took the money and ran."

"I know, but what if?"

"Gigi, what's with you?" Sandro asked. "The plan worked! You got your money. He got the restaurant. A win is a win. You taught me that."

"It's not a win if I lose him!" she cried.

Her voice bounced around the car. The desperation laced through it left her terrified. Sandro heard it, too.

"Gigi! You're in love with the guy!"

"Don't say that!"

"I'm sorry," he said gently. "I have to say it."

"Oh no!" Gigi dropped her head on the steering wheel. Sandro was right. She'd played the game and won. She'd got her inheritance and was on track to producing films again. And yet, all she could think about was whether Myles was happy with the way things had turned out, happy enough to stay committed, because, really, they could announce their separation by the end of the year. So long as their little scheme never came to light, a quickie marriage wouldn't destroy their careers.

"Gigi," Sandro said. "You're in love with him. I figured it out on your wedding day. The way you look at him…it's beautiful."

She perked up and wiped flyaway strands of hair from her face. "Do you think he loves me?" Sandro hesitated, and her heart tanked. He was Myles's best friend and would surely know what he was thinking. "He doesn't, does he? I mean… he likes me fine, but it's not love. Or he still loves that Natalie person."

"Hey! Take a breath! You're spinning," Sandro said. "And leave Natalie out of this."

"But you said he wasn't over her."

"Hold on! I never said that!" Sandro protested. "He stopped dating after they split. That's all."

"But why?"

"To put his career first," Sandro said. "Natalie resented him for refusing to make the sort of compromises normal couples would. That was the problem. He figured any relationship would end the same and gave up."

"Oh." In that case, she liked her chances. Their relationship was based on chasing dreams.

"Do you know she blamed me for their breakup?" Sandro asked.

"I didn't."

"She DMed me to say I should have intervened on her behalf. As if I could make Myles do anything he didn't want to do. And I can't speak for him, either, Gigi. The only person who can tell you how he feels is Myles."

"I know," she said softly.

"How are you two getting along?" he asked. "Has it been easy living together?"

There was so much their friends did not know. They assumed they had separate rooms and led separate lives, but nothing could be further than the truth. Some days, she couldn't remember a life before him. Twice now, she'd flown back to LA for business. Each time, he'd taken her home from the airport, cooked and listened while she rattled on forever about the meetings she took and the contacts she'd made. Never once did he tune her out, like most men did. He even turned off his phone so they wouldn't be disturbed. Those moments brought to light how lonely she'd felt over the years, and how full she felt now.

Myles poked his head out the back door and, with a hand gesture that she understood, signaled that her dinner was ready.

"It's dinnertime," she told Sandro. "I'll call you soon."

"Domestic bliss!" Sandro exclaimed.

"It's a perk!" she cried. "When you marry a chef, you eat well."

"I'm familiar with the rule," Sandro said. "I didn't marry him, but he'll never get rid of me."

# ACT III

*Scene: Interior. Day. Phone Call.*

Publicist: There's still time to get ahead of the story and plug any leaks. Let's draft a list of names, people who might have, intentionally or not, let something slip. Hopefully, it's a short one. It's likely we needed more than one NDA. That's my fault.

Client: Umm…

Publicist: Umm… What?

Client: About that NDA…

# Twenty-Two

*When you marry a chef, you eat well.*

The pleasure didn't end there. Their skills weren't limited to the kitchen. Watching Myles knead dough was foreplay enough, to be sure. But waking up to hands roaming her body, his palms pressing her knees apart, his mouth on her, sucking, tasting, as if starved for her. He didn't stop until she was satiated. There was no way to share all this and not come off as bragging.

"What are you smiling about?"

Myles came out of the bathroom, freshly showered and shaved, glistening, gorgeous.

She reached out and tugged at the towel around his narrow waist. "Come here."

"No, Gigi. No!" he cried. "I'll be late for work again."

"Don't you own that restaurant?"

He cupped her chin, rubbed his thumb along her bottom lip. "Jointly, with you."

"I thought you were the boss." She sat at the edge of the bed and wrapped her legs around his. "Was I wrong about that?"

He kissed her. "Guess I'll have to show you."

The ring of her phone disrupted those plans. She couldn't help but grab it off the nightstand and check the caller ID. It was Stella, her publicist.

Myles backed away and retreated to the closet. "Guess it'll have to wait."

"Don't go!" she cried. "It's not important. I'll call her back."

Her words rang false, even to her own ears. Stella never called just to say hi.

Myles came out of the closet in a pair of jeans, a soft grey tee, and the white uniform jacket slung over a shoulder. "Take the call," he said. "Trust me. It'll be sweeter, later."

She blew him a light kiss. With a heavy heart, she answered the phone.

As it turned out, Gigi's gut instinct was right. Stella had catastrophic news.

"My sources say a *Miami Post* reporter has been poking around asking about your marriage, seeking to expose it as a sham."

"How would they know this?" Gigi cried.

"Apparently, someone overheard a conversation with Sandro."

"Shit!"

"Yup…any idea who they could be?"

Gigi's mind was reeling. "No! Are you sure about this?"

"That's what my sources say."

"Oh my God…"

"No one has reached out for comment, so there's still time. Unfortunately, if a tabloid gets wind of this, it'll spread like wildfire."

Gigi eased back into bed and closed her eyes. Why was the world out to destroy her one chance at happiness?

"Our plan is simple," Stella continued. "Deny. Deny. Deny."

They would have to be more proactive than that. "That's not enough. We've got to plug the leak."

"Exactly," Stella said. "We've got to get aggressive. This is not a good look for you or Sandro. Obviously, I've reached out to his publicist."

This was all her fault. How could she be so stupid to implicate Sandro like this?

"Are you still there?" Stella asked.

Throat tight, Gigi said, "Give me a second. I'm freaking out."

"Don't freak out!" Stella cried. "This is what you pay me for. I'm prepared to go to war."

"Right," Gigi said. "It's war."

"Let's start by drafting a short list of names, people who might have been around when you and Sandro were chatting and, intentionally or not, let something slip."

She didn't have the nerve to tell Stella that the list could be quite long, despite that she and Sandro had been careful.

"It's likely we needed more than one NDA in this affair," Stella continued. "At least Myles is covered."

"Why would Myles tell on himself?" Gigi snapped.

"For money, attention, revenge… Who knows? People do strange things."

"Not Myles."

"Exactly! The NDA practically guarantees it."

All this talk of NDAs made Gigi's stomach churn. "Umm…"

"Umm… What?" Stella asked.

"About that NDA…" Gigi said tentatively.

"What about it?" Stella asked, her voice rising with alarm.

Stella would have to wait for her answer. With her phone clutched to her chest, Gigi sprinted from the bed to the bathroom and emptied the contents of her stomach in the toilet.

War wasn't for the weak. Gigi got up from the bathroom floor, showered and brushed her teeth. With her hair still wet, she drove to Diablo and stormed the kitchen, disturbing the peace of the lunch crew.

"Hey, Mrs. P," Delia, one of the line cooks, said. "Don't forget tonight's party."

The grand closing… It had slipped her mind. Yet, she pasted a smile on her face and said, "I never forget a party!"

Myles looked up from his computer desk tucked in a corner. "Hey, gorgeous, I wasn't expecting you."

Gigi did not feel gorgeous. For one thing, she'd puked her guts out just an hour ago. For another, in shorts and sandals, not a lick of makeup, she was sure she looked as wretched as she felt. Yet, Myles leaning back in his chair, beaming at her, had the power to ignite her from the inside out. Did he know this?

"Something's come up," she said cautiously. They weren't alone, even though it felt that way. "Can we talk?"

"Sure." He shuffled some papers and locked the computer. "Would you like breakfast? I could whip up eggs and potatoes. I could fry cheese. I've got the good stuff, straight from DR."

"Thanks, honey, but not today." Her stomach cratered at the thought. She zeroed in on a crate of grapefruits and grabbed one. "May I have this?"

He looked at her quizzically. "You may have whatever you like. Coffee?"

She clutched the fruit in both hands. "Just this."

He approached and took it from her. "I'll cut it."

A moment later, they sat in the empty dining room, a plate of grapefruit, halved and sprinkled with sugar, before her. Gigi tried to delay the inevitable fallout as much as possible, but Myles wouldn't let her. "If you're not going to eat, you're going to talk."

She pushed aside her plate, resigned. "I have something to tell you that can potentially change our lives."

Myles went still. "I'm listening."

She gulped and nodded and gulped again. "A local reporter is snooping around, asking questions, trying to expose us."

"Oh."

There was something about that "oh." Gigi couldn't put a finger on it.

"Stella… She's my publicist and she's incredible…"

"Oh?"

It occurred to her that Myles likely didn't date women with publicists, and agents, and managers, trust funds, and so much emotional baggage.

"Someone overheard Sandro and me talking," she said in a breath. "I'm not sure how that came about. We were very careful, and our text messages were cryptic enough. Do you think they hacked my phone?"

"No, babe. I don't."

He had no way of knowing this, but Myles's quiet confidence reassured her. "We have to make a list of people who know the whole story. Stella is appalled we told our wedding guests without having them sign NDAs."

"An NDA, really?" Myles asked. "That would've been awkward. They're our closest friends and family."

"I know, right?" Gigi picked up a grapefruit and licked the sugar coating, anything to keep from meeting his eyes. "She expected you to sign one, too."

He brushed that off. "That's no problem."

Stunned, Gigi could only manage a pointed stare.

"What?" he said. "I'd do anything to make you comfortable. I'll sign one now."

"I don't want you to."

"Why?"

She would have thought it was obvious. "Because I trust you!"

His expression changed slightly, then he extended a hand. "Come with me."

Gigi followed him to the patio deck. It was set up with bar-height tables and a pair of rattan swings. The slatted ceiling was strung with fairy lights. In the evenings, the bartenders stirred up cocktails and sometimes a live band played. In the daylight, it was hauntingly quiet. They sat facing each other on the swings, their feet touching. It was such a peaceful moment, if only they weren't talking NDAs, potential scandals and all the drama she'd brought to his life.

"Is that all you wanted to tell me?" he asked. "The reporter… the leak… That's all?"

"That's a big fucking deal!" she cried. "Don't you care about your reputation?"

"I care about you," he replied. "I care about Sandro's reputation, very much so. If anything, we have to keep him out of it."

"What about you, and your reputation?" she asked.

He shrugged. "I'm a chef. The worse my reputation, the better."

"You don't mean that."

"What are they going to say?" he asked. "I married a beautiful woman. We bought a restaurant."

If only it were that simple. "You married a spoiled, entitled, rich girl who couldn't wait to inherit a fortune and roped you into a scheme. That's what they'll say."

"Put like that, it doesn't sound good."

"It sounds like trash, Myles!"

"That's not what I did, though, is it?" he asked.

Her thoughts took a tumble. "I…can't answer that."

"You don't have to."

"Either way, it doesn't matter, Myles," she said. "The media will turn on you, and I can't let that happen. I won't! I'd rather tell the world I tricked you into marrying me to get my hands on the money. They already think I'm a rich bitch. Nothing I do will change that. They'll eat it up. They'll *love* it!"

"You'd take the fall, then?"

"Absolutely."

"Sorry. Can't let you do it," he said flatly. "I took vows to love, cherish and protect you."

"Myles…this is serious. Stella is livid."

"Tell Stella to take a breath," he replied. "Also, tell her I don't care what people think. Please don't stress out over this. You haven't eaten in days."

"Yes, I have!"

"No, you haven't."

"Let's focus on what's important. Okay?"

Having always been a media darling, hottest chef and all of that, he had no idea how vicious a full-on media assault could get, to say nothing of social media.

Myles slid off the swing and pulled her to her feet. "*You* are important to me."

Gigi leaned into him and pressed her forehead to his chest. All these weeks, he'd been her rock, her true ally. He would never know how much it meant to her. "I'll make this up to you."

"Stop worrying so much. That's all I ask."

Franklin, a line cook, called out to them from the patio door. "Sorry to interrupt! There's a seafood delivery! Thought you might want to take a look."

"Handle it," Myles shot back. "You know what I like."

She, too, knew what he liked. Above all, Myles liked his peace. His routines. His slow and quiet life. She would wage war to protect that. He wasn't the only one who'd made promises before God, drunk priest or no drunk priest.

She gazed up at him. With the tip of a finger, she traced the line of his thick brows, the cut of his jaw and his strong nose. "I don't think our friends betrayed us."

"Me, neither," he murmured into her hair. "Michelle wouldn't, and Carl doesn't have the energy or inclination."

"That leaves my family."

"I'm ruling out Beth," he said. "She'd do anything to avoid scandal."

"True," Gigi said. "That leaves Gabe."

"It could only be him," Myles said. "I don't think he means any harm. He could be acting out of a misguided sense of duty."

"Oh, sure!" Gigi cried. "Betray me out of duty, why not? It makes total sense."

He rubbed her back. "Don't be bitter."

"Too late," she snarled. "I am bitter. When I'm done with Gabe, he'll regret he ever opened his mouth."

# Twenty-Three

Gigi got a hold of Gabe over the phone.

"Mrs. Garcia-Paris! What a surprise!" he cried. "Hey, wait! Did you take his name, or did he take yours?"

Her brother's tone was cutting; good thing Gigi was armed with indifference. "Where are you?" she asked. "We need to talk right now."

"The Coral Reef Yacht Club."

The way his voiced curled around every syllable of the establishment's name! He loved his status symbols. Gigi wasn't a member. However, her parents had lifetime memberships; she was likely grandfathered in. "Stay there. I'll be right over."

"No problem," he replied. "I just wrapped a meeting with a client, but I'll stick around."

She arrived at the club thirty minutes later, disheveled and disgruntled. At the front desk, she worked to convince the clerk that she was meeting her brother. The woman did not object, but her sharp gaze betrayed her skepticism. She was this close to shouting, "Do you know who I am?" when Gabe crossed the lobby to meet her. He looked every inch the well-heeled country club member in an impeccable suit, his dark hair brushed back. Gigi, on the other hand, well…never mind.

"There you are! It took you long enough."

She offered a one-word explanation. "Traffic."

"Uh-huh." He gave her a long, assessing look and marched her away from the front desk. "Marriage doesn't suit you," he said. "I did warn you, though. You can't say I didn't."

Gigi pushed out a response through clenched teeth. "And I warned you to stay out of my business."

"You need a drink," he said. "I got us a table by the pool. We can chill and catch up, like old times."

He was in a delightful mood, for a traitor.

"Sorry," Gigi said. "My memory isn't what it used to be. When was the last time we chilled over drinks by a pool?"

"Never," he replied. "I blame myself."

"As you should."

She'd tried with him; she really had. Over the years, every olive branch extended was snapped into twigs. Gigi was over it.

"Come on," he said. "It's nice out."

She followed him out down the marble steps, her flip-flops clicking unbecomingly on the marble floor. At the table, Gabe handed her a cocktail menu she had no intention of ordering from. Instead, she went straight for the pitcher of ice water and poured herself a glass.

"I think about it all the time," Gabe said. "If I were better at keeping up with you, maybe you would have listened when I tried to stop you from making the biggest mistake of your life."

"Myles is not a mistake," she corrected. "I've never been happier."

"Don't take this the wrong way, but it doesn't look like it," Gabe said with some concern. "You look a mess."

"Because you're trying to sabotage us!" she cried.

He shushed her and pointed to a table set up for a luncheon directly across the pool. "Do you want the ladies of the Greater Miami Organization to hear us?"

"So, you do understand discretion!"

"I just don't understand you," he said wearily. "What are you going on about?"

"Georgina!"

Both Gigi and Gabe snapped to attention at the whipping sound of Beth's voice. They craned their necks to see the woman in a prim tweed jacket paired with a pencil skirt charging toward them in stiletto heels.

"Mother, what are you doing here?" Gigi asked, although

the answer was obvious. She only had to connect the dots from Beth to the luncheon table.

"Never mind me," she said. "How could you leave the house dressed like that?"

"Calm down, Mom," Gigi retorted. "I'm sure my father's reputation will survive the scandal of his daughter looking a little disheveled for one day."

"The thing is, you look unwell," Gabe said. "Are you feeling all right?"

"No, I'm not," she replied. "I'm under the weather. Thanks for asking!"

"The husband you hired said you were happy with him," Beth said. "What happened?"

"It's your fault I had to hire him," Gigi said. "Maybe you should remember his name."

"Ah," Beth said. "He told you of his little visit."

"We're partners," she retorted. "Of course, he told me. What are you still doing in Miami? I figured you'd be back in the great state of Texas by now."

"I'm staying," she said. "I don't have anyone in Houston anymore."

"Face it, Mother," Gigi said. "I'm all you have."

Beth glanced from Gigi to Gabe. "Sure, but what's brought you two together?"

"That's what I want to know," Gabe said.

Beth pulled up a chair. "So do I."

Gigi had a strange sense of déjà vu, confronting her mother and brother again.

"Gabe leaked the story of my marriage to the press," she said flatly.

"Ha!" Gabe clapped slowly, shaking his head. "Good one!"

Heat spread from Gigi's chest to her face. "A local reporter is asking questions. He has a source."

"Well, it ain't me." As chill as ever, Gabe flagged down a waitress, ordered a beer and offered to buy Gigi and Beth drinks. They both turned him down. "What?" he said to Gigi. "No margarita this time?"

"No, thanks." She couldn't stomach anything so tart. Besides, she needed a clear mind to crack this mystery. "If you didn't leak the story, who did?"

"It wasn't me," Beth said. "I don't air dirty laundry. I burn it, and make sure it never sees the light of day."

"That's actually good advice, Mom."

"I warned you this would happen, didn't I?" Beth said. "There was no way you could keep something like this a secret. And what did I tell you about secrets? They will haunt you your entire life."

"You ought to listen to your mother," Gabe said, lighting a cigar. "She's making sense."

Gigi slumped into her seat, defeated, but not too defeated to snatch the lit cigar out of Gabe's hand and stomp it out in a stone-carved ashtray. The rich aroma was too much to bear. "Sorry. I can't."

Gabe shook his head. "First you make false accusations against me, now you assault me. You know, I hoped we could patch things up."

"We can," Gigi said. "Just not today. All right?"

"Do you really think I'd rat you out to the press?" Gabe asked, bewildered. "Why would I? What's in it for me? Money? I don't need it. Attention? I don't want it. That leaves only one thing—revenge."

"Bingo," Gigi said.

"If you think so little of me, I really have nothing to say."

Beth, who was usually quick to intervene when Gigi and Gabe were at each other's throats, was oddly silent. Lips pressed shut, she stared at Gigi with wide eyes.

"What is it, Mom?" Gigi asked. "You're freaking me out."

"You've gotten yourself pregnant, haven't you?" Beth said.

Gigi closed her eyes. Her mother's words drilled through her. Could it be true? Had she gotten herself pregnant? It would explain the heartburn, nausea, vomiting, loss of appetite, plus the humming sense of contentment despite it all, which she'd attributed to her feelings for Myles.

"Well," Gabe said, glib as usual. "Good luck getting an annulment now."

He spotted Lou right away, at his usual seat overlooking the finish line, his face turned up to the sun, a folded horse race program on his lap. Myles sat next to him and propped up his feet.

Lou stirred from a nap and cleared his throat. "Look who it is! The great Pedro Garcia's son-in-law! I should congratulate you on your marriage."

"Thanks," Myles said, his eyes on the empty track. "Who's the favorite today?"

"I don't really bet on horses," he said.

"No way," Myles said. "You come here for the beer?"

"And the ambience," Lou added.

"If you say so."

"Baseball is my game," he said. "That's where I put my money."

"Is gambling on Major League games legal in Florida?" Myles asked.

"There are ways around it."

"I'm sure of it," Myles said dryly.

Lou clasped his hands. "To what do I owe the honor of this visit?"

"Respectfully, I'm here to ask you to shut the fuck up."

"Hey now!" Lou said with a nervous chuckle. "Don't get feisty."

It had hit Myles as soon as Gigi left to confront her brother: she wasn't the only one who'd discussed the plan with Sandro. He and Sandro had openly and repeatedly discussed Gigi and the proposal. At any time, Lou could have overheard them. He couldn't forget the night he'd heard footsteps in the dining room. Now he knew for certain that he hadn't imagined it.

"I know you spoke to the press," Myles said.

Lou stared at the track; his eyes followed a trainer leading a horse to the stables. "I might've overheard some things," he said. "I might've shared those things with an old buddy of mine, a retired reporter, over a beer or two. He doesn't mean any harm."

"I don't know what you thought you heard."

"I heard enough," Lou said. "First you and your little actor friend make a marriage pact that involves the legendary Pedro Garcia's daughter. Next, a mysterious development company makes a sweet offer on my land. Finally, I hear the restaurant that you love so damn much is staying open! Wouldn't you know it? How wonderful for all involved!"

"Lou—"

"I might be old, but I'm not an idiot," Lou interrupted. "I can connect the dots."

"And so can I," Myles said, unbothered. "I know a reporter or two, and here's what I'll tell them. I worked tirelessly to make your failing restaurant a success. When you were ready to sell, I paid above market price so you could retire in style. I was a good steward and a good business partner. And how do you repay me? By extorting my wife who, by the way, is still grieving the passing of her father, the legendary Pedro Garcia."

Lou chuckled without humor. "I didn't think you had it in you."

"You have no idea how far I'd go to protect the ones I love."

"Love, huh?" Lou said with a smirk.

"That's what I said."

Myles stood and stretched. It was a fine day and the air smelled of freshly cut grass.

"Leaving so soon?" Lou asked.

"I've got a restaurant to run," Myles answered. "Don't make me come out here again."

# Twenty-Four

Gigi was home, locked in the bathroom, standing over the toilet and waiting for the tip of a urine test strip to turn pink. Was it one line or two? Either way, in three minutes or less, she would know for sure whether she was pregnant with Myles's child or battling severe heartburn. Although the instructions clearly advised against it, she clutched the plastic wand between pinched fingers, staring at it, instead of laying it flat on a clean, even surface. It had the power to predict her future. Worried it might snap, she loosened her grip slightly, oh so slightly, just as the faintest pink line was starting to form. Naturally, she screamed, jumped and dropped it into the toilet.

If that wasn't a sign, she didn't know what was.

She fished it out and disposed of it then slunk off to the bedroom. The bedsheets smelled of Myles. *What if he doesn't want this?* It was a fair question. Yes, they'd been playing house, but this was real, potentially. They couldn't fake their way out of it. Ever since her mother had pronounced her pregnant, and even cracked a smile at the idea of being a grandmother, Gigi knew how desperately she wanted it to be true. *What if he doesn't want me?*

Done with the hemming and hawing, she grabbed her phone off the nightstand and sent Myles a text message. We have to talk. It's important.

His response left her confused. Don't worry. I took care of it.

Clearly, they weren't on the same page.

Despite everything, she had a party to attend. Gigi revived her party girl persona for the grand closing and showed up in one of Myles's shirts paired with a feather-lined miniskirt. Good thing, too! What was billed as a late-night gathering on the deck had all the trimmings of a New Year's Eve bash with live music, a photo booth and a bar. Tatiana, an event planner in training, was given carte blanche, and it showed.

Gigi waded through a sea of gold and silver balloons in search for Myles. Instead, she ran into the lady of the hour. Tatiana hugged her and fit a tiara on her head. "Welcome to Gigi's!"

"Excuse me. What?"

"We're reopening as Gigi's, and we couldn't be more thrilled."

"That can't be true."

A banner above a chocolate fountain said otherwise: *Gigi's in the District.*

Okay... It was a little long, but she liked it overall. Oh God... now she was crying and not in a subtle way. What was happening to her?

Tatiana hugged her again and handed her a napkin stamped with her name.

Gigi blew her nose. "Where's Myles?"

"Over there, with Alessandro."

Now, that was a surprise. "Sandro is here?"

"Everybody is here!" Tatiana cried and danced away.

This also proved to be true when she bumped into Nina Taylor and Julian Knight.

Nina kissed her cheek. "It's so good to see you, again!"

"Same here," Gigi said. "Julian, thanks for coming."

"I'm here for the oxtail empanadas," Julian deadpanned in his charming British accent.

The British actor was of Jamaican descent and his love for Caribbean flavors was well documented. So was his quick wit. But lord, he was handsome! He had the profile of an emperor. Unfortunately, his good looks had held him back. He'd been typecast as an action hero the moment he broke onto the scene. He and Nina had smartly and expertly turned all of that around.

"Looks like we'll be working together in the future," Julian said.

"I can't commit to anything until next year," Gigi replied. She would hate to lose this project, but she had to be honest. The lawyers informed her it could take a good six months to sort everything out.

"That's fine," Nina said. "That gives me time to work on the script."

"And wrap up some other things we've got going on," Julian added. "We'd like to have you over at the house sometime soon to talk it over."

"Don't you mean mansion?" Gigi teased.

"Yeah, well..." Julian let out the self-deprecating laugh of a proud homeowner.

"With you here, in Miami, there's an opportunity for a serious partnership," Nina said. "We could build something. The local film industry needs a boost."

*Building something in Miami...* That was the way forward; Gigi was sure of it.

"Sounds exciting, Nina."

"Great! I'll call you and we'll set something up."

Next, Gigi ran into Michelle and Carl, both of whom gushed over Diablo's new name. Then, she crashed into Sandro. As ever, he was as bright and warm as the sun. "G., you did it! You pulled this off. I'll never doubt you again."

He was a little too bright and sunny for Gigi to take right now. "We're not in the clear. You've talked to Felix, right?"

Felix was Sandro's longtime publicist. He was good, but not as good as Stella. It was possible he'd dropped the ball.

"I have, and he has some ideas. Still, for the most part, it's handled. Don't worry about it."

Seriously, if one more person told her not to worry! "Handled how, exactly?"

"Don't you know?"

She shook her head, feeling helpless. "It's been a long day. I can't play twenty questions."

"Speak to your devoted husband. He'll tell you."

She looked around. "Where is he?"

"Right here."

Myles was behind her, wrapping his arms around her waist,

kissing her neck, calling her gorgeous, and she had to get him alone.

"Could you please excuse us?" she said to Sandro.

"No problem," he said with a little grin. "I'll catch up with Julian."

Gigi grabbed Myles's hand and dragged him off through the back door, the kitchen, and into their private storage room.

He switched on the light. "Why are we in here?"

He was as relaxed as Sandro, and she couldn't take it. "Myles! We're still in crisis mode," she reminded him. "I don't think Gabe is the leak and—"

He touched a finger to her lips. "It's Lou. He overheard me on the phone with Sandro one night."

"What is wrong with that man?" Gigi cried, exasperated.

"I took care of it."

His voice was chilling. She was reminded of his favorite movie, *The Godfather.* "He's not in the trunk of your car, is he?"

"I promise he's alive and well." He pulled her to him by the hips. "I love the feathers. Can't wait to ruffle them later."

"Really? What do you have in mind?"

"I—"

"Nope! Never mind!" God, she was so easily distracted! "Tell me what you said to Lou."

"Forget him," he said. "No one is going to make you miserable, Gigi. No one is going to harass my family for their own twisted enjoyment and get away with it. I won't have that."

She reached for his hands, curled her fingers around his. "I come with so much baggage. The last thing I want is to complicate your life."

"How could you? I love you."

"You *love* me?"

"Yes, Gigi," he said. "I'm in love with you. Don't you feel it?"

If he hadn't said those words tonight, she might've crumbled into dust. She needed his love too much to go without it a single day. "I do."

"Do you love me?" he asked.

"Yes!" she cried. "I love you, and it's making me a little crazy!"

"You can't put that on me," Myles said. "You were this way when I met you."

"And still, you love me," she marveled.

"I do," he said. "I wondered if you'd consider keeping our marriage going, forever. What do you say?"

"Yes," she said in a breath. "I say yes. Myles, I want to be your wife, for real and forever."

"For real and forever," he repeated.

The air stirred around them. Gigi couldn't believe her crazy good luck. Myles was her husband. He was family. He was quiet nights, long talks, warm meals, home…finally.

"Gigi, babe, we should make love in this closet once and for all."

"Yes, definitely."

He slipped a hand under her skirt and squeezed her thigh. She slapped it away. God, she was *way* too easily distracted. "We still have to talk!"

"Is there something we haven't covered?" he asked.

There was a hint of a challenge in his voice, as if he were daring her to speak up. If there was anything Gigi couldn't walk away from, it was a dare.

"I think I'm pregnant."

"I think so, too."

"You do?"

"You wouldn't eat anything for days, not even fried cheese."

"I miss *queso*…"

"You'll have it again."

"How did this happen, Myles?"

"Come on…" he teased. "You know how."

"Okay, but how do you feel about this?"

While she waited for his answer, the deep-rooted fear of rejection, like unpleasant morning nausea, crept up again.

"How do I feel about having more of you to love?" he asked, incredulous. "Like I must have done something right because I'm one lucky bastard."

With a squeal of joy, she tried hiking up her skirt. "Now, let's make love!"

A knock on the door put an end to that. It was Sandro. "Hey, you two! Come out! You can do what you do in the closet later!"

Myles took her face between his warm hands and kissed her. "I'll tell him to get lost."

"What's the point? He never will!"

Another knock. "I can hear you."

Myles raked his fingers through his hair. Gigi smoothed down her skirt. They exchanged a look and he opened the door. Sandro greeted them with a knowing smile.

"This better be important," Myles said.

"I just got off the phone with Felix."

"Who's that?" Myles asked.

"His publicist," Gigi said somberly. "This is important."

"And?" Myles asked.

"He recommends I tell the truth," Sandro replied.

The truth? Wonderful! Her future kids would read all about how their dad married their mom to cash in on their granddad's money. What a legacy!

"The whole truth?" Myles asked, bewildered.

"Don't be crazy," Sandro said. "The truth from my perspective."

"What does that mean?" Gigi asked.

They were in the clean kitchen, just the three of them, scheming as usual, while a party raged outside. This was just who they were, at this point.

"I'm going out there to give a speech," Sandro said. "I've asked Tatiana to post it on social media, and I'm willing to bet she won't be the only one. Either way, Felix will ensure it goes viral."

"I don't follow," Myles said.

"It's called taking over the narrative," Sandro explained. "I'm going to tell the story of how I schemed to set up my two best friends. How I arranged their first dinner date, and even sent champagne to their table. It took some work, but I knew they'd be perfect for each other. I knew they'd do great things, like breathe new life into a restaurant that's been a haven to many of us over the years." Sandro paused for a response. When none came, he pushed on. "To wrap it up, I'll wish you luck and happiness, because you two deserve it."

Gigi was sobbing by the time he was done. Sandro had done more than set her up with his friend. She'd turned to him in desperation, and he'd saved her life. She could never thank him enough.

"What do you say, G.?" Sandro asked.

"It's a brilliant idea," she said. "How will I repay you?"

"With a part in your next movie," Sandro suggested. "I've been talking to Nina and Julian. It sounds like a hit."

"You got it!"

Sandro turned to Myles. "Are you in?"

Myles pulled him into a sloppy hug. "You're a genius. You know that?"

"Yup. And it's about time you figured it out." He broke free from Myles and smoothed his shirt. "I've got to look good in this video. I'm in the running for Sexiest Man Alive this year."

"You got my vote," Gigi said.

"All right. Meet you outside."

Sandro headed out. Myles suggested they follow suit, but Gigi grabbed his arm. "Wait."

"What is it?" he asked, concerned. "Are you okay?"

"I've never been better," she assured him. "It's just…it feels like we renewed our vows just now."

Myles cocked his head. "It does, right?"

"There's just one thing," she said. "You forgot to kiss the bride."

He drew her to him. "What was I thinking?"

Gigi took his face between her hands. "My love…" she whispered just as his mouth claimed hers.

Every promise they ever made now and forever sealed with a kiss.

## BUSINESS NEWS

The Heron, the seafood restaurant on North River Drive, has been sold for $3.6 million, according to the *Miami Today Business Journal*. The 3.2-square-foot lot was purchased by Miami Realty LLC, in an all-cash deal, with plans to open a second location of the popular restaurant Gigi's.

## VANITIES

GG Cinema has greenlit *At Dusk,* with writer Nina Taylor-Knight making her directorial debut. Actors Julian Knight and Alessandro Cardenas to costar.

## POST-CREDITS SCENE

*Scene: Outdoors. Midafternoon.*

*A young mother paces a deck trying to calm a fussy baby.*

Husband: Hand over my darling girl. I made her favorite mushy peas. You're hungry, aren't you, baby?

Wife: Mushy peas is great, but how's the paella coming? Will there be enough for all of us?

Husband: I think I have it under control. This isn't my first time hosting a party.

Wife: It's the first my mom is attending! She's so picky.

Husband: Don't worry, gorgeous. If she's anything like you, I'll have her eating out of my hands in no time.

\* \* \* \* \*

# OVERNIGHT INHERITANCE

## RACHEL BAILEY

For Vassiliki Veros,
friend and fellow romance novel obsessive.

Here's to many more late-night chats
about books and all good things!

# One

Mae Dunstan—or Mae Rutherford, as everyone at the party was calling her—stood at the soaring doors to the patio of her aunt Sarah's house in the Hamptons and sighed. Behind her was a glittering party in her honor, filled with the rich, the famous, and the beautiful, and all Mae wanted to do was escape.

In front of her was the velvety night sky and the promise of a few minutes of priceless solitude.

Before she could think better of it, or be called back, she stepped over the threshold. Each step into the backyard brought a decrease in noise and light, and, enveloped by the warm summer air, her entire body relaxed a little.

Since arriving in the US three weeks ago, her life had been a whirlwind, with people pulling her in all directions. Of course, it had been bound to happen once people found out she was a lost heir to a billion-dollar fortune, and now everyone seemed to want a piece of her, whether details, due to their morbid curiosity, or money. The fortune hunters were the worst. Men who were attempting to charm their way into her bank account by way of her DMs and then her bed.

She stepped farther into the manicured garden decorated with fairy lights and took a breath. It didn't help much. She'd barely been able to breathe since arriving from Australia. No, before then. Since her brother Heath had told her that the father they'd been hiding from for her entire life was dead and that they were now both billionaires. She still wasn't one hundred percent sure that it wasn't a mistake and someone would arrive soon to make them hand the money back. At least then her life would return to normal—the elementary school teaching job that she'd had to take leave from, the lifestyle of a small Australian town—instead of the circus it had become.

A patch of darkness along the tall, thick hedge that separated her aunt Sarah's house from the closest neighbor beckoned her with promises of peace, so she headed for its sanctuary. Once encased in the shroud of darkness, she wrapped her arms around herself and looked up at the stars that shone in the moonless sky. The angles of the constellations were different to those she'd grown up with in the southern hemisphere, but being able to see a sky full of twinkling stars was one of the few familiar things she still had.

"Party a bust, is it?"

She jumped several inches off the ground and swung around. No one was there, but leaves were rustling on the other side of the hedge.

She peered through but the foliage was too thick to see much. "Are you seriously lurking out in the bushes?"

"I could ask you the same question." The deep voice sounded amused.

She casually shrugged a shoulder, then realized he couldn't see the action. "I just needed to get some air."

"You're a fair distance from the party. I, however, am strolling along a pathway in my own yard. So tell me—" he lowered his voice "—why are you hiding from what sounds like an impressive event?"

This man was a stranger, and she was hardly going to spill the secrets of her heart to someone she couldn't even see. Even though part of her wanted to. The only person she really knew in the entire country was her brother, and Heath was wrapped up in his new fiancée, Freya. If she told him she wanted to talk, then of course he'd be there for her, but he'd spent his whole life looking out for her, working with their mother to keep them all safe, and now that he'd found happiness with Freya, Mae couldn't bear to taint that with her doubts and fears.

"I am enjoying the party. I'm just taking a moment to admire the night sky right now."

"Liar," he said softly.

Mae frowned at the hedge that separated them. "You don't know me."

"True." There was a pause and she heard the clink of ice cubes in a glass. "Which proves my point. You're talking to someone you've never met and can't even see instead of being inside at that party you say you're enjoying."

Annoyingly, he was right. "You're not there either."

"Wasn't invited," he said wryly. "Besides, I only arrived about half an hour ago."

"Arrived?" Despite herself, her curiosity was piqued. Since she'd landed on American soil, almost every conversation had been about her. It was a relief to talk about someone else, especially someone not connected to her situation.

"From New York. I have an apartment there where I live most of the time. I'm here for the weekend." The ice cubes clinked again. "Now you know my secrets, tell me why you're out here instead of in there with the who's who of the Hamptons' social scene back in the house."

She closed her eyes for a long moment. Maybe she should. It would be a relief to say it aloud, and didn't people say that it was easier to tell your truths to a stranger...?

"I don't fit in," she said in a rush. "These people, I don't understand them." Mortified, she covered her mouth with a hand, but he didn't reply, so she dropped her hand so she could clarify. "Don't get me wrong, they all seem lovely, but I can't seem to connect with anyone."

"Ah, there's your problem. A party in the Hamptons isn't a place where you make soul-deep connections. Everyone has their guard up. Did you meet anyone famous?"

"Several." She'd been stunned into either silence or babbling several times when she'd been introduced to people she recognized from movie screens or music videos.

"Part of their mind was on whether you had a phone and were going to sell photos of them, or repeat something they said to the gossip columns, so they had their guard up. And if you met someone rich, they were waiting for the pitch."

"The pitch?" she said, drawing the word out as if that would make its meaning clear.

"How you were going to ask them for money." His tone was neutral, matter of fact. "Maybe an investment, or a donation to charity, or straight up handout."

Her mother had always told them that money didn't buy happiness. Sure, having enough for the rent and food was vital for everyone, but after that, money made things worse instead of better. "That's an awful way to live."

He coughed out a laugh. "Better than the alternative, though. Besides, you get used to it."

Mae noted that he included himself in that group, which made sense. "Which type are you? Waiting to be betrayed or waiting for requests for cash?"

Sebastian Newport's face heated at the comparison of him to the Rutherford family and their friends.

"I'm nothing like them," he said with more intensity than he had intended.

"Strange," she said in her cute Australian accent. "You have a house in the Hamptons that you're using for a weekend and an apartment in New York as well. I dare say that it's unlikely you're on the poverty line. So this conversation is either about you waiting for me to prey on you, or…"

"Or?" he prompted through a tight jaw when she didn't continue.

"Or I'm the one who should be wary of you."

"You think I arranged this meeting to prey on you?" He'd been pacing in his own backyard, trying to wind down after the rush to get out of the city and then settle his infant son, Alfie. Once Alfie was asleep, Sebastian had poured himself a generous scotch and, baby monitor in hand, walked outside. Weekends always involved a fight with himself—he hated being so far from work, and his instincts shouted that he needed to be available, weekend or not, but he'd promised his late wife that he'd find more of a work-life balance for Alfie's sake. And deathbed promises were hard to break. So, during the week, his son was primarily cared for by a live-in nanny, while Sebastian devoted himself to long days at the office, and on weekends, it was just the two of them, here, at their holiday home. The last thing he'd been thinking about when he walked out here was meeting a woman through the shrubbery.

"Maybe you didn't set this meeting up, but your own theory means that everything at parties is transactional or avoiding it becoming transactional."

He chuckled. "Touché. But you forget. I'm not at your party."

"Which puts this conversation outside your theory."

Sebastian sank his free hand deep into his trouser pocket. "It's almost outside reality."

"Sounds about right," she said, her tone dry. "My whole life is practically outside reality at the moment."

He hesitated. She might think this was an anonymous encounter, but he'd guessed her identity from her first few words. The lost heirs of the Bellavista fortune, Heath and Mae Rutherford, were all anyone in their world was talking about, and he'd heard his neighbor Sarah was hosting a party for Mae tonight. Add her Australian accent to the equation, and her confusion about how this circle of society worked, and there was no one else this could be but Mae Rutherford.

He was low-key uncomfortable that their encounter in the darkness was anonymous only on one side, but he was enjoying talking to her and wasn't sure she'd continue if she knew who he was. Her aunt and brother must not have warned her that the other major stakeholder in the company they'd inherited owned the house next door, or she'd have been wary. Hell, she'd probably have ignored him from the start. But he meant her no harm. In fact, talking to her was the most fun he'd had with another adult in a long time. She was like a breath of fresh air, and he sorely needed one of those right now.

"Why weren't you invited?" she asked. "Didn't Sarah know you'd be here for the weekend?"

He sipped his drink before replying, "There's some history." That was true, even if it was an understatement. "We generally avoid each other now. But I hear she throws excellent parties."

"It's great, but…this is going to sound stupid."

"Go on," he said, trying to sound encouraging.

"I really don't know how to enjoy myself in there. With all those people."

He remembered being in the same position when he'd started attending society parties as a teenager, and he was hit with a wave of sympathy. She'd likely hate him when she found out who he was, and there was nothing he could do about that. Until that happened, though, one thing he could do for Mae Rutherford was share the insight he'd gained as a teen.

"All those people are showing you a facade," he said. "They've worked out how they want other people and the world to see them and they've slipped that mask on before arriving. All you need to do is work out what mask you want to wear. What face do you want to show them?"

"What if I don't know the answer?" The words emerging from the hedge between them were tentative. Vulnerable.

"Maybe start with working out what you want, and go from there." He rolled his shoulders, feeling the weekday stress beginning to recede.

"You mean what I want out of *life*? That's a pretty broad question."

"True." He watched the blinking lights of a plane crossing the night sky, giving her a moment to process her thoughts. "Do you know the answer?"

"Not really," she admitted on a sigh.

He couldn't imagine not knowing something as basic as your life's direction. He'd had his entire life planned out when he was still in elementary school. Mind you, curveballs, such as his wife dying just over three years into their marriage, had made him start to wonder if he was really in charge of his own destiny after all. For now, though, he was focused on Mae.

"I'm going to suggest that you have some resources behind you if you're at one of Sarah Rutherford's parties and you have possible contacts in the other guests. What do you want from that?"

A twig snapped in the shrubs, in roughly the same place her voice was coming from. "Why do I have to want something from it?" she asked, sounding a little annoyed.

"Everyone wants something." He knew that from experience. "What's the voice in your heart whispering? Fame? Power? Influence?"

She was silent for so long that he began to wonder if she'd left. Then she said, softly, "To make the world a better place."

He almost snorted in disbelief but thankfully caught it in time on the off chance she was serious. Did people like that really exist? People filled with hope and goodness?

"There's a lot of things that aren't great in the world," he said, probing. "What, specifically, would you like to make better?"

"I'd like to help children. And mothers who are trying to protect them."

The simple sentiment hit him hard in the solar plexus, and he practically staggered with the weight of it. Everyone knew that her father, Joseph Rutherford, had been a terrible human being, and many suspected that his wife had run to protect their little boy, Heath. Heath had reappeared on the scene a few months ago, and it was later revealed that he was a package deal with Mae. Their father hadn't known of her existence, which meant her mother had to have escaped once she knew she was pregnant. Sebastian's own father—and Joseph Rutherford's business partner—wasn't someone he thought of fondly, but he'd been an angel compared to Joseph. Mae's mother had probably done the right thing by running far, far away, and, as a parent himself, he respected her choice.

"That's," he began but had to stop and clear his throat. "That's a good idea. If it's what you want to do, then slip on the mask of someone who can get it done and head back inside."

He heard a long intake of breath and could imagine her straightening her spine and getting her game face on.

"Thank you. I'm ready." There was a crunch of leaves, as if she'd taken a step. "Nice to meet you, shadow man."

He waited until her steps faded, then whispered, "Likewise, Mae."

Mae felt taller, surer. She'd left the party less than half an hour earlier, wanting to be as far from the people and their world as she could. One conversation with the stranger next door and she felt different, and was reentering the party with a sense of purpose. She began to talk to the people she met about their passions and what charity work they did, feeling her way and looking for clues of what she could do with these new connections.

She wasn't staying in the US forever—she'd spent most of her life in Australia and thought of it as home—but while she was here, she could do something to help women who were in a similar position to the one her mother had found herself in when she realized she was pregnant with her.

Aunt Sarah approached from the champagne bar, the skirt of her turquoise dress swirling around her knees. "You seem different than the last time I saw you." She smiled, and her kind eyes crinkled at the corners. "Less like a startled bird."

Mae chuckled. She really did like Sarah. "I just had an interesting conversation with your neighbor."

Sarah stilled. "Which neighbor?"

"The one over the hedge there," she said, pointing.

Her aunt swore under her breath and Mae was momentarily surprised. She'd obviously only seen Sarah on her best behavior in the few weeks she'd known her. Then she registered that Sarah's expression was stormy too. Shadow Man had said there was some history between them and that they avoided each other when they could.

Mae lifted her hands, palms out, placating. "I'm not sure what the problem is between you, but he was really lovely to me tonight. Gave me some good advice too."

Her aunt's eyes narrowed. "I'll just bet he did."

"Okay, what am I missing?" This seemed like an over-reaction for neighbors who didn't see eye to eye.

Sarah glanced around, then beckoned her to follow until they reached a secluded corner on the other side of the kitchen. "I was planning on letting you settle in a bit longer before plunging you into meetings with the lawyers and accountants to explain your inheritance to you. But for now, how much has Heath told you about what your father left in trust?"

"We haven't had much time to talk in detail yet. Just that after our father died, most of his wealth was left for Heath, and you've been the executor, overseeing it in the meantime. And that once you and Freya found him and proved his identity with the DNA tests, he split the money fifty-fifty with me."

"That's the story of the money," Sarah said, inclining her head in acknowledgement, "but do you know anything about the composition of the estate?"

Mae thought about conversations she'd had with Heath and came up empty-handed. She really should have asked more questions. "Not really."

"Okay, here's a quick overview. You've both inherited a portfolio that contains cash, bonds, and investments. But the main component is stock in a property development company that my father, your grandfather, and his business partner started—Rutherford and Newport. That company passed to their sons—your father, Joseph Rutherford, as well as Christopher Newport. They ran it together for many years, despite disliking each other intensely. They both tried to buy the other out several times, but neither would sell. When your father died and we couldn't find Heath and didn't know about you, Christopher thought he'd won. But I refused to sell the stock and, instead, employed a team to work in the company, to keep the business going and keep the seat warm for Heath, and now for you too."

Mae gave Sarah a spontaneous hug. "I can't believe you kept the faith all that time that you'd find him."

"I never gave up hope." Sarah reached out and cupped

Mae's cheek. "And then finding you was such a special bonus."

The touch, the boundless love, reminded her of her mother's love for her, and she found herself smiling. "So what does all this have to do with your neighbor?"

Sarah flicked a glance at the window that faced her neighbor's property, appearing lost in thought for a long moment. "That man is Christopher's son, Sebastian Newport. Christopher is in the process of retiring, and Sebastian has stepped up to take over most of Christopher's duties. So the man who 'gave you good advice' has a vested interest in any decision you make."

Mae's heart stuttered and her stomach sank before she remembered something crucial. "I didn't tell him who I was. I could have been any guest at the party."

"Mae," Sarah said kindly. "How many guests here tonight do you suppose have an Australian accent? And don't doubt that he has a thick dossier on his desk covering every detail about your life that his investigators have been able to glean so far. He would have known exactly who you were."

Mae's chest filled with heat and anger. "Sonofabitch."

"Yeah," Sarah said and handed her a glass of champagne.

# Two

Sebastian Newport leaned back against the marble kitchen counter as he threw back his second coffee of the morning and prayed it kicked in before his son woke. Thankfully, Alfie had always been a good sleeper, unlike Sebastian.

Of course, it hadn't helped that he'd stayed awake for hours last night, replaying the conversation with Mae Rutherford in his head. He'd tried hard to marry the image of her from the photos in his dossier with the captivating voice he'd heard through the shrubbery but hadn't been able to quite make it click. Last night, she'd been wary and uncertain in a new world. The pictures—private investigator photos in which she hadn't been looking at the camera—had shown a smiling, confident woman. And he couldn't help but want to know more.

The faint tune of his front doorbell sounded, and he instinctively stiffened in case it woke Alfie. He'd changed the shrill buzzing to a gentle classical-music-inspired sound, and had set the volume to low, but he still waited a beat, listening to the baby monitor, just in case. When there were no stirring sounds from the nursery upstairs, he slid the monitor into his pocket, shoved off the counter, and headed for the front door.

With one hand wrapped around his coffee mug, he unlocked the door with the other and swung it open to reveal the woman he'd just been thinking about. He blinked, wondering if it really was her or he was being too quick to judge. But the long, dark, wavy hair, piercing gray eyes, and dimples gave her away. And the clincher was how much she looked like her aunt. This was Mae Rutherford.

She wasn't smiling, happy and bright, like in the photos. She wasn't smiling at all. Her almond-shaped eyes gave the impression of gathered storm clouds, ready to break and rain down mayhem.

"Do you know who I am?" she asked, before he could say anything.

"Hello, Mae."

"How do you know?" A frown dug across her forehead.

"As I'm sure you've guessed, I recognize you from photos. Though I have to say, they don't do you justice." The photos were, well, flat. This woman before him was so full of emotion and intensity that it was spilling out around her, as if he'd be able to feel it if he reached his hand out to the air near her face or arms. And damn if he didn't want to try...

"When did you first know it was me?"

*Ah.* "I guessed it was you last night, if that's what you're asking."

She tipped her head to the side, so her hair swung across her shoulder. "Did you know the whole time?"

"Pretty much. Your accent is rare here, so I put two and two together."

She folded her arms tightly under her breasts. "Why didn't you tell me? Why let me think our talk was anonymous?"

He shifted his weight to his other foot. He'd asked himself the same question while lying in bed last night. "I was relatively sure you would have walked away, and I was enjoying our chat."

She didn't speak for a moment, just held his gaze with sparking eyes, nodding slowly. "So, the advice you gave me last night. It's starting to seem that it was more like manipulation than advice."

He winced. That was a fair conclusion, and one he would have drawn himself had their roles been reversed. And yet…

"It might seem that way to you now, but I treated our conversation last night in the spirit of two strangers meeting through shrubbery. I gave you the same advice I would have given anyone in that situation."

"You'll excuse my incredulity."

The stirrings of a smile pulled at his lips, but he managed to keep it from forming. "If it helps, it's not the same advice I'd give this morning, to your face."

She narrowed her eyes. "I know I'm going to regret this, but, what's your advice this morning?"

"Sell to me."

"Sell to you?"

"Sell me your family's half of Bellavista Holdings. We both know you're out of your depth, so sell it to me and walk away with a very large bag of cash."

"Did you just call me dumb?"

"Absolutely not. I wouldn't know anything about teaching school, but it's something you trained to do. I've been training my whole life for *this*. So, sell to me."

"First of all, this is preemptive. Heath and I don't even own it yet. The legalities are still being sorted out. But even so, what makes you think I'd want to sell a company I'd only just inherited? Especially to you, when there's so much history with my family."

"Because I was there, talking to you last night, and you don't want to run a business. But the money you'd make on the sale, well, that could be put to all sorts of good purposes."

"What I do or do not want is—"

Sebastian held up a hand as faint noises came through the baby monitor in his pocket. Not crying, just the sounds of Alfie waking up. The crying would start soon, though.

"Nice meeting you, Mae. I have to go," he said and moved to close the door.

"We are not done," she said.

"True," he said. "We'll continue this another time. Right now, I need to go."

"You do not get to walk away, just because I caught you out—"

Alfie's vocalizations were changing, as if he were working himself up to a cry. "Look, if you're not done, then fine, but I really have to go. You're free to stay or leave, but either way, shut the front door behind you."

He turned and headed for the stairs, taking them two at a time, just as Alfie's wail exploded through the baby monitor.

Mae stood on the threshold and watched Sebastian's retreating back, not really sure what had just happened. She'd been primed for a confrontation—had lain awake most of the night planning for one—and been determined to get some answers. But she hadn't gotten far before he'd…left. And had that been a baby's cry? The sound had been muffled and faint, but it had sounded like a baby.

She frowned as Sebastian disappeared around a corner upstairs. Then she glanced over her shoulder at the border to Sarah's place next door. The sensible thing to do would be to pull the door shut and head back to Sarah's. But then, no one had ever accused her of being sensible.

Besides, Sebastian had invited her in. Sort of.

Feeling a little like she was trespassing, she closed the door and followed him up the stairs. The house had the air of slightly faded opulence, with its heavy wooden furniture, thick rugs, and expensive drapes, as if the place had been tastefully decorated many years earlier but not been updated. Huge portraits in gilt frames filled the walls, and elaborate light fittings hung from the center of the rooms on either side of her. Mae might have been staying with Sarah for a few weeks already—both here and at her New York City apartment—but she was still adjusting to the realization that people really lived like this.

At the top of the staircase, she turned left—where Sebastian had disappeared from sight—but all she found was an empty hall. Pausing, she heard low murmurs, so she followed the sound to the first door on the right.

Inside was a nursery, and unlike the other parts of the house she'd seen, this one was newly decorated. Fresh mint-green walls, buttercup-yellow checked drapes, and matching bedding. It felt bright. Happy. She stepped inside in time to see Sebastian reach into a crib and lift out a toddler, maybe eighteen months old, maybe a bit younger.

Transfixed, she watched as he laid the baby on a changing table, smiling down at him. Then, with one square, tan hand on the baby to keep him safe, he reached with the other to a cabinet above the table for a diaper. The movement showcased his strong, broad shoulders, and she was momentarily distracted. He murmured to the baby as he worked, changing the diaper in economical movements.

He glanced up, seeming to notice her for the first time, and she fought the instinct to shrink back behind the door. The moment seemed too private, too intimate to be observed by a stranger. But Sebastian wasn't angry.

"Meet Alfie," he said and lifted the baby again, holding him to his chest, high enough that their faces were side by side. The intensity of two sets of ocean-blue eyes was startling. Alfie had long lashes and his T-shirt had ridden up to show some adorable, chubby baby belly.

Damn, he didn't play fair. She'd been all worked up and annoyed at him when she'd arrived, and now the wind was totally taken out of her sails. First, when she'd seen him, and his masculine beauty had hit her square in the gut, and, after she had recovered from that, with the realization that his baby was a cherub.

"Hi, Alfie." She waggled her fingers at him. "How old is he?"

"Fourteen months," Sebastian said and tickled his son's belly. "You're getting big, aren't you?" Alfie gurgled in agreement.

"Come on," he said to her. "Alfie is hungry."

"Sure," she said, with no real idea what she was agreeing to.

Sebastian turned for the door, swiping a plush toy elephant from the crib on the way out.

She followed them down to the kitchen and waited while Sebastian settled Alfie into a high chair. This morning was quickly becoming surreal. She'd come over to his place to confront him, maybe yell a bit to get it off her chest, but here she was, standing in a kitchen, watching him with a darling baby.

"I prepped a fruit platter for him earlier, but you're welcome to coffee instead."

"Is his mother still asleep?" she asked, then realized how inappropriate the question was. Did he even have a ring on?

"It's just the two of us," Sebastian said with a shrug that looked practiced. "Isn't it, Alfie?"

"You're divorced?" she asked, unsure why she was pushing the point.

"Widowed." He didn't look up as he slipped a bib over Alfie's head and laid the plate on the high chair's tray.

Her heart clenched tight. "Sorry. I shouldn't have pried."

"It's okay. You're hardly the first person to ask. We get that question a lot," he said, finally looking up. There were those eyes again. Ocean blue and too magnetic for her peace of mind. She needed to focus.

She had a million questions—how did he run Bellavista Holdings when he was a single parent to a baby?—but she didn't know him well enough to ask.

"Okay, I'm ready," he said, squaring his shoulders.

"For what?" she asked warily.

"You said at the door that we weren't done, and I said it would have to wait. You can continue now."

"Oh, right." It seemed wrong to be cranky at a man in front of his infant son, so she said, "You know, I'm still getting my head around our family connection. Sarah told me that your grandfather built this place at the same time my grandfather built the one next door."

He blew out a breath and nodded. "They were best friends. They'd hoped the connections would travel down the generations, but, as you know, it wasn't to be."

"Did you know your grandfather?" She watched Alfie concentrate as he picked up a blueberry and popped it into his rosebud mouth.

"I knew my grandparents well." A smile flitted across his face. "And yours. My own parents didn't like having me underfoot and would send me up here to stay as often as they could."

"I'm sorry—that must have been rough." To have your own parents not want you must be an awful feeling. She might not have had any contact with her father, but that was a completely different thing to growing up with a parent who didn't want you around. Her mother had spent time with her and Heath every chance she got.

"It wasn't so bad." His eyes had a faraway look for a long moment. "I much preferred being here with Nan and Pop. If it had been up to me, I'd have grown up with them."

"Does your father spend time here now?"

"Here?" He handed Alfie a sippy cup. "Never sets foot in the place. Too far from the bright lights and easy convenience of city living. Besides, the house is mine—Pop left it to me—and my father likes to be in places where he rules the roost."

Alfie finished his fruit platter and waved his arms in the air. Sebastian wiped them over with a damp cloth and then lifted his son out of the chair and held him against his well-muscled chest. Again, she had to remind herself to focus on the issue at hand.

"I have to tell you, Sebastian," she said, leaning back, "you seem to be volunteering a lot of information for a business rival."

He coughed out a laugh. "I'd hardly call it *volunteering*. You're asking a lot of questions. I'm just trying to answer them."

"Unless," she said, undeterred, "this is all calculated. You're trying to give the appearance of transparency, while hiding the real secrets deep."

"Or—" he raised an eyebrow pointedly "—I have nothing to hide."

"That's what you want me to believe."

"Because it's the truth," he said as Alfie patted his cheek—a pale hand against his father's olive skin.

She regarded him for a long moment. "I'm going to work this out, Sebastian Newport. Work *you* out."

He grinned. "You know, I think you meant that as a threat, but I'm strangely looking forward to it."

Mae walked down Sebastian's driveway, then back up the path to Sarah's house—no way to cut through between these houses. A thick hedge ran the full length of the border, ensuring that no one accidentally had to see anyone from the other's house. Two houses, built side by side by best friends, now divided by an impenetrable tangle of leafy shrubs—the symbolism was not lost on her.

As the house came into sight, she saw Sarah's driver and all-round right hand, Lauren, depositing a couple of bags into the trunk of her aunt's black Suburban and waved.

Lauren called out, "Heading back to Manhattan in about twenty minutes, Mae," and went back inside.

Heath appeared with a backpack and smiled when he caught sight of her. "You missed breakfast."

"I'll grab something to eat in the car," she said, still distracted by her conversation with Sebastian.

He slid the backpack into the trunk alongside the other bags, then turned and leaned back against it. "Did you take a walk?"

She glanced at the hedge. "Went next door to talk to our neighbor."

"Newport?" Heath was suddenly alert.

Given that she and her brother jointly owned the share in Bellavista Holdings, she should have checked with him first. But facing Sebastian was something she'd had to do alone. "We sort of met last night and I needed to ask him something."

"Get any answers?"

"Not really." She dug her hands in her pockets. "Did you know he has a baby?"

He screwed up his face in thought. "Don't think I did." He surveyed her face and frowned. "Don't you go softening toward him just because he has a kid. It doesn't take morals to procreate—just look at our own father. It means nothing."

Mae nodded. He was right, but… There was something about the way that Sebastian had smiled at Alfie and cared for him that had raised questions in her mind. Their father might have produced children, but from all accounts, he hadn't been caring to them.

She rolled her shoulders, searching for perspective. "What do you know about Sebastian?"

"Not a lot, personally." He shrugged. "I only met him a couple of times, and the best thing I can say about him is that he's better than his father."

And they both knew that counted for nothing. "Ethical? Transparent?"

"Well, I trust him about as far as I can throw him, and he's a fairly big man."

She snorted. "So no trust at all. But how many people have we trusted in our lives anyway? Adding Sarah and Freya into our circle of trust in the same year must be a record for us."

He winced and then shoved his fingers through his dark blond hair. "Freya says that I'm hypervigilant, because of our upbringing. She says it's a trauma response."

That made a lot of sense. Some of her earliest memories were about realizing that her responses to things were different than those of other kids. "It kept us safe, though."

"That's exactly what I said to her." He grinned.

The lack of trust was usually something they reserved for other people, but when Heath had found out about their inheritance, and about their father's identity, he'd kept it a secret from her. Mae understood his need to investigate before exposing her to risk, but it still stung. She'd let it go at some point, but she wasn't ready to do that yet.

"So," she said, digging her hands into her pockets, "using your power of hypervigilance, tell me more about your impressions of Sebastian Newport."

"When I went into the office to look around, he tried a pretty basic divide-and-conquer move—tried to get me away from Sarah and Freya to talk alone. I didn't fall for it."

She shifted her weight to the other foot. "Did you find out what he wanted to say to you alone?"

"Oh, yeah," he said, nodding. "To talk me into selling my half of the company to him."

Mae sucked in her bottom lip. It was the same thing he'd asked her. "Were you tempted?"

"To be honest, selling would be the easy option."

"But…?"

"At the time, you didn't know about the inheritance and it wasn't my decision alone, not to mention, it wasn't then—and still isn't—in our names. Besides—" he crossed his arms, seeming less certain now "—it seemed like it was something we should think about."

Mae waited a beat. She knew her brother, and there was something else, something deeper, here. "Think about what? As Sebastian says, we don't know anything about property development."

"It was something our grandfather built. His life's work."

She rocked back on her heels. That was not the answer she'd been expecting. "We can't keep a huge company out of nostalgia, Heath."

"I get that. But we owe it to ourselves, and everyone whose livelihood depends on the company, to at least think it through first. I realized during my visit to the office that walking in and upending things without a thought to the people it employs, is something our father would have done."

A cold shiver raced across her skin. That one line affected her more than anything else he could have said. "Do you have a plan?"

"It's on my list of things to do," he admitted. "I'm still getting my head around the investments and the whole portfolio."

"Now that I'm here, I can help with that." Through his

will, their father had left everything to the only child he'd known about—Heath—but her brother was sharing it with her fifty-fifty, and she needed to step up to the plate.

"That would be great. To start, Freya and Sarah have given me a mountain of reports to read, and we need to visit the businesses we own or have shares in."

"Ugh. Reports? That sounds like homework, and I'm normally the one who gives homework to other people." She was joking and he chuckled, but there was a kernel of truth to her statement. All those business reports were completely outside her wheelhouse.

"There's a charitable trust that looks more your style. Maybe start with that—read up, visit whoever is overseeing it, whatever—to ease your way in. Then dive into the other stuff once you're up to speed."

Mae took a breath and tried not to feel overwhelmed. She looked back up at Sarah's house and scuffed her foot on the gravel drive. "Do you think Sarah would mind if I stayed a few extra days?"

He frowned. "Alone?"

"I just need to catch my breath." The thought of heading back to Manhattan made her head hurt, with the noise and the bustle and the people expecting things of her that she wasn't sure she could deliver. "I could join you in a couple of days."

"I'm sure she'll be fine with it, as long as you're back for Friday night."

A small family dinner to celebrate Heath and Freya's engagement was planned for Friday. Of course, she knew that her idea of a small family dinner and Sarah's would be vastly different, but she was looking forward to raising a glass to her brother and his new love. "I wouldn't miss it. Besides, I was planning on dropping over to see

Mum's family one night this week, so I'll come back before Friday."

"That's a good idea. If Lauren can't come back and get you, I'll come out on the bike and pick you up."

He opened his arms and she stepped into a bear hug. Since their mother had passed, Heath was the only person in the world she truly trusted, and she was grateful they were in this together. "Love you," she murmured.

"Love you more," he said.

# Three

Later that afternoon, Sebastian adjusted Alfie on his hip, and knocked on Sarah Rutherford's front door. He hadn't been here since he was a child—back when he'd stay with his grandparents, and they'd bring him over to see their friends. After that generation had all passed, the invisible walls had gone up and any connection between the families had dissolved. In fact, more than that, his father and Joseph Rutherford had become archenemies, and the distance hadn't improved since Joseph's death.

The door opened and Mae stood there, her storm-gray eyes wide, her hair pulled back in a ponytail. The air whooshed out of his lungs. Some people might not call her beautiful—her thin features were a little too severe to meet traditional beauty standards—but what were standards worth with a woman like Mae Dunstan? There was so much vivacious life emanating from her every pore that she glowed. And he couldn't look away.

She didn't speak, perhaps surprised to see him again this soon, and his lungs had stopped working, so he simply stood, drinking her in. Until Alfie squirmed in his arms and broke the spell.

Seb cleared his throat. "I was wondering if we could have a word. Maybe alone."

"That figures," she said, crossing her arms under her breasts. "I heard you like the divide-and-conquer strategy."

"What?" He'd been hoping to avoid a confrontation with the whole family while he had Alfie with him. Babies his age should be protected from tension. "No, I just—"

She waved a hand. "The others left a couple of hours ago."

"You stayed behind without them?" He frowned. She was new in the country, which made it surprising that they had left her out here alone.

She arched one eyebrow. "Wasn't aware I needed your permission."

He readjusted Alfie in his arms. This wasn't going the way he'd hoped. When Mae had left his place earlier, he'd thought they had something of an understanding, but her guard was up again. "Can we start again? I've come to make you an offer."

She nodded, her expression unchanging. "To buy the company from us."

"Not this time. Though that deal is still on the table if you've changed your mind."

"We haven't, but okay, then," she said, her tone challenging. "What's your offer?"

He did his best to look as professional as he could while standing uninvited on the stoop of his family's nemesis, his hair mussed in the breeze, wearing casual clothes, and carrying a baby. "Come into the office and shadow me for a week."

Mae's eyes narrowed. "Shadow you?"

"You can see the company from the inside, and you'll see that I'm not trying to do anything underhanded."

"Is this another version of divide and conquer? Get me on my own and bamboozle me."

Mae Dunstan really was the most skeptical person he'd ever met. He liked that about her. "It just seems like the fastest way to cut through all the suspicion and speculation."

"What would shadowing entail, exactly?"

"You'd sit in on meetings and appointments. I'll have calls on speaker, and you can read anything I work on." It might be weird and awkward at times, but she and her brother owned half the business, which would make it easy enough to explain her presence.

"If you're hiding something, wouldn't you just plan that only things you're willing for me to see would be on your schedule for that week?"

Alfie began to fuss, so Seb pulled the plush elephant from his pocket and handed it to him. "You're smart," he said to Mae. "You'll work out if I'm trying to defer appointments to the next week or not taking calls from certain people."

Mae watched Alfie for a beat, then looked back to him. "What sort of access to information do I get?"

She was wavering. He gave her the most charming of his smiles. "You can ask me anything, and I promise to share as much information as I have. Also, you can ask the rest of the staff anything and have free access to all files."

In fact, the more she asked, and the more understanding she gained of the business, the faster she'd realize she was out of her depth and agree to sell the company to him. He'd answer every question she had, and then some. Drown her in answers. She expected him to be underhanded, but there was no need to be when the truth would do a better job.

"What do you get out of it?" she asked, her chin tipping up.

He met her gaze squarely and answered sincerely. "I'm hoping you'll find that, not only do I have nothing to hide, but once the veil is ripped away, you'll see that property development isn't the most exciting line of work. I predict that, at the end of the week, you'll be more inclined to sell to me."

She pressed her lips together and a dimple appeared on her cheek. Then she nodded. "Okay, I accept. But just so you know, it's only because I want to see what you're up to."

"You're not very trusting," he said, trying not to grin and failing.

She shrugged. "Family trait. When do you want to do it?"

"Whenever you have time is fine by me."

"This week?" She tucked some strands of flyaway hair that had escaped her ponytail behind her ear.

"Sure." He'd see if his assistant could reschedule his Monday morning to give him some time to bring Mae up to speed, but since that was the only change he'd make to his week, the timing didn't matter much. "When are you headed back?"

She chewed on her bottom lip before replying, "I don't have a firm plan yet. As I said, the others already left."

"You're welcome to travel back with Alfie and me," he said. Alfie usually slept most of the way, and it would be an early start to the plan to overload her with the honest reality of the company. "I'll be driving back tomorrow afternoon."

She regarded him for a long moment, then nodded. "Okay."

"Great." Sebastian let out a long breath. He'd achieved his goal, but part of him wondered if Mae had somehow gained the upper hand.

Mae fiddled with the seat belt in Sebastian's SUV. Alfie had fallen asleep within minutes of leaving, and she and Sebastian had made polite small talk, but her tolerance for chitchat was low, and she'd about reached her limit. Especially since sitting this close to him was making her restless. His woodsy cologne was drifting across the confined space, filling her senses, and every time he checked his mirrors before overtaking a car, or his hand moved to activate his turn signal, he seemed even closer and her skin buzzed.

For the past day and a half, she'd drifted around Sarah's weekend home, thinking about Sebastian and the coming week. With no one there to distract her, she'd thought about him more than she otherwise would have. A couple of video calls to friends back home in Australia had diverted her attention for short periods, but her thoughts always returned to this man beside her. To the fall of his wavy hair over his forehead. The way his lips moved as he talked, shaping themselves around the words, or pulling out into a smile. The warmth that bloomed under her skin every time he fixed those blue, blue eyes on hers.

But an alarm at the back of her brain had been sounding since he'd made his offer. No, before that. It had probably started when she confronted him at his front door and he hadn't reacted as she'd expected.

*Don't form a crush on Sebastian Newport.*

Her life had been turned upside down—she was in a new country, staying with family she hadn't known existed a few months ago, had inherited more money than she could have imagined, and she had no idea what she was doing. This was the very worst time to develop a crush on anyone, but the person who seemed to be at the center of so much of it? The person Sarah and Heath both told her was the enemy? Yeah, he'd be a stupid person to crush on.

If only her heart didn't beat a little faster every time he was near...

"When does our deal kick in?" she blurted out, needing to stop her thought spiral.

"The shadowing?" He glanced at the rearview mirror, then back to the road. "I get into the office at about eight tomorrow, so whenever you arrive after that."

She was looking forward to that. Heath had already visited the office, and now she wanted a turn to visit it on her own, to look around and form her own opinions. "What about the questions? You said I could ask anything."

"We have a drive ahead of us, and we may as well use that time constructively, so I'm happy to answer questions now, if that's what you're asking."

Now that he'd agreed, she hesitated. There was something she really wanted to ask, but didn't know if it was too personal. Heath always said she pushed too far, but...

What the heck. He could always tell her to mind her own business.

"Tell me the story about your wife and Alfie."

He threw her a sharp glance. "I meant ask me anything about the company."

She knew that's what he'd meant, but she was determined to understand what made him tick, and to do that, she needed to see him from all sides. "This is relevant to the company. I'm interested in how a single father to a baby is able to run a company of this size. This question is for context."

He shrugged one shoulder. "Okay, I'll allow it, but only in the spirit of complete transparency."

"Your commitment to the cause is noted," she said with mock seriousness.

As he smiled, his eyes crinkled at the corners, and then his expression changed, becoming nostalgic. "Ashley and I met when we were kids. Her parents knew mine, which meant we crossed paths occasionally, but they lived in Upstate New York, so not enough that we grew up together. By the time we were in our late teens, everyone around us had decided that we should be together. We liked each other and had a lot in common." He shrugged. "It seemed like a good idea at the time, so we started dating, and then I proposed."

"That doesn't sound like a love story for the ages," she said, then bit down on her lip. Insulting the man's marriage probably wasn't the best start to working together for a week.

"It might not have been a great, passionate affair to start with, but we grew to love each other. Ash was a great partner to have by my side, and she was an excellent mother." He glanced at the back seat in his rearview mirror. "For the time they had together."

"How long did they have?" Watching his profile, she saw his jaw tense.

"Almost five months."

"What happened?" she asked, her voice just above a whisper.

"Cancer." He swallowed hard, his Adam's apple moving down in the strong column of his throat. "She had treatment, but it was aggressive and took her fairly quickly."

The tragedy of Alfie losing his mother that young, too young to even form proper memories, made her chest ache. "You've been raising Alfie on your own since then?"

"Pretty much. My mother isn't on the scene, and I wouldn't let my father near Alfie even if he was interested. Ashley's parents are great, but they're upstate. They try to see him regularly, and we visit them as much as I can manage."

For a couple of minutes, she just watched the road, absorbing it all. Though she was watching him out of the corner of her eye too. She suspected he wouldn't appreciate it if she stared at him, but she'd been raised by a single parent who'd had no support. She knew how big a job it was, and he was running a huge, complex company as well.

"How *do* you manage?" she finally asked.

"I'm lucky," he said with a rueful smile. "I have a live-in nanny who does a lot of the day-to-day care while I'm at work."

That *was* lucky—most single parents couldn't afford

a full-time nanny. Though he'd just parented solo all weekend.

"You didn't bring the nanny to the Hamptons?"

He rolled his shoulders back, stretching, then relaxed his grip on the wheel again. "When Ashley," he began, but his voice rasped, so he cleared his throat. "When Ashley knew she wasn't getting better, she made me promise a bunch of things. One of them was that I'd find some sort of balance between work and parenthood, for Alfie's sake. I have the nanny for the weekdays and I try to get up to the Hamptons on the weekends where it's just the two of us. I don't always manage it, but I'm doing my best."

Mae sat back in her seat. That had been a whole lot more honesty than she'd expected. "You weren't joking that you'd answer anything."

"I'm an open book." He rubbed a hand around the back of his neck before putting it back on the steering wheel. "Actually, that's not true. Normally, I hate sharing private information."

"So this is all in aid of being able to buy the company off me?"

"Yes," he said. "No, not only that. There's something weirdly honest between us. I think it's from the way we met. It was like we were in a little bubble, apart from the world that night."

"You knew who I was, though," she pointed out, still not quite ready to let that go.

"I did, but it still felt…different. You don't believe me, which is fine, but I was being honest with my advice in that conversation."

She thought about what he'd said back then, his voice surrounding her in the inky-black night, and had to admit that he was right. It had felt different to any other conversation she'd had in her life. Chances were that he was conning her to get complete control of the company, but she had to admit one other thing too…

Listening to his deep, smooth voice through the hedge on a moonless night was the real moment she'd started developing a crush on Sebastian Newport.

# Four

The next day, Mae stepped out of the elevator into the reception area of Bellavista Holdings. She'd left early and walked to get her bearings, but five minutes into the walk, she'd regretted her decision. Not only had the streets been busy, but she had taken a wrong turn and then had to hurry so she wasn't late, and now she was hot and rumpled.

She didn't have any business clothes, so she had borrowed a pantsuit from Sarah, and it was scratchy and a little too loose. The outfit was a long way from the linen and cotton sundresses she wore with open-toed shoes back home in Noosa.

The reception area was large, with a lot of glass and reflective surfaces. It was light, bright, and sterile. From behind a long desk, a guy wearing a headset smiled at her. "Can I help you?"

"My name is Mae, and I'm here to see Sebastian Newport."

He glanced at a screen. "Do you have an appointment?"

"Not really, but he—"

"I'm sure he did," the guy said, heavy on the condescension. "Mr. Newport has a heavy schedule, but if you'd like to take a seat, I'll see what I can do. Or you could call and make an appointment with his personal assistant."

Mae hesitated. "He really will be expecting me. If you could just—"

From her left, a woman came barreling into the reception area, hair in disarray, the bright yellow glasses on top of her head in danger of falling off. "Mae?"

"Yes?"

"I'm Rosario, Mr. Newport's PA. Did you meet Reuben?"

Mae glanced around, feeling more out of her depth by the minute. The guy at the desk raised an eyebrow. "We met briefly. She didn't have an appointment, so I was just about to call you—"

Rosario threw up a hand. "This is Mae *Rutherford*," she said, emphasis on the surname.

Reuben's eyes widened. "Oh, I'm so sorry, Ms. Rutherford. I had no idea. You'd be surprised how many people show up unannounced and ask to see the boss."

"It's fine, really—"

Rosario turned. "This way," she said over her shoulder.

Mae followed her into the elevator for a quick trip up one floor, then down a wide corridor, with offices off each side and people in each one, tapping away at keyboards, or talking into headsets. She was used to school grounds, which were similar, full of movement and noise, but they also had flow. This just felt busy, with everyone in their own spaces, disconnected and isolated.

They reached the end of the hallway and entered a large office.

"This is mine," Rosario said, "and through that door is Mr. Newport's office. You can go in."

"Thanks," Mae said and only hesitated a second before grabbing the door handle. As she entered, she caught sight of Sebastian on his cell, writing something on a notepad, talking faster than she'd heard him in all the conversations they'd had. He was clearly in control of the conversation, though the topic was beyond her, as he used words she didn't recognize in this context, his tone firm yet collegial.

She was glad one of them was in control of themselves. She was having trouble just getting air into her lungs.

When she'd seen him in the Hamptons, he'd been casually put together in shorts and T-shirts. Now, though... Now his suit was charcoal, the cut emphasizing the breadth of his shoulders and his narrow hips. The white business shirt beneath contrasted with the smooth olive of his skin, and the deep blue patterned tie at his neck sat in a perfect Windsor knot. Why did the suit make such a difference? An alarm in her brain told her that if she didn't get a proper lungful of air soon, she'd probably swoon, and that was something she didn't want to do, so she gulped in a breath.

He glanced up and saw her, and a slow smile spread across his face, changing his features from something that might be carved in marble—coolly beautiful—to something warm, appealing. She wanted to reach out her fingertips and touch...

Catching herself again, she straightened. She couldn't be sidetracked by a nice smile. She'd agreed to shadow him for a month so she could find out what was really going on in the company. Naturally, he was going to try and hide things, no matter what he'd promised. He'd made no secret of his goal to convince her to sell to him, so now she just had to see what exactly he was hiding.

She was fairly certain he was going to try to ditch her—perhaps get her to talk to other staff when he had top secret meetings, or ask her to grab coffee when he wanted to open a sensitive file. She'd keep focused and would not be swindled. Spending her days teaching young children had made her good at spotting attempts at distraction. She could dig her heels in if she had to.

She headed to the other side of the room, where a cream chaise sat under a window. The view of Manhattan was expansive. Buzzing and gray-toned, a world away from the ocean's deep blues, the white sand, and the greenery of the national park of her laid-back hometown in Queensland. Heath looked to be putting down roots here, and she couldn't imagine her life without her brother nearby. Could she get used to this view? The pace of life here?

Sebastian wound up his call and she turned as he stepped around his desk. "Mae. You're here."

"Isn't this the time we agreed to?" Had she misjudged how long it had taken to walk here?

"The time is good." He set his cell and pen on his desk. "I wasn't one hundred percent convinced you'd show."

He crossed the room and stuck out his hand. She shook it, feeling the smooth, warm skin of his palm slide across hers and then lock their hands together. Awareness skittered across her skin.

He indicated the chaise, and she perched on the edge, not wanting to get too comfortable. He took a seat at the other end and ran his fingers through his dark, wavy hair.

"I've cleared as much of this morning as I could, but since we only made this plan on the weekend, I haven't had a chance to move a meeting with some lawyers. It's starting—" he checked his watch "—well, about now, but it will be boring as all hell, so Rosario will show you around and introduce you to the staff while I'm there. After that, I have some clear time to take you through a few things."

Mae narrowed her eyes. Was he trying to have a meeting in secret within minutes of her arrival? "This deal is for shadowing you. I'll come to the meeting."

Sebastian regarded her for a minute, then shrugged. "Suit yourself."

Within minutes, Sebastian was ushering her into a large meeting room on another floor. The size of this business and the number of people working at it was impressive. They sat around a long table among a bunch of young, smug and hungry-looking men and women in matching suits—some on the same side as them and some opposite. After jovial handshakes, the meeting was suddenly underway, with all in attendance puffing up as they argued about a subclause in a contract. It was tedious. But worse was the manner in which they were arguing—if this had been her first graders, she would have stopped the meeting and spoken to them about manners, beginning with "Don't speak over the top of other people, and if you're going to ask a question, at least wait for the other person to answer."

After an eternity of listening to them, with an occasional comment from Sebastian, Mae opened her notebook and wrote: *They all need to learn constructive listening. And how to compromise.*

She slid the notebook to Sebastian, who was sitting

beside her. Other people in the room were passing notes, so no one even noticed.

Sebastian read the note and smothered a smile before jumping into the conversation again by asking one of the lawyers a pointed question. A minute later, he scrawled something below her comment with his left hand and slid the notebook back, their hands brushing as he did. The light contact set off butterflies in her stomach.

*They don't get paid to compromise. They get paid to win.*

She watched the arguing back and forth for a few more minutes before adding another line.

*This is going around and around in circles. Never been so bored.*

With barely a reaction, and while seeming to not lose a moment of the lawyers' conversation, he wrote a reply and then pushed the notebook back to her.

*Told you so.*

This time it was her turn to squash a smile. And then she sat up straight and made more of an effort to follow the conversation. And not get too distracted by the man beside her.

By lunchtime, Seb was desperate to find his equilibrium. After the meeting with the lawyers, he'd shown Mae an empty office that she could use as her base for the week. It was only a few doors down from his, but it would have given her some territory of her own. She could have taken files in there and had some peace and quiet to read, or had privacy to meet with members of his staff. Instead, she'd banded together with Rosario—when had they become friends?—to find a small, wooden desk and move it into his office.

He stared at it, blinking. Mae had moved the chaise from under the window and put her desk there. In the middle sat a laptop, and neatly aligned to the side was an in tray, and three pens. She and Rosario had talked for a full ten minutes about pens and stationery before she'd made her selections.

From her new swivel office chair, all she had to do was turn her head sideways and she'd see the Manhattan view, but if she looked straight ahead, as she was doing now, she looked at him.

"What's next?" she asked.

His plan had been to order some lunch in and spend time running through his week with Mae. But having her at that desk, so close, making his breath catch every time he caught sight of her... He swallowed hard and tried to ignore the shiver skittering across his skin. The office was too small, too intimate and he suddenly wanted to be someplace busy, where they weren't the only two people in the room.

"Lunch," he said, standing and gathering some pages he needed to show Mae. "There's a place down the street we can go."

"Great. I'm still in sightseeing mode, so any chance to see somewhere new is good with me."

They walked to a nearby upscale restaurant, and Seb firmly told himself that he wasn't choosing it to impress her, since he occasionally had business meetings there. But he knew he was lying to himself. It had nothing to do with the business they—and their families—had together; it was just him showing off for a woman.

"Here it is," he said as they reached the tall doors, which were being opened by a man in full uniform.

Mae's gaze darted around, and then she spied a hippy place over the road. "Can we go there?"

It was a hole-in-the-wall joint that had signs out the front saying "vegetarian" and "half-price Mondays." Not somewhere he'd ever consider going. But Mae's eyes were bright with hope and his heart swelled to see it, so he said, "Sure," before he'd even thought it through.

"This is adorable," she said once they were seated.

He wasn't sure he'd call any place that served food adorable, but what he did know was that the air was stuffy, the chairs were hard, and the tables were small. Mae's dimples were showing, though, and he decided that the hard chairs were worth the sight.

After they'd ordered, he reached into a satchel he'd brought with him and laid five pieces of printed paper on the Formica tabletop.

Mae ran a finger across the top page. "What's this?"

"I had Rosario print out my schedule for the week. It will help as we discuss our plans."

She leafed through the pages. "You sure it wasn't to intimidate me?"

One corner of his mouth pulled up, and he had to fight to keep the smile at bay. That had definitely been part of it, and she'd seen right through him. He wanted her to see how busy this job was, how complicated it was, so she could just agree to sell to him. But mainly, they needed to discuss how this shadowing would work, and this seemed to be the easiest way.

"I cleared this morning to help you settle in—"

"Except for the bunch of matching lawyers all in a row that you were going to exclude me from."

"—except for the meeting with the lawyers this morning." He spread the pages across the table. "This way you can see what your options are. You can choose which meetings you attend, and what hours will be most interesting to you."

"If you're doing all of this, then I will too."

That was the response he'd been expecting, however, his load was heavy and she wouldn't last the entire week if she tried to do everything. "If you burn out within a few days, you won't get to see a proper scope of our work. It'd be better to choose the things that most interest you, and then we'll work out what to do about the rest."

Her chin tipped up. "Are you saying I couldn't handle your schedule?"

"I'm not bragging about my hours. I've been trying to scale it back ever since Ashley died and haven't got it to the level I'm comfortable with yet. Though I do leave at six o'clock each night now, which allows Alfie some consistency in his routine. Whenever possible, I get the nanny to bring him in for a visit during the day but, often, that's difficult."

"Admirable," she said, her gaze not faltering. "But teachers are no strangers to a busy schedule."

Was he missing something? There was no way a teacher would put in the hours he did. "Don't you normally work nine till three? No need to be a hero and cram everything in just because you feel you have to—there's no judgment."

"Nine until three?" she said with a snort. "We dream of those hours. After the kids go home, teachers mark assessments, do lesson planning, answer emails from parents, attend in-service training, have meetings with the school administration or other key people, etcetera, etcetera, etcetera. Plus, that work also spills into the weekend and holidays, and now with easy access email and messaging platforms, families and senior management often expect us to be available twenty-four-seven."

Their food—something called a wellness bowl for her and a simple pasta for him—arrived and he moved the pages into a stack to make room while Mae chatted with the waitress. From her flushed cheecks, it looked as though he'd touched a nerve about her teaching schedule. It must be something she had to explain a lot, and he was sorry he'd made her do it again.

Once the waitress left, he reached out and laid a hand on her arm. "I didn't realize about your hours. I was seeing it from my own point of view and didn't think to ask what hours you normally worked, which made my comments patronizing."

Her warm gray eyes widened—from the apology…or the touch of his hand? He shouldn't have done it, should remove his hand, would never normally dream of touching someone in a professional setting. Technically, she didn't work for him, and he wasn't carrying out any business with a representative from another company. No, it was much worse. She was a Rutherford, and he was potentially shooting himself in the foot by making things messy. Because things were *bound* to get messy. And yet…neither of them had moved. Her skin was soft beneath his, warm, and the pulse at the base of her throat beat fast. What would it be like to kiss her? To feel all that vitality and life in his arms? Writhing beneath him?

The intensity of the image in his mind too much to bear, he pulled his hand back, looking down at his pasta. That was not a path he could allow his mind to take. There was too much at stake.

He cleared his throat and picked up his cutlery. "Just

so we're clear, my hours are eight till six. I used to work later, but I cut back when I became a single dad."

"Noted," she said and studiously picked up the printed pages containing his schedule, avoiding eye contact. "What's this note on the lunchtime slots?"

"I've blocked out lunch with you each day." His voice was tight, but there wasn't much he could do about it. "That way, we'll have a chance for you to ask questions or debrief after meetings."

"I appreciate that." She put the pages down and picked up her spoon, still not looking at him.

He shoved a forkful of pasta into his mouth and tried his best to ignore that his body was hungrier for Mae than for food.

# Five

Mae arrived for her second morning of shadowing Sebastian and stopped by Rosario's desk.

"Morning," she said and held out a cup.

Rosario reached for the cup. "Morning. What's this?"

"A French vanilla cappuccino made with oat milk." Mae had listened closely yesterday when Rosario had ordered a coffee and made a mental note. "Is it too early for it?"

"No," she said with feeling and then took a sip and sighed. "It's perfect timing."

Mae smiled. For this week to go smoothly, Rosario was the key person, even if Sebastian probably thought it was him. Besides, she liked the other woman.

"Before you go in," Rosario said, tilting her head to Sebastian's office, "you should know that there's...a situation unfolding."

Mae instinctively looked across the space, but the

closed door offered no clues. "Okay, thanks for the warning."

She opened the door and poked her head around. Sebastian was standing in the middle of the room with a baby in one arm.

"Alfie!" Mae rushed over, surprised at how happy she was to see him. "How are you?"

Alfie offered a quick smile and then turned his head into his father's shoulder. Apparently, just because they'd met a couple of times didn't mean they were friends.

"Morning, Mae," Sebastian said, sounding weary. She looked from the baby up to the father, noting the dark smudges under his eyes, and olive skin a little paler than usual.

"Do you normally bring him into work? I thought it was his nanny who brought him in."

"Never on my own, or I wouldn't get work done. Emily does bring him in sometimes." He blew out a long breath. "But she got sick overnight, and I took her up to the ER. Of course it meant waking Alfie too, so we're both pretty tired. Emily has a stomach bug. The doctor suggested she have a few days away from Alfie even after she feels better to ensure she's not contagious, so we don't know how long until she can come back."

Mae stroked Alfie's chubby little arm. "What will you do?"

"I have calls in to all the agencies, but there seems to be some sort of shortage of experienced nannies. Maybe they're all enjoying the spring weather somewhere, I don't know. For today, Ashley's parents are on their way down from upstate to help. They should be here soon." Sebastian walked to the chair behind his desk and sank into it, Alfie on his lap. "I've had to clear my morning again."

Her instinct was to offer to help, but she wasn't sure exactly how. Before she could think it through, raised voices from Rosario's office floated through the doorway. "I want to see him."

"I'm afraid that's not possible," Rosario's calm, firm voice countered.

"We had an appointment this morning and I'm here." The voice sounded like that of an older man. An annoyed older man. "I want to see him. Now."

Sebastian pinched the bridge of his nose, took a deep breath, then stood, Alfie still in his arms.

"Do you want me to…?" Mae said, putting her hands out, not really sure of the best course of action.

"No, it's fine," he said and opened the door, revealing a man of about seventy wearing a tweed coat. "Mr. Sheridan. I'm sorry about our meeting. As you can see—" he looked down at Alfie, who was starting to fuss, kicking his legs "—my hands are relatively full this morning, which is why my assistant changed our time."

The other man planted his feet. "Well, I'm here now."

"Okay, then come on in," Sebastian said, a determined smile plastered on his face.

Mae stepped back, out of the doorway, not really sure what she should do.

"Mr. Sheridan," Sebastian started, before Alfie covered his mouth with his chubby little hands. Sebastian removed them and adjusted the toddler. "Mr. Sheridan. Laurence, if I may?"

"You may not. I'm Mr. Sheridan to you, and I want the meeting I was promised."

For a suspended moment, Alfie seemed to stop breathing, his little face turning red, and then he let out a wail.

Mae stepped forward and stuck out her hand to their visitor. "Nice to meet you, Mr. Sheridan. I'm Mae."

He regarded her suspiciously. "I came for a meeting with him—" he jerked a thumb at Sebastian "—and I won't be foisted on someone else. I need to meet with the owner."

Sebastian turned sideways so he could speak over Alfie's head. "Then it's your lucky day. This is Mae Rutherford, and she owns 50 percent of the company."

Technically, she and Heath owned 25 percent each, but now wasn't the time for nuance. She grabbed a chair from in front of Sebastian's desk and took it over to her little wooden desk. She had no idea what she was doing. Her only aim was to smooth things out somehow. "Would you like to sit down?"

Mr. Sheridan looked from her to Sebastian and back again. "Thank you, I will."

As she took her seat on the opposite side, she met Sebastian's gaze over their visitor's head. He mouthed, "Just go with it."

She laced her fingers together on the desk in front of her and smiled as if she were meeting a student's parents at a parent-teacher conference. "How can I help you, Mr. Sheridan?"

He ran his hand over the wood. "This is a good desk. Solid."

She nodded. "Not too big, not too small."

"Exactly." He threw a look at the huge glass monster of a desk on the other side of the room. "Too much desk for any one person, that one."

"Plus," Mae added, "I'd be looking at my own legs all day. I want to focus on the work instead."

He grinned. "You're not like the other suits."

"To be honest," she said, peeking over his head at Sebastian as he entertained Alfie with a bunch of pens, "I'm an elementary school teacher. My family owns half of this company, but I don't usually work in the office."

"Good to hear it. All these business people in their fancy suits and their hair slicked back like it's the forties. Gives me the heebie-jeebies."

Mae couldn't hold back the laugh. He'd summed up the lawyers at the meeting the day before. "They're great talkers," she said, "not so great at listening."

He slapped a hand on the desk. "That's it in a nutshell."

"I'm right here," Sebastian said, leaning a hip on his desk.

Mr. Sheridan turned to him. "Why *are* you still here?"

Sebastian's brows drew together comically. "It's my office."

Mae bit down a grin. "Actually, he's not so bad. Now, tell me why you're here, Mr. Sheridan."

"Larry. The name's Laurence, but you can call me Larry."

She caught sight of Sebastian mouthing, "Oh, come *on*," and grinned back at him.

"Okay, Larry. I'd love to try and help."

Almost forty minutes later, as she walked back in from seeing Larry out, she found Sebastian sitting on her desk, a drowsy Alfie still in his arms.

"That was impressive," he said.

"I didn't fix things." Larry had multiple offers for his small property, and he was ready to sell, but wanted a bunch of assurances. First and foremost, that his house wouldn't be pulled down and the land used to build a skyscraper. Turned out, that was exactly what Bellavista Holdings had planned. A stalemate.

"You got him to discuss his terms and start to consider he might need to compromise, which is more than anyone else here has been able to do."

"I feel for him, though." It was the house he'd bought with his wife when they'd first married. They'd raised their kids there and he knew almost everyone in the neighborhood, who would all be affected by the decision. But the prime location meant that even if he sold to a private person, they'd likely be tempted to sell to a developer soon after. He was just trying to do his best for his community.

"Hello?" A soft voice came from the door and a middle-aged couple walked in, clearly trying not to make too much noise. "Is he asleep?"

Sebastian smiled. "Close. His eyes are starting to droop."

"Oh, my heart," the woman said, crossing to the baby and smoothing the hair from his face.

Sebastian looked down at his son too, and his features softened, his gaze full of love. Mae's father had been completely absent from her life, so fathers were always a curiosity to her. When her mother had found she was pregnant for the second time, she'd taken two-year-old Heath and disappeared to protect them all, and Mae was both grateful and proud. It had left her fascinated by fathers with their babies—nothing quite tugged at her heart the way Sebastian unashamedly loving his son did.

"Can I hold him?" the woman asked.

"Sure." He carefully transferred Alfie to his grandmother's arms. "He might be too sleepy to be excited now, but once he wakes up and realizes you're here, he's going to be beside himself."

"My sweet baby," she whispered and kissed the soft, wispy hair on his head.

Sebastian waved a hand toward Mae. "This is Mae Rutherford, though I think she prefers Mae Dunstan. One of Joseph's missing children. Mae, this is Amanda and Barry, Ashley's parents and Alfie's grandparents."

"Oh," Amanda said, eyeing her eagerly, "so lovely to meet you. I have to admit, after reading about your re-appearance I've been a little curious."

"A *little* curious?" Barry said, chuckling. "She's been following any crumbs of the story she can find."

Amanda blushed. "Well, we have a family interest. You're the people who share Sebastian's company. And our little Alfie will inherit it after him, so you'll have to excuse me for wanting to snoop a bit."

"It's fine," Mae said. "I'm sure I'd do the same in your position." In fact, she and her brother had been raised to be suspicious, so they would have done much more investigating than simply following the crumbs of a story.

Amanda turned back to Sebastian. "What's the latest about Emily?"

"She's doing okay. She's gone to stay with her parents, and the doctor advised that we should wait a few days after the last time she has symptoms before she starts caring for Alfie again."

"Glad to hear she's okay," Barry said. "You said you're trying to get an agency nanny?"

Sebastian nodded, wrapping a hand behind his neck. "I'm expecting a call back soon. They said they'd have someone here by the end of the day."

"You know," Amanda said, "we could take him. It's only a couple of weeks before our monthly days with him anyway, so we could bump that visit up. The nursery at our house is always ready, Sebastian, just in case you need us."

"She means," Barry said, "just in case she gets the chance to have an extra day or two with Alfie."

Amanda grinned and held the baby a little tighter for a moment. "I can't deny that."

"Well, if you're sure," Sebastian said. "It would certainly be less disruption for Alfie to go to a familiar environment with people he loves than adjust to a new nanny for only a few days."

"Oh, we're sure," Amanda said, her eyes lighting up.

"Right, then." Sebastian went behind his desk to grab his suit jacket. "We'll head back to my place now and pack his bags."

Mae watched everything unfold in front of her, feeling more like a casual observer than a part of the scene. She was here to shadow Sebastian, but this was a private family situation, so perhaps she could hang out in his office in case any other Larrys arrived. "Is there anything specific you want me to do here while you're gone?"

Sebastian frowned and glanced at his desk. "Not really. There's nothing you're up to speed with to work on. I still have some time cleared this morning, so why don't you come with us, and we'll have our working lunch early today?"

"I can do that," Mae said and grabbed her bag.

She, Sebastian, and Alfie caught a cab over to his apartment while his in-laws followed in their car. They didn't chat much, since Sebastian was focused on Alfie in his baby seat. He was talking to his son, telling him about the trip he was about to have with his grandparents and all the toys he'd pack to take with him, and when he told him how much he loved him, Mae had to swallow past the lump in her throat.

Packing bags went fairly smoothly, partly because Sebastian seemed to be in a routine of leaving each weekend, but he also just seemed to know where everything was. Of course, being a single parent meant he had to be on top of his kid's things. Still, since he had a full-time nanny, she'd expected he'd stumble a few times.

Amanda fed Alfie a banana while Sebastian got things ready, and by the time they waved Alfie and his grandparents off at the door, she could see the strain around Sebastian's eyes. They were left standing together in front of the closed door, neither of them speaking for a couple of moments.

It was different than the stress on his face when she'd arrived at the office this morning—that had been more about the frustration of trying to do too many things at once and not succeeding at all. This stress, though. This was deeper.

When children arrived on their first day of school, they were often excited to see all the new things. But the parents? They tended to fall into one of two groups. Those that blinked back their emotions and pretended everything was fine. And those that needed reassurance that they and their child would be okay. The expression on Sebastian's face seemed to put him squarely in the second group. Seeing his uncertainty pulled fiercely at her heartstrings.

"Does he go with them often?" she asked gently.

He loosened the tie at his neck. "They come down and spend a day with him every couple of weeks, and we planned that he'd do an overnight trip to their place every month, but I often manage to find an excuse to put that off. Luckily, they're understanding."

"Do you want to talk about it?"

He blinked hard and looked at her, confused. "Talk about it? I'm fine. Really."

"Okay, then," she said, not believing him for a minute.

"It's a bit early to go for lunch." He undid his white shirt's cuff buttons and rolled the sleeves up to his elbows. "Do you want a coffee here first? Or we could go back to the office."

After a hectic twelve hours, taking his nanny to the ER and having Alfie at work, then having his son leave for a few days, she could see that he needed a beat to catch his breath. That was something she could help with.

"A coffee would be great, thanks."

She followed him into the kitchen and leaned back against the counter as he operated a state-of-the-art coffee machine. He talked as he worked, explaining something about Bellavista Holdings, his talking getting faster as he went, until she stepped close and laid a hand on his forearm.

"Sebastian," she said.

He looked up sharply.

"It's okay to be sad."

"About the deal with Johnson Developments?" he said slowly, as if he was missing something.

"About your little boy leaving with his grandparents." She withdrew her hand and let her arms hang at her sides, wishing she could do more.

He shrugged his broad shoulders and went back to finishing up with the coffee. "I've been away from him before."

"Thanks." She accepted the mug he handed her. "Just

because you've been away from him before doesn't mean that this time isn't hard."

He picked up the second brew, wrapping his long fingers around the mug, then he closed his eyes for several seconds before opening them again. "It's always hard."

"Did it get worse after your wife passed?"

"From the day he was born, I never really wanted to leave him. But while Ashley was alive, it was bearable… at least it was until she got sick." He turned to face her, resting his hip on the counter. "But since Ashley died, I feel this primal need to be there for him all the time."

The load on his shoulders was huge—he was trying not to let anything slip with the company or his son—and her heart ached for him. "I guess it's harder because Ashley's parents are hardly just around the corner. And your father wouldn't be any help."

He turned so his buttocks rested back on the counter, then he crossed his legs at the ankle. "I keep Alfie away from my father as much as I can. I can't think of a worse role model." One corner of his mouth hitched up. "Except, of course, your father. He was an absolute asshole."

"I've heard that," she said drily and grinned, mainly because Sebastian had broken the tension, but also because it was a relief that someone wasn't sugarcoating the truth. "Can't say I'm sorry to never have met him. What about your mother? Did you say she'd moved away?"

A humorless smile flashed across his face for a moment as he placed his mug on the counter. "She walked out when I was about nine."

She blinked, trying to make sense of it. "Your mother left you with your father? A man who everyone says is a despicable human being?"

He placed his hands back on the counter, fingers

splayed, in a move that should have been casual but somehow looked formal since he was still in a crisp white business shirt and dark pants. "She decided that I was just like him, and she wasn't putting up with two of us. Moved out, met a guy richer than my father, and moved to Texas. I've barely seen her since."

"You are *kidding* me," she said, her skin growing cold.

His beautiful mouth twisted. "Wish I was."

"Holy hell. At least I had one good parent." As if pulled by a magnetic force, she moved closer to Sebastian. The body heat emanating from him called her to move even closer, but she dared not. "Hang on, if you were raised just by Christopher, how did you turn out…" Her voice dried up as she realized she was rushing headlong into saying something that would give away her growing fascination with him.

He grinned, his eyes shining. "Mae Dunstan, were you about to compliment me?"

"Don't let it go to your head," she said dismissively. "From what I hear, the bar to be a better person than your father is a very low one."

The lines around his eyes crinkled. "It was still a compliment."

"It might have been," she said, looking at her nails and feigning disinterest. "We'll never know now."

He reached for the hand she was holding up and, unable to resist, she reached back. He slid his fingers between hers, the intimacy of the move sending a shiver racing across her skin, the heat of his palm against hers making her heart quicken.

"I choose to believe it was going to be a compliment," he murmured, his voice low, "and that you're finally starting to believe that I'm not full of nefarious plans."

She was drowning in his blue, blue eyes, trying not to get carried away and read too much into the situation, trying to keep things light. "Would an honest, straight-up guy use words like nefarious?"

"This one does." He tugged her closer, until her feet bumped against his. "This one uses a whole heap of words that might surprise you."

"Yeah?" she said, but her voice sounded breathy to her own ears.

"We could start with *want*."

Her heart skipped a beat, and the whole world seemed suspended before it kicked back in and thudded against her ribs. "Want?"

"It's been going around and around in my mind since we first talked on that moonless night." The intensity in his gaze was scorching. "Before I even saw you."

She swallowed. "What did you want?"

"To touch you." He released her hand and wrapped an arm around her back, sending sparks through her blood. "To kiss you."

She took the last step to close the gap between them and looked up into his eyes, with less than an inch separating their bodies. "I wanted things too."

He swiped a thumb along her bottom lip. "Whatever it is, you can have it."

"That's a hell of a promise. You don't know what I'm going to ask."

"With you looking at me like that? I don't care." His voice was deep and smooth, and she started to sway as if hypnotized, and then she was being lifted and placed onto the counter, and he was standing in the V of her legs, his uneven breath on her mouth. "Tell me what you've been wanting."

"I want…" She had to fill her lungs to make a sound. "I want…"

"Tell me, Mae." His chest rose and fell, rose and fell, working overtime. "Tell me what you want, and I promise—"

"To touch you," she said on a whisper. "And I want you to touch me."

A groan was ripped from his throat and he leaned in and kissed her. It was hard and it was hungry and it was everything she'd dreamed it would be. She lifted her legs and locked them together behind his hips, holding him against her and spearing her fingers into his hair. His mouth was hot, decadent, and he held the sides of her face in his hands as if she were precious.

Then his hands roamed down, undoing the buttons on her jacket and slipping underneath it, sliding over the smooth cotton of her shirt, leaving a trail of fireworks despite the barrier to her skin. She felt his fingers spread out on her back as he leaned her backward. She'd never had a kiss go from zero to one hundred so fast, and she was trying to keep up, wanting more, wanting everything he had. His erection pressed against her, and an insistent pulse beat at her core as she started thinking about where they could move to, and how far away his bedroom was. Then she was struck by the thought that the bedroom would have been his and Ashley's…

She looked around the kitchen with new eyes, spotting a collage of photos on the refrigerator—Sebastian with a tiny Alfie, Sebastian and Ashley, the two of them with Alfie… She was in another woman's kitchen, another woman's apartment. It had been long enough for Sebastian to move on, but this still felt…wrong. And then she remembered everyone else who would be upset by this kiss, including her own family, and it was as if the whole world had crowded into her brain, and the moment, their connection, was lost.

She pulled back, dragging in air to fill her lungs, needing a moment to think things through. This wasn't a random hookup; anything they did together had consequences for a range of people. If this was going to happen, it couldn't happen on impulse, when he'd been feeling vulnerable and she'd tried to cheer him up. The whole thing was a hot mess on so many levels.

"What's wrong?" He dipped his head to meet her eyes. "Hey, did I do something wrong?"

"No, no. I just…" Her gaze drifted to the fridge again. "We shouldn't be doing this."

He eased back, then cocked his head to the side. "Why not? We're consenting adults."

She bit down on her lip, wondering how a person should bring up a dead wife with a man she'd just kissed. "This might sound weird to you, but this feels like Ashley's home, and…"

He laid a finger over her lips and sighed. "That doesn't sound weird. In fact, I haven't brought another woman here to the apartment for that reason. This kiss…" He looked up at the ceiling. "This was unexpected."

"Definitely unexpected. And possibly unwise."

He winced. "Now that the blood is starting to return to my brain, I think you might be right. Unwise."

"My brother, my aunt, your father, they'd all be horrified that we were blurring the lines," she said, pushing the point home. "Even Alfie's grandmother commented on the company being Alfie's future inheritance. This situation is bigger than the two of us."

"You're right. One hundred percent. And yet…" He

cupped the side of her face and she leaned into the touch. "It's hard to make myself care about any of them right now."

She pressed her palm against his chest—the solid muscle, the heat emanating through his snowy white shirt—maybe instinctively, to hold him at bay, but found herself gripping his shirt in her fist and pulling him down again. He came willingly.

This time, when he captured her mouth, it was slow, gentle, honoring her, tempting her. And after only a few moments, he broke the kiss, leaning his forehead against hers, his warm breath fanning across her cheeks.

"I can't think of anything I want less than to end this kiss, but if we're going to stop, we probably should head back to the office. We need some sort of impediment, like being in an office with no privacy, to stop us from taking this further."

Everything inside her rose up to object. It felt wrong to be kissing him here, now, at all, but it felt just as wrong to not be kissing him. This was a lose-lose situation and was really just about picking the lesser of two evils. Which meant they had to stop.

She slid down from the counter and began straightening her clothes. "And if we're serious about not taking this further, then we need to go now. Like, right now."

His expressive eyes filled with regret, and he nodded. "Let's go."

As they walked out the door of his apartment and headed down to the sidewalk to hail a cab, she'd never wanted to throw caution to the wind more in her life and turn right back around.

# Six

For the rest of the day, Sebastian focused on his work and nothing else. Or he tried to. Mae was sitting at her desk. In the same room. Lighting up the space as if she were the midday sun. He could walk over there and kiss her if he wanted to.

And he wanted to.

*I want you to touch me.*

He'd almost combusted on the spot when she'd said that. And now none of the figures on the spreadsheet made sense.

Instead of the working lunch he'd planned, they'd ordered sandwiches from a place that delivered and eaten at their desks. To keep her occupied, he'd told her to ask Rosario for any company files she wanted. The two women had carried some boxes of old files in, and Mae was also going through files on the company server. He'd had a meeting in the boardroom, but Mae had been absorbed in something she'd found, so she'd waved him away and kept reading.

It was annoying that she could concentrate on work so well when he was still consumed by their kiss.

Rosario came through and picked up a couple of packages off his desk that needed sending. "I'm heading out—I'll see you both in the morning."

Surprised, he glanced at the clock. Six o'clock. "I lost track of time in the spreadsheet." Although he was lying about what had consumed his thoughts so much, he wondered if it was obvious to anyone else. "Thanks, Rosario. I'll see you in the morning."

After she left, he stretched his arms over his head in an effort to look casual. "I'm thinking of working late to make up for the time I lost this morning." Another lie. Alfie was with his grandparents. The house would be empty, nothing to rush home for. And worst of all, the kitchen would be full of memories of Mae sitting on the counter, kissing him as though she would die if she didn't. No one had ever kissed him with so much desperation.

Mae put the lid back on an open box and stood. "Have fun. I have somewhere I need to be."

"Well, that sounds mysterious." And, again, here he was, drowning in memories of their kiss while she seemed to be going about her day and evening, even going out to socialize.

She flashed him a smile, her dimples peeking out. "I'm dropping over to see my mother's family."

He frowned. For some reason, he only ever thought of her as a product of the Rutherford side of her family. "Did you know them growing up?"

"No," she said, grabbing her satchel. "When my mother ran, she cut all ties. She never saw them again."

Well, now he felt like a louse. Of course she wasn't thinking of their kiss when she had this on her mind. He turned his computer screen away and leaned back in his chair. "Are you going for dinner?"

"Just a visit." She picked up her coat and draped it over her arm. "Joseph Rutherford really screwed them over on a number of levels. The O'Donohue family lost their daughter and sister, but he also systematically harassed them after she left, just in case they knew something. Or maybe it was petty revenge—who knows?"

"As previously mentioned, I can attest to the fact that he was an asshole."

She tipped her head in acknowledgment and leaned a hip on the corner of her desk. "So now Heath and I have inherited all this money, and we want to share it with them."

He could imagine how well that had gone down. "Let me guess, they don't want a cent of anything that Joseph owned?"

"That's a big part of it, but they think of it as our money and say we should keep it."

Large amounts of money affected people in different ways. Some were keen to share it, while others would throw their best friend under the bus to get their hands on it. Still others didn't like to touch it. For them, small amounts were fine, but once large sums were mentioned, they took a big step back. And given their front-row view of Joseph Rutherford's use of money, it probably wasn't surprising that her mother's family wanted nothing to do with it. Mae seemed confused by their reaction, though. "You see it differently?"

"It's more than we can use, and the O'Donohues have suffered terribly because of Joseph. At the very least, we should be able to make some reparations with his money." She lifted a hand, palm out.

It was a good justification. "You know, if he was still alive, they'd have the chance to sue him for stalking and harassment, so giving them a settlement seems very reasonable."

"Easier said than done," she said, rolling her eyes.

He rested his elbows on the chair's armrests and steepled his fingers under his chin as he thought the problem through. "Do you have ideas about how to get them to accept it?"

"Not really. I was going to try logic again, but Heath has tried a few times already and it hasn't worked so far. I said I'd take over trying." She tucked some long, dark hair behind her ear. "One of the underhanded things Joseph did was buy the company that my grandparents and three of my uncles worked for. He did it so he could get reports on them from their managers—looking for suspicious vacations, etcetera. But that now means that Heath and I own that company. I'd be very happy to hand it over—"

"You can't," he said, interrupting her. "That would insult their pride. They don't want a handout from their newly discovered grandchildren. They'll want to give, not take."

"That's the same conclusion we came to, so we haven't even offered it." She looked so downcast that he felt compelled to fix this for her. Offer her something uncomplicated that she could accept.

"What if you took them on as consultants?" he said,

sitting up straight. "Pay them for their expertise about the business."

She fiddled with the strap of her bag. "Would that be enough money?"

"Some consultants get paid an exorbitant fee. The price can be the amount you want to give them, and then they have earned it, not been handed it."

She turned to the window for a long moment before turning back to him again. "That could work. I don't suppose…?"

"As it happens," he said, grinning, "I have a free night if you want me."

Her eyes flared and everything around them stilled. He hadn't meant to remind them both of the kiss that morning, of everything they'd said they wanted, but now that it was there, it was like a living, pulsing thing between them.

"I didn't mean—"

She held up a hand. "I know you didn't. And, yes, thank you for your offer, I'd love to have someone with a good business brain there when I talk to them about being paid consultants."

He shut his laptop and stood. "Then I'm at your service."

They caught a taxi over to her grandparents' house in Brooklyn, and together, she and Sebastian laid out the plan to her mother's family. The O'Donohues were grateful for the offer, but saw through it immediately and graciously declined. Disappointed, but not surprised, she and Sebastian said goodbye and then shared a taxi back to Sarah's place. He'd said he'd take it on to his place after it dropped her off, but as it pulled over, he found himself paying the driver and getting out with her.

"Sebastian?" Mae said as he came to stand on the sidewalk beside her.

"It's a nice night." He rocked back on his heels. "Thought I'd walk some of the way home."

She looked up at the exterior of the building, then back to him. "I'd invite you up…"

"You can't." The very idea was ludicrous. "I'm not welcome in the enemy camp."

"I wouldn't say *enemy*," she said diplomatically.

"Really?" He allowed his incredulity to flow into his voice. "What would you say?"

She opened her mouth, but no words came out.

He chuckled. "It's okay, Mae. You don't have to spare my feelings. I've lived in the middle of this family feud my entire life. It's the same at my father's place."

Her expression was suddenly full of sympathy as she nodded. "Will you be okay at home tonight?"

He put on a mock stern face. "Are you seriously asking if I'll be okay in my own apartment overnight?"

"You know what I mean," she said, not diverted by his teasing.

He did. She wondered of he'd be okay without Alfie. "I'll be fine. Amanda has already sent through a bunch of videos of the things he's done this afternoon, so I'll console myself by watching those." He was being tongue-in-cheek, but there was an element of truth in there too.

"Thank you for coming with me tonight and trying." She pulled her bottom lip into her mouth and let her front teeth scrape over it as she released it.

He sank his hands into his pockets, willing himself not to respond. "It wasn't a problem. I liked your grandparents. They're stubborn, but that's not a bad thing."

"Well, good night." She leaned forward and kissed his

cheek, and as she did, the world faded away. The traffic sounds disappeared; the other people on the sidewalk and the buildings all evaporated from his awareness. All he could see was Mae. All he could hear was her breathing so close to his ear. She seemed to have frozen, perhaps waiting for him to make a move. Perhaps she was as paralyzed by whatever was between them as he was.

"Mae," he said, his voice rasping. "I want…"

"I know," she said near his ear. "I want too."

She pulled back and met his gaze. "But we won't. We can't. We're fighting over a company."

"Are we fighting, though?" He had to ask the question that had been bouncing around in his brain. "It feels like we're on the same page most of the time."

She arched an eyebrow. "You still want Heath and me to sell you half the company, right?"

"It's the only thing that makes sense." Getting to know Mae had only supported that conclusion.

"Then yes—" she tipped up her chin "—we're still fighting."

She had the most beautiful chin. Rounded, with skin that was silky smooth, and he wanted to cup it in his hand and draw her face toward him so he could kiss her senseless. His breathing was labored, as if they were striding along the pavement, not standing still, and hers seemed to be uneven too. Who were they kidding?

"Not sure how many business fights you've been in," he said, knowing the answer. "I've been in quite a few, and none of them have felt like this."

"Felt like what?" she asked, her voice faint.

"The wanting."

She stared into his eyes for a second too long. "And

that's exactly why we're not going to complicate it even more."

"You're right. Good point." He kept forgetting that, and he really needed to do something now to get them back on track. "I'm totally out of line. I was emotional today because of Alfie leaving. I don't know what to do with myself tonight because he's gone, and I've gotten carried away. I shouldn't use all of that to complicate things between us."

"That's all this has been?" she challenged, her beautiful gray eyes stormy.

"Yes." *No.* "Sure."

She gave a quick shake of her head. "You're kidding yourself."

"Well, what's your suggestion, then, Mae? What do we do about it?"

She simply looked at him for an eternity, her eyes unreadable. "How about this? Heath is staying at Freya's place and Sarah is out until late. I'm going up now, and on the way through, I'm going to tell the doorman that a guy named Sebastian Newport might be dropping by, and if he does, to send him up."

He drew in a sharp breath. "If he doesn't drop by?"

"Then I'll see him at the office tomorrow."

"And if he does?"

"Then two consenting adults would have to work out what they're going to do about the inconvenient thing that's between them." She turned and said, over her shoulder, "'Night, Sebastian."

He watched her walk to the door, stop to say a few words to the doorman, then disappear into the building. And he'd never been so torn in his life.

* * *

Once she'd made it inside Sarah's apartment, her heart pounding, Mae couldn't make herself leave the foyer. She'd just crossed a huge line with Sebastian. Dropping her bag on the floor, she drew in a shuddering breath. They were in an impossible situation, and inviting Sebastian Newport upstairs had been a very bad idea, and yet…a little kernel of hope flickered in her chest. Hope that he'd be as reckless as she'd been.

She groaned and pinched the bridge of her nose. "This is ridiculous," she whispered.

Getting her hopes up was just setting herself up for disappointment since she had zero idea what Sebastian would do. She told herself to head for the kitchen and make a coffee, or sit on the sofa, or something. Anything. Yet she remained with her feet planted on the tiled foyer floor…hovering. Wishing. Wanting.

*So much wanting.*

Footsteps sounded outside and then a sharp double-knock. Mae's heart stalled and then burst back to life, beating double time. He'd actually followed her. She reached for the door, then hesitated, her belly filling with butterflies. She should have used the few minutes before he'd arrived to brush her hair or refresh her lipstick. Maybe change into something new. Pop a breath mint. But it was too late, so she smoothed her hands over her trousers and tucked her hair behind her ears, hoping she was enough as she was. Then she took a deep breath and opened the door.

Sebastian strode in, and she took a step back because he didn't seem to be stopping. She wasn't fast enough, though, because he crashed into her, grasping her face with his hands as his mouth landed on hers, hot and hungry. Suddenly light-headed, she wrapped an arm around his waist to keep her balance and kissed him back. Heat licked through her body, a deep need, unlike anything she could remember feeling. Without breaking the kiss, he kicked the door closed behind him and slid his hands to her thighs, lifting her. While she wrapped her legs around him, locking her ankles, he turned and walked her backward until her shoulders hit the door with a light thud. The exquisite pressure of the hard planes of his torso pushing up against her breasts made her moan, but their kiss swallowed the sound.

When they finally wrenched themselves apart—moments? Minutes? A lifetime?— later, she rested the pad of her thumb against his bottom lip and whispered, "You came."

He stared at her for a beat, his blue gaze unreadable, their heavy breathing the only sound in the apartment.

"Here are my terms," he said, his focus on her unwavering. "We agree that this is not the start of something. It is a onetime only deal. We shouldn't have started this in my kitchen, but since we did, we finish it now." He adjusted her weight by placing his forearms under her buttocks. "There will be no repeats—we just get it out of our systems and move on. And we don't talk about it after I leave this apartment tonight. Those terms acceptable to you?"

She would have agreed to fly to the moon in that moment if it had been a condition for him to start kissing her again. "Deal."

He lowered his head, his mouth finding hers for another brief kiss that scorched her system. "Where's your room?" he asked, his voice unsteady.

She unlocked her ankles and slid down his body, relishing the feel of him so close. "This way." She took his hand as she stepped away, but he didn't follow. "Sebastian?"

"Are you sure, Mae?" His gaze was intense, but wary. "Less than ten minutes ago, down on the sidewalk, we agreed this shouldn't happen." He lifted their joined hands and gently kissed her knuckles. "Us getting carried away and you regretting it in the morning is not my idea of a good time, so I need to know that you're sure."

The air around them was heavy, as if carrying the weight of this moment. Of her choice. But there was no choice to be made. There was only the need, and the want that thrummed between them. She knew why he was checking—she'd been the one to pull away in the kitchen. That kiss had been unexpected and overwhelming, and that combination meant that she'd needed to step back to give herself a chance to think things through. To process. She was done processing now.

"That conversation was about why we shouldn't do this. What we didn't cover was why we should."

He cocked a brow. "Yeah? Got many reasons on that list?"

"Just the one," she said through a dry throat. "Right now, I feel like I'll die if I don't have you even once."

A slow smile spread across his face. "Lead the way."

Making it through the apartment took much longer than it should have. Sebastian caught her on the staircase and turned her in his arms, the extra height of the stair meaning she didn't have to stretch up to kiss him. And once they reached the hall, the absence of his touch was too much to bear, so she turned and reached for him, and he pulled her tight and kissed her hard.

Somehow they made it to her room, and as soon as they were through the door, she was in his arms again, his breath hot near her ear. "Now, where were we?"

"Where were we?" she asked, trying to get her brain to work, which was difficult when she could smell the intoxicating, warm musk of his skin. "You were asking if I was sure?"

"Earlier." He sucked her earlobe into his mouth and gently bit down.

Her blood fizzed through her body like champagne. "Deciding if you were coming upstairs?"

"Earlier."

Everything outside this room was a distant memory, but she forced her mind to work. "When we were in your kitchen?"

"That's the one," he murmured against her skin. "Tell me what you want, Mae."

The possibilities flooded her mind, and she swayed, her grip on his shoulders the only thing keeping her upright.

"Everything," she whispered. "I want to touch you, and be touched by you. To kiss and be kissed by you. To drown with you. I want everything you have to offer."

"Done." He kissed her again, pressing his thigh between her legs, providing delicious pressure where she craved it the most.

"And what about you?" Her hands roamed over his back, his sides, wherever she could reach, learning the shape of him, committing it to memory. "What do you want?"

His eyes flared. "I want to hear you say my name."

"Sebastian?" she said, knowing she was missing something, since she'd used his name countless times over the past few days.

"Not like that." He leaned in, murmuring at her ear, sending sparks zinging across her skin. "I want to hear you moaning it when you're lost to sensation. Screaming it when you find your release. I want my name to be your whole world for tonight."

As she snaked her hand down his chest, across the flat of his abdomen, and farther to the bulge of his erection, she whispered, "I don't think that's going to be a problem." His breath hissed out from between closed teeth. She traced the outline of his shape, teasing him, building, wanting him to be as desperate as she was. Then she palmed him through his trousers, cupping him, and his hips bucked, thrusting into her hand.

She found his belt and was fiddling with the buckle when his hands came down to stop hers. He swore savagely under his breath.

"I don't have a condom," he rasped. "Didn't need them when I was married and haven't been seeing anyone since. I'm assuming, since you haven't been in the country long…?"

Her stomach sank and she winced. "I didn't bring them from Australia and haven't had a reason to buy any since I arrived." Which right now seemed like a massive oversight. "I don't want to stop to get some, though."

"I'm not even stopping for earthquakes or hurricanes," he said and kissed her.

The intensity of the kiss kicked up a notch, setting her aflame. The pads of his thumbs stroked over the front of her bra, but her hands were greedier, trying to touch all of him through his clothes at once.

Breaking the kiss, he turned her and pushed against the closed door, his arms coming around from behind to find the button and zipper at the top of her pants. He released the closure and slowly pushed them down, taking her underpants with them, smoothing his hands over her bare buttocks as he went. A rush of cold air hit her flesh and her head swam.

"I knew your ass would be delectable." He kissed one cheek, his tongue flicking out, and then he softly bit her.

All the air left her lungs in one long whoosh and her legs swayed. "Maybe give a girl a little warning next time?" she said once her lungs were working again.

He stood, his front sliding up her back, and then his breath was at her ear. "Now where would the fun be in that?"

She coughed out a laugh.

He undid the buttons of her shirt and tugged the sides apart. He wrapped one arm around her stomach, and the other up and over her shoulder, sliding his hand down into the cup of her bra. With his body pressing into her from behind, the hand holding her against him started to inch downward, overwhelming her with sensation. And then his hand reached the juncture of her thighs and he cupped her, pressing lightly.

"Oh, God," she said, her vision swimming.

"What was that?" he murmured beside her ear. "Was that my name you were trying to say?"

She started to reply but broke off as he gently sucked at the sensitive skin on the side of her neck, and, this time, had no trouble remembering to say his name. Every nerve ending was sensitized, every inch of her skin yearning for his touch. The hand he'd placed between her legs began to move in a slow, rhythmic pattern, and the hand still inside the cup of her bra explored, gripped, caressed. Her head dropped back onto his shoulder and she melted into him. Her entire universe was Sebastian—his hands, his mouth, his hard body behind her.

"Sebastian," she whispered, unable to summon her full voice, but needing to say his name, to add the extra layer of connection between them.

"An improvement," he murmured, "but I think we can do better."

The toe of his shoe nudged her feet farther apart as he slid a long, strong finger down low, then another, moving into the slickness he'd created, driving her out of her mind. Her knees buckled, and the hand at her breast moved down until his arm wrapped tightly around her waist, taking her weight onto his frame. Near her ear, his breathing was ragged as he talked dirty and whispered sweet nothings in equal measure. She tried to focus on everything she was feeling, to commit it all to memory. Since their deal was for this one night only, she wanted to remember every second. But it was no use—she was too lost to sensation, overwhelmed by the rising, swirling currents inside. And as her world came apart, his name was wrenched from her throat, the only word that made sense, the only thing that seemed real.

For long moments, she simply stood, the sound of her harsh breathing filling the room as she leaned back against him. Once she could breathe freely again, she opened her eyes and turned in his arms. "That was…"

"Yeah," he said with a satisfied smile. "It was."

"And now it's my turn." She pushed against his shoulders, and he dropped his arms.

He cocked a brow. "You can barely stand on your own."

"I'm recovering fast," she said, grinning.

She unbuttoned his shirt and pushed the fabric back over his shoulders and down to his wrists. She paused as she undid the cuffs, then he slid his arms free. The shirt hung from his waist, its tails still tucked into his trousers and secured by his belt, but she didn't care; she had free rein to explore every inch of the warm olive skin of his chest. She ran an exploratory hand over the crisp hair covering his pecs, down over the solid muscles of his abdomen, loving the way his breathing matched her movements.

Leaning in, she allowed herself the luxury of pressing a kiss to his collarbone, then the base of his throat. His pulse throbbed there, strong and fast. She slid her hands down his sides, bringing them to rest on his hips, and they anchored her as she explored his chest with her lips, her tongue, her teeth. She dropped lower, onto her knees, and felt a shudder run through his body.

Clasping the zipper, she undid his trousers and let them pool at his ankles, then hooked her thumbs in the sides of his briefs and lowered them to the floor. As she leaned back, he stepped out of the discarded clothes, shoving them to the side. Looking up, she met his eyes and then took a moment to let her gaze roam down, over the expanse of skin on display, and her breath caught high in her throat.

Then she brought her attention to his erection, encircling it with one hand as the other rested on the solid muscles of his thigh. The skin was soft and burning hot, and as she moved her fingers lightly, Sebastian groaned and speared his fingers through her hair.

She looked up and smiled. "Let's see if I can make you say *my* name."

Then she leaned forward and took him in her mouth and he gasped. She experimented a little, looking for sensations and rhythms that he liked, peeking up at his face to gauge her success. His eyes were closed, and his chest was rising and falling quickly with every breath.

"Mae," he said, his voice tortured, and she grinned.

She leaned back, releasing him, and before he could question her or complain, she gently pushed him back onto the bed. She wanted him stable for what she had planned.

His eyes flashed to hers, but she crawled onto the bed with him, over him, and his mouth curved into a lazy smile. "Come here," he said, then he pulled her close and groaned.

The scorching heat of him against her bare skin sent a shiver down her spine, but she kept her eye on the prize. "Not a chance," she said, smiling back. "I'm going to finish what I started."

She kissed a trail over his chest, down his stomach, her nails scraping across his abdomen as she went. And when she reached his erection again, hot and solid in her hand, in her mouth, she returned to her experimentation, more confident now that she knew how he liked to be touched.

"Goddamn it, Mae, you're going to kill me." She glanced up to find him propped up on his elbows, watching her, his blue eyes dark with desire, his jaw tensing and releasing.

She stopped what she was doing long enough to echo his words from earlier. "A good use of my name, but I think we can do better."

As she took him into her mouth again, her fingers and

palms working as well, he flopped back onto the bed, groaning. It was gratifying to know that he was as powerless and as lost to need as she was.

As his need built, she watched his beautiful body fill with tension, his muscles cording, and his arms moving restlessly, from cradling her head, to grasping handfuls of the bed covers, and back to tangling his fingers in her hair. As he found his release, he cried out her name, and she'd never felt so triumphant in her life.

# Seven

The next morning, Mae walked downstairs, hoping that no one would guess from the smile she was attempting to hide that Sebastian had spent the night. She'd reluctantly sneaked him out the front door just after four o'clock, when everything was quiet. With a gentle kiss in front of the elevator, he'd whispered, "See you at work," and was gone. Sleep had been impossible after that—she'd lain awake replaying every second of their time together.

She ran into Heath at the front door. He mainly spent his nights at Freya's place, but in the mornings, when she left for her job as a forensic accountant at the FBI headquarters, he headed over to Sarah's. He and Sarah were still going through various business files and legal details about the inheritance during the day, and she'd be doing that this week with them too, if the opportunity to shadow Sebastian hadn't come up. She loved her brother and was coming to love her aunt, but this time with Sebastian? It was precious—and not only because she stood to learn the ropes of the company she'd partially inherited.

Heath held up a paper bag. "I come bearing bagels."

She snatched the bag and opened it to draw in the scent. "See, this is why you're my favorite brother."

"From a pool of one," he pointed out. "Though, to be fair, that's the reason you're my favorite sister."

She grinned and headed for the kitchen, where she found Sarah making coffee and chatting to Lauren.

"Morning," her aunt said.

Mae handed her the bag. "Heath brought bagels."

"And *that's* why he's my favorite nephew." Sarah took the bag from Mae and kissed Heath's cheek.

Heath pumped a fist. "Man, I'm really creaming the competition in the categories where I'm the only candidate."

Lauren chuckled as she took a mug of coffee Sarah handed her. "Morning, Heath. Morning, Mae."

Heath pointed at Lauren. "I wasn't sure if you'd be here for breakfast or not, so I got enough bagels just in case. I guess that makes me—" he raised his eyebrows hopefully "—your favorite future son-in-law?"

"Maybe," Lauren deadpanned. "So far, you're ahead of both of Freya's ex-husbands, but let's see how it goes, hey?"

Heath clutched his chest. "I'm wounded."

Mae grinned and began pulling bagel toppings from the fridge. Over the years, people had sometimes commented on how she'd missed out on having an extended family, growing up with just a mother and a brother, but the three of them had always been close. Now that she had Sarah, as well as all the O'Donohues from her mother's side, and even Lauren living downstairs—all of a sudden she had a bounty of riches in terms of family. Her heart was full from having them all in her life, and she just wished her mother was here to see it, to be part of it.

Her thoughts drifted to Sebastian, alone in his apartment. He'd been abandoned by his mother, his wife had died, and his father was horrible. Now, with his son gone for a few days, he had no family at all. It made no sense how much luck and arbitrary circumstances affected whether a person had family around them or not.

*I'm not welcome in the enemy camp.*

They walked through the kitchen to the dining table, carrying food, coffee mugs, and plates.

As she took her seat, Mae looked at the other three. "Can I bring a plus one to the dinner on Friday?"

Sarah's eyes lit up. "Of course you can."

Her brother frowned, and she could see his wheels turning. "Who?"

She grabbed a bagel and put it on her plate, attempting to look casual. "Sebastian."

Sarah's butter knife clattered onto her plate. "Sebastian *Newport*?"

Lauren's concerned gaze cut to Sarah then back to Mae, but she remained silent.

"Yes," she said simply and cut her bagel.

Sarah and Heath exchanged a glance, before Sarah said, "You said you were there to investigate, not…make friends."

Her brother was very still. "I don't trust him."

That didn't surprise her. Their entire childhood had revolved around them hiding from their father and being suspicious about new people in case they were private investigators. They'd changed identities more than once and moved around a lot. If Heath *hadn't* been suspicious it would have been weird.

"I'm not sure I trust him either, but I do know that there's a lot of bad blood between the families, and the cause was our father and his. Not him, and not us. If we're going to find a way forward, we at least need to find a way to talk to each other that's not combative."

Heath regarded her in silence for a long moment. "You know what you're doing?"

Honestly, she had no idea what she was doing, or what she was feeling, but she said, "Absolutely."

He nodded and went back to his breakfast.

Lauren cut into a banana and arranged the slices on her bagel. "It doesn't have much to do with me, but in case anyone's interested, I won't mind if there's an extra person at my daughter's engagement dinner."

Mae threw her a grateful smile, and Lauren gave a small nod before biting into her breakfast.

"I'll extend the booking," Sarah said with a valiant attempt at a smile.

"Thank you," Mae said and stood, snagging the bagel from her plate. She kissed both her brother and aunt on the cheek, mouthed "Thank you" to Lauren, took her plate back to the kitchen and went to her room to get dressed for work. The room where the sheets were still rumpled from her encounter with Sebastian. She bet they still smelled like him too.

Less than an hour later, she walked through Rosario's office, placing a French vanilla cappuccino, with oat milk, and a paper bag containing a pastry on her desk.

"Mae, I'm so glad you came to work here," Rosario said with a smile that bordered on adoration. "Best boss ever."

"Hey." Sebastian appeared in the doorway. "You know she doesn't actually work here. I'm still your boss."

Rosario lifted her hands, palms out. "You don't bring me coffee. My loyalty is fickle."

Mae went to her shared office and headed for her little wooden desk. "Morning, Sebastian."

"It's all making sense now," he said, one side of his mouth hitched up. "You agreed to shadow me so you could woo my staff into switching loyalties. You were the one with the nefarious plan."

"I can write down the way she likes her coffee for you if you think it would help," she said sweetly, and heard his chuckle from behind her.

As she sat down at her desk, she noticed a square box tied with a red ribbon. She glanced at Sebastian, who gave her a self-satisfied smile, and opened it to find an assortment colored pens, sticky notes, striped paper clips, highlighters, and a bright-orange notebook.

She gasped. "You got me stationery?"

"I had some spare time this morning without Alfie at home, so I left early. When I passed a stationery store, I remembered you said how much you like it." He casually shrugged one shoulder. "I figured you needed some for your desk."

"Thank you," she said, lifting each item out of the box and admiring its beauty.

He rubbed a hand across his jaw. "No need to be too grateful—it went on the office expenses."

It was more than that, though. He'd thought about her and had stopped to pick out some things he thought she'd like. Her heart swelled in her chest. She lined each of the items up along the side of her desk, then folded her hands, looking at them. Then she looked back up at him and smiled. "What's on the agenda today?"

"Back-to-back meetings I'm afraid." He swiveled in his chair to face his computer screen. "First one starting in ten minutes in our boardroom, then we're darting across town for the next. No time for one of our lunches either, since we're catching up from yesterday. We'll just grab something on the go."

No time to go out for lunch? That was when she was going to ask him about the engagement dinner. Maybe she should just get it over with now instead. "Sebastian?"

"Mm-hmm?" he said as he stood and started collecting things he'd need for the meeting.

"Are you busy Friday night?"

His brows drew together. "Not really. Amanda and Barry are keeping Alfie over the weekend."

"Then you should come to dinner with us," she said brightly.

"Who is 'us' exactly?" He looked over, his deep blue eyes narrowed.

She counted off on her fingers. "Heath, Freya, Lauren, who is Freya's mom and Sarah's best friend, Sarah, and me."

"You want me to have dinner with the heart of the Rutherford family?" He put his things down again and crossed his arms. The action brought her attention to his fresh white shirt, and the muscular chest beneath it that had been pressed against her breasts the night before. Suddenly, there wasn't enough oxygen in the room.

"Yes," she managed to whisper.

"Why?" he said, his voice full of incredulity.

She shook herself and forced her attention back to the

conversation at hand. "Because we're toasting Heath and Freya's engagement."

"Sure," he said pointedly, "but why invite *me* to it?"

"Because I think we need to move past this idea of who is from what family and preconceptions about things and just meet each other as people." Was she the only one who saw it like that? How people were just people and should be judged on their own merits?

He was still clearly less than convinced. "Now who has a secret agenda?"

"Lord above," she muttered to herself. "What *possible* secret agenda could I have to invite you to dinner?"

"I can't imagine, Mae." His voice was taut, his jaw set. "You tell me."

She'd already offered him the justification that Heath and Sarah had accepted, yet he wanted more. What else could she tell him when he wouldn't see the need to build bridges between their families? Gazes locked, they waited, as if in a standoff.

A little voice inside her mind nudged her to acknowledge the truth. Yes, there was a need to bring the families together, but there was something deeper that she was scared to admit. Something terrifying. And now that she'd realized what it was, she could no longer be a coward. She needed to say it out loud.

She blinked and then softly said, "I'd like you to be there."

He held her gaze a moment longer and then nodded. "Then I'll come."

Sebastian arrived at the hotel at five minutes to seven to find Mae already waiting for him on the sidewalk, beside the door. She was wearing a lilac wraparound dress that hugged her curves so close he almost stumbled on the pavement. The vibrant color complemented her dark brown hair, and her gray eyes took on the lavender tones in the dress, and he had the thought that she should be on the big screen. Had he once thought she wasn't traditionally beautiful? He'd never seen anyone look more exquisite.

He reached her and leaned down to kiss her cheek, drinking her in. "Hello, Mae."

She grabbed his forearms and went up on her tiptoes to kiss his cheek in return. "I'm so glad you made it."

When they separated, she was looking up at him, smiling widely, her dimples twinkling in her cheeks. Her joy was infectious, so he smiled back. "Thanks for inviting me."

"Come on, let's go in." She led the way through the ornate marble lobby with expansive ceilings. Everyone knew this hotel, and Seb had often thought about staying a weekend here just for the experience, but had never seemed to find the time.

Mae took him off to one side, then led him into the hotel restaurant, finally stopping at a private dining room. The room was small but lavishly decorated, from its crimson fabric wallpaper to its elaborate chandelier. The tabletop was marble, and the seats of the chairs were upholstered in the same crimson fabric as the walls. It would have been a comfortable room to spend a few hours, except for the four sets of eyes that had watched his approach and were glued to him now.

"This is Sebastian," Mae said. "I think you know everyone except Lauren?"

He nodded. "Sarah and I have crossed paths a number

of times over the years, and I met Heath and Freya only a few months ago."

Some stilted small talk followed, in which he tried to make nice with people he was in the middle of a battle of wills with. Entrées came and were cleared away, and Seb continued to chat, mainly with Sarah and Lauren, both of whom were clearly assessing him.

Once the waiter had refilled all their glasses with champagne, Sarah raised hers and said, "To Freya and Heath."

Seb joined in the chorus of the others repeating, "To Freya and Heath," and then half listened to the discussion about wedding plans. Most of his attention was on Mae, at his side. Every time she moved, she brushed his shoulder or his arm, and it was throwing him off-balance.

The waiter brought their main course, and Seb glanced across the table to find Heath staring at him. In a business context, he'd take on Heath Dunstan, no question. But, despite their joint business interests, this was not a business setting, and Seb didn't know what the rules were. Mae turned to speak to Lauren, at her other side, and casually brushed against Seb's arm again, and he watched Heath pointedly follow the casual contact.

"Mae," Heath said, "can I have a quick word?"

"Not just now," Mae said, using a sweet voice that Seb was coming to recognize as the one she used when she knew exactly what she was doing to mess up someone else's plans.

"Heath," Sarah said, snagging Heath's attention away. "I was just talking to Freya about a proper engagement party."

"I thought that's what this was," he said.

"No, this is a small family gathering. I've been thinking about something bigger, with all your friends. I'll take care of everything, of course, plan all the details."

Heath and Freya exchanged horrified looks.

"Here's the thing, Sarah," Heath said gently. "Freya and I both hate parties. We've attended your others because they're yours, and we love you, but it's no kindness to us to throw us a party."

Lauren laughed behind her hand, and made eye contact with Sarah, toning down her amusement to offer unspoken support once she saw how crestfallen Sarah was. Seb watched the two older women a bit longer. Hadn't Mae said they were best friends? There was something too attentive between them for mere friendship. They both always seemed attuned to the other no matter who was talking or where they were. If those two weren't secretly a couple already, then they should be. He checked out the others around the table and wondered if they all knew.

Across from him, Heath put down his cutlery. "Are we going to talk about the elephant in the room?"

Seb stilled. Had Heath just worked it out? Or had Seb given it away by watching the women too closely?

Freya made a valiant effort to redirect the conversation to the history of the room they were sitting in, but Heath persisted, saying, "Everyone here is okay that there's something going on between these two?"

Seb was horrified to realize that Heath was waving a hand at Mae and him. He hadn't expected to be welcomed with open arms, not when their families had been fighting for years, but it still felt like a punch to the gut that he was deemed so wildly unsuitable for Mae.

"There's nothing between us," Mae said, but she undermined the statement by putting a reassuring hand on his thigh. Heath didn't miss the move.

Sarah leaned forward. "Heath, this is hardly the place…"

"I'm okay with it," Lauren said and took a slug of wine.

"What?" Heath said. "After everything you put me through when I wanted to be with Freya?"

"Freya's my daughter." Lauren gave the table an enigmatic smile. "Besides, I've mellowed."

"You have not," Heath said.

Lauren raised her glass to Seb down the table. "Single parents have to stick together."

Seb tried to smother a smile, but was unsuccessful, so he simply raised his champagne glass back to her. He knew that would probably infuriate Mae's brother more, but there weren't a lot of good options given the circumstances.

Hoping to defuse the situation, Seb pushed his chair back. "If you'll all excuse me for a minute, I need to find the restroom."

Before he was even out of earshot, he heard Mae telling Heath to let it go. He blew out a long breath. He'd known coming tonight would be a disaster, but when Mae had said she wanted him here, he'd found that he couldn't say no. He seemed to have an ongoing issue with his ability to deny Mae Dunstan anything she asked for.

When he was done and walking back through the hotel lobby, he saw Heath waiting for him up ahead and groaned.

Heath stepped into his path and didn't bother with a greeting. "I don't know what sort of game you're playing with my sister."

Seb sank his hands into his pockets and prayed for strength. "I'm not playing a game."

Heath took an infinitesimal step forward. "You should know that when my mother found out she was pregnant with Mae, she took me and ran. Changed our names, falsified Mae's birth certificate, moved countries with us several times, all to keep the two of us safe."

"I know that," Seb said, confused. Everyone in the state knew that. His cell in his pocket vibrated but he ignored it—the man in front of him needed all his attention.

"Then," Heath said, menace in his eyes, "you'll understand that after all my mother's efforts to protect her, I'll be *damned* if I'm going to let you walk into my sister's life and take advantage of her. It would be dishonoring my mother's sacrifice if I allowed it."

Part of him was glad that Mae had someone in her life willing to go to bat for her—except for the short period of his marriage, Seb had never had that, and Mae deserved all the support. The other part wanted to de-escalate the situation, get through the dinner, and go home. His cell vibrated again, and again he ignored it. "I know what she's been through—"

"You don't know anything about what we've been through," Heath said, then turned on his heel and strode away.

Seb watched him leave, then rolled his shoulders back, trying to release some tension. His cell vibrated again. He drew it out and found a message from Mae.

Where are you?

Torn, his thumbs hovered over the cell.

Maybe it's best for everyone if I leave.

The reply was instant.

Is Heath with you?

He almost grinned at how fast her mind went to her brother. She must have suspected what he'd been up to, which also meant there was no point avoiding or sugar-coating the truth.

Not anymore.

I will kill him.

Seb rubbed a hand behind his neck, even less keen to return to the table now that he knew that fratricide was being contemplated. While he was still working out a plan, he saw Mae striding toward him, dragging Heath by the hand.

When she reached him, she dropped her brother's hand and looked from Heath to Seb, and back again. "What the hell, Heath?"

"I could say the same to you." He pointed at Seb while keeping his eyes on Mae. "What exactly is going on between you two?"

"I'll tell you what." Security near the front door looked over, so she dropped her voice to a harsh whisper. "None of your business is what's happening."

Heath angled his shoulders to exclude Sebastian, and, if anything, Seb was grateful. Mae wasn't in danger, and there were about a thousand places Seb would rather be right now. But she wanted him there, so he waited.

"Since when do we keep secrets?" Heath hissed.

Mae's eyes widened and even Seb could see that that had been a trigger of some kind.

"Since you started it." Her voice was laced with barely contained anger. "Finding out about our father and Sarah. The inheritance. You did it on your own, without telling me, until it was pretty much all settled."

Heath rocked back, shock all over his face. "Hang on, that's not fair. You know why that was."

"I know your own justification for it, sure," she said, pointing a finger at his chest. "Now I'm doing my version of how to approach all of this on my own. So you can back off."

"But—"

"I. Said. Back. Off." Her voice was low and lethal and both men took a small step back.

Heath glared at his sister for a long moment, then headed back to their private dining room.

Once he was out of sight, Mae's face filled with pain and her shoulders slumped. Sebastian reached for her and brought her into the circle of his arms, holding her tight. She felt good there. Right. As if nothing in the world could be bad as long as she was there.

"You don't fight with him often, do you?"

"No," she said against his shoulder as her arms wrapped around his back. "But that one had been coming for a long time. I hadn't forgiven him for keeping secrets. Still, I shouldn't have done it here, or in front of you." She tipped her head back. "I'm sorry. That must have been uncomfortable to see."

"Not as uncomfortable as it would have been for you to be in the middle of it."

"And what's worse is I'll have to apologize to him later.

He was out of line, but I shouldn't have lost my cool. Not in public, anyway."

"Do you want me to get you out of here?"

She sighed and pulled back. "Thank you for offering, but no. We need to go back, finish the dinner, and then I can go. It's not just Heath's night, it's Freya's too, and I really like her."

"Then, let's go." They disentangled themselves and walked back to their table with a respectful distance between them, but the imprint of her body still hummed against his.

Sarah and Lauren watched their approach, one with an expression of concern and the other looking intrigued. They took their seats as Freya was whispering to Heath, her brows drawn together, but her fiancé merely gave a curt shake of his head and mouthed, "Later."

The whole scene was excruciating, even compared to dinners with his father. The difference was that he hadn't cared about his father from quite a young age, so he could easily dismiss or ignore whatever he was saying. He'd grown very accustomed to tuning his father out. But, he realized, he cared a lot about Mae. He didn't want to be the cause of a rift with her family, especially with her brother after all they'd been through together.

Worst of all, what if Heath had been right? Seb hadn't set out to take advantage of Mae, but maybe, subconsciously, that was part of what he'd been doing? He was Christopher Newport's son, after all. Even his own mother thought he was like Christopher, so perhaps he'd been kidding himself about his own motives all this time?

While stilted conversation went back and forth around the table, Seb took his cell from his pocket, set it on his thigh, and typed a message to Mae.

I don't belong here. I should leave.

He heard her phone vibrate and saw her look down seconds before his cell vibrated on his thigh.

You can't.

He turned to her and raised his eyebrows, snagging his water glass at the same time for cover. His phone vibrated again.

You said, whatever I want, I could have it.

A bolt of heat shot through his system.

Mae...

He didn't know if that had been a warning or a plea, but, either way, he couldn't look at her.

You promised. And I've decided. I want you. Tonight.

He almost choked, and took another sip of water. He checked the table, but no one seemed to be paying them attention. But then he had a horrible moment of doubt. Surely, she wouldn't use him to get back at her family? This had to be about more. But he had to check.

Is this because you're mad at your family?

She leaned over and whispered in his ear, "I want what I asked for before, but more. So much more. I've wanted it since we were in your kitchen." He felt her hand on his side. Clearly, she wasn't bothering to hide things from the others now, and he had no idea how he felt about that. His cell vibrated again.

Check your jacket pocket.

He slid a hand into his pocket and found the hard, smooth surface of a hotel room key card. He put more effort into keeping a poker face at that moment than he ever had in his business negotiations. When had she even booked a room? His hand was unsteady as he typed on his cell.

Are you seriously doing this?

From the corner of his eye, he saw her smile.

No one ever accused me of being sensible.

With that, Mae stood and gathered her purse from under her chair. "I'm feeling tired, so I'm going to make it an early night. Congratulations again, Freya and Heath. I can't tell you how much I'm looking forward to having a sister. Sebastian, would you see me home?"

"Yeah, sure. Thanks for having me tonight," he said to the others. "It was an honor to be invited." He pushed his chair out and stood beside her, feeling as if the rug had been ripped out from underneath him. "After you," he said, mainly because he didn't know where they were going.

They walked out, side by side, and once they reached

the lobby, she took his hand and changed direction, heading for the bank of elevators. And just like that, Sebastian was dizzy with want.

# Eight

As they neared the door to the room she'd booked, Mae slowed down and tried to catch her breath. Since she knew the room number, she'd been the one leading the way, but it was somehow important that Sebastian be the one to open the door. There was a second card in her purse, but him doing the honors would make this a choice they were making together.

His hand was still wrapped tightly around hers, and when they stopped, he produced the key card from his pocket. He held it aloft for a beat, and when she nodded, he inserted the card, pushed open the door, and held it for her to enter.

A few steps inside, the sound of a soft click from behind told her that the door had been closed, and she turned, hoping he'd dispense with preliminaries like last time. Instead, he stood there, magnificent, his chest rising and falling, with an intensity in his features she didn't understand.

"Mae, I need to check something. Is this really what you want?" Small frown lines appeared across his brow and he lifted a hand to absently rub at them, before dropping it back to his side again. "Am I really what you want?"

Caught off guard, she almost laughed at how ludicrous the question was, but stopped herself in time. "It was your pocket that I slid the card into." She'd thought that was a pretty clear signal. "Besides, who else would I want here?"

"It's..." He blew out a breath. "We had our deal in place—that last time was a one-time-only deal. Then you argue with your brother about me and now here we are."

"Sebastian, no—"

"I need to know that you want this—" his eyes narrowed, assessing her "—and it's not you proving something to yourself or whatever."

That explanation made sense, but was there more to it? She bit down on her lip, thinking it through. Had *he* been swept away with her putting the card in his pocket and wanting to get out of the dinner...and was he now having second thoughts?

"Sebastian, do you want to be here? You laid out your terms that night at my aunt's apartment, and I'm the one who's crossed the line by inviting you here. If you'd rather leave, it's fine. Honestly." She tried to emanate I'll-be-fine vibes, when that was the opposite of how she felt inside, but he deserved have the choice to walk away if he wanted to.

He drew in a shuddering breath. "Mae, I really want to be here. In fact, I'm so far beyond want right now that I can hardly see straight. Which is why I need to know that you do too."

A weight slid from her shoulders and her body felt as if it were filled with champagne bubbles. *He wanted her.* Wanted this.

"I paid for this room before Heath was being a jerk," she said, taking a small step closer.

He cocked his head to the side. "When, exactly?"

"Before you arrived. I got here early and took the room." She'd come with Sarah and Lauren but had told them to go ahead to the private dining room, taking the chance to sneak over to reception.

His eyebrows shot up. "You had this planned?"

"Not planned, exactly." Planned sounded too definite. But hoped? Absolutely. "Let's say I was keeping my options open."

He reached into his back pocket, pulled out his wallet and produced a condom. "Maybe I was keeping my options open as well."

Arching an eyebrow, Mae lifted her purse in front of her chest and pulled out an entire box of condoms.

Sebastian laughed. "When you're in, you go all in."

"I'm what you might call an all-or-nothing kinda gal," she said, fluttering her lashes.

"I've noticed." One corner of his mouth hitched up.

She hesitated. "Noticed it in a bad way?"

He closed the distance between them and slid his arms around her waist. "I like it."

"Well, then you're going to love this," she said and began unbuttoning his shirt.

He leaned in, pausing when his mouth was so close that his breath fanned over hers, and said, "You're right. I do."

And then he kissed her and she was once again drowning in her need for him. His tongue pushed against her lips—seductive, carnal—and she forgot about the buttons on his shirt, winding her hands up behind his neck, holding his head in place.

She'd kissed and been kissed before, but it had been nothing compared to kissing Sebastian. The need he didn't attempt to disguise, the desperation she couldn't have hidden if she'd wanted to. He slid his hands down to her hips, pressing her closer as she speared his hair with her fingers, giving her all and taking as much from him.

Eventually, she dragged her head back, sucking in lungfuls of air, almost dizzy with wanting.

"I have to tell you," Sebastian said around his own panting breaths, "I'm feeling torn about this dress."

She glanced down. "You don't like it?"

When she'd bought it, the dress had made her feel good about herself, flattering her nicely. And when she'd put it on earlier in the evening, she'd thought of him and smiled at herself in the mirror, hoping he'd be taking it off later.

"I'm torn," he said, toying with the neckline, "because I like it so much that I'm a little sad it has to go. But it does. Have to go. Now."

Her knees buckled, and she swayed in the safety of his arms. "There are two ties. The one you can see on my left side, and, on my right, there's a secret hook as well as the tie."

"Now, that is useful information." He kissed her again, a quick, scorching press of his lips to hers and then dipped his head to focus on the task. He pulled at the first tie, and one side of her dress dropped, leaving a length of material wrapped against her torso. The light pressure of his fingers at her side as he searched for the hook was torture—the touch, muffled by the fabric, was nowhere near enough. And then he found the hook, unclasped it, and the rest of the dress unraveled from around her.

As he slid the two panels of soft material apart, the pads of his fingers brushed lightly against her ribs, leaving a trail of sparks on her bare skin, and she gasped. Too soon, his fingers were gone, and then his hands were on her shoulders, slowly easing the dress down her arms. In moments, her dress was gone, leaving cool air swirling against her flesh.

Surprised, and impressed, that he'd worked it out so easily, she gave him a lazy smile. "That was fast."

"I can be fast when it's important. And this was very important." He leaned past her and carefully draped her dress on the hotel room's plush velvet chair.

As his gaze roamed her body, he set his warm, strong hands on her shoulders, first tracing circles and patterns, then moving down her arms, across her back, and a soft moan escaped her lips.

She glanced up at him, mesmerized by the wonder and appreciation she found in his features. "What do you want, Sebastian?"

"I want to see you this time," he said without hesitation.

Meeting his eyes, she reached behind her back and found the clasp on her bra. It took her a few seconds to release the catch—despite only having one glass of champagne at dinner, she was feeling more than a little inebriated. It had nothing to do with the champagne. She was drunk on him. It was all him. It was Sebastian's effect on her, making her fingers tremble, making her light-headed.

She pulled her arms from the lace straps, and let the bra fall from her fingertips to the floor. Then she hooked her thumbs in the sides of the matching underwear and slid them down to her ankles before kicking them away, along with her shoes. Sebastian's eyes flared as he drank her in, and she stood tall, feeling beautiful under his gaze.

"Mae," he said, his voice a hoarse whisper. "You're…" He stopped, cleared his throat, and tried again. "Everything about you is exquisite."

He reached for her and she melted into him, tugging at his belt buckle even as he kissed her, wanting to remove the last fabric barrier between them. On one especially rough tug on his belt, he laughed and laid his hands over hers, stopping her until she looked up at him.

"What about you?" Releasing her hands, he cupped her face and brushed a featherlight kiss on her lips. "What do you want?"

"I want…" She had no idea if this was another one-time deal or if it was the start of something, but just in case, she wanted to experience everything with him at least once. "I want you inside me this time."

"Well," he said, swallowing hard, "it would be a shame to waste all those condoms."

This time, when he kissed her, his hands had free rein over her body, and he took full advantage, from teasing her breasts to skimming across her stomach until he reached the delta of her thighs, an area he gave special attention to until she was writhing against him.

When his hands moved on again, she wrenched away and sternly said, "Trousers, Sebastian."

Grinning, he dispensed with his pants, and she allowed her gaze to roam over him, from the rigid erection he'd just freed, to his strong, muscular legs, up to his chest with its expanse of olive skin, dusted with dark hair.

"My turn," she said and scraped her nails across his pecs.

As a shiver ran through his body, he dropped his hands. "No argument here."

She circled behind him and pressed a kiss to the spot

between his shoulder blades. Last time, everything had happened so fast that there hadn't been time to stop and smell the roses. Or, more precisely, to smell him. She pressed the side of her face against his back, luxuriating in the feel of his skin, the heady scent of him. He remained still, giving her the space to explore as she chose, so she traced her nails down into the arch of his lower back then over the rise of his ass cheeks, caressing them for the pure pleasure of it.

Circling around again, she found his eyes closed, the tension in his expression betraying what it cost him to stay still while she played. She stood up on tiptoe and touched her lips to the sculpted perfection of his mouth, and his arms were suddenly around her, lifting her off the ground as he kissed her hungrily, then gently lowered her to stand again, all without breaking the kiss.

"My turn?" he asked when they came up for air.

"Nearly," she said, snaking her hand down to grasp his erection. He already felt familiar, velvety and hot, and she stroked him the way he liked it. Knowing how Sebastian liked to be touched, having the freedom to simply reach out and do it was exhilarating.

He brushed his mouth over the shell of her ear and, his voice gravel-rough, said, "Now it's my turn."

"For now," she conceded, releasing him.

He drew her earlobe into the heat of his mouth and scraped his teeth across its flesh, igniting fireworks in her blood. Then he kissed his way down the side of her face, her neck, nipping at her collarbone before circling the peak of her breast with his tongue. Her heart raced in an erratic beat, but before she could find her equilibrium, he'd moved on, sweeping kisses across her stomach and then kneeling before her. As he threw her a smoldering glance, she steadied herself with her hands on his shoulders and held her breath. He parted her with his fingers, then rubbed her with his thumb, using downward strokes. She made a loud, involuntary noise but couldn't make herself care. All that mattered was Sebastian and what he was doing. Then, slowly, oh so slowly, he leaned forward and his tongue swept the path his thumb had taken.

"Sebastian," she said on a strangled breath.

Without missing a beat, he gripped her hips to steady her, his mouth making blissful magic, and the world around her dissolved into a burst of light and sensation.

She was vaguely aware of him lifting and moving her, and when she blinked her eyes open, she was straddling his lap on the side of the bed. She smiled, feeling pretty good about the world.

"Hey," he said softly.

"Hey, you." She reached her arms above her head to stretch, her muscles still buzzing.

"Whoa," he said. "You might want to give a guy some warning if you're going to do that. My entire system could have overloaded."

She pushed gently at his shoulder. "I think you can take it."

"Think of my poor heart," he said, hand on his chest, all faux dramatics, even though his jaw was tense and his muscles were bunched. It was costing him to be light and charming when his body was screaming for release.

Grinning, she maneuvered and wriggled until she was tighter against him, and all traces of humor evaporated from his features.

"This," he hissed through his teeth. "This is what I want."

"Just this?" she said innocently, squirming just a little.

His breath caught. "Maybe you're right and I can handle more."

"Care to prove it?" she said, raising an eyebrow in challenge.

Eyes dancing, he lay back on the bed, and she lifted herself on her hands and knees above him, leaning down for his kiss, the heat rising inside her again as his hands stroked and teased her flesh. Just as the urgency began to creep back into her blood, he changed their positions and then stood, taking all his warmth and beauty with him. He held up one finger before disappearing for intolerable seconds, and then he was back, sheathed, and she pulled him down to her on the bed, needing the feel of his skin on hers again. As he kissed her, he rolled her beneath him, his delicious weight pressing her into the mattress. Everything inside her began to feel frantic, needing him more than anything, wanting it all, whatever *it all* was.

Honestly, it all came down to him. Sebastian. Lately, it seemed that it always did.

She reached a hand and laid it on the side of his precious face, wanting to appreciate the moment, commit this view of him to memory. He stilled for endless seconds, seemingly lost in the moment with her, the only sound in the room their heavy breathing. And then he whispered her name and reached down to guide himself inside her, and she wrapped her legs around his waist, shifting to adjust, reveling in the intimacy of the contact.

He began to move, and she caught his rhythm and moved with him, the coiled tightness inside coming faster than she'd expected, growing stronger, until the world exploded and she clung to Sebastian as if he was the only thing anchoring her to reality.

As he chased his own peak, Sebastian continued his rhythm, and in his moment of release, he called out her name.

When she drifted off to sleep a little later, it was that moment that she replayed in her mind, and she smiled.

Mae woke slowly, stretching catlike before opening her eyes. Spontaneous stays in expensive hotels were one aspect of being rich she could definitely get used to. She rolled over to find Sebastian already awake and sitting up on the bed.

She smiled sleepily. "You're awake early."

"I have a toddler," Sebastian said with an eyebrow quirked. "This is not early."

As her brain began to engage, she frowned. He was wearing the same shirt and pants from dinner the night before, though they were more rumpled now. "You're covered in all those clothes." She slid a hand across his covered stomach. "Can't say I approve of that."

He lifted two cups. "I had to put the clothes on to get the coffee."

"Then I do approve." She sat up, stretched again, and took the coffee he handed her. He'd brought her a Grande Americano, just as she liked it? "This is an excellent way to start a day. Much better than sneaking you out of Sarah's apartment at 4:00 a.m."

"Also better than sneaking out of a family dinner that turned messy."

She sighed. "I'm so sorry about that. It must have been awful for you."

"It wasn't all bad." He shrugged. "Freya seems great. And I liked Lauren."

"She was definitely on our side, which surprised me."

Sebastian sipped his coffee, his gaze thoughtful. "Is there something between Sarah and Lauren?"

"I think there's a lot between Sarah and Lauren. They're boss and employee, but most importantly they're pretty much best friends." They always seemed in sync with each other, the way long-term friends often were.

He cocked his head to the side. "Nothing more than that?"

"I don't think so." She pulled her legs up under the covers so she could wrap her free arm around them. "Why?"

"I just thought I saw a...connection."

Mae considered it, thinking back over the interactions she'd seen between the two women. "I doubt it. They've been friends since before Freya was born, so if there was something there, surely they would have acted on it by now?"

"Maybe," he said.

"Though that does make me think I should try some matchmaking for Sarah. I love to see people find their person."

"I'm glad you think that, because I have something to ask."

"Me too," she said and took a sip of coffee, savoring the deep, rich taste. "I was thinking about coming into the office again and doing another week." The week had gone so quickly, and there were a couple of things she hadn't been able to resolve during that time. Larry Sheridan's situation was one—she wanted to ensure that he was okay with whatever Bellavista decided to do—and a couple of changes she'd been supporting Rosario in making with the admin staff.

"I have a better plan." He reached over and took her

hand and his gaze became more intense. "We should get married."

Mae blinked. She hadn't been awake long, and her brain wasn't firing on all cylinders yet, but it sounded like he'd just…proposed? That made zero sense.

"This is from left field," she said carefully. "When did you decide this?"

A frown line appeared between his brows. "Last night your brother accused me of taking advantage of you."

Mae shot up from under the covers. "Heath said *what*?"

"It's okay," he said, holding up a hand. "Under the circumstances, it wasn't completely out of line."

"Yes, it was." Because of the way she and Heath had grown up, with the two of them and their mother keeping their identities secret, and only being able to rely on each other, they'd all tended to be overinvolved in each other's lives. And since their mother's death, when it had become just the two of them, she and Heath had looked out for each other more than most siblings, which could lead to overstepping. It was time to end that. She'd be having a word with her brother in the very near future. Again. "I'm sorry he said that to you. I know it's not true, and that's all that matters."

He swallowed hard and looked down at their joined hands. "Even though it wasn't my intention, it did start me wondering if I've been subconsciously taking advantage of you. I mean, I do have my father's genes, and that's what he'd do. But if we get married, it puts us on even footing, which fixes everything."

"Fixes everything?" She tried to put all that together in her head, but it didn't add up. She took a slug of coffee, set the cup on the side table, and said, "Okay, explain that to me."

He twisted so he was completely facing her. "If we're married, then there's no question of motives anymore. We'd be on the same team. It won't be the Rutherford-Dunstan family versus the Newport family, it would just be Mae and Seb, the dynamic duo." His eyes filled with enthusiasm, and he tugged on her hand, inviting her to join his excitement. "When you split your inheritance with Heath, you could ask for Joseph's shares of Bellavista, and once my father retires, the two of us would own the entire company. I'll help you learn everything you need to know, and we can run it together. And Alfie and our future kids will inherit the combined company."

Mae stared at him with growing horror. "Is this a proposal for a marriage or a proposal for a business merger?"

He shrugged that away, seemingly unconcerned. "Why can't we have the best of both worlds?"

The coffee in her stomach turned sour. Was there a chance that she'd been right in her suspicions at the start? That he was playing a long con, and this was another step in his plan? "Sebastian," she said slowly, "I don't think this is a good idea."

He stilled, the passion in his eyes ebbing. "You seemed to like being with me, though."

"Sure, but that's not really enough to be considering a lifelong commitment." And it felt weird to even have to spell that out.

"It's all relative. Ashley and I grew to love each other more once we were married, but if I compare my feelings at the time of making a commitment…" He shrugged one shoulder. "I already feel closer to you than when she and I got engaged."

There was silence in the room for several beats as she wondered if this was what rich people were really like—

very little about how rich people operated made sense to her—or if this was just a Sebastian thing. Either way, this conversation was getting surreal. He really was speaking as though he believed intimate relationships were transactional. She needed a moment to think, and this wasn't a conversation she wanted to have while she was naked and he was dressed. Stepping from the bed, she slipped on her underwear and the lilac dress, then, taking his hand, drew him to the armchairs off to the side.

"I haven't had a committed relationship before," she said once they were seated. "It didn't seem right when I couldn't share the truth about who I was and knowing we might have to move with little notice again, so I kept things light when I was involved with someone. So, I'm definitely no expert, but, Sebastian, I don't think this is how proposals are supposed to work."

His gaze on her was unwavering. "Well, I've only ever done the one proposal before now, so I'm no expert either, but I think they should work however we want them to work. It's just between us."

So many thoughts were crowding her brain that it was difficult to separate them. She tucked her hair behind her ears. "You've raised a few different things here, and they seem to be all tangled together." The only thing to do really was to address them one by one, and the easiest one to start with was the company. "Sebastian, I don't want to work at Bellavista. Being a businessperson is who you are, but it's not who I am."

He tipped his chin. "You just asked to come back for another week," he said, surprised. "I've seen you in the office, and you clearly love it. Plus, Rosario tells me that all the people you met so far only had great things to say about you. You're a natural."

Rosario was lovely to have passed nice feedback about her to Sebastian, but working in an office for the rest of her career, chasing profits instead of doing good, going to meetings with those smug, hungry lawyers and people like them, sounded awful. "A main reason is I wanted to follow up on Larry—I'm the sort of person who finishes what I start. And—" she glanced down, butterflies filling her stomach "—to be completely honest, I wasn't ready to say goodbye to you."

It shouldn't have been awkward to say, not after he'd just proposed, but his idea of marriage was about business, and she was admitting something deeper. But then he was there, kneeling in front of her, and he tipped up her chin with one finger. She looked into his deep blue eyes, and found herself trapped by the emotion there.

"Mae," he said, his voice gentle, "I told you that you could ask for anything you wanted. You didn't have to invent a story about coming into the office. Why not just ask to keep seeing me?"

"I thought that was just about..." She didn't want to say aloud that she thought he'd only been talking about sex, in case she'd misjudged him.

"It's about everything," he said simply.

Unable to help herself, she leaned forward, and he met her halfway. The kiss was sweet and soft and full of tenderness and promises.

When they pulled apart, she laid her hand on the side of his face. "Here's a counteroffer. What you and I have had so far has been hurried and clandestine. What I'd really like is for us to start dating. I appreciate that part of your reasoning for the marriage proposal was to protect me, but it's been just over a week since we met, Sebastian. Regular people don't get married that quickly."

He huffed out a laugh. "You might be right. Okay, dating it is." He leaned in and kissed her again and then murmured against her lips, "What time is checkout?"

"I arranged a late checkout when I booked the room last night."

His eyes widened comically. "Miss Dunstan, were you planning on seducing me this morning?"

"You bet I am," she said and let him lead her back to the bed.

Three weeks into their new dating arrangement, Mae decided to surprise Sebastian for lunch. They'd managed to spend some time together most days, getting to know each other more like a normal couple, and she'd spent some time with Alfie, too. She and Sebastian had managed to have lunch a couple of times a week, and dinner at his place after Alfie went to bed, and he'd left a few gaps in his daily schedule to meet up with her. She hadn't stayed the night with him, though. After his proposal, she was wary of sending mixed signals, so she was trying to keep them firmly in the "just dating" territory. But the warm call of his body every day was making it harder to say no, and to leave his apartment and head home.

She'd spent the rest of her time with either Heath or Sarah, dealing with the rest of their inheritance. On Thursday, she'd passed the morning at the office of their charitable trust, which was easily her favorite of the offices, and had some free time before an afternoon meeting with Sarah.

There were options to fill her time, but she was always itching to see Sebastian nowadays...

In the past, if things were going this well, she would have split and run because she was raised to believe that if it looks too good to be true, it probably is. She was trying to be optimistic, though. To believe in Sebastian. Believe in the two of them together.

So she drew in a breath and decided to drop in and see him in her free window of time.

When she reached Rosario's desk, the other woman was on the phone. Mae put the cappuccino she'd brought in front of her, and when Rosario held up a finger, Mae nodded and stood back to wait. She put the call on hold. "It's great to see you, Mae."

"You too, Rosario. Is Sebastian in?"

She shook her head. "He's having lunch with Ashley's parents. Since it's her birthday, the first one since she died, I think they were going to do something to commemorate it."

"Oh, of course," Mae said, trying not to betray her feelings. Maybe it was nothing, but was it weird that Sebastian hadn't mentioned this at all? She'd seen him last night and he'd sent a text at 7 a.m. to say good morning, but there had been no mention of something this big. She considered the other side of the story, for balance. Perhaps he was thinking it would be awkward for her? Still, she was going to have to mention to him that secrets were a deal breaker for her.

Rosario pointed to her headset. "Give me a minute to finish this call before you go, though. I was hoping to talk to you today."

"Sure," Mae said and glanced out the window.

An older man with gold-rimmed glasses and an angry face stormed in, pushed past her, and opened the door to Sebastian's office.

He stomped back and scowled at Rosario. "Where is he?"

"I'm sorry. I need to put you on hold again for a moment," Rosario said into the headset's microphone. To the man, she said, "Mr. Newport, he's not available right now."

Mae was suddenly on full alert. This was Sebastian's father, Christopher Newport. Sebastian looked nothing like this pasty-faced man with sandy hair—he must have taken after his mother in looks.

"I can see that," Christopher said. "I asked *where* he was."

Rosario didn't flinch or falter. "I'm afraid he didn't tell me. I'm only his assistant."

"This is unacceptable—" He froze as he caught sight of Mae waiting to the side, all color draining from his face. His mouth opened and then closed again.

In the background, Mae heard Rosario going back to her call and ending it. "Mr. Newport, I can take a message and pass it to Sebastian when he gets back."

Christopher didn't take his focus from Mae. "I assume you're Joseph's other missing brat. At least you look more like the Rutherfords than your brother."

Mae weighed her options. Even if she hadn't already known what sort of man Christopher was, it was clear now that nothing good was going to come out of his mouth and she should step outside until he was gone. But this man had been her father's business partner and rival, and she expected to see something of her father in him—more than she'd seen anything of her father in his sister, Sarah, so morbid curiosity kept her there.

Besides, this was Sebastian's father and observing him for a few moments might give her more of an insight into the man who occupied her every waking thought.

And so she stuck out her hand. "Good to meet you, Mr. Newport. I'm Mae Dunstan."

He stared at her hand without reaching for it, then looked back up at her. "I'd heard rumors that Sebastian was taking a leaf out of my book, but I didn't believe it."

"I'm sorry," she said. "I'm not sure what you're referring to."

He smirked. "You look like your aunt."

She'd heard that often enough, but it still didn't make sense. "So I believe. Not sure how that relates to Sebastian."

He tipped his head to the side in what he probably thought was a suave gesture. "Sarah and I used to be together."

"You and Sarah?" she said, incredulous.

"What? You think I wasn't good enough for her? She was obsessed with me back in the day."

Magnificent Sarah, obsessed with this buffoon? "I find that hard to believe."

He lifted his chin in the air. "I almost had her father convinced to leave his share of Bellavista to her. Then once I married her the whole company would have been mine."

A creeping chill spread across her skin. Something about his words seemed very off. "What about Joseph?"

"Your father was a jerk." He'd spat the words with contempt. "And stupid too. Sarah was the brains of the family, and their father knew it. And if I'd pulled my plan off, you and your brother would never have seen a cent either."

"That's an interesting story, but you obviously didn't pull it off. Heath and I inherited everything, so something went wrong."

His eyes shifted to the doorway. "I changed my mind," he said with less bluster.

"She dumped you, didn't she?" His shoulders bunched up and Mae smiled. "Took her a while, but she ended up seeing through you."

"She didn't see anything. I decided to tell her the reality of our situation and she freaked out. She might have been smart but she was naive about the world."

"Hang on, you had a grand plan to get control of the company by seducing and marrying Sarah, then getting her father to change his will to leave his share to her. And then, what? You ruined it all—why? Did you fall for her and tell her everything? And she realized what a contemptible human being you are and walked out. Is that it?" She could see from the look in his eyes that she'd put it all together.

"Don't look so self-righteous. Sounds like you and Sebastian are doing the exact same thing to *your* brother."

"Wait, what? I would never try and cut Heath out of his share."

"Right. Then it's just Sebastian working alone. Hopefully he'll propose soon and all this can be yours." He swept an arm around the office.

The cold, sinking feeling she'd had through the entire conversation finally became a sharp bar of ice in her gut. She glanced at Rosario and back again.

Christopher guffawed. "Oh, that is rich. He's already proposed, hasn't he? Gotta hand it to the kid. I often wondered if he had too much of his mother in him to do anything good with the company, but looks like he's got it all shored up. Welcome to the family, sweetheart."

He walked out the door, laughing. Mae didn't move.

She felt like a grenade had just gone off and she wasn't sure if she'd survived or not.

Rosario rushed around the desk and put an arm around Mae's shoulders to guide her to a chair. "I'm so sorry. I hate him—we all do. Most of us only stay for Sebastian. Just ignore everything he said. He shoots his mouth off all the time, and I don't think he knows what he's saying half the time."

Mae found a smile to reassure Rosario that she was okay. She needed to talk to Sebastian, but she couldn't call or text him if he was at some sort of memorial for Ashley.

"I might just leave Sebastian a note on his desk, if that's okay."

"Of course it is. And I'll tell him that you were here if he calls to check in."

"Thank you."

But what could she say in a note?

If the proverbial apple had fallen right at the base of the tree, then there was nothing left to say. And if it hadn't? She squeezed her eyes shut and tried to ignore every instinct she had, because they were all screaming to run.

Don't look back, don't falter, just run.

She opened her eyes, picked up a pen, and started writing.

# Nine

Sebastian opened his car door, sank into the driver's seat, and leaned his head back on the headrest with his eyes closed. The lunch with Ashley's parents, extended family, and assorted friends for her birthday had emotionally wiped him out. Such a senseless waste of life to cancer—their daughter, their cousin or niece, their friend, Alfie's mother, his wife.

He missed Ashley's companionship, her sensible advice, and most of all, he missed parenting with her. Every time Alfie hit a milestone, it was bittersweet because Ashley couldn't see it. They might not have started as a love match, but they'd come to love each other, especially through Alfie.

Alfie had been the center of attention today, and Ashley's friends and cousins had taken turns holding him, needing that connection to her. They'd prearranged that Amanda and Barry would keep him overnight and bring him back in the morning, since they needed to hold their daughter's son more than anyone today.

His cell rang and Rosario's name flashed up. There had been a message from her earlier to call and he'd planned on using the drive back to do it anyway. He started the car and answered the call. "Hey, Rosario. I'm just heading off now."

"I know this is a terrible time to bother you, but something's happened you'll probably want to know about."

He stifled a groan. "If that's the architect about the plans I said I'd have back this morning, tell her—"

"It's Mae."

He broke off immediately, heart in his mouth. "What about Mae?"

"She came in to surprise you for lunch and ran into your father. He was as unpleasant as you'd expect, but he's suggested to her that you're seducing her to get her shares in the company."

He almost ran off the road. "You *have* to be kidding me."

"It was like a slow-motion train wreck. I watched it happening, could see it getting worse, but there was nothing I could do. I'm sorry."

"None of this is your fault, Rosario. Not a thing." The fault was all his father's. "Why would he even say that? If he really thinks I'm playing a game, why would he alert her?"

"Honestly, I think he just got carried away with his story about dating Sarah when he was young and being a blowhard, and totally lost sight of who his audience was. But, yeah, if you *were* capable of something like that and were using Mae, then he'd have shot the Newport plan in the foot."

Seb gripped the steering wheel tighter. "How did Mae take it?"

"She seemed rattled. I tried to talk to her after, but I think she just wanted to get out of the office." She drew in a breath. "There's something else."

"Hit me," he said and braced himself.

"Mae asked where you were and I assumed she knew about the lunch for Ashley and had just forgotten, so I told her. I'm sorry if I've put my foot in it."

He winced as he made a left-hand turn. Poor Mae, double blindsided without him there to explain. "Again, that's not on you. That one's on me. Do you know where she went?"

"She didn't say, but she did leave you a note on your desk."

"I'm on my way. And thanks for the heads-up."

He disconnected and tried Mae's number. She didn't pick up, so he left a message, apologizing for not being around today and asking her to call him. He should have been up front about today, and at the very least told her in the text he'd sent her this morning where he was going, but he'd needed some time to get his head around the day first. Once he'd arrived there, he'd realized why.

They'd all visited the grave site first, in a picturesque cemetery partway between Manhattan and her parents' place, and then had lunch together at a local café to reminisce. Laying the flowers at her graveside, his feelings had suddenly made sense. He was there to say goodbye to Ashley before moving into the future with Mae. Having a future with Mae without doing this first would have felt like a betrayal of his first marriage. He'd needed to tell Ashley.

The others had let him have some time alone to stand beside the marble headstone, which he'd appreciated.

He'd given her an update on Alfie, told her how proud she'd be of her son, promised her he was still prioritizing finding work-life balance. And then he'd asked for her blessing to move on with Mae.

In that moment, as he'd told Ashley about her, he had been hit with a bone-deep certainty that he loved Mae. He'd told Ashley that he loved her too, but that his love for Mae was different. Ashley would have understood—they'd never lied to each other about their feelings, and she'd known that he loved her as his best friend, his ally, and the mother of his son.

Mae, though? She was everything. His here and now, his future, his everything. He could barely breathe when he thought of her.

He tried her cell again a few times on the drive back, but she still wasn't answering. Once he finally reached the Bellavista headquarters, he had to force himself not to run to his office to find her note. He smiled and exchanged greetings with various people in the hallways and told someone from accounts that it was okay to send through some files.

When he stepped through to Rosario's office, she said, "I've cleared your afternoon."

"You are an angel," he said, without stopping.

In the middle of his glass-top desk was a folded slip of paper with his name written in her neat handwriting. Barely restraining himself from lunging at it, he picked it up in controlled movements and opened it.

*Sebastian,*
*Rosario told me where you are, and I'm sorry you have to go through this, because Ashley's birthday will be a rough day for you.*

*I haven't called or texted because I didn't want to interrupt, but the thing is, I'm mad at you, but I don't want you to see me mad on a day like today. So, I hope you're okay, and tomorrow we need to talk.*
*Mae*

His stomach turned over and made a new knot. This mess needed fixing, now. First, he had to find her.

He was still holding the piece of paper in his hand when his father blustered past Rosario and into his office.

"There you are," he said in his too-loud voice. A voice that had grated on Seb his whole life. "I've been looking for you. What's the point of having a personal assistant if they don't know where you are?"

Seb folded the note and put it in his shirt pocket. "Dad, it's not the time."

His father stabbed a finger in the air in the general direction of a wall clock. "These are business hours and I need an update on the Sheridan property, which is a business matter, so this *is* the time."

Seb glanced up at him, the man who'd sucked any joy from most things in his life and who might now have ruined his future. "What did you say to her?"

"Who? Rutherford's daughter?" He flicked a hand as if this was beneath his notice. "Nothing much. I'll give her one thing, though. She at least looks like the Rutherfords. Still not convinced her brother's part of their gene pool. Not that their features sit well on her. Not really a looker, is she?" His father laughed.

Seb drew in a breath through his nose. Blowing his top at his father wouldn't help anything—besides maybe his mood—and would only waste time. The day his father handed over the reins of the company and stepped away couldn't come soon enough. On that day, Seb was going to tell him exactly what he thought of him and then walk away from him forever. Today, however, yelling at his father would only delay finding Mae.

So all he said was, "You're an ass," and then pushed past him and out the door. Finding Mae was all he cared about. Any interaction with his father would have left her feeling awful, which meant he didn't want to wait until tomorrow, as her note had suggested. He needed to check if she was okay today. Now. If she really didn't want to talk, then he could wait, but only when he knew she was fine.

As he stepped out of the building onto the sidewalk, he tried her number again, and she still didn't answer. So he did the unthinkable. He called Heath.

"Newport," Heath said on answering, his tone dry. "What a *delightful* surprise."

He didn't bother with niceties. "Have you seen Mae today?"

There was silence on the line, and he was just starting to wonder if Heath had walked off without disconnecting to annoy him, when Mae's voice came on. "Sebastian?"

"Thank goodness," he said, his shoulders slumping in relief. "I've been trying to call."

"My cell is turned off. I didn't want to talk to anyone, and I thought you'd be busy for the rest of the day."

It was so good to hear her voice again. "Where are you?"

She hesitated before admitting, "At Freya's place in Queens."

"Can I come over there and see you?"

"You'd better not." Her voice had dropped to practically a whisper. "Everyone here is pretty anti-Newport at the moment."

And that was fair. His father made enemies more easily than he made friends. But he still wanted to see her. Emily, the nanny, was having some friends over to his apartment while Alfie was away, so his options were limited. "I'm going back to the office," he eventually said. "When you're done at Freya's, come and see me, no matter how late."

"I don't know, Sebastian." Her voice wavered. "I wanted a bit of time to think it all through."

"Alfie's with Amanda and Barry, so I'll wait the rest of the evening. Hell, I'll wait all night, just in case you decide to come."

"I'll see," she said and disconnected.

Seb dragged himself back up to his office and closed the door behind him. Mae's desk was still sitting at the window. He couldn't imagine his office without it now. What he wouldn't give to see her there, smiling across at him.

When the rest of the staff left for the night, Seb ordered in dinner and worked through his backlog of paperwork, trying not to check the clock every five minutes.

Just before midnight, Mae arrived.

"Hello," she said softly from the door. "I wasn't sure you'd be here this late."

"Hello," he said, drinking her in. "I told you I'd wait until morning, if necessary." She was so beautiful that his chest ached to look at her. "You want to come in?"

She wandered over to her desk and sat on its edge. "Your father said some things to me today," she said without preamble.

"I heard." He stayed in his chair, not wanting to spook

her away now that she was so close. "I'm sorry about that. It was unforgivable. He's a despicable human being."

"No argument from me. He said he dated Sarah when they were younger, and he tried to manipulate the situation to get his hands on the Rutherfords' half. Something that Heath has confirmed. Did you know about that?" she asked, her chin tipping up.

"I've heard the story a few hundred times, yes."

"He also seemed to think you might be using the same playbook with me." Her gaze on him was laser sharp as she watched for his reaction, testing his father's theory against what she could see.

"Mae, after everything we've been through so far, you can't still suspect me of running a long con?"

She shrugged one shoulder. "My mother taught us to be suspicious precisely because of our father, and people like your father."

"I'm not him." He speared his fingers through his hair. He didn't just want to smooth this out so they could move on. He'd never really had anyone in his corner before, someone completely on his side, believing in him. To an extent, Ashley had been, but he kept her shielded from a lot of his family stuff, so she hadn't needed to take a stand by his side. With Mae, it was as if his chest had been ripped open from the start, with his beating heart on offer to her, vulnerable to her. More than anything, he wanted her to see him for who he really was. To look into his heart and know. To believe him. Believe in him.

He stood and crossed the distance to her desk. Not wanting to touch her yet, to risk swaying her through their chemistry, he shoved his hands in his pockets and left a couple of feet between them.

"I realized today that I love you, Mae. The only other

person in my life I've ever really loved this much is Alfie, and I thought that was different because it's how you feel about your child. But, Mae, I love you with the same intensity. I'd die for you. I know you think we've been going too fast, and I'm not expecting you feel the same, because it's too soon for you." He paused, sucked in a breath and opened his heart to her. "All I want is for you to see me. Neither of my parents ever saw me, and I'd kept parts of myself hidden from Ashley, so she never had the chance to see me even if she'd wanted to. You've been different from the start, though. I've kept nothing hidden. I need you to see the real me and that I'm nothing like my father."

Mae rose and took his hand, threading her fingers through his. "I do see you." She placed a palm firmly on his chest. "And I see your heart. I just sometimes get tangled in my own head. The programming my mother instilled to keep me safe hurts even as it helps. And being in this world—my father's world—was bound to trigger it more than normal."

He closed the distance separating them. "Not sure if you noticed that I slipped into that speech that I love you."

A corner of her mouth hitched up. "I did happen to notice that."

"You don't need to say it back," he clarified, in case she thought he was pressuring her. "I just needed you to know."

She drew in a trembling breath. "You were right that this is going too fast for me—I'm not in the same place as you. I'm not sure I *can* be in that place. If I can ever be as open and vulnerable as you just were."

"I'm willing to take the chance." Mae was worth the chance.

He rested his forehead against hers and slid a hand behind her neck, a shiver running up his spine at just being able to touch her again. She lifted herself up on her tiptoes and leaned into him, kissing him, drawing out the desire that was always near the surface when he was around her. Breathing her name, he kissed her back.

When they came up for oxygen, he said, "Come to the Hamptons with me. Alfie and I will be heading up tomorrow."

She grinned, her dimples flashing. "You mean today?"

He glanced at his wristwatch. "I guess I do. Amanda and Barry are bringing Alfie back during the day, and then we'll head up after I finish work. Come with us." In the weeks they'd been dating, they'd spent most of the first weekend in the hotel bed after her family's disastrous dinner, and the next weekend, she'd said she had something on. But they could spend this weekend together, with no Rutherfords, no nanny, no work. Just them. "Spend the weekend with us. Alfie can sometimes be a handful when he's awake, but he has an early bedtime."

She chewed her bottom lip and then nodded. "Okay. I'd like that."

He kissed her again and the world seemed a whole lot brighter.

They made it up to Sebastian's house in the Hamptons just at sunset the next day, and Mae was hit with a strong sense of déjà vu. The first time she'd been in this driveway, she'd just walked over from Sarah's house next door to confront Sebastian and get some answers, and the second time had been when she'd accepted a ride back to Manhattan with a man she barely knew. This third time, she was arriving as an invited guest to stay the weekend with the man she wanted to spend every waking and non-waking moment with.

Alfie had fallen asleep in the car, so Sebastian transferred him straight into his crib in the nursery while Mae carried in her bag and some of the food bags she'd brought.

Within an hour, they were out back, sitting by the pool in wooden deck chairs, a glass of white wine each, and the baby monitor on the small table between them. The pool lights cast a glow around her, the balminess of the summer night nothing compared to the warmth flooding through her.

"So this is what this side of the hedge looks like," she said.

Sebastian indicated a spot farther down the paved pathway with his glass. "That's where I was standing. And I think it's almost as dark now as it was that night."

"It was a moonless night," she said, looking up at the small sliver of moon in the sky, It seemed like forever ago. "I couldn't see a thing on my side of the hedge, let alone you over here."

He nodded sagely. "Good for all the hiding you were trying to accomplish."

"And I was very successful at it, except from the chatty neighbor with the voice like melted chocolate."

He glanced over, eyes comically wide. "Mae Dunstan, was that another compliment? I need to bring you to the Hamptons more often—it agrees with you."

She chuckled, happier than she could remember being in a long time. "It's certainly more relaxed here," she said as she stretched her legs out and flexed a foot. "That aspect of it reminds me of home."

"Are you thinking of going back to Noosa?" he asked, tapping his nails against the side of his glass.

"Not sure I can. Sarah's lawyers are working on it, but I was in Australia under a false identity, so I'd have to apply for a visa again." She'd originally just taken leave from her teaching job, but with the citizenship and visa situation, she'd had to resign so they could fill her position. "Heath seems to be putting down roots here—he's even selling his beach bar in Noosa—so New York seems as good a place as any to set up a life."

"From my own selfish perspective, I'm glad to hear it." He reached for her hand and linked their fingers. "What about what you'll do here—have you thought more about that? Perhaps run a certain company with a man who has a voice like melted chocolate?"

"If you're going to let the compliments go to your head, I'll be more careful handing them out." She grinned, knowing full well that never complimenting Sebastian again would be impossible. "I still don't see myself working at Bellavista Holdings. But I've been thinking more about what you said that first night—working out what I want to do with this financial privilege I inherited."

"And what is that?" he asked, rubbing his thumb along the back of her hand.

"I still want to do good in the world." She was embarrassed to voice those words aloud—it sounded like an impossibly naive thing to say—but she knew Sebastian would take her seriously.

"I have no doubts at all that you'll do it," he said, his tone so strong and sure that it brought tears to her eyes.

She blinked a few times to clear her eyes, then decided to divert the focus to him. "What about you? Do you ever think about the world you're leaving for Alfie and want to do something good? What do *you* want? You know, if you'd been born to another family that didn't own half a property development company, what would you want to do?"

He took a sip of wine as he thought. "To be honest, I think it would still be the same. I like the world of property development. I like seeing evidence of what I've achieved, and helping to change the landscape of the city. I can't even imagine myself not doing it."

He did seem well suited to the work, and his staff respected and liked him. She took another sip of her wine. "Before I can do good in the world, though, I still want to do something for my mother's family, especially my grandparents. It just seems wrong that they suffered so much from my father harassing them and losing their daughter. His money should *do* something for them."

He shrugged. "When I met them, they were pretty adamant about letting you and Heath keep the money."

"Which is why I need a plan." She and Heath were in one-hundred-percent agreement that the O'Donohue family deserved a share of the money; the only question was finding a way to give it to them that they'd willingly accept.

"As a father," Sebastian said, glancing at the baby monitor, "I think about Alfie's future more than my own now, and money is framed that way in my mind, like I'm thinking a few steps ahead. So maybe you could talk to your grandparents about setting up college funds or trust funds for the grandchildren. That moves money into their family, while bypassing their concerns about the adults profiting."

The beauty of the idea unfurled in her imagination.

"You know, I think that would work. You are a genius, Sebastian."

"Another compliment," he said, raising his glass to her. "We are definitely coming back here every weekend."

"I could get on board with that," she said, leaning back to look at the twinkling stars. It was such an amazing place that she could imagine spending a lot of time here. "I've been thinking more about the company Heath and I own that my grandparents and uncles work for."

"I remember it. We tried to offer them paid consultancies and they outright rejected the offer."

Her grandparents had been far more curious about Sebastian and his connection to her than they had been about the offer. "What if we broke up the company? I was reading some stories where employees banded together to buy the company they worked for. What if we combined that idea with that thing some businesses do where they hand out stocks as bonuses?"

"You want to give the employees stock bonuses that will total the entire capital of the company?" he said, his voice full of amused wonder.

"Pretty much. Maybe offer 5 percent of stock to each of twenty long-term employees, which would of course include my grandparents and uncles, and those twenty become like a co-op, and run it together. If it's treated like a bonus and goes to other staff as well, then it's all aboveboard and my grandparents would still have the option of giving their shares away to other employees if they didn't want them." She hadn't been able to stop thinking about it since she'd found the stories online. "What do you think—is it doable?"

Sebastian set his arms wide on the arms of his chair. "I think, Mae, that your mind is an amazing thing, and that your idea has some interesting possibilities that we will discuss. Tomorrow. But right now, I think you should come over here and join me on this chair." He was smiling; she could hear it in his voice.

"Why would I do that when I have a perfectly good one over here?" she said in a breathy voice, all faux cluelessness.

"This one has me," he said simply, but with certainty.

Laughing, she stood, finished the wine and then deposited the glass on the small table. "You might need to scootch over a bit so I have some room."

"I'm afraid that's not possible," he said, snagging her hand and drawing her down on top of him. "Sharing this chair is a contact sport. Full-body contact, to be precise."

She stretched out against him. "I think I can live with that," she said and kissed him.

# Ten

Just over two weeks later, Mae let herself into Sarah's apartment, feeling pretty pleased with herself. With Heath's blessing, she and one of the lawyers had set up generous funds for each of her cousins that could be used for education or other purposes their grandparents approved. Her mother's parents had finally been happy with a money-related plan when she'd explained that it was for their grandchildren. She still had plans to distribute the company's stock with them as well, but she was taking it one step at a time. Once her family's needs had been squared away, she'd turned her attention to finding a solution for Larry Sheridan, and this morning, the pieces had finally fallen into place.

She found Heath and Sarah at the table in the formal dining room, documents spread across its entire surface.

"I'd really like Freya's take on this one," Sarah said.

Heath glanced up. "She said she'll meet me here after work, so we can get her to look at it then. I never thought having a forensic accountant in the family would come in so handy."

Mae dropped her bag on a small table nearby, and Sarah looked up, saw her, and smiled.

"You were out early this morning," her aunt said. "Gone before I even made it to breakfast."

"There were a couple of last-minute things I wanted to check out or clear with people before I present my plan to you both."

Heath sat back. "That sounds intriguing. And vaguely alarming."

Mae slid into a chair across from them and squared her shoulders. "Our charitable trust was set up as a tax write-off, and historically, it just donates minimal amounts to established organizations. I'd like to change that so that we take on projects of our own as well."

"Like what?" Sarah asked, tapping a pen against the papers under her hands.

Mae bit down a grin and tried to appear like a serious businesswoman for her pitch. "There's an old house in Brooklyn that's on the market. The owner is Larry Sheridan, and he originally bought the house when he married and lived there with his wife and raised a family. Now he's widowed and retired and needs to downsize, but wants his house to somehow do good for his neighborhood. I spent some time talking to him and a few of his neighbors, and I think this would be a perfect opportunity for us to do something good."

Her brother leaned forward, resting his arms on the table. "What are you thinking we do with it?"

"The yard would make a great playground for the local kids." She'd spoken to a bunch of the kids from Larry's neighborhood and realized how much she'd missed working with children. They'd been enthusiastic and creative with their ideas of what their neighborhood needed. "And if we do some alterations to the house, we could make it a community center."

"I like that," Heath said, running a hand over his chin as he thought.

"Thank you." She beamed at him. "Sebastian inspired me."

Heath and Sarah exchanged a glance.

"What?" Mae said.

"You already know what we're going to say," Heath said, gentling his voice as if she were a child getting bad news. "We don't trust him. He's been trying to influence your decisions since that first night, when you met through the hedge."

Mae frowned. How had the conversation gone from her exciting plan to an attack on Sebastian? "He didn't tell me to take on this project specifically. He doesn't even know about it yet—I wanted to run it by you two first. He just helped me think about what I wanted to do with my life, and that's when I realized I wanted to do something with the charitable trust."

"So after all this time of having you shadow him, and then dating," Heath said, "he's managed to convince you that you don't want anything to do with a business that he's trying to get control of?"

She crossed her arms and steadied her voice. "That wasn't his aim at all." If they knew Sebastian the way she did, they wouldn't be questioning his motives. "In fact, he proposed to me weeks ago and suggested I could work in the company with him if I wanted."

Sarah was suddenly alert. "Proposed? What, exactly, did he say?"

Mae winced as she realized how that would sound to Sarah and what memories it would trigger. "I know where you're going with this, because I met Christopher and he told me what happened between you two."

"Oh, did he, now?" her aunt said, her voice full of disdain, though Mae knew it wasn't for her.

"And at face value, Sebastian's suggestion was similar, but the motivation was completely different. He loves me." Her chest warmed as she said those words aloud for the first time.

"Christopher said he loved me too," Sarah said, her lips tightening.

Heath watched the exchange, then jumped in. "So, let me get this straight. A man from a family that we have an intergenerational feud with..." He held up one finger. "...gets a private investigator to compile a thick dossier on you..." Another finger. "...then *accidentally* meets you on a night when everyone knows where you would be..." A third finger. "...then convinces you to share his office for a week and gets you on-site..." A fourth finger. "Then he starts dating you and proclaiming his love..." He held up a thumb. "And then—" he held up a finger from the other hand "—uses the *exact same strategy* his father used on Sarah forty years earlier to scam our family and gain control of the company that started this whole feud."

Mae shifted her weight. "When you put it like that, it doesn't sound great, but that's not how things really happened. Some of those things were my decision."

Gently, Sarah said, "Tell me you at least saw the dossier he has on you? So you know what information he's been working with?"

Mae thought back and couldn't remember it ever being

mentioned once she'd started at the office. "I never asked to see it."

Heath and Sarah exchanged another glance.

"I don't know what you're implying," Mae said. "Sebastian and I have no secrets. I told him that secrets were a deal breaker for me."

Sarah nodded. "Then would it hurt to take a look at the dossier?"

Mae pulled out her cell. "I'll call him now and ask to see it."

Heath frowned and looked down at his hands.

"What now?" Mae asked, exasperated.

Sighing, Heath met her eyes. "If there's anything there and you give him notice, he'll doctor the file."

"Assuming he hasn't already," Sarah added.

"Okay," Mae said, standing. She'd had enough of this questioning of Sebastian's motives. "Let's go."

"Now?" Heath said, glancing around at all the pages they'd laid out.

"Right now." Mae used the voice she saved for times her class needed to be pulled back into order.

Instead of standing, Sarah rested her elbows on the table and cupped her chin with her two hands. "Why are you fighting so hard about this, Mae?"

"Because I think I might have a future with Sebastian," she admitted, "and that's not going to work if you two keep trying to sow seeds of doubt for the rest of my life."

"You're serious about him?" Heath asked, gaze unwavering.

Her gaze didn't waver either. "I am."

Heath's eyes narrowed a fraction. "And you have enough faith in him that you're willing to take us there, giving him no warning."

"I believe in him," she said simply. "He's a good man."

Heath pushed his chair back and stood. "Okay then."

Sebastian rose from his chair and circled around his desk to see the photos his site surveyor, Lisandro, had opened on a tablet.

"This one," Lisandro said, "lines up with the drawings."

Sebastian nodded. "Send it to me."

From the distance, he heard Mae's voice floating down the hallway and he found himself smiling. She'd left before he'd woken this morning. He'd missed her being the first thing he saw more than he could have guessed.

"Lisandro, do you mind if we postpone this?" he said, straightening. "I need to check on something."

Lisandro picked up the tablet, saw Mae come into Rosario's office, and smothered a grin. "No problem."

Seb had been catching various members of his staff giving similar reactions when Mae walked into the room, and he could hardly blame them. He was well aware that his expression changed when she was around. His whole being transformed whenever he saw her. Hell, whenever he even thought about her, his pulse picked up speed, and his heart swelled in his chest, as if she'd cast a spell over him.

After Lisandro left, Seb crossed to the door to greet Mae, only then realizing that she had her brother and aunt with her. The happy glow he'd felt ebbed away, replaced by caution. These two people were no fans of his.

"Good to see you all," he said and stepped to the side of his doorway. "If you're here to see me, you'd better come in."

The three of them filed into his office. Mae came over

and kissed his cheek, her dimples flashing. The other two seemed less pleased.

"Why does this feel like an ambush?" he asked, only half joking.

"Nothing nefarious," she said, and her use of the word from previous conversations about secrets and cons put him on alert. She slid her hand into his. "We just dropped by because I'd like to see the file that your private investigators compiled about me."

Mae was still smiling at him, but it was strained now, and the other two were wearing poker faces.

"Right now?" he asked.

She nodded. "If it's no trouble."

They were here about an outdated briefing file put together long before he'd met her by a team of private investigators who were no longer working the case? What did they think they were going to find? Hacked documents of national importance?

He cocked his head, trying to understand. "Why didn't you just ask when you were here? Doing it this way feels like a test of some kind."

"Does it?" Heath asked, eyes narrowed. "Is it a test you can pass?"

Seb looked from person to person, trying to read the situation. There was an undercurrent here that he was missing. He caught Mae's eye. "Can I talk to you for a minute?"

Heath crossed his arms over his chest. "What is it with you always wanting to talk to people in private?"

"Heath, don't," Mae said to her brother, then turned back to Seb. "Of course."

Unwilling to leave her suspicious family members

alone in his office, he drew her down to the other end of the room. "What the hell is going on here, Mae?"

"Sorry," she said, her shoulders slumping. "This is bigger than I'd intended—I sort of lost control of the situation along the way."

"What situation is that?"

She tipped her chin so she was looking directly in his eyes. "I was defending you, saying you had nothing to hide, and we somehow ended up here."

"Right," he said, wrapping a hand around the back of his neck. "But why did I need defending, exactly?"

She closed her eyes and winced, as if realizing she'd just given away more than she'd intended. Then she opened them again and her beautiful gray eyes were clear and certain. "If we want a future together, then we need everything out in the open once and for all. No room for doubts. So I wanted to prove to them that you're an open book to me."

Seb sighed, all the fight leaving his body. "Okay, sure." He turned his head to the door. "Rosario? Can you get the private investigator's file on Mae, please?"

"Can do," his assistant called back, then her tone changed as she said, "Mr. Newport, I'm afraid this isn't a good time."

From Rosario's office, his father's voice boomed, "I'll go in there whether or not it's convenient to you or my son." Then Christopher appeared in the doorway, scowling. "What the hell happened to the Sheridan property?"

Seb cast his mind around, working out what his father could mean. "Nothing, as far as I know. I was just meeting with Lisandro, the site surveyor, who was out there a couple of days ago—"

"Well," his father interjected, "something's happened.

I just got off the phone with Laurence Sheridan and he says he's not signing the contract. Has another buyer."

Seb's gut twisted. "I don't know anything about this."

"You should know everything about that property," his father spat. "We'll lose a mountain of money if this doesn't come off. We've already invested too much."

Seb racked his brain. He'd spoken to Laurence Sheridan himself last week. The man had been disappointed that Mae wasn't there, but they'd ended up having a productive conversation, and Seb had asked the lawyers to draw up the contract.

Mae stepped out from behind him, into the center of the room, chin tipped up. "It was me."

Seb frowned. "What was you?"

"I'm going to buy the property for our charitable trust. We're going to build a playground for the kids, and a community center, and make it into something that contributes to the neighborhood."

Seb's blood chilled as he absorbed what she was admitting. "You met him here in my office and then used information you learned while speaking to him on behalf of Bellavista Holdings to follow up outside the company and then bought the property?"

Her mouth opened but no words came out. She simply stared at him, a deer in headlights. He wasn't sure she knew what lines she'd crossed, but she was clearly picking up from his tone that there was a significant problem.

His father swore loudly. "You stupid girl. Besides the fact that you just lost your own company's money, you can't take information you got while here and undercut it with your own offer. You idiotic—"

Seb stepped forward to stand between Mae and his

father just as Sarah drew in an audible breath from her position near the door.

"Stop right there," she said, her voice threaded with steel.

His father froze, then very slowly turned and caught sight of Sarah for the first time. "Sarah," he said, his voice hoarse.

"Don't you dare attack Mae over what's the right thing to do. You have fewer morals and ethics than a slab of concrete." Her expression was one of complete disdain and disgust.

"Sarah," his father repeated, looking in danger of swaying on his feet. "I—"

She prowled closer, pointing a finger at his chest. "You have never done a principled thing in your entire life, Christopher Newport, and you have the gall to stand there and yell at a woman who is trying her best to do something good."

His father took a step back and Sebastian blinked. He'd never seen his father back down from anyone. He was starting to wonder if he'd dozed off at his desk and this entire meeting was an elaborate, bizarre dream.

Sarah turned to Mae, her gaze softening. "He's right, though. When you told us about the plan, you left this very important part out."

"Wait, what?" Stunned, Seb looked down at Mae. "You've been working on a plan and told them, but you didn't talk to me about it? Even though it's a property you know I'm in the process of buying?" The betrayal bit so deep he almost stumbled. He straightened his spine, tensing himself. This couldn't be true.

How had he been so blind?

Mae's loyalty was to her brother and aunt, and likely

always would be. To be fair to her, he was the one who'd said he loved her, the one who'd proposed marriage. She'd never professed her love for him and had fought to keep their relationship status casual.

She'd been accusing him or questioning him about whether he was conning her since the first morning she'd arrived on his doorstep. Had that been to cover her own agenda?

*The lady doth protest too much.*

The words rang in his mind like a slap in the face. Had she been stringing him along, holding him at arm's length this entire time? Playing with him? Maybe not to get her hands on Laurence Sheridan's property, but he could suddenly clearly see that there was a huge imbalance in their relationship. He'd opened himself to her, prioritized her over everyone, let Alfie get to know her, even told Ashley about her. In return, she still wasn't on his team. She'd been able to just cut him out of something this huge and see no problem in her priorities.

He'd thought that, for the first time in his life, someone had seen the real him; he'd have someone he could support who would love and support him back. Maybe that had been an unrealistic fantasy, but the little boy whose mother had left him with a monster of a father had clearly been too desperate for things to work out with Mae. So desperate that he'd read the situation—and her—all wrong.

"You inspired the whole plan," Mae said, her eyes wary now. "When we were talking about what I want to do and I said I wanted to make the world a better place and you said I should go for it." She threw out a hand. "Well, that's what this is."

His ears buzzed. Even aside from the personal element, there were layers to the corporate angle of this situation that he needed to address, and he had no idea where to even start.

"You idiot!" his father bellowed at Mae. "You have no idea what you've—"

Seb turned to his father and snarled, "You heard Sarah. You have no ground to stand on in attacking Mae. She's one hundred times the person you are, you pitiful excuse for a human being."

His father straightened to his full height, seeming to swell to the size of a much larger man. Seb had seen the same move countless times in his life, and it suddenly struck him that he was done. Done with his father, done with this company, done with everything.

Done.

There was no way he was going to stand side by side with his father against Mae. In fact, he didn't want to be on the same side as his father at all. His father had never been on his team. The only team Seb had was with Alfie.

He held up a hand. "Before you say anything, listen, because you may as well save your breath. I'm out. I'll hand over the projects I'm in the middle of to the team, and then I'm walking out that door. And once I've gone, I don't ever want to see you again."

His father's face was scarlet, his breath audible. "You can't walk out!" he yelled. "This company is our family legacy."

"I don't want it," Seb said and slid his hands into his pockets.

"If you leave," his father said, his face turning ugly, "I'll disinherit you. Cut you and that crying baby of yours out of my will entirely."

"Great." The relief he suddenly felt was dizzying. "Then at least we're clear about that."

His father stepped toward him with a raised arm, his eyes bulging, face so red it was starting to look purple. "You ungrateful—"

Sarah jumped between them. "Christopher!"

His gaze slid down to Sarah's, and he drew in an unsteady breath. "Sarah," he said, his voice cracking on her name, "you—"

"There is *nothing* you could say that I want to hear. It's time you left." She swung her arm and pointed at the door.

His father shot a baffled look around the room. "But this is my—"

"Out," she said, and with only another moment's hesitation, he left.

After he went through the door, no one moved or said anything for a long moment. Seb was reeling. He'd just crashed and burned his career, and given up the company he'd planned on leaving Alfie one day. His father appeared to still be in love with Sarah, and Mae's family hated Seb more than ever.

Worst of all, Mae had undermined him, and he'd realized their entire relationship had been one-sided. He glanced down, half expecting flames to burst through the floors.

Sarah blew out a breath. "I think we should get going." She headed for the door, then paused, with a hand on the doorjamb. "Good luck, Sebastian."

"Yeah, I have places to be," Heath said and followed his aunt.

"Sebastian," Mae said softly from his side. "I'm sorry."

He couldn't look at her. He knew that if he saw her,

he'd fall at her feet and accept any crumbs of attention that she was willing to throw his way, and he couldn't live like that.

"I know," he said through a tight jaw, forcing a smile. "Look, I have a lot to do here. I need to tie things up and hand projects over, say goodbye to the staff, and a million other things."

"Do you want me to go?"

His heart screamed *no*, but following his heart for the first time in his life had led to this mess. He'd always tried to keep his heart protected—only Alfie had really breached its defenses. Then along came a brunette with an Australian accent and an infectiously positive attitude to life and, without hesitation, he'd handed her his still-beating heart and thrown a grenade into his life.

What would that life even look like now? And, more importantly, *who was he* without his grandfather's company? He'd lived and breathed Bellavista Holdings since he was old enough to say the words. And he had no idea where to even start finding those answers.

The only thing he knew for sure was his devotion to Alfie.

"That would probably be best," he said, still not looking up as she slipped out the door.

# Eleven

That night, Mae sat at the marble-topped table Sebastian had reserved at a chic SoHo rooftop restaurant and straightened her napkin and cutlery again. He'd booked this place a couple of weeks ago, when things had been bright and sparkly between them. Now the timing seemed excruciating. In fact, she wasn't even certain that he was coming. She'd sent him several texts to confirm and he hadn't replied. She took a mouthful of the wine she'd ordered when she'd arrived.

She glanced past the lush greenery that spilled from pots and climbed posts, looking for a familiar tall frame. The sounds of glasses clinking and laughter from other tables blended with the soft bubbling from the water fountains, and all of it made the wriggling bundle of nerves in her stomach ratchet up several notches. Where was he?

Something had changed between them in his office today. She knew the moment it had happened—his features had morphed from confusion to granite, hard and cold. It had been more than cutting himself off from his father, something that they would have discussed and she could have comforted him about only yesterday. No, this was something concerning Sebastian and her, and she couldn't remember being this agonizingly worried about anything before, which, given her childhood, was saying something.

Movement in her peripheral vision snagged her attention, and then Sebastian was there, devastating in a charcoal jacket over a deep green shirt that set off his tan skin, his dark wavy hair sitting formally in place. His expression was troubled, and as their gazes met, he smiled with exquisite politeness.

"Sorry, I'm late," he said as he took his seat.

Nothing about his approach or lack of greeting eased her nerves. "Did you get Alfie to bed okay?"

Seb nodded. "He had a big day at a baby gym with Emily, so he crashed pretty quickly."

"Oh, good." So it wasn't Alfie that had held him up. "Do you want to order dinner or start with a cocktail?"

"We may as well jump straight to dinner," he said and picked up the menu.

It didn't appear that they were going to linger over their night. She'd already scanned the menu several times, so she used the time to surreptitiously observe him. Ocean-blue eyes flickering back and forth as he read the options, that beautiful mouth, which she'd felt all over her body, now tense and unyielding.

The waiter came and they placed their orders, and he filled Sebastian's glass from the bottle Mae had ordered. She sipped her wine, wondering how to break the tension.

"Mae," he said, looking at her properly for the first

time. "I apologize for my father. Yelling at you like that was inexcusable."

"I appreciate you saying that, but it's not your responsibility to apologize for him." She ran her finger through the condensation on the side of her wineglass. "I liked your defense of me." It had been worth having someone yell at her to hear his words.

*She's one hundred times the person you are.*

"It was true," he said and shifted his weight in his seat.

"Have you heard from your father since…" *The dumpster fire that I triggered in your office…*

He gave a curt shake of his head. "And I don't expect to. He's probably still in shock that I rejected the most important thing in his life." His broad shoulders lifted in a shrug. "Plus, he has nothing to hold over my head anymore, and he doesn't like any conversation where he's not automatically on top."

"Do you really think he'll cut you out of his will?" She'd been shocked at how quickly and easily that had happened.

"I'm certain of it. I'm literally no use to him anymore."

He didn't seem particularly worried. Six months ago, she'd been a teacher with no savings to speak of, and Sebastian had been the classic rich guy who'd inherit even more wealth, and now she was the one who'd inherited money beyond her dreams, and Sebastian was about to lose most of his. Sometimes the world was unpredictable.

There had been something else unexpected in that conversation. "You know, Christopher reacted weirdly to Sarah."

"That caught me by surprise," he said, leaning back in

his chair. "The only thing I can think of is that he's still in love with her after all these years."

The first time she'd met Christopher, he'd talked of Sarah. "He told me that when they were younger, he was conning her, and then he decided to tell her everything, and that's when she dumped him. So maybe it started as a con but he fell for his mark."

He took a sip of his wine and put the glass back on the table before replying, "Makes sense."

"Do you know what you'll do now?" she asked, wishing she could cross this divide of polite conversation.

"No idea, to be honest. I'll take some time and think it through." He looked at her and there was finally a glimmer of the real him showing, sharing something real, so she took a deep breath and forged ahead.

"Sebastian, what changed between us today? I know it was wrong to show up like that, and I wish I could take it back, that we could start today again. You were right that it turned into a test, but you have to believe that's not what I meant it to be."

He turned to look out over the expansive views and twinkling lights, but she had a feeling he wasn't seeing any of it. A slight breeze rumpled his hair, and she yearned to reach over and smooth it.

"You told me once," he finally said, turning back to her, "that you'd never had a committed relationship before, and I thought at the time that it would be me. I'd be the one you'd fall in love with and commit to." A deep groove appeared between his brows. "But I don't think it will be. Maybe it's the way you grew up, always keeping people on the outside of your core family. Not trusting anyone completely except Heath, and maybe now Sarah, and having to keep your guard up around everyone else. I wish it weren't this way, but I think I'll always be part of 'everyone else.'"

"How can you possibly think that?" she said, dumbfounded by the direction of his thoughts. *This* is what was troubling him? "I've let you in so much."

He pinned her with an intense stare. "Do you love me, Mae?"

She hesitated. How did you even know if you were in love? She had feelings for him, absolutely, but he was right that she'd never formed a deep attachment to anyone outside her family—they moved around far too often when she was growing up for that. So if she'd never loved before, how could she even recognize it now?

Sebastian nodded. "There's my answer. I've said from early on that I'd give you anything. *Everything.* But it hasn't been a two-way street, has it? You've wanted to keep things light between us, and I don't mind going slow if that's what you need, but, Mae, I don't get a sense that you truly believe we're going somewhere. You've been testing me in a range of ways since we met. Always asking if I'm conning you, or trying to trip me up, or bringing your brother to my office to demand to see an old document. I can't build a life with someone who's always expecting the worst of me. I've had two parents who saw me that way. It would destroy me to spend my life with someone else who did."

Her stomach turned. "I don't think the worst of you. I think you're amazing."

"Can you really deny it?" he challenged. "Deny that every time something happened between us, that your first thought was you couldn't trust me for some reason? That I was trying to con you or manipulate you in some way?"

She ran back through the time they'd been together, and her doubts, and her fears about trusting him, and she had to admit that it was true—every time something had happened, she'd questioned his motivations, either in her head or by asking him directly. And, looking at it from his perspective, that had been grossly unfair. He was a good man, and he'd shown her over and over that he could be trusted.

"I'll do better." She leaned forward and reached for his hand across the table. He took it and squeezed her fingers, holding tight. "I can change."

"I have Alfie, Mae," he said and released her hand. "Taking on a serious relationship based on a promise that the other person can change is a risk I can't take. He's already lost his mother. I don't want to be casual with you for a couple of years, have Alfie come to love you and then find that I don't pass some test you've given me, and you leave. Alfie would be devastated all over again."

Panic was rising from her toes all the way up through her body, and she swallowed hard, trying to contain it. Was he really saying that it was over? That *they* were over?

"Where does that leave us?" she asked and bit down on her lip to stop it from trembling. "Do you still love me?"

He sighed, and it was a bone-deep, sad and weary sound. "I can't turn it off like a faucet, so yes, I still love you. But this relationship isn't going to work for me. We need to end things here, tonight."

Her chest started to crumble in on itself, folding into blackness, disappearing, threatening to suck down and destroy her.

Sebastian's cell sounded from his jacket pocket. He never ignored a call when Alfie wasn't with him, so she wasn't surprised when he drew it out and looked at the screen.

"It's my father's number," he said, frowning, but he didn't move to take the call.

"Are you going to answer it?"

"Can't see the point," he said, and his finger moved to dismiss the call.

"Answer," she said quickly. "Don't get caught in regret later. If he acts like a jerk, then disconnect, but at least answer." Sebastian had already lost so much today. If there was a chance that his father had realized what he'd done and wanted to make amends, then she didn't want Sebastian to miss the opportunity to lose one less thing.

He frowned at her, looked down at his screen, and then answered.

Mae tried to give him some privacy by looking at the panoramic view, but his voice, unusually staccato, broke through. He was already standing as he disconnected.

"What's wrong?" she asked.

"The hospital found my number on my father's phone when they were looking for a next of kin. He's had a heart attack. He's not conscious but they're working on him."

"Oh, God."

"Look, I have to go." He moved around to her chair and bent to press a kiss to her cheek. "If you need me, you know where to reach me."

"It's not like we won't ever see each other—you have a house next door to my aunt's," she said lightly, unable to bear the tension surrounding them.

He gave her a tight smile. "Be happy, Mae."

And then he left, taking a part of her with him.

* * *

Mae made it home and checked a few rooms before she found Sarah in her favorite blue wingback.

"Hey, sweetheart," her aunt said. "How was your dinner?"

Ducking the question for now, Mae crouched beside the chair. "I know you don't like Christopher much, but given your complicated history, you should know that he's had a heart attack and has been taken to hospital. Sebastian is on his way there now."

Sarah's eyebrows shot up, then she let out a breath. "I'm sad to hear it, but it's been a long time since I loved, or even liked, Christopher Newport."

"I think he loved you too," she said, thinking back over the conversation with Sebastian. "Maybe even still does."

Sarah smiled sadly. "Love is wanting more for the other person than you do for yourself."

That sounded borderline unhealthy. She might not know what love was, but it couldn't all be about giving and not looking after yourself. Sebastian had just ended things with her for his own sake, and she didn't doubt at all that he loved her.

"Surely, that's not true," she said, thinking it through. "Well, maybe it is, but it's only part of the truth. Love is more complicated than that. Heath and Freya prioritize each other, but they also prioritize themselves. That's why they work so well together."

Sarah tipped her head in acknowledgment. "Heath and Freya are two of the lucky ones."

Mae moved across to a small sofa and sank into the cushions there. "Can I ask you something? It feels a bit out of line, maybe too personal."

"You can absolutely ask." She picked up a mug from a side table, took a sip, and replaced it. "I reserve the right to not answer, but I can't imagine anything I won't tell you."

"Have you been in love with Lauren for all these years?"

Sarah stilled, her eyes going big and round like those of an owl. "That's a strange question."

"You're not together, are you?" Mae asked, suddenly worried she'd put her foot in it and was talking about a relationship that they were trying to keep secret.

"*Lauren and me?* Of course not." Her eyes slid to the door and back. "Why would you think that?"

"But you're in love with her," Mae said, even more sure. Sebastian had been the only one to see it. The kid who'd had no love in his life had grown into a man who could spot love when no one else could.

And offer it to someone as undeserving as her.

Sarah fixed her with a stern glare. "It would be very inappropriate for me, as her employer, to have feelings for her."

"Freya told me about her father, that Lauren was the family's housekeeper, and when they found out she was pregnant, Freya's biological father and his wife kicked Lauren out."

"Asshole." Sarah scowled. "Heath fixed that situation a few months ago, though."

"I heard that too, but also that you fixed things for Lauren at the time. Took her in when she was pregnant, gave her a job as your chauffeur, and yelled at her former boss until he agreed to pay child support for Freya."

Sarah smiled. "Ah, that was a satisfying day."

"And," Mae said, bringing her point home, "that's why you've never told her that you love her, isn't it?"

Sarah opened her mouth, clearly about to deny it, and then appeared to give in. She lifted her mug and took another mouthful, this time keeping the mug in her hands. "She's already had to put up with the advances of one boss—she certainly doesn't need that in her life again."

That was a reasonable position to take, except that—depending on how long it had taken them to fall in love—it might have been twenty years, maybe even twenty-five or more. That amount of pining should be illegal. Logic was the key, though. If Sarah could be swayed by pure emotion, she would have said something already.

*Love is wanting more for the other person than you do for yourself.*

Mae's heart broke a little more, thinking of Sarah being in love with Lauren for most of the time that Mae had been alive, seeing her every day, and loving her so much that she'd rather Lauren was comfortable and safe in her job.

"You have a very different power dynamic between you," Mae said, tucking her feet underneath her legs. "You're good friends. And she'd know that if she didn't return your feelings, her job wouldn't be at risk."

Sarah looked shocked. "Of course it wouldn't be at risk."

"Then tell her." While her own heart was raw and bleeding, she needed to see at least one other couple finding happiness. "What have you got to lose?"

"Have you told Sebastian that you love him?" Sarah said pointedly.

She recognized an attempt at diversion when she saw

one. She and Heath were the masters at diversion—they'd practiced it most of their lives whenever someone asked an awkward question about their history. "That's different."

"Oh, is it?" Her aunt narrowed her eyes. "Please do tell."

Mae looked at her aunt, her face so similar to the one she saw in the mirror each day, and gave up. It would be good to tell someone. "We've already tried a relationship, but it exploded."

"Oh, Mae. I'm sorry." Sarah pushed to her feet and joined Mae on the small sofa, placing an arm around her shoulders. "But he knows you love him, right?"

"How do you know I do?" she asked, curious. Why would Sarah think that if Mae hadn't been sure?

Sarah grinned. "That defense you mounted for him today. That came from a place of love."

Mae digested that. It might not be a perfect definition of love, but, she really did need to be honest with herself—whatever definition she used, she absolutely, one hundred percent, completely loved Sebastian. Hell of a time to realize it, obviously.

She rested her head on Sarah's shoulder. "I do love him, and, no, I haven't told him. In fact, I didn't even reply when he point-blank asked me at dinner tonight." She winced at the memory. "He's been much smarter and braver about it than I have."

"I was wrong about him." Sarah stroked a hand over Mae's hair. "Maybe I was too caught up in my distrust of his father, but I saw the way he looked at you today, the way he defended you to his father. The same way you defended him to us. That man loves you, and he has a good heart."

A tear slipped out the corner of Mae's eye, and then another. She swiped them away, but they were coming too thick and fast, so she spoke through them. "It's too late. He ended things with me tonight."

Sarah sat with her until the tears stopped and then twisted to face her. "You said he's at the hospital with Christopher?"

"Yes, he was heading over when I came up here," she said, scrubbing at her face with the inside of her wrist.

"Regardless of what happened at dinner tonight, they have no other family, so Sebastian has no one."

Mae had been thinking about that after she left the restaurant, but had decided she was the last person he'd want to see. Now that she'd released some of her emotions, though, she could see more clearly. She needed to check on him. If he didn't want her there, she'd leave. But she couldn't leave him alone at the hospital.

She drew in a shuddering breath and stood. "On my way. And you have someone to talk to as well."

Sarah opened her mouth, as if to deflect again, then closed it and nodded.

Mae smiled.

She caught a taxi, and, when she arrived at the hospital, searched through the emergency department until she spotted him. Her heart tripped over itself at the sight of him. How had she ever doubted that she loved him? He had his head in his hands, so he didn't see her approach.

She plopped down onto the seat beside him. "Today has been wild."

Startled, he looked up. "Okay, you have to stop ambushing me or there will be two Newport men in there with heart attacks."

"Any news?" She bumped his shoulder with hers, offering support but trying to keep the boundaries he'd set.

"No." He flipped his hand over to reveal his cell. "They said they'd call when they have news or he's stable enough for a visitor, but where else can I go?"

"Let's go outside and get some air." She stood and held out a hand, and, after a quick glance at the doors to the treatment rooms, he took it.

They walked outside into a warm summer night.

"Not that I don't appreciate you coming," he said after a couple of minutes, "but why are you here? We left things between us in a fairly final place."

"Same reason you're here for your father." She stopped so she could see his beautiful face. "We're the same about that—we show up when people need us, regardless."

He held her gaze for a heavy moment and then pulled her into a hug. "Thank you."

They strolled in silence for a few more minutes until Sebastian let out a long sigh. "He probably doesn't even want me here. It's less than a day since he said he was disinheriting me, but he's my only family. I'm not even sure where my mother is living now, so, besides Alfie, he's the only family I have left."

"Families are complicated," she said, and given their entangled circumstances, she knew it was an understatement. "He's a horrible human being, but he's still your father, the man who raised you, so you're bound to be conflicted."

"Thank you for understanding." He cupped the side of her face with his large palm. "You always do."

She sucked her bottom lip into her mouth, keeping herself steady at the warm contact of his hand on her face, and waited until he dropped the hand and shoved it into his trouser pocket before she let herself take another full breath. They set off walking again, and she said, "Hey, here's some news for you."

He coughed out a laugh. "Not sure I can handle any more news."

"You'll like this one. You were right about Sarah and Lauren. Well, from Sarah's side anyway. I nudged her a bit—"

"I can imagine," he said, smiling.

"—and she's going to tell Lauren how she feels." It was the one bright spot in this wretched day.

"You've done a good thing, Mae. After seeing them together, there's no way it's one-sided. I'm glad for them."

"Me too." And since Sarah was going to tell Lauren how she felt, Mae needed to do the same. "This is really crappy timing, but there's something I need to say too."

He shrugged, as if resigned. "Go on then."

"You asked me at the restaurant if I loved you and I didn't reply straight away. That's because I'm not always great at recognizing how I feel about things." She stopped walking again and he stopped too, watching her intently. "But I do. I love you, Sebastian. So much."

He reached for her and pulled her face to his, their lips crashing in a kiss that was hungry and desperate, and she melted against him. Her brain was trying not to read anything into the kiss because the day had been turbulent, and it was just a kiss, after all, but her heart was full of hope. They broke away and he rested his forehead against hers as they caught their breath.

"Is there any chance for us?" she whispered.

He squeezed his eyes shut tightly and stepped back.

"All my life I've had my guard up, even with Ashley. Always waiting for someone to leave or kick me while I'm down. I have no idea why I let you in so easily, but now that my guard is up again, I don't think I can bring it back down. I am sure I don't want to. I love you, Mae, but I can't spend my life constantly proving myself to you."

That was fair. It might break her heart but she couldn't blame him for needing to protect himself and his precious son.

His cell chirruped in his pocket and, lightning fast, he had it out and at his ear. She watched the conversation, watched the color drain from his face, and then he disconnected and carefully put the cell back in his pocket.

"Sebastian?" she said gently.

"It was too late." He looked at her, his eyes wide and unseeing. "They couldn't save him."

She pulled him close and wrapped her arms around him. "I'm so sorry."

"This doesn't seem real." He rubbed his hands over his face, as if trying to wake himself up. "And it's all so messy, I don't know what I'm supposed to feel."

She took his hands and held them between hers. "There's no 'supposed to' in these situations. How do you feel?"

"Numb."

"That's probably normal." Unlike Sebastian and his father, Mae had been very close to her mother, and when she died after being hit by a car, Mae had felt numb for days.

He looked back at the hospital over his shoulder. "They said I could go inside and say goodbye and collect his personal things."

"You want me to come with you?"

He released her hands and stepped back, his face blank. He stuffed his hands into his pockets. "I think I should do this alone."

She'd expected that, and she tried not to care that it stung, because he really did need some time alone to say goodbye to his father. "Call if you need anything."

He nodded, turned, and left.

She watched him walk away from this little moment outside time, and wondered if she'd ever feel this close to Sebastian Newport again.

# Twelve

Mae stepped out of the elevator at Bellavista Holdings just over a week later, surrounded by her aunt, her brother and future sister-in-law, and one of their lawyers. An invitation had arrived a couple of hours ago to attend a meeting in the boardroom. The message was from Rosario, and she'd apologized for the short notice and said they could bring along anyone they wanted, but mentioned nothing about the reason for the meeting. After a quick conversation, they'd decided that whatever the meeting was about, having Freya's forensic accounting brain and one lawyer would be useful, so Heath had rung Freya at work and asked if she could get away for a couple of hours, and Sarah had organized one of her lawyers to attend.

That left Mae to stew in her own thoughts. She hadn't seen Sebastian since the night at the hospital—the night his father had died. She'd composed hundreds of texts in her head since then, even started typing several of them, but had deleted them all. He'd made the decision to stay apart and she had to respect that, no matter how wrong it felt or how much she physically yearned to be near him.

Rosario was there waiting, and they had a quick, catch-up conversation as she showed them into the boardroom. She'd missed Rosario. Sebastian's assistant had become a good friend, and she was sorry to lose that.

Once in the boardroom, Rosario took Mae to a place beside the head of the table that had a coffee waiting. "Grande Americano. That's right, isn't it?"

Mae laughed and hugged her, saying, "Perfectly right, thank you," and took her seat. Heath, Freya, Sarah, and their lawyer all sat in a row beside her.

Within minutes, Sebastian entered, and her heart swooped and then clenched tight in her chest. He looked as commanding and in control as that first day in his office, and her body ached for all she'd lost. He was followed by a group of six women and men in suits, most she recognized from when she was shadowing Sebastian, but she couldn't remember any names. Like the suits at the first meeting she'd attended in this room, they were all matching in their attire and their severe, slicked-back hair, and all looked smart, dispassionate, and focused.

Sebastian took the seat beside her, at the head of the oval table, and for a suspended moment, she was paralyzed with longing. His profile was heartbreakingly beautiful—how had she forgotten how beautiful it was? His woodsy cologne drifted over to surround her, teasing her senses, and his mouth moved to form words to the person on his other side, but she didn't hear any of them. All she could do was drink him in. And try to stop her hand from reaching out to touch the fire that burned so brightly from within him that it warmed her from where she was sitting.

Then he swung around and caught her gaze, and for a moment so tiny, so brief that she almost missed it, his eyes filled with pained longing that matched her own, then disappeared as his features smoothed out.

"Mae," he said, his voice as steady as a rock. Then looked beside her. "Heath. Thank you for coming. I know it was short notice." His gaze traveled to the others in her group, and he greeted them one by one, and she was glad, because she wouldn't have been able to get her voice to work—not without it giving away every foolish and messy thought inside her.

Sebastian shook out his wrists, bringing her attention to his strong, tan hands against the snowy white of his shirt cuffs, and leaned his forearms on the table as he took control of the meeting.

"I'm sure you're all aware that my father threatened to disinherit me," he said, and the room fell into deathly silence. "There's a chance he would have followed through, but he died before he could, so we'll never know." He paused, swallowed, then continued. "All we can do is move forward, and that means I've inherited his half share in Bellavista Holdings. The other 50 percent, of course, is jointly owned by Mae and Heath."

There was nodding around the table, and Sebastian made brief eye contact with everyone on her side. "Because of the way things were left with my father, I considered selling my share. Drawing a line under it. The company, and the rift between the descendants of the original owners, has caused too much pain over the generations." He looked over at Sarah and they exchanged a nod of acknowledgment.

"Instead," he said, straightening, "I'm bringing you a proposal today to turn this company and its capital into a force for good.

"Someone asked me a question recently, a question that was so sensible, so obvious, that it's replayed in my mind ever since. It was this—do you ever think about the world you're leaving for Alfie and want to do something good?"

Mae bit back a gasp, peeking around to see if anyone had realized it was her question, but they were all transfixed by Sebastian. Her pulse thudded in her ears as she turned back to him, desperate to know where he was taking this.

"The answer I found is that I want Alfie to grow up in a better world. Also, after just losing my father, I've done a lot of soul-searching about the sort of father I want to be. I want Alfie to grow up with a dad who sees the world the way good people see it." He glanced down at her, his mouth quirking at the corners. "The way Mae Dunstan sees it."

He held her gaze and she couldn't look away. The air was completely sucked from the room, and she couldn't draw breath, and the terrible truth was that she didn't care. As long as Sebastian was looking at her, as long as she was looking at him, within touching distance, nothing else mattered.

Heath cleared his throat. "So what's your proposal?"

Mae tore her gaze away and looked down at her hands crossed on the notepad.

"I want to change the company's vision statement to center on projects that improve quality of life in tangible ways. The perfect example of this new model would be purchasing Laurence Sheridan's property, which sits in a neighborhood that needs more communal spaces, and building a multilevel playground for the local children."

He drew something from his pocket, and the screen behind him flared to life, showing drawings of an amazing playground, with slides and swings, but also, a four-story wooden fort, with rope netting instead of walls, and interior stairs, climbing poles, and slides. Beside the fort was a metal climbing pyramid that was at least half as high, with a spiderweb of rope in all directions to make paths for a child's ascent. "These are initial ideas, and the plan is for the designers and architects to work with local children on the final design before commencing work."

"Good God," Freya whispered from the other side of Heath.

"In Mae's original idea, the plot would also have a community center. Our planner—" he nodded to a woman at the far end of the table "—suggested using the entire plot for the playground to maximize the opportunity, and buy a separate space for the Evelyne O'Donohue Community Center." Another slide flashed up behind him with a drawing of a welcoming building that had her mother's name emblazoned across the front, and she heard Heath's breath catch.

She looked from the screen to Sebastian and back again. He was still talking, and she tried to take it all in, her eyes swimming with the tears she was trying to blink back.

"Of course," he said, flicking the slide to one with graphs and numbers, "this is one idea, an example of the type of project the company would take on. To carry this out, we might take a commission from a charitable trust, or we might take it on as a pro bono case."

One of the suits took over and started explaining financial specifics, and Freya asked a couple of money-related questions, but Mae wasn't listening to any of it. Sebastian had turned everything around because of something she'd said? Her entire body trembled with the enormity of it.

She scribbled a note on the paper in front of her and slid it to him.

*Did you call me sensible?*

He subtly took the paper without looking away from the discussion in front of him. After a few seconds, he glanced down, saw her note, and scrawled something with his strong left hand beside it, and passed it back to her.

*Very sensible. You're starting to blend in with all those suits on the other side of the table.*

She smothered a grin and wrote her reply in big letters across the bottom of the page.

*You take that back.*

He looked at her then, and she was in danger of drowning in his blue, blue eyes. The meeting, the rapid-fire questions that were being asked and answered around the room faded away, and all there was in her entire world was Sebastian.

Someone called his name and he jerked, as if pulled from a trance. He turned to the suits and elaborated on a point that needed clarification, then he wrote on the notepad and slid it over to her.

*It's good to see you, Mae.*

He faced the table again and cleared his throat, and the other conversations died down. "That's the crux of it. Obviously, there's more that needs to be discussed and worked out, but I wanted to share the overall vision with you now. I realize it's very different to the company's past, but I'm committed to this new direction. I'll understand if you don't want to be part of it—profits will obviously go down. If you're not on board, I'd be happy to talk about buying you out, or we could split the company in two and I'll take my smaller company in this direction."

Mae looked at Heath beside her, then at the others on her team. Freya gave a subtle nod, meaning that the numbers at this early stage had passed her assessment. Sarah's eyes were wide and sparkling, and the corner of her mouth was hitched up, so she clearly approved. The lawyer gave a noncommittal head tilt, which she took to mean that there were no red flags. Finally, her gaze landed on her brother. They were literally half a world away from where they'd been less than a year ago, in an Australian beachside town, living as a bar owner and a teacher. They'd gone from just the two of them against the world, to Heath planning a life with Freya, having their aunt Sarah in their corner, and joining the large O'Donohue family. The enormity of the changes in such a short time made her head spin. But in this moment, it was just the two of them again, brother and sister, deciding their path forward. Did they focus on building more money that they didn't need, or did they join Sebastian in making the world a better place? There was no doubt in Mae's mind what the right path was, but Heath owned the shares with her and had a say about it.

Her brother's dark gaze softened, and he leaned over to whisper in her ear, "Your call."

Mae straightened her shoulders and turned back to the man she loved, bursting with pride for him. "The Rutherford-Dunstan side of the company would be thrilled to work with you in transforming Bellavista Holdings into your vision of what it could be."

A slow smile crept over Sebastian's face and her heart lurched in her chest.

"Thank you," he said, and she knew that was for her alone, for believing in him, the way he'd just shown he believed in her. Then he looked down the line at the others on her side of the table. "Just to be clear, the profits are going to slump to a trickle. We can still take on projects that will make us money if they also fit our new company vision, but I can't guarantee that stream of income."

Heath shrugged. "We have enough to live on already. This is what we want to do."

Sarah leaned forward. "My involvement as the executor of my brother's estate is all but over, but if you're looking for another investor in this new Bellavista Holdings, then I'm very open to that discussion."

The meeting wound up and, as her group was leaving, she tried to catch Sebastian's eye, but he was busy with the suits tightly crowded around him. Sarah linked her elbow through Mae's, and with a last look over her shoulder, Mae left the building, her head spinning.

Lauren was waiting on the curb with Sarah's black town car and the others started to pile in. "I think I'll walk," Mae said.

"You sure?" Heath asked beside her.

She nodded. "I need a moment to clear my head."

"Okay." He grabbed the door to lower himself in, then turned back and gave her a lopsided smile. "I like him," he said, then he was gone.

She filled her lungs with the New York air, the sounds and the pollution, the buzzing energy, and the sparkle, and started to walk.

Her cell vibrated in her pocket. She took it out and saw Sebastian's name.

Where are you?

She glanced around.

About two buildings north of yours. I'm walking.

The reply was immediate.

Wait there.

With trembling fingers, she slipped the cell back into her pocket.

In an impossibly short time, she heard her name being called, and she turned to find him approaching, slowing from a jog to a walk, breathing heavily. He'd left his suit jacket somewhere behind, and his face was flushed from exertion.

"Did you run all that way?" she asked, confused.

"I might have." He rested his hands on his hips as he caught his breath. "Including the stairs, when the elevator was taking too long."

She smothered a smile. "You told me to wait, so there was no need to rush. I was right here. Waiting."

"There was a need," he said. He speared his fingers through his hair, leaving the dark waves rumpled. "I'd hoped to talk to you at the end of the meeting, but I turned around and you were gone."

Maybe she should have waited, but just because he'd changed his mind about the company didn't mean he thought any differently about her.

"It was a good meeting, Sebastian. A good proposal."

One side of his mouth hitched up. "You liked it?"

"I've never been prouder of anyone in my life than I was of you in that meeting today." Her chest swelled just remembering what he'd done, what he'd achieved in so little time, and what he wanted to do.

"Mae, I…" His voice trailed off and he turned to look at the traffic for what felt like an excruciatingly long time before looking back at her again. "I can't believe how badly I screwed up things between us. You should have been allowed to question me, to double-check things until you felt you could trust me, and I—"

She laid a hand on his arm, interrupting him. "No, Sebastian. You were right to call me out on that. My childhood was a training ground in the art of being suspicious, and then I landed in the middle of an ongoing feud between two families. That was a bad combination—a perfect storm."

"And I knew those things." He grabbed her hand from his arm, lacing their fingers together, and then let their joined hands hang across the space between them. "I should have been more patient, or…something."

"It wouldn't have helped. I was trapped in that spiral and couldn't even see through it enough to realize that it *was* a trap. And you caught the brunt of it all. I'm surprised you put up with it for as long as you did. You've been a saint."

He huffed out a laugh. "Hardly."

"Regardless, I'm glad you called me on it, or we'd still be stuck inside that spiral." Being with him now felt different. Even though they were just standing on the pavement, talking, her shoulders felt lighter with the freedom to trust him as her instincts had told her to all along. Her guard wasn't up, not even a little bit, because she knew that no matter what happened from here, she'd never need it around Sebastian.

"So, you don't doubt my motives for today?" He cocked his head, watching her closely. "Think I might have an ulterior plan?"

"Honestly, it didn't even cross my mind. Not once. I can see your heart, Sebastian." She placed her free hand on the left side of his chest, feeling the steady thump-thump beneath her palm. "You were showing me right from the start. You showed me who you were, and I'm sorry I didn't see clearly then. But I see it now. The real Sebastian is shining from your eyes. It's in the way you care for Alfie. The way you went straight to the hospital despite the appalling way your father treated you your whole life. It's in the way you were open enough to new ideas that you changed the whole damn company. It's in the way you've treated me every second we've been together. Your heart is huge, Sebastian. And I trust it."

"Thank you," he said, his voice hoarse, and he captured the hand that sat on his chest so their four joined hands formed a cross between them.

The way he was looking at her now, the way he was holding both her hands tightly, it was dangerous. It was letting a glimmer of hope spark back to life. "You," she began, but her voice shook, so she stopped and tried again. "You told me I could ask for anything…?"

His gaze didn't waver. "That still stands. You ask, and I promise I'll give it to you."

"I want a life with you. With you and Alfie. Everything else is negotiable, as long as we're together."

She felt a shudder run through his body and watched him close his eyes tight for a long moment. "Done." He leaned forward and brushed the gentlest of kisses on her lips. "The easiest promise to fulfill, because it's what I want too. Though I have to warn you that my negotiation skills are highly tuned, so get ready for some intense rounds of talks at the kitchen table. Where we live, who cooks dinner, what we watch on TV, where we vacation—"

"I'm not worried." She raised one brow. "I have bargaining chips."

"That you do," he said and released one hand to snake around her back and draw her closer for another kiss. This one was deeper, needier, and she felt the dampness on her cheeks from her own tears at the sheer joy of kissing him again.

Even once the kiss ended, they stayed tangled together, and she rested her head on his chest, her arms tight around his waist, luxuriating in the feel of him.

"You know," she said as a thought occurred to her, "I never did get to see that dossier about myself."

"It's outdated," he said, shrugging. "I'll write you a new one."

She arched her neck back so she could see his face. "What would it say?"

He didn't hesitate. "Mae Dunstan is a woman who is not at all sensible yet is quite often the most sensible person in the room." He cupped the side of her face with his palm. "She has dimples in her cheeks and starlight in her eyes, and my love for her is bigger than I thought love could possibly be." He dropped a kiss on her nose. "I'd accompany the written report with a photo of you in that lilac wraparound dress you wore to your brother's engagement dinner. Tell me you still have that dress."

"Of course I do. It's my favorite dress." It reminded her of Sebastian. She made a mental note to wear the dress again soon. "That's a good dossier report, but it needs a matching piece. One on you."

A group of people bumped them as they pushed past, but Sebastian barely seemed to notice. "What would it say?"

She thought for a moment. "Sebastian Newport is a serious businessman who sometimes surprises everyone by making unbusinesslike decisions. He has eyes the color of the ocean and a mouth that's pure, sculpted perfection, and my love for him is deep and trusting and endless. I'd accompany it with a photo of you with your blue shirt unbuttoned and your tie askew."

He frowned, as if confused. "You forgot a voice like melted chocolate."

A laugh gurgled up and burst from her throat. "You remember that?"

"I remember every compliment you ever gave me, Mae. To be fair, there weren't that many, so it's not hard. Mostly, you described me with words like nefarious," he said, his expression angelic.

"Hey, that one was yours. But point taken. If it helps, there was pretty much a constant stream of complimentary thoughts in my head. I'll have to remember to start saying them aloud."

He chuckled, shaking his head. "I love you, Mae."

"I love you more," she said and kissed him, ignoring all the bustling people on the sidewalk and the traffic noise and everything else except Sebastian.

# Epilogue

Mae carried two pies out the back door of Sarah's Hamptons house, Alfie darting around her feet. Alfie's third birthday party was underway—her mother's family and Alfie's grandparents had all made the trip, so the backyard next door was packed. To make up for asking people to come this far out from Manhattan, they'd offered everyone beds for the night. Fortunately, between them, they had enough space. Around the time they'd married, Heath and Freya had offered the neighbors on either side of them exorbitant sums of money to sell so they could have a strip of three houses in the family. Both owners had refused, but the people with the place across the street had heard the story and stopped by. The house's owners had made a good profit, and Heath and Freya had landed a home over the road from the rest of the family. Sarah and Lauren spent a lot of time in the Hamptons now, and since Freya had given birth to their baby girl, Stella, she, Heath, and the baby had been out here a lot too. So Mae and Sebastian tried to get out as often as they could.

Her cell dinged, and with a bit of juggling, she saw the message from Sebastian.

Where are you? Amanda and Barry want to see Alfie.

She smiled and wrote her reply with one thumb.

On my way back. At hedge gate.

Sarah and Lauren caught up to her, their hands linked and their faces radiating the joy of new love. Well, love that was new in the sense that it had been over two decades in the making.

"Need any help?" Sarah asked.

Mae threw her a grateful smile. "Amanda and Barry are looking for Alfie."

"On it," Lauren said and held out a hand to the little boy. "Come on, Alfie, let's find your grandparents."

"*Yesss*!" Alfie said and grabbed both the hands offered.

Mae watched them walk through the little gate, her heart so full it barely fit in her chest. Alfie's happiness, Sarah and Lauren finally finding each other, that little gate…

After she'd moved in with Sebastian, she'd found a pair of pruning shears and cut a hole in the shrubbery, around the exact spot where she and Sebastian had had their first ever conversation. The gap had been just big enough to squeeze through—it was harder work to cut through a thick hedge than she'd expected—but she'd been happy with her work. Soon after, Sebastian had widened the opening and installed a cute little wrought-iron gate. Mae loved that gate. It wasn't just about the ease of access, it was symbolic of this large family—*her* large family. A shortcut to her aunt next door, with her brother and his wife just across the street. She had more people she loved, and who loved her, than she'd ever dreamed possible. Sebastian, too, had gone from a unit of just him, his son, and his father, to losing that one parent and now being surrounded by this chaotic, loving extended family.

Heath and Freya appeared with a sleeping Stella resting on Freya's chest, snuggled tightly in a wrap, and Mae's heart melted a little more.

"Hey," Heath said, "Sebastian was looking for you."

"I spoke to him," she said, her gaze still on her sweet little niece. "He wanted Alfie for Amanda and Barry. Sarah and Lauren have taken him through."

Heath edged closer. "Can I help with those pies?"

"I'm fine—" she began, but Heath took them anyway.

"What are they?" He took a deep sniff. "One cherry and one…?"

"Apple." Alfie's favorite. "A special request from the birthday boy."

"Excellent," he said as he turned and headed back to the party.

Knowing the birthday boy's uncle would get the first slice, Mae shared a look with Freya.

Freya raised an upturned palm. "Sometimes I think it's his newfound obsession with pie, not me, that keeps him in the country."

Mae laughed, partly because it was so ludicrous— anyone who saw the way Heath and Freya looked at each other knew the truth. Even so, she slid Freya a sly grin. "Let's hope he never has to choose."

"Let's hope," Freya said, smiling, and followed her husband back to the festivities.

Alone for the first time that day, Mae took a moment to look over the party, feeling like the luckiest person in the world.

Her cell pinged.

Happy?

A buzz zipped through her bloodstream at the sight of Sebastian's name on her screen.

Very.

Close your eyes.

She did as he asked but couldn't keep the smile from spreading across her face.

Within moments, she felt his arms slide around her waist and she leaned back into his solid strength. She'd never had a home with long-term security and stability. In the circle of Sebastian's arms, though, she'd found her home.

"How happy?" he murmured at her ear.

Her eyes drifted closed. "Deliriously."

"Me too," he said and kissed her temple. "Which got me thinking. We said we'd wait to talk about having another child until Alfie was used to you and the new arrangement."

She nodded. It had been one of their negotiations about what they wanted from their future. "When everyone else is used to it too, especially Amanda and Barry."

"And they are inside right now telling everyone that you're their daughter-in-law. Though there's some debate, especially among your cousins, about whether you're actually a daughter-in-law-in-law."

Mae laced her fingers through his. Ashley's parents had been grieving a daughter, and Mae had been missing her mother. They'd quickly bonded. Mae had gone from growing up with only a mother and a brother, and then just having a brother, to now also having honorary parents-in-law, her aunt Sarah and Lauren, a sister-in-law in Freya, her mother's large family, and best of all, Sebastian and Alfie—the loves of her life.

"So," Sebastian said, "I'm ready."

The world stilled. She turned in his arms. "You are?"

"Whenever you want to start trying for a little sibling for Alfie, I'm ready."

She stood on her tiptoes and kissed him. A breeze danced around them and the leaves of the shrubbery rustled, and Mae felt completely at peace. She had family and a life here—she had roots—and would never need to run again. And more than that, she had a future.

"I'm ready too," she said. "But for now, let's go back to our guests. We're missing out on all the fun."

"And the apple pie," Sebastian said. "Let's find out if your brother left some for anyone else."

They stepped out of the gap in the hedge, into their own backyard and their future. Together.

\* \* \* \* \*

# MILLS & BOON

## *Desire*

# IS COMING TO AN END

**From January 2024, Mills & Boon will no longer publish books in the Desire series.**

Check out our other series, featuring billionaires, royals, and stories of sizzling seduction.

Whether you love an enemies-to-lovers romance or fake dating, a marriage of convenience and everything in between, we've got a romance for every reader.

## millsandboon.co.uk

# COMING
# SOON!

We really hope you enjoyed reading this book.
If you're looking for more romance
be sure to head to the shops when
new books are available on

## Thursday 4th
## January

To see which titles are coming soon, please visit
**millsandboon.co.uk/nextmonth**

MILLS & BOON

# afterglow BOOKS

**Introducing our newest series, Afterglow.**

From showing up to glowing up, Afterglow characters are on the path to leading their best lives and finding romance along the way – with a dash of sizzling spice!

Follow characters from all walks of life as they chase their dreams and find that true love is only the beginning...

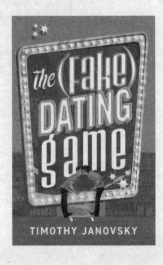

Two stories published every month. Launching January 2024

**millsandboon.co.uk**

# LET'S TALK
## Romance

For exclusive extracts, competitions and special offers, find us online:

**f** MillsandBoon

**X** @MillsandBoon

**⊙** @MillsandBoonUK

**♪** @MillsandBoonUK

Get in touch on 01413 063 232